I0599369

Robin Goodfellow

The Goblin Chronicles, Volume 1

S. M. Sutton

Published by S. M. Sutton, 2026.

ROBIN GOODFELLOW

First edition. January 13, 2026.

ISBN: 979-8992352924

Written by S. M. Sutton.

Table of Contents

To Faith—The dreams are yours. The dreams are mine. Both our lives are intertwined. My only wish for you, it seems, is to make them all come true - your dreams.

Her Whispered Words

You struggle with the memory,

trying to recall;

the dream from your childhood,

it didn't seem real at all.

The room filled with light and shadow;

your remembrance full of holes.

Her golden hair hung in waves;

Her sapphire eyes held your gaze;

Her essence sweet, like springtime in May.

Her whispered words;

a spell, hidden deep down in your soul;

you'll not recover what you lost, the part of you she stole.

Her slender fingers held at bay; a Trillium.

She gave the flower's name to you

and in the name, she told it true;

the one who picks the flower new,

will wake the magic left in you.

Wake Robin. Wake Robin. Wake Robin.

The years will pass;

the time will come

and when the hour strikes;

you'll protect a maiden fair,

she too has golden waves of hair.

When your task is done,

you'll find you've lost your chance,

regret you didn't dance the dance,

to match your steps in life with her;

to hold her in your arms,

as she became impervious to your many charms.

Her whispered words;

echo loud,

the Trillium's leaves wither,

you've missed your chance to be with her.

I tell you now, good fellow;

the flower will fade from white to yellow.

If you fail to act in time;

the death of love will be a crime.

Fate, as fickle as the wind that blows,

the enchantress, the only one who knows;

how you alone can break this curse.

A simple rhyme; an easy verse.

Wake Robin. Wake Robin. Wake Robin.

INTRODUCTION: A Ride Born of Desperation

Robin woke with a start. His body clammy, a cold sweat had broken out across his dark skin. His father, Lancer Goodfellow, had roused him from the comfort of his blankets in the middle of the night, making it clear they needed to be silent. The lad dressed and followed the Goblin King out into the cool, damp night. Lancer handed a shovel to his son to carry and picked up a bundle of cloth. Robin followed, groggy, struggling to keep up with his father's long strides. Atop the hill in the fortress cemetery, he could see two horses tethered to a tree on the edge of the meadow. Confused by his Da's actions, Robin knew it was best to keep his questions to himself, so he said nothing, watching as his father dug a small grave. Lancer gently placed the bundle down into the dark opening, took up the shovel, and began filling in the deep hole. The smell of freshly turned earth hung in the damp air all around them.

Lancer bid Robin lay the shovel against an old oak and instructed him to bring the horses over. Leading the animals, the lad saw the goblin king place a small bouquet of trilliums on the grave and wipe a rare tear from his rough cheek.

With no explanation, they'd ridden their horses into a lather as if a pack of wolves was at their heels, though Robin could see nothing chasing them. His father brooked no questions on the journey. Robin noticed Lancer carried a small package strapped to his chest, partly hidden beneath his heavy cloak. The lad sensed his father was in a highly agitated state. Hours later, his body exhausted from lack of sleep, they finally stopped. The young prince recognized it was a castle they'd arrived at. Darkness surrounded them, but Robin could hear waves crashing against the shore as they dismounted.

A stable boy, rubbing the sleep from his eyes, came and took their horses away. Robin found he could barely keep his own eyes open. It was the Fae Queen herself who deposited him in a guest room. Her long, golden hair shimmered in the candlelight. Robin couldn't help but think how beautiful she was. Humming a soft tune, she rocked him back and forth until she felt his body slacken, laid him down, gently pulling the bedding up to his chin. She cupped the side of his face with her smooth, warm hand and bid him good night. About to exit the room, the Queen turned to glance back at the young Goblin Prince, a thoughtful look on her face, then closed the door behind her. Robin's breathing slowed, and he fell into a deep sleep.

THE MOON HAD RISEN, glowing, with wispy clouds moving across its face, creating shadows. The goblin prince lay under a comforter, looking around the dark room. A moonbeam shone like a spotlight through the window, lighting up a scene on a tapestry that hung from ceiling to floor. A wall-hanging that depicted Fae dancing under the stars. After a moment, he realized he could hear voices talking low, with urgency, just outside his door. Of the voices, he recognized one as his father's. Robin threw the covers aside and slipped from the bed without a sound. He pressed his ear to the door, his goblin-enhanced hearing allowing him to make out most of the conversation.

"I'm begging you, Lennox," Lancer pleaded. "Don't turn me away, denying my request! This child is special. I can't let Morveena ruin her the way she is damaging my sons."

"I don't doubt your concerns, Lancer," King Lennox responded, sympathy resonating in his voice, "But, if she ever found out the child had not been stillborn, that it was *you* who stole the babe and brought her to *us* to hide away? Well, let's just say that none of us will be safe from the wrath of that woman. Under Goblin law, you can't set the marriage aside now that she's borne you a child. You're stuck with her. What makes you absolutely sure she will believe the baby was stillborn? That woman has an evil heart. She practices dangerous magic—blood magic. I'm not convinced that this is the right course of action, my friend."

Queen Aleta laid her hand on her husband's. "Lancer has come to us for help, my love. There is no one else he can trust with this task. We must save the babe from its mother."

Lennox looked deeply into his wife's eyes, then slowly nodded his agreement.

Lancer turned, picked up the bundled package he had carried against his chest all the way to the Fae castle, and extended his arms, offering the child to his oldest friend, Lennox Stargazer. The Fae King heaved a heavy sigh, but before he could take the infant from Lancer, Aleta stepped between the two men.

"As you've requested, Lancer, we will aid you in spiriting the child away to be fostered in a suitable home, but I have conditions. We will never reveal where or with whom we placed her. Once we take your daughter from your hands, she must be dead to you, as you will claim she is to her mother. This you must promise."

Lancer clutched the swaddling close to his chest. His voice broke. "I understand why you demand such a promise. If Morveena ever suspected I had lied about the stillbirth... We would all be in danger. It's better that I never know where you fostered her, never ask for that information. Even if I beg you in the future, never tell me. Never. Promise me you will never disclose her location to anyone, including me."

"I trust your word, Lancer, but remember, time has a way of changing all things. We would do well not to forget that blood magic can influence even the best intentions in the world. It would be simple enough to assuage all our fears. Agree to allow me to wipe your memory of this deed. It would be safer for everyone." Aleta inclined her head, then added, "I'm afraid this is not negotiable, old friend."

Lancer Ian Goodfellow took the Fae Queen's hands into his own, kissed the backs of them, and lifted them to his face. "Assuage your fears. Take my memories."

"When the new sun rises, you will forget this night's deeds. If ever you think you recall the babe, it will only seem a dream," Aleta told him.

Pity from his oldest friend shadowed the Goblin King as he turned to leave the room. His newborn daughter, hours old, was now cradled in the arms of the Fae Queen. He stopped; eyes cast to the floor. Lancer didn't turn back to look at them, but in a low whisper, said, "Hide her well. My vision has foretold that this child will save the goblin race in the future. I showed both of you the birthmark and sent Lennox a vision of how the child will look when she becomes a young woman. Robin and I will leave at first light. I'm grateful for your help and will forever be in your debt. We must be back home before Morveena rouses from the drugs the midwife had given her when the pain from the birth became unbearable. Then, I must be ready to act out my greatest stage role and deliver the saddest tale I have ever told in my life."

"Lancer," Aleta called softly. "May I ask why you brought the boy with you on this dangerous errand?"

"He's safe enough. Knows nothing about the errand or why we are here. Rob watched me bury his dead sister." The queen raised her eyebrows at the idea of a staged burial.

"I think it wise to allow me to set a small glamour on him that will help him forget this night's dark visit. If memories try to surface, he will only recall the burial in the cemetery. I promise he is not in any danger from the deed of this night's betrayal. Before you go, let my magic help keep the lad safe." Aleta squeezed the Goblin King's shoulder, looking for permission. Lancer granted it, wanting to keep his youngest son safe.

Robin scurried back to the bed when he heard footsteps coming toward the door. But it wasn't his father who entered the room. The Fae Queen swung the heavy wooden door open without a sound and came to his bedside. Looking down at the handsome lad, she watched his chest rise and fall in the innocence of pretended slumber. Her full lips caressed his ear as she whispered comforting words, then brushed his forehead with a light kiss, and laid a trillium on the bedside table. Robin fell back asleep until his father woke him.

"Come on, lad. We need to get back home." Lancer picked up the trillium, twirled it back and forth between his forefinger and thumb, a faraway look in his eyes, deep in thought. "Rob," he tossed the trillium on the bed, took his son by the shoulders and kneeled down to face him. Keeping his voice low so only the two of them could hear, he said, "Remember what I tell you now, Robin Wilum Goodfellow. Whatever else gets wiped from your memory, you'll never forget the secret I'm about to share with you. The bundle you saw me bury this night was not your dead baby sister. That was a ruse to save the babe from Morveena's cruel hand. Understand?" The lad nodded and swallowed hard; the fear of keeping a secret from his stepmother gripped him. "You must promise one day to find your hidden sister. Being fostered out, no one will know her real identity. No one will know where she was raised. All will believe she died at birth. Start the search thirteen years from now. If I can, I will help you. But if I am unable, you must do it on your own. Valvina Ariana Goodfellow is the future key that will save the goblin people, Rob. You must be the one to keep her secret, to keep her safe. I'm sorry to lay such a heavy task at your feet, son, but you must bear the burden of finding her."

"How will I know her? What will she look like in thirteen years?" Robin whispered.

Lancer leaned in and breathed the description of a birthmark that his sister bore. The father let his forehead rest against his youngest son's brow, and he formed a vision of how his lost daughter would look years into the future, just as he had for Lennox. Planting a light kiss on the top of Robin's head, he pulled a knife from his pocket and slashed his palm. Knowing what his father intended, Robin held out his small hand, bracing for the sting. The two of them clasped hands, mixing blood. "Swear it." Lancer ordered.

"I swear it, Father. I will find Valvina Ariana Goodfellow one day and protect her with my life."

Lancer roughed up Robin's hair, patted his shoulder. "There's a good lad."

The two of them hadn't gone a quarter mile from the northern Fae castle when the sun popped up on the horizon, triggering a twinge, an ache at the base of their necks, specific memories fading, and certain details firmly planting themselves for future recall.

Later, Robin learned Lancer had told his stepmother that he'd buried the tiny body while the Queen lay drugged from the difficult birth to save her from the trauma of seeing her dead child. Robin recalled the eerie cemetery scene, realizing Lancer meant him to be a witness to the burying of his stepsister. A recollection he kept to himself. With a profound fear he didn't understand at his young age, his memory of that night's events remained muddled. The details scrambled.

Years passed, and over time, it all but faded away. The only thing he could clearly recall was the beautiful, golden-haired woman who murmured soft, sweet words and rocked him peacefully to sleep. It must have been a dream, as no one else had been at the cemetery with his father. As he grew older, the vision came and went in his dreams from time to time, but he could never recall her whispered words, nor who had breathed them into his ear.

Robin Wilum Goodfellow grew up with a constant emptiness he felt at the loss of his baby sister. Each spring, he would slip away in secret and lay a bouquet of trilliums at the unmarked gravesite beside the old oak tree. He took precautions to be sure no one ever saw him do it, especially his stepmother.

PROLOGUE: A Waxing Gibbous Moon

(Thirteen years later)

In a small village in the northern reaches of Sharas, a waxing gibbous moon rose high, bright light swallowing the shine of the stars. A soft blanket of peace covered the night.

Until it didn't.

Darnell Dru Brogan had been on the night watch for the last three evenings. The young Fae was serious about his job. Night watch to Darnell meant he was doing his part to help keep his village safe. But a third late shift in a row found his eyelids heavy in the warm, humid air, with only the singing of tree frogs for company. His mind strayed, unable to keep thoughts at bay of the smooth skin and full lips of his latest crush, Selma. Eyes glazing over, imagination claimed his attention. Darnell dreamed of how pleasant it would be to kiss her. In his second to last thought, he imagined Selma's sensual lips pressed against his, her lithe body fitting alongside his own, a moonbeam highlighting her silver hair.

His last thought? Wondering when his older brother, Badger Bartholomew Brogan, would return from trading. Badger had gone south a fortnight ago to a neighboring Fae settlement. Darnell hoped Badger might return with something special Darnell could give to Selma to garner her attention, perhaps provide a reason to gift him with a kiss.

Life left his eyes, his body slumping forward, blood from his severed jugular spurting out in time with the last pumps of his beating heart. Darnell never made a sound as death took him in its arms and claimed him for its own.

Invaders slaughtered all the Fae on the night watch. They torched the village, fire raging over thatched roofs. Screams shattered the peace of the night. Twelve additional raids were taking place all along Sapphire Lake's southern shore.

Thirteen villages burned to the ground. Villages occupied by humans. Villages occupied by the Fae. Villages occupied by goblins.

The ground was soaked red with blood.

Be it human, Fae, or goblin blood, it was red all the same.

Badger, Darnell's older brother, returned home a week later to find the butchery and char. He sat next to his dead brother's body, filled with grief, when a thought struck him hard. Badger jumped up like a wild animal, racing through the village again. Finally, he came to a stop, alone at the Elder's fire ring. A noise emanated from him, echoing across the inlet. The sound was that of a wounded beast, broken.

He'd missed the details in his first desperate search through the small village. Going back for a second look, he found all the male Fae butchered. Some with cut jugulars, like Darnell. Others with throats ripped out. He hadn't realized the part of the picture he'd missed. Besides the male Fae, all the elders, men, and women alike, were dead. But in his mad search, he'd failed to notice the fact that the women and children had vanished. They weren't among the slaughtered. Only the Fae males, the strong, and the Elders, the weak, were slaughtered.

Badger wasted no time in burying the dead. The trail was already cold. He could not allow it to grow colder. A week had gone by before his return. He tracked the shuffle of footprints leading away from his village. There'd been no attempt by the raiders to hide their trail. When he came to the next settlement, the stink of char, blood, and death assaulted his nose before he even crossed the border of the goblin hamlet. There, he found the same destruction. Goblins massacred. All the males. All the elders. Some had been friends. A path worn in the dirt continued across the long grasses of the meadow, trampled, showing him the route leading north, then west along the shore of Sapphire Lake.

Badger pushed on. He found a man clinging to life, lips moving, whispers escaping with the last of his breath. The male Fae put his ear next to the dying man's mouth, desperate to hear his last words, "Killed us all. Gobs, Fae, Men. Monsters took the women. Took the children. Claimed them as slaves. Their fate. Slaves. Monsters all." His breath hitched in pain.

"Who?" Badger screamed at him. "Who took them? Where are they taking them?" Tears rolled down his cheeks as he realized he was shaking a corpse. With strong shoulders slumped in defeat, his body shuddered with sobs as he gently laid the man back down. When he wiped his tear-streaked face with rough hands, he glimpsed a small shadow darting behind a tree. He was up, leaping over the dead man like a white-tailed deer. When he caught up, Badger found the shadow belonged to a child. Guessing her age, maybe six or seven years old, she was half mad with terror. He'd cornered her against a rocky outcropping, the lake water glittering in the sun as small waves rose and fell behind them. Badger held out his hands as if he were dealing with an injured animal, making soothing noises. He assured the goblin child that he would not hurt her, that he was only there to help.

Her dress, shredded, strips of material fluttering in the wind, was nothing more than rags on her tiny frame. Badger inched closer, making soft cooing noises. Looking out at the endless water, then back at him, deciding. The waif fell to her knees. Badger took a careful step toward her, then lifted her, wrapping the child in his arms, rocking back and forth as the water lapped at his feet. Time stood still until she gave in, her stiff body going limp as she laid her head on his shoulder, eyes catatonic.

The young Fae male found a sheltered cove on the beach out of the wind, blocking the child's view of her burned village. She whimpered as he peeled her hands from around his neck. He laid her down, opting to take a chance to leave her long enough to retrieve his pack. Rushing back, he was relieved to find she hadn't moved an inch. Pulling his blanket from the pack, he wrapped her in it. The child's open eyes held a dead gaze as he gathered small pieces of wood near the treeline. She was silent as he dug out a bowl in the sand, laid the kindling in to start a fire. But the smell of smoke caused the survivor to let loose a loud, repetitive keening. Ignoring it, he filled a pot with water, pounded three thick branches into the ground with a rock, forming a tri-pod. Then, he settled the handle in the crook of his makeshift potholder and put it over the flames to boil. All the while he worked, talking over her distress. Offering kind, soft words of reassurance. When he had tea made, he gathered her back in his arms, tucking the blanket around her. She quieted as he sat on the ground, rocking, giving her sips of the hot liquid. Waves on the lakeshore lulled them into drowsy exhaustion, and the two of them fell asleep. The fire burned down to coals, winking out as the moon rose.

At sunrise, Badger set his charge aside and stood to stretch. Stirring the coals to life, he began cooking dried grain in a fresh pot of water. Pulling a precious jar sealed with wax from his pack, he started to tear up. He'd purchased it when trading, intending it for Darnell's sweet tooth. When the grain reached a consistency of soft mush, he filled a wooden bowl and drizzled Darnell's maple syrup over the contents. When he came back to sit near the child again, her eyes tracked him. Badger pointed at his chest and said, "Badger." Then he pointed at her, raising his eyebrows. He repeated his name, asking, "You?" He could hear her stomach growling with hunger from where he sat. Badger coaxed her to come and eat. Her hunger won out over her fear. She crawled over to his side. He tapped his chest again, saying, "Badger."

Then pointed at her, asking, "You?" Using two fingers, he scooped a mouthful of the cooked grain into his mouth. She stared at him. A small drip of saliva fell from the corner of her mouth.

He tapped his chest again. "Badger. You?"

She tapped her chest, whispered, "Tula". He rewarded her by handing over the bowl. She put her mouth to the edge of the vessel, used her fingers to shovel the food in, barely breathing between gulps. "Easy now. Easy," he cautioned.

When she had licked the wooden bowl clean, her face, and hands were a mess. Sand granules stuck to all the sticky places on her skin, so he gathered her skinny frame into his arms and walked right into the lake's cool water. Dunking them both under, he began scrubbing the dirt from both of them. Washing her hair first, then his own. When they were clean, her lips blue, fingertips wrinkled, Badger took her back to shore and pulled a clean shirt from his pack. After he pulled her rags off, he gave her the shirt. It came down to her feet, so he took a small length of rope, tied it around her waist, then laid the blanket back across her shoulders. Settled, he handed her a cup of hot tea. He set about putting on a fresh shirt himself, his wet leather pants sticking to his damp skin as they slowly dried in the morning wind.

The sun climbed its way overhead to begin its descent toward the horizon. Badger fed Tula again, breaking off a hunk of cheese to share, giving her a hard biscuit to dip in her tea. When she finished licking the crumbs from her fingers, he cradled her in his arms again as the sky turned dark, stars glittering above.

Badger whispered in her ear, "I cannot help the dead," he told her. "But if I am to have any chance of helping those taken alive, I need you to tell me who raided and in which direction they went?" Tula's body began shaking. She buried her face against his shoulder, moaning. He lifted her chin to look into her eyes. "Tula. It's only you and me now," he imparted to her, his voice soft. "There aren't any others to help us. Only you can help me find them. You must be strong. You must be brave. There is only *you* to tell me."

A single tear slid down her cheek. Tula watched one slide down his. "Fae took my mother," she murmured.

"Fae? You're sure?" he questioned.

Violent shaking took hold of her thin body. "No. That's not right," tears running down both cheeks. "Goblins took my mother. Killed my father, my brother." A loud moan escaped her again. He stroked her hair, letting her work through it. Then, "No, no, no!" she shook her head. "It wasn't Fae or Gobs. It was men. Men took my mother, killed my father and my brother."

"Little one, are you confused? Take your time, Tula. Time to remember. It's important. Which was it? Fae, goblins, or men?" Badger coaxed, stroking her cheek with his rough thumb, pushing the tears off her soft skin. Images flashed through her mind's eye; screams of terror rang out that only she could hear. She saw them all—Fae, goblins, and men. Her body cringed in terror.

Tula's eyes rose to meet his. She looked all around them to be sure no one could hear. Then she confessed in a whisper, "It was monsters." Her small forefinger pointed toward the lake. "They sailed away," her finger pointing across the vast waters of Sapphire Lake.

Badger couldn't have known it then, but those were the last words Tula ever spoke.

One thought overrode all his others. He would need to get word to Robin Goodfellow.

PRELUDE: The Trillium

From the moment he saw her, he was smitten. So severely, in fact, it felt as though an iron fist reached in, grabbed his heart through his massive chest muscles, and squeezed without mercy. Time froze. He struggled for breath. Never had Robin Wilum Goodfellow found himself captivated by such beauty. Watching her, he found himself a prisoner of her power, a power she was unaware of. Sweat poured down his face as he witnessed this sweet creature moving through the forest. He noticed butterflies made her smile and felt his knees weaken. She glanced here and there, searching the ground in sweeping motions. She stooped. In fascination, he watched as she reached out, pinched off a morel mushroom, placing it in the basket she carried.

Not wanting to frighten her, Robin pressed his muscular body against a tree, immersed, blending in, the bark becoming his camouflage, hiding him.

Dropping to her knees, picking two more morels—some folk referred to them as roons or roonies—she laid her walking stick across the ground, pointing to the next one she saw. Then, taking her time, surveying a small area, her blue eyes honed in on yet another mushroom. Her face lit up as over twenty of them, inches from one another, stretched out before her, eyes able to see the elusive honeycomb-shaped caps. She crawled on the forest floor, delight obvious at picking such a bountiful rune patch.

It was a beautiful spring day. Robin was there quite by accident.

Or by fate, if you believe in such things.

The Goodfellow had ventured deep into the rich forest land while hunting with a group of lads. Without meaning to, he'd gotten separated in his own quest for the spring treasure. Mushroom country, some called it. He was aware that somewhere in the background, a rose-breasted grosbeak was singing a spring serenade.

Standing, she turned full circle, scanning the ground again, as any good mushroom hunter would. Robin caught his breath, swept away in her power with a full view of the young woman before him. She wore dark leather leggings that enhanced her long, slim body, and a soft deerskin top laced up the front. Golden hair, twisted into a braid, hung below her waist. He counted an additional thirteen tiny beaded braids on the left side of her head. Then, watched in slow motion, as those long-beaded braids swung as she moved, making clicking noises, bead to bead, sounding like drums in his ears. Time stopped when she looked straight up, almost locking her eyes with his. Blended as he was beneath the tree bark, concealed, he knew she couldn't see him. The ash tree supported his weight, his heart encased in the bark. He held his breath, lest he betray his presence and frighten her away. He yearned to know this girl.

A grosbeak landed nearby and broke the spell, or perhaps the spell began as the bird's song erupted, celebrating spring. The hunter turned her booted heel away from him, adjusting her shawl over her shoulders, revealing a muscular build. Taking up a walking stick, she continued the search for mushrooms, her wicker basket nearly full.

Admiring the forest floor while moving, she found the ground a riot of white, yellow, and purple violets. Small patches of Dutchman's breeches and squirrel's corn decorated her path. Everywhere, as far as the eye could see, were Trout Lily, wild Ramp's leaves, Lily of the Valley and Trillium; here and there, like the heralds of the woodland, rose Jack-in-the-Pulpit, the trumpets of spring's arrival. She seemed graceful among them as she moved away.

Robin caught up with her, angling in from the east. It charmed him when she dropped to her knees again, pulled a knife that hung sheathed from her belt. He could see several pouches hanging from her waist when she bent to dig. Finishing her work, she admired the handful of wild leeks known as ramps. Braiding the long leaves of the wild onions together, with their pungent smell in the air, she secured them to her belt with a leather strip.

"Oh, hullo," Robin tipped his hat. "I see you found my secret mushroom spot," he joked. "A good day for 'shrooming, yeah?" He held his own basket up for her to see.

"Hullo. Looks as though you've done well for yourself. I don't think I've met you before. Are you new to the area?" She asked, bending to pick another.

"My clan moved near here last summer. Haven't been out and about much to meet people, but my luck changed today," he offered her a smile. "Robin Goodfellow at your service." He grabbed his hat off and swept it down as he gave her a theatrical bow.

That made her smile, and he knew he would try to get her to give him another. She didn't offer her name and turned away in the opposite direction. "Good luck with your hunting. I've got to start back home. Cook will be delighted with these mushrooms. Lovely to meet you," she called over her shoulder, long strides taking her away.

"But I didn't get your name, lass," he called.

She waved, hurrying through the woods. He stood watching when she bent at the waist, spotting something on the ground.

The grosbeak above him broke out in fervent song. Robin's heart pounded. Drums beat in his ears again. His entire being quivered; his Goblin sight allowing him to see her long, slender hand reach out, touching a Trillium.

He froze in place.

Colors swirled before his eyes. She glanced around to see if anyone was watching, now far enough away from the stranger in the woods that she couldn't see him. Turning back, she ran her fingers down the stem of the lovely flower...just to the sweet spot of picking. Robin felt overwhelmed, energy surging, coursing through his powerful body, not sure exactly what was happening to him. Out of the blue, cutting through the fabric of his being, he heard shouting! Shouting of...he shook himself, coming out of the trance, trying to grasp what was transpiring around him.

He focused on the shouting. A name! An old woman's voice, shrill, with intent to do bodily harm, calling out a name.

Fervent with worry.

Commanding.

He turned at the last moment, enhanced Goblin sight making him able to see his woodland muse snatch her hand away, leaving the trillium unpicked, causing a cold sweat to break out across his body.

Jumping up, she ran through the forest like a graceful deer, calling out, "I'm here, Nursie, dear," she answered to the shouts. "Coming, darling. Here, Evy, here I am."

A gust of wind came up. He lost her voice among the rustling of the forest leaves; gurgling of the river's flow; singing of birds.

The sun beat down upon him, forehead damp with sweat, Robin stood dazed for a moment. He had the presence of mind to pick up his own mushroom basket, spilling out a few. The woven container overflowed with spring's bounty.

That shouting.

Clarity struck him like lightning. It was a name he'd heard shouted.

Not just any name.

Her name.

Her name was Faith.

"AND JUST WHERE HAVE you been, young lady?" Faith's nurse demanded.

Faith released her deep-throated laugh, saying, "Don't fuss so! Look darling, I've got enough mushrooms to serve for Spring Feast tonight."

The old nurse was a solid woman. She kept her long gray hair twisted in a tight bun at the nape, giving her thin face a rather severe look. The elder frowned her usual disapproval in Faith's direction. "It's not respectable for young ladies to be running about the forest unattended. It's unsafe! Dedo told me You were in danger!"

"Dedo!" Faith exclaimed. Her eyes narrowed. Blast that meddling gargoyle! She made a mental note to deal with him later. "Come now, Nursie, you're vexed for no good reason. Cook will prepare us a feast this evening of roonies and ramps. Let's go see if Garrett has caught us trout to dine on; don't tarry. Fresh asparagus should definitely be on the menu, and oh! Wouldn't it be lovely to have watercress with dandelion greens, the perfect spring mix?" Faith salivated.

The old nurse muttered to herself. She informed Faith that Estella and Andrew were gathering asparagus. To keep up with the ball of energy moving almost in a dance through the woods, she hustled, both of them picking fiddlehead ferns as they went. Working up an appetite, Faith imagined the delicate round spirals sautéed in butter.

By the time the Nurse reached the river's edge, she was not at all surprised to find a trail of boots, leggings, and top leading to Faith's walking-stick leaning against a tree. The basket of morel mushrooms on the ground below and all her other woodland paraphernalia lying in a heap, as though she'd vanished. Evy heard a splash as the girl jumped into the river.

Faith let out an excited "whoop!" as the water enveloped her. "Come on in, Nursie. It's just the thing after an afternoon of hunting mushrooms under the scorching sun!"

The nurse shook her head and yelled out a caution, "Hurry out, Lovie! You'll catch your death!" After all, it was spring. In Evy's mind, the water was still freezing in temperature.

Faith had to admit her nimble fingers were becoming numb. But she loosened the braid in her hair and dunked her head, letting the water flow through her long tresses. She came up, standing full, sputtering, sunlight glistening on the water, small clothes clinging to her skin as she made her way shivering to the river's bank. The water swirling about her feet and ankles made them feel like blocks of ice, as if pins were pricking them everywhere. But that wasn't enough to stop her from stooping and picking handfuls of fresh watercress at the edge of the riverbank.

Emerging, water streaming from her hair, Faith put the cress on top of her basket, making a cool, damp cover to keep the mushrooms fresh. Then she lay down in the grass, letting the afternoon sun dry and warm her. Evy sat on the bank above.

After a while, Faith called up to her, "Be a dear, won't you, and go on ahead. Tell the house we'll be celebrating Spring Feast tonight. Let's make it special and dress for a festive evening! I feel like music and dancing, don't you, love?" she queried.

Her nurse smiled and sighed. "I do. But I'll not leave you alone in the woods. The sun's going down. Get dressed and let's be off together," Evy said with authority.

"Oh, Nursie darling, you do fuss so." Faith got up, followed the trail of her clothes, dressing as she picked up her things. Finished, she looked around. "Where are my boots?" she muttered to herself and began walking in a widening circle, searching for them. She must have cast them off somewhere when running down the hill to get into the water. "We're losing the light, Evy. Maybe you could ask Garrett to take the message up to the house while I look for my boots. He'll be near the footbridge at his favorite fishing hole, just three bends up the river." Faith said, searching in the tall grass and ferns along the bank.

"We'll be going back to the manor together, young lady."

"I'm not quite ready to leave yet, Nursie. I can't find my boots," Faith told her, frustrated.

"Well, you'll have to come back for them another time," the nurse prodded. "The sun's gone down." Faith acquiesced, hoisted up her belt and fastened it, her gear and pouches swinging.

The two women walked in silence along the river's edge. Evy turned to keep her eye on her charge, just in time to see the sun sink below the horizon.

"Please, my lady, hurry along. There's so much food to prepare for a fine feast tonight." The older woman shivered, pulled her shawl closer, glancing about as though looking for wild beasts.

"What worries you, Evy?"

"Rumors. Rumors that goblins have settled in the area. If that's true, you stay away from them, missy!"

"Oh, Nursie," Faith laughs, "if it is true, it's likely they'll be looking to meet people and make friends. I have no quarrel with goblins, and neither should you."

"Hmph! Just you mind what I say. Being friendly with goblins only ever brought bad luck, I say. It's not safe to be out alone at night when they like to sneak about."

Faith let the comment go, knowing that arguing with the old woman would get her nowhere. She hooked her arm with Evy's and, tired as the older woman's legs were, they kept a steady clip through the woods back toward the fortress. Back to home and haven. She had no intention of divulging to Evy that she'd met a handsome young male goblin in the woods that very afternoon.

CHAPTER 1: Spring Feast

After delivering her gathered fare, Faith marched from the kitchens straight to the fortress's womb. The entire household would turn out for the Spring Feast celebration. Every year, she helped Estella and Andrew prepare the Great Hall for dinner and dancing. The three of them talked as they set up the ballroom together, mouth-watering aromas wafting into the open space as the cook was preparing the food gathered that day.

"Estelle. Andrew. Did you know anything about me? I mean, before I came to live here?" Faith inquired.

"That's a strange question to come up, my lady. No, we would have said, wouldn't we, Andrew?" answered Estella.

"Of course we would," Andrew nodded in agreement. "I remember the day you arrived. Practically a newborn babe when the Watsons adopted you," Andrew says. "Reatha just took you in her arms as if a spell had been cast upon her." Andrew drifted off, recalling fond memories. He picked up an empty wine barrel, hoisted it onto his shoulder and trudged off toward the kitchens to replace it with a full one.

Estella touched Faith's shoulder and said, "Never mind Andrew's orphan talk. What brought these questions to your mind, lass? We've always been your family here at Robert's Fortress and always will be. I hope *you* think of us as your family and this place as home. We love you, dearie! Everyone here, I dare say." Estelle finished shyly.

Faith hugged her, saying, "Stell, I love all of you too! You've been family all my life. That will never change. This is home. Heavens, I'm not planning to go anywhere! Oh! I've just had a thought." She put her hand to her mouth. "Stell, do you think Nursie knew anything about my real parents?"

"I wonder," Estelle reflected. "But you'll have to ask her yourself, Lady Faith. It was Evy who brought you here as a babe, so she might know something. Guess we never thought to ask," Stell finished.

Faith turned around from her task and looked at Estella, her face registering shock. "Stell," Faith said, her breath catching, "are you telling me

Nurse did not live here with all of you before I came here as an orphan? Nurse *came here* with me? How could I have never learned this?" Faith demanded. "She must know something about my actual family. I must go at once and find out!" Hurrying across the ballroom floor, leaving a startled Estella behind in her hurry to find Nursie.

"You've picked a poor time to be inquiring about the past. Nurse will have her hands full preparing for the Spring Feast, dearie. Faith!" Stell shouted after the girl, her words falling on deaf ears. "Ah well, my Lady, go then, I can finish up the mopping by myself," Stell muttered to herself.

Andrew came back into the hall. "Who are you talking to, Estelle?"

"Never you mind, Master Andrew," Stell responded. "Let's get this job done. I still need to dress up for the festivities. Mark my words, tonight is going to be full of mischief," she nodded to herself. "I'd bet gold on it. If I had any, that is."

BREATHLESS AND ANXIOUS, Faith knocked at Nursie's door. The gala was to begin in a little over an hour, but her need to know consumed her common sense. She was an orphan. Chances were there weren't even any records of her birth. The question burned like a candle flame at the back of her mind. She couldn't let it go. Knocking harder a second time, she cracked the door open. A small orange glow shone from the embers in the room's fireplace. Faith called out, "Nursie? Evy? I need to talk to you before the party. Nursie, are you here?" Silence.

Frustrated, she did not close the heavy door behind her with grace. Faith hurried down the hallway to her own room. The grandfather clock chimed, announcing that it was already half past the hour. Her questions would have to wait. She needed to wash up and get dressed. That would leave little time to confront Dedo about sending the Nurse out after her in the woods earlier.

A FIRE ROARED IN THE massive stone fireplace, making her room cozy. Pacing back and forth in front of the flames, Faith was lecturing in a louder than usual voice as she struggled to control her emotions.

"You are interfering with my life again!" accusing the empty room. "We had an agreement. Your word given! I thought I could trust you. Does it even bother you to know that my heart feels betrayed?" Faith choked on those last words. Standing with her hands on her hips, she glared upwards at the solid stone structure in front of her, flames dancing in the firebox. Two stone gargoyles that had candle holders strapped to their backs stared right back at her; chins held in their hands. Her eyes drew further up the stones, stopping when she found his shape.

It took a keen eye to pick him out, camouflaged as he was among the rocks. He sat stone-still, squatting in apparent comfort with his arms wrapped around his knees, watching.

"Have you nothing to say in your defense?" Faith asked.

Silence. More watching.

"So, I'm right. My heart means nothing to you, Dedo?" she hung her head in despair.

The stone statue turned slightly, so she could not see his anguish, then schooled his features. "I have done you no wrong, my lady," Dedo responded in a quiet voice. "As for your heart, as you well know, I would never willingly cause you pain," he maintained his stoic look.

"Dedo," Faith asked, "did you or did you not send Nursie out to look for me in the woods? You scared her nearly to death by telling her I was in danger! Do you deny it? Are you saying Evy made it up? You must think me a child? A fool?" she finished.

"I think you are neither," Dedo said.

The two gargoyles holding lit candles on the mantel kept their chins in their hands. They maintained their stony silence. Faith shook a finger at the two of them. "Not a word from either of you!" she chastised them. Turning their heads, the two small gargoyles looked at each other, rolled their eyes, and returned to their original positions. Dedo frowned at them, but then Dedo almost always frowned.

"Faith," Dedo said in his calm, matter-of-fact way, "I gave you my word I would not interfere with your life. Your comings. Your goings. Your carefree nature. I gave the promise with the caveat, unless and only unless I thought you were in danger. You. Were. In. Danger. So, I sent the nurse, as was my right. My whole life, I've done my best to protect you. It was *you* who left me no choice," he finished.

"Oh, Dedo," Faith chided him, amused as he attempted to flip the tables on her, "please, spare me. I was picking morel mushrooms. Roonies. What danger could I have been in? I am curious to hear you spin a tale to explain how this is my fault."

Stone silence. Moments ticked by. Then he hissed a question at her. "What else did you find to pick besides spring feast mushrooms?"

Faith defended, "Oh well, let me think. If you must know, I also found a fine selection of ramps, fiddleheads, and watercress! Yes, Dedo, the woods were full of dangerous butterflies and siren songs of returning spring grosbeaks. Did young Master Garrett playing hooky from his chores give you cause?" She glared at him.

"Young Master Garrett has no place in this conversation. You know," Dedo said as the two of them locked eyes, his turn to accuse, "for such a smart girl, sometimes you can't see the forest through the trees." He tsked. "Admit it. You were about to pick a Trillium when you thought no one was watching, were you not? Even though you know it's forbidden."

The Lady Faith's eyes took on a sudden look of surprise. "I...I," she stammered.

Sensing he had the upper hand now, Dedo continued. He lifted a finger from his knee, pointed at her, "You. Were. Going. To. Pick. A. Wake-Robin." He let it sink in, went on, "Knowing full well Robin Goodfellow awaits...The. Very. Moment." Dedo was careful not to raise his voice as he continued. "The desire to pluck a trillium overcame you, and it was only the cries of your dear Evy that brought you back from the brink. Do you know why you were so affected? Of course not. You accuse poor Dedo of treachery. Not a thought about Dedo, only having your best interests at heart. Never a moment spent thinking about what a loyal servant Dedo has been. Alas, I must tell you, He. Was. Right. There. The Prince of the Goblins, Robin Wilum Goodfellow, was in your wood! Yet, it is your loyal Dedo who takes your tongue-lashings in good sport. And I might add, who *saved you?*"

Like the little drama-queen she had always known him to be, Faith watched Dedo as he brought his arm up, swaying as he put the back of his hand to his forehead. Acting as if he were going to faint because he couldn't believe her lack of concern over committing such a foolish act. He carried on, "Evy and I have warned you all your brief life not to pick a 'wake-robin.'" He turned back to look at her. Tapping his foot in irritation, he waited for her to respond. "Have *you* nothing to say for yourself?" he queried.

"What do you have against the goblin people?" Her anger flashed before her guilt returned. "Look, the two of you have been spewing that old worn-out warning ever since I can remember!" She recalled the earlier chance meeting that afternoon. Robin had introduced himself, but she had withheld her own name, not knowing why. He seemed a perfect gentleman. But Dedo had a point. She didn't know any of the details about Robin Wilum Goodfellow and his clan. It had been years since goblins had interacted with anyone in the area.

There was a knock on her chamber door. A humbled Faith looked up at Dedo. Having once again taken his usual squatting position. It looked as if he were pouting. "Dedo," Faith whispered, "I admit I was in the wrong; please forgive me. My accusations weren't said to hurt you. It's just I thought you were interfering!" she pleaded. "I guess I can see now you were only concerned for my safety."

Stone silence.

She huffed at his stubbornness. There wasn't the slightest chance she was going to disclose having met a young man today while mushrooming. Especially one who had introduced himself as Robin Goodfellow. Best to keep that little secret to herself.

Another knock at the door, louder than the first. Faith went to open it. Lenny and Lester, the mantel gargoyles, turned to look at each other and winked. In doing so, candle wax dripped across the fireplace mantel. Garrett rushed in without waiting for an invitation.

Her friend was gasping for breath, as though he'd run all the way from the fortress kitchens. Nursie had lit a fire under him, still angry at finding him truant on the river's edge, shirking his duties in favor of fishing.

"Faith," he gulped for air, "you won't believe it!"

"What won't I believe, Master Garrett?" Faith asked, amused, her left eyebrow raised, encouraging him to get to the point.

"We've got visitors, Faith! They arrived after the gate had closed. In the dark! Demanded the guards open up! All of them on horseback."

"Who are these visitors?"

"Oh, right!" Garrett exclaimed as he felt his face flush red, showcasing his embarrassment because he had forgotten the 'who' part of the details in his rush. "They said they're all cousins of yours, Faith! Robert invited them to the Spring Feast. They even brought along the venison for roasting they'd hunted on the way here. I didn't know you had any relatives, Faith?" Garrett rushed on. "The sooner you get ready for tonight's celebration, the quicker you can meet them."

Stunned by the announcement, Faith asked the visitors' names.

Color flooded his neck and cheeks again. Garrett thought for a moment, then admitted, "I am sorry, Faith, I was so excited for you, I didn't think to ask." Backing out of the room, turning as he reached the door, Garrett shouted over his shoulder, "I'll meet you downstairs, Faith, for the festivities. I'm going to finish my chores, clean up, and put on my best."

The fire crackled. A log fell across the grate, sending up a spray of sparks. Dedo closed his eyes in deep thought, already knowing who had come to the fortress. He worried about the 'why' of their coming.

Faith stood for a moment in shocked silence, staring at the door Garrett had closed behind him. Visitors. At her fortress. Her home. Claiming to be her cousins? How is it possible to have any relatives outside the fortress? She was an orphan, fostered here.

She felt lightheaded at the idea that perhaps her world was about to change.

AN HOUR AFTER GARRETT delivered the news, Faith reached the gathering hall, bustling with activity. It appeared she was the last to arrive. Excited as she was, it had taken her longer than usual to get ready for the party. Voices and laughter rolled out of the hall to meet her in the entryway. Heartbeat speeding up, she felt her skin go clammy. Grinding her teeth together, she tried to ignore her stomach clenching. Her nerves had frayed over the last half hour. She was about to meet people claiming to be related to her.

Individuals she knew nothing about.

Zip. Zero. Zilch.

No names, no background. Not even a hint of information about where they were from. She couldn't help wondering why they were here? What family connection made them related to her? Maybe this was some kind of trick?

She stood out in the foyer, gazing into the great hall, filled with people. Memories of growing up at the manor flashed before her eyes. She thought about how everyone in the Pureheart family was close and loving. Those girls were all adopted. Garrett's parents adored him. Her friends' relationships almost seemed the opposite of the cool, remote affection that was offered to Faith. Not that she had felt unloved, Robert and Reatha treated her with kindness. They were caring people. It was just that she'd never felt she quite fit in.

Her stomach fluttered just before she entered the ballroom. Setting the past aside, she replaced it with the details of the guests in the room. Nervous, she wiped her sweaty hands against the sides of her dress. Had Nursie seen, would have admonished her. Excitement was at war with her fears. Stepping across the threshold, she told herself she was ready to explore any possibilities that might present themselves. Curiosity became her catalyst in finding out how having actual blood relatives might change her life.

The room was aglow with bright light, fires burning at both ends of the vast room. To calm herself, Faith took the time to notice all the favorite things she loved about Spring Feast. Vases of fresh flowers decorated every table. The sideboards filled with steaming trays of asparagus, bowls of sauteed, buttered morels with wild ramps. Fried trout, stuffed with wild onions, fiddlehead ferns, and morels; roasted venison made a perfect accompaniment to the watercress and dandelion greens salad. Creamy butter pats lined the table next to baskets of warm loaves of bread. The cooks had made Morel mushroom soup. Evy had prepared her special morel sauce for the venison. The dessert table featured baked pies made from last summer's canned blueberries.

She spotted the small group of strangers talking with Robert and Reatha. The musicians began tuning up. Dancing would begin as soon as everyone had finished the meal.

The newcomers turned as one to find her standing in the archway just as the bell rang, signaling everyone to be seated for dinner. Robert made a toast, followed by a quick introduction of names, but insisted the guests line up at the buffet tables to fill their plates before the food got cold. Faith was seated on Robert's right, Reatha on his left. Val Pureheart, her best friend, occupied the chair on Faith's other side. With the special meal finished, dishes cleared away and coffee served, Robert cleared his throat as a way of taking the floor. "So, Master Travis, you seem to be the oldest, of course, we're wondering," he pointed to Reatha and those from his household, "how you all came to be searching for our own Lady Faith?" He patted her hand to reassure her.

Using direct eye contact, Robert held his silence, a skill demanding a response. The cousin's eyes darted around. Travis personified a casual attitude, long legs stretched out in front of his chair, crossed at the ankles. "Umm..." he started.

Brittany stood, walked behind her brother, put both her hands on his shoulders and spoke up, "Sir Robert, if I may? I would love to speak to your question. It's for your benefit. If the question doesn't involve weapons, drinking, gambling, or women, I am afraid my brother would not be your best choice for information." Her statement brought a few laughs from the group, along with some rolled eyes.

"By all means, please do." Robert waved his hand, encouraging her to continue.

Ever the drama queen, Britt walked around her audience as though she were on stage, making sure she had everyone's full attention.

"Our father," she pointed to herself and her brothers, Travis, and Shaun, "Jake answered a summons nine years ago to attend a meeting with the leaders in our region. The purpose was to discuss the perceived threat that increasing factions of goblins were moving into the mid-lands. That topic, coupled with more attacks along the shores of Sharas's Sapphire Lake, sent fears spiking. In addition, rumors were on the rise from travelers north to south of invaders attacking small villages north of the mid-lands."

Brittany took a deep breath before continuing, making eye contact with the audience. "Little was known about these raiders. Coastal attacks on Sapphire's shores had only happened half a dozen times. The predators slaughtered the villagers, left the hamlet burned to the ground, with no witnesses alive to tell of the details." She scowled.

"Lady Brittany," Sir Robert interrupted, "Troubling news, no doubt, but if this all began nine years ago, are you suggesting it is still going on? If true, why haven't we heard of it until now? We all know that the goblin population has been growing throughout the mid-lands. As they find places to settle, occasionally they cause some minor trouble, but there's been no violence in recent years. We do our best to welcome them into the community, but generally, they keep to themselves. Are you implying that the Goblin clans are responsible for the killing and the raids? What in heaven's name does all of this have to do with Faith?"

"She's coming to that, good sir," Shaun yawned.

Brittany waited to garner everyone's attention again before continuing. You could have heard a pin had Nursie chanced to drop one from her sewing basket.

Faith looked around the room and saw the visitors' faces staring back at her. "Well, cousin," Faith's voice was steady, "don't leave us on the precipice with a cliffhanger. Go on with your story." Travis pulled a flask from his vest, twisted the cap off, and took a swig. Sir Robert reached his hand over, holding a mug of hot coffee, signaling to Travis he should put a splash from his flask into Robert's cup. Travis raised his eyebrows, then laughed a hearty belly laugh, sloshed in a generous amount, clapping Sir Robert on the shoulder.

Pleased with her recital so far, Brittany smiled around, ready to resume. Shaun stood up and said, "I think it's best if I take the story from here. We'll be here for days if you continue, Britt. Too much detail, just need the nitty-gritty."

Brittany's eyes squinted into angry slits, glaring down at the brother upstaging her performance. Before she could erupt into a tirade, a behavior she exhibited from time to time, another of the visiting group stood. Surprised looks appeared on the stranger's faces.

Mariella, one of their younger cousins, said, "I'm afraid that would be 180 degrees too far a change in the telling, Shaun. I'll carry on at the 90-degree mark between the two of you."

Shaun politely nodded his agreement. Brittany sat down with a smirk.

Faith remained calm. Finished with her meal, dishes cleared away, she handled her nervousness by sketching in a small bound book she had pulled from a deep pocket, now balanced in her lap. Her artistic hand was capturing the likenesses of her visiting cousins as the story unfolded.

Mariella was smaller than the others, but she had a grace about her. Faith captured her poise on paper. The audience rapt, she continued, "Faith," addressing her directly, "Lennox Stargazer was the ruler of the Northern Lakes in Sharas," she stated, paused for a moment, hoping the statement would mean something. When there was no reaction from Faith, she resumed her telling. "You see, Lennox and his wife, Aleta's realm, had been ransacked. Aleta taken. She's been missing for years now. The assumption, whispered without a shred of concrete proof, has always been that the goblin king, Lancer Goodfellow, was responsible for her kidnapping."

Val noted the sudden appearance of all the faces on the rocks. She draped a protective arm around Faith's shoulders. No one else seemed to notice. Faith continued sketching, not having looked up yet.

"For those who know this story, I will be brief. For those first hearing it, please hold your questions, and we will answer as best we can at the conclusion. After the demise of Lennox's realm, the goblin population spread throughout the northern peninsula of Sharas. With no leadership, any of Lennox's people still in those lands were barely scraping out a living. As often as not, they worked for the goblins, growing food or selling goods."

"The goblin clans became rich with new claims on the resources ranging from the waters to the woods. They confiscated plunder from the mines they had taken over. A new enemy had come to the shores of Sharas. This adversary made no distinction between the victims it assaulted. Fae, goblins, humans, and others were all killed without prejudice or preference by this foe."

"Gossip, of course, ran wild. People claimed the usurpers had faces like bears or wolves. Most referred to the invaders as Beast-Men. We now know they are a race called the Gugwe. An enemy who plunders towns, kills, rapes, and takes women and children as slaves. The assaults are more frequent every year."

"In summary, the goblin populations have grown in the north, the mid-lands and the southern lands of Sharas, as they are pushed further south from the invaders. But it is the Beast-Men who are consuming the resources of the northern peninsula, your true home, Faith! We've received communication that the usurpers plan to spread even further south."

"We have to live in harmony and work together again with all the other races. All the citizens of Sharas. Rumor blames the goblins for the attacks. I, for one, do not believe it is the goblin people taking slaves and killing, but in fact, the Gugwe."

Mariella turned and faced Faith. "Aleta Stargazer has been missing for almost fifteen years. Her husband never gave up searching for her. Lennox Stargazer came to my mother, Mari, Reatha's sister, two years ago." She nodded at Reatha Watson. "He said he was on the trail of recent gossip, suggesting where his wife was being held. He insisted we find you, bring you on a quest to restore the kingdom that is yours."

Faith's eyes left her sketchbook and opened wide as saucers. Her forehead crinkled in confusion as she struggled to reconcile the reference Mariella had made between her own mother, Mari, and Faith's foster parent, Reatha. If these strangers were her cousins, as they claimed, and Reatha was sister to this young woman's mother, Mari...

She forced herself to drop the path her thoughts were headed down and instead locked eyes with Reatha. The betrayal she felt was easily confirmed. Guilt was written across Reatha's face. Turning back to Mariella, Faith said, "It's clear there's been a mistake made somewhere along the way. I've never heard of the people of the Northern Kingdom, much less about a ruler named Lennox Stargazer or anyone named Aleta Dawn Stargazer. Goblins in the Northern Kingdom fighting with those migrating to the mid-lands and southern reaches are no concern of mine. The goblins that live around here are peaceful among our human population. I cannot understand what any of this has to do with me?"

The cousins turned and gaped at Lady Reatha. It was clear Faith had been told nothing about her heritage or the history of her people. Reatha stood, reached out a hand toward Faith. "That's enough for tonight. Faith, come with me. You and I need to have a private conversation. Please excuse us."

"I don't think so, Auntie Reatha. Let's get all the game pieces out on the board," Travis said. He held Reatha's chair out for her to sit again. "Finish it, Mariella. Faith has a right to know," Travis encouraged.

Mariella gave her full gaze back to Faith, sympathy softening her features. "You are the heir, Faith. King Lennox Stargazer and Queen Aleta Dawn Stargazer are your parents. You must have wondered why we came here? Speculated about how we came to know of your existence? It was King Lennox himself who set us on this task. Your father planned to have us meet him in the north to raise an army to take back the lands of our people. He gave us instructions that when we found you, we were to send word through the People of the Rocks. The gargoyles." Mariella raised her eyebrows, wondering if any of this was making sense to her estranged cousin. "Our search brought us here on a mission to convince you that you must lead our people in a fight for our homeland. *Your homeland, your people.* You're needed to help in the quest to find your mother, our missing queen, or your father, our missing king."

"Queen? King? And if you find neither? Faith asked.

"Then you must take up the mantle and rule in their stead as heir to the Northern Fae Kingdom." With her last plea, Mariella sat.

Faith stood. She looked to Reatha, Nursie, and her Uncle Robert. No one stirred. Turning back to Mariella, she asked, "Are you suggesting I am some kind of royalty? Proposing that I am the daughter of a king and queen? Bloody hell! That would make me a...a princess," voice winding up three octaves.

She stomped her foot in anger. "What a tale you've spun. I'm afraid you've wasted your time. I am no more a princess than any of the rest of the humans who live here in Robert's fortress. Being adopted, many would find the very suggestion that I am your long-lost princess amusing; I can assure you. Do you expect me to fight against the goblins? I have no quarrel with the goblin people," she stammered, confused.

"No. Not the goblins. Our people have a common enemy with the goblins. With all the citizens of Sharas. It's the Beast-Men, the Gugwe. We must unite to fight the Gugwe. I know this must be a lot to take in. It is obvious you didn't know about your ancestry, but our prayer is that you will take up the responsibility for your people. Help us," Mariella held out both her hands, palms up, with the question in her eyes as she gazed at her newfound cousin.

"You say 'our people' have a common enemy with the goblins? I don't understand. I thought all of you were goblins. That the goblin race are your people?"

Faith felt overwhelmed. Such an outlandish story after so many years of quiet, simple living. It was too much to take in at once. The room was too warm. She felt anxiety building in her chest, felt trapped. Her eyes swept the room for an escape route. It was boiling in here. Sweat trickled down her back. Her cheeks flushed. Nauseas, acid rolling in the pit of her belly, Faith looked up to where Dedo usually sat and found the space empty. She did not understand everything Mariella said. Felt there were holes in the overall story she couldn't piece together. Her mind jumped from one detail to another as she tried to make sense of Mariella's tale. It seemed as if the room were spinning.

Reatha jumped up again. "Please! Let me talk with her in private! Can't you see the distress you're causing her?"

"She wouldn't be under stress if you had been honest with her long ago," Brittany quipped.

"How dare you!" But before Reatha could do anything to remedy the situation, Faith's lashes fluttered. Dizziness seized her as her heart began thumping against her chest. Then, her eyes rolled back into her head, and she dropped to the floor like a sack of potatoes.

WHEN FAITH OPENED HER eyes again, it surprised her to be looking up from where she lay on the cold stone floor. A crowd had gathered around. Had she passed out? Why was everyone staring at her?

Val was crouched next to her on her knees, holding Faith's head and shoulders protectively in her arms. Faith leaned back against her friend, shocked when she noticed numerous faces looking back at her-rock faces in the fireplace.

So. Many. Faces.

Glittering auras filled her peripheral vision, and she realized for the first time maybe she wasn't the only one who could see Dedo and his kind. Now...now of all times, they were showing themselves! She'd never known so many people of the rocks lived here. Faces of every shape and size stared out at her from the fireplace. Val whispered in her friend's ear, trying to calm her.

Body jerking, Faith cried out in pain, then shock. "What's happening?" she wailed. A wave of vertigo made her head spin. Motion sickness swept over her body, skin pebbling as she broke into a cold sweat.

Val held her steady. "It's alright. It will be all right. I'm right here with you." Val looked at the crowd in panic, whispering to herself, "Oh gods, not now! She's changing. It's her time."

Faith doubled over when her best friend released her to give her space. Garrett reached out to catch Faith, but Val pushed him back. "Wait!" she commanded him. Their best friend let out an animal-like groan that echoed across the room. Reatha bit down on her knuckles. Nursie rocked in her chair by the fire. Dedo reappeared, watching from the stone chimney. All the visiting guests had eyes that glowed with excitement.

Coming to a stand, her balance off-kilter, Faith swung her head to the side and retched. Her silk dress ripped out in the back, blood soaking into the material that now lay in shreds to her waist. She whimpered in pain as full, five-foot opalescent wings sprouted open on her back, connected to her shoulder blades.

CHAPTER 2: The Goodfellow

The sun had dropped below the horizon as Robin led his band of lesser goblins away from the woods surrounding the fortress, where he'd introduced himself to Faith. The group moved through the forest without noise, except for a sort of "swishing" caused by their speed, if anyone had been around to hear.

Zepher stopped in mid-stride, planted his feet and called out, "Ho there, Robin! We've passed this tree before. I'm sure of it. In fact, I remember seeing it at least three times now. What's what?"

Robin shook with laughter. "It only took you seven times around in a circle to discover, Zepher. You're catching on quicker." The group laughed at Zepher, at themselves, as they hadn't discovered the jest either. Robin tossed Zepher a chunk of green rock candy for his clever detection. "Let's get a move on home, lads. We've got food to prepare for Spring Feast," Robin suggested. In no time, they covered the ten miles to the cave entrance of the old mine they'd taken up residence in. They greeted the guard on duty at the entrance. Down, down and down they traveled through the dark, damp tunnels. Bits of mica shimmered here and there along the stone walls. When the ground leveled out, the passageway opened onto a wide cavern where the clan made their home. Flickering wall torches lit the vast space.

Robin and the lads had gone out early in the day to gather spring's bounty to celebrate the equinox. Springtide was the time of year his father had disappeared. The season always made Robin melancholy, thinking about Lancer Goodfellow. But Robin loved nature's annual rebirth and renewal: green growth, flowers blooming, trees budding, leafing out, not to mention the animal and bird courtships. It was seven long years ago his Da had mysteriously disappeared, and Robin still missed him. He'd looked up to his father, respected him, so he'd done his best to stay close to the clan members, knowing it would be important to his father. The youngest Goodfellow had devoted himself to becoming a powerful warrior to protect the people, something he thought would have made Lancer proud. Robin often took time to listen to the tales of older clan warriors, hoping to learn from them and show them respect. He made it a point to memorize any war stories they shared about serving under Lancer Goodfellow. He kept his heartfelt wishes close to the vest, hoping against all odds that Lancer still lived. Even if he did not, Robin committed to striving every day to live a life that honored the noble code his parent had portrayed. Attempting to emulate leadership, integrity, honesty, intelligence, ambition, loyalty, compassion, courage, gratitude, humbleness, kindness, and a trait he admired above all, Lancer had been open-minded. Robin had to work harder on some attributes than on others. But he accepted responsibility when he fell short in any area, acknowledged his lack, re-doubling his efforts to become better where he had fallen short.

The hunting party he had taken out totaled thirteen, including Robin. He had lost track of the lads while searching for mushrooms. Then, he found himself distracted by the lass he'd met in the forest. Still, his basket was full of roonies. Two of the lads carried a small deer on their shoulders. With the animal's legs lashed to a sturdy tree branch, they carried it on their shoulders between them. All the members of the hunting party had pouches attached to their waists, bulging with fiddlehead ferns and wild asparagus. Shouts of welcome were called out as the party returned to the clan's hold.

Faith. Faith. Faith.

Her name, a silent mantra, over and over in his head until the shout of his own name broke his reverie.

"Robin! Robin, did you hear me?" growled the voice.

Ah...Rupert. Robin came back to himself. Several people moved throughout the domed room, doing various tasks and chores amid the stalactites. Soft yellow firelight flickering against the dome's walls created an ethereal cast Robin found comforting.

"We expected you hours ago. Everyone is starving! Where have you bloody been?" Rupert's gravelly voice demands.

"Peace, Rupert," Robin said, holding up his hand, forefinger, and middle fingers extended. "The lads and I are here now with a bounty for our Spring Feast. Nothing else matters, yeah?" Robin dismissed his brother's ugly mood and took his mushroom basket over by the fire, ignoring the eyes that were burning against his back. Finally, Rupert walked away, crossing the cavern, pissing and moaning under his breath as he went, as usual.

Zeeka was nearby, already sorting the asparagus the lads had given her. She was a favorite of Robin's, and Robin a favorite of Zeeka's. She had been their camp cook ever since Robin was a young lad. Getting on in goblin years, her dark, long, frizzled hair, streaked here and there with silver, stood out against her black leathers. Her lesser goblin face, a dark brown, was further creased with wrinkles, but most were laugh lines at the edges of her black, shiny eyes. Lesser Goblins were about a third of a size smaller than the Greater Goblins. Her flat nose crinkled as she smiled at Robin, saying, "Rupert's in one of his black moods, don't ya know? Oh, now... don't these look lovely!" she exclaimed over the basket of mushrooms he'd handed her.

Robin produced a small, hand-picked bouquet of violets. "You look lovely today, Mistress Zeeka. I picked these just for you."

She beamed at him. "The lads have already built up the fire, put the deer on the spit. Smells bloody wonderful, don't you think?" she breathed in.

Robin agreed. "Would you like some help with the mushrooms, fiddleheads, or asparagus?"

"Oh, Robin, such a good fellow you are! But no, no. Yer helpin' me fix the food would only add more fuel to Rupert's fiery thoughts. Not your place, no dearie, not for a high goblin such as yerself. Off with ya now. No need to give Rupert any more tales to tell your mother. I thankee as always for your sweet offer. Instead, you can give me your promise for a turn or two when the music is playing aft this fine supper." Zeeka winked at him.

"There's no difference between you and me, Zeeka," he said, relating to her reference in calling him out as a high goblin. He turned, leaving the mushrooms with her.

"Well," she winked at him, "there's a topic for serious debate to be had over a mug of ale. The sooner you recognize the difference, the better off you'll be. No trick of yours is going to change the lot of a lesser goblin," Zeeka wagged her finger at him. "I know your tricks and jests well. I still remember when you were a wee lad, and you changed out the sugar in my canister for salt for a quick laugh." His cheeks reddened. "And how about that prank you pulled on Master Cornerstone? Yeah, you turned the clock forward when he was eating the noon meal, and he let all the students out two hours early. Ha! Then, there was that time you and Cazzidy snuck a gallon of beet juice into the batch of soap I was making and everyone's hands turned red when they washed them." Robin was squirming to leave now, but Zeeka continued to remind him of his childhood pranks. "Ya can rest assured, laddie, no one's forgotten when you stuffed the toes of Morveena's shoes with wool and she thought her feet had grown two sizes larger overnight. Of course, there was a bit of hell to pay for that little yuck, yuck, hmm? The tables turned, and your best friend got the laughs one day when he replaced all the eggs in my basket with hard-boiled ones. Oh, and I'll never forget about the two of you pulling one over on Bedwer when you put that sticky honey all over his broom handle, waited around until closing time to watch him fumble with it, hmm?"

"Point taken, Mistress Zeeka. We'll have a serious discussion over a mug one day soon, I promise."

As was his habit, Robin went round the cavern, greeting others, catching the day's news as the name Faith, Faith, Faith, beat through his head like a drum.

Robin Wilum Goodfellow was known by one and all in the camp. He was a striking figure. His older, sour brother, Rupert Gregor Goodfellow, was short and rotund, with the shining red eyes and black hair that greater goblins seemed to share. Rupert's hair stuck out in all directions. It gave him a perpetually shocked look and seemed to enhance the ugly, snarled expression he often wore. Zeeka had told Robin once in a hushed whisper, Rupert seemed to have been born with a scowl. As soon as she said it, she clapped a hand over her mouth, peered around to be sure no other goblins had heard her dangerous words. Words like that could draw Rupert's unwanted attention.

Robin was the polar opposite of his brother, Rupert. Built like his father, Robin was tall, his body rippling with muscles. He had the striking features of the greater goblins, in a handsome, roguish sort of way. Oddly, his chin and nose were sharp, not mashed down like most other goblins. With hair hanging to his waist, it was a shining mass of black dreadlocks. The younger goblin prince sported numerous tattoos, each with a personal meaning known only to himself. Robin's eyes were a disturbing green, unlike any other goblin north or south of the great waters in Sharas. He was the second son of Lancer Ian Goodfellow, King of the Goblins.

Rupert was the probable Goblin Kingdom heir as the first son. Being the first son alone didn't grant him the status of heir. Goblin kings could choose their successors. Historically, it had been a tradition that first sons were named successors for the last five hundred years. Since Lancer Ian Goodfellow was missing, there seemed to be no question of Rupert becoming the next king. Robin worried that the older Goodfellow prince would rule in Lancer's stead, a fact that weighed heavily on their clan. Goblins lived extended lives in the absence of war. If Rupert became king, the people would be stuck with him as a leader for a very long time. Until that nightmare came true, Robin felt they were already getting a taste of how awful it would be. The clan was already living a bad dream with Morveena ruling as Queen Regent in Lancer's absence.

Walking the entire length of the cavern, Robin called out to each person, waved, shared a nod, and gave a smile here and there. He would stop, clap his hand on someone's shoulder, give or receive some news or a clever quip. He would tell a joke to lighten someone's mood, felt rewarded when they beamed at him, pleased that he'd noted them.

His circuit ended at the far end of the domed cavern. There, a collection of stalactites and stalagmites formed an archway where the rock rose a level, creating a platform. Robin looked up and bowed his head as the hazel eyes that met his held him with a steady gaze. "Good evening, my queen."

There, on a natural stone-formed seat, sat the self-proclaimed gem of the Kingdom. She wore a dark green velvet corset, brown leather leggings, and soft tan leather boots. Goblins did not wear shoes or boots, and Robin was no exception. The boots on the female before him made her stand out. She wore her red hair long, curls cascading down her back, setting off those gold-flecked eyes. Slim and fair-skinned, her caramel color was like the coveted cream the cooks always asked the lads to steal for them from a neighboring dairy farmer. Hundreds of tiny freckles dotted her face. Goblins had skin colors that ranged from light brown to dark black. Her unusual features made her beauty enchanting and unique. Robin stopped at the edge of her dais, stood facing her. Unfortunately, he knew her beauty was external only. Not one ounce of her outward looks gave her any inner beauty. Inside that façade lived a monster. Rupert stood behind her, his hand on her shoulder, hers reaching up, covering his, as he whispered in her ear.

Those hazel eyes held Robin's as if by magic. She nodded to Rupert, bringing both her hands to settle in her lap. "Robin," her voice named him like the softness of silk, "always comes to greet me last. You've said hello and spread your cheer to most everyone in the camp. How nice of you to bother with wishing me a good evening." She gifted him a smile that didn't meet her eyes. "Rupert brought me news of your Spring Feast gathering. He talked with the lads who were hunting with you," she informed him.

Robin stood tall, waiting, thinking it was likely Rupert threatened the lads by looking for negative information. The firelight flickered in the dome. Attendants added more logs to the central fire behind them. Red hair shimmered in the light. He had to admit she looked regal as their queen regent sat drumming her fingers on the arm of the stone seat, long, sharp nails clicking against the stone.

"The lads reported you *disappeared*," she said with suspicion, "while hunting today. You *must*," she emphasized, her eyes closing to slits, "tell me every detail. What kind of leader disappears from those under his command while out on a hunt?" she questioned, her words dripping with sarcasm. "What minor detail diverted you from your duties this time, Robin?" she taunted him.

The woman in front of Robin snapped her fingers. A lesser lad appeared with a goblet of wine for the queen. He'd been a member of the day's hunting party. Both his eyes were swollen and blackened, and Robin could see a thick bandage where his forefinger was broken. Or missing. Wine was not offered to Robin, but she signaled the servant to provide a goblet to Rupert, turning his brother's scowl into a leering smile. This was the type of thing Rupert considered a win over his brother. The servant cringed in fear as he proffered the wine. Rupert's eyes met Robin's, savoring the moment. Robin knew the lads wouldn't willingly betray him. He also knew there was nothing he could do to save them from Rupert's cruel treatment.

"Good evening, Mother, Rupert." Sidestepping her request for details, Robin bowed at the waist. "There are disturbing rumors of small clans of goblins going out on raids. Villages are being torched, people killed or kidnapped. After the deaths, those responsible are said to hold a looting party." He met their individual gazes eye to eye. "I thought we had all agreed to keep violence down, stay hidden and peaceful until we can sort out the Gugwe raids. Rumors can be dangerous. Especially if what the Gugwe are doing is being blamed on the Goblin people. At some point, we may need to create alliances with the other races of Sharas to fight the Gugwe." Neither of them responded.

"Training as many of the lads as possible in all the clans is my top priority, at least until we are better skilled and better armed to protect the lands *father* claims," he pressed his point, making sure not to refer to his father in past tense.

"Yes," Rupert hissed at him, "and I thought I assigned the job of training the clans to you and your sidekick! You and Cazzidy have the responsibility to keep the clans peaceful. It is your job to recruit and train soldiers to fight with the weaponry we've bought for you. It seems the two of you are falling short of the leadership skills entrusted to you, *brother*," the last word had been spit out of Rupert's mouth with disgust. "If goblins are staging raids anywhere in Sharas, you had better be investigating and putting a stop to the behavior. Perhaps Mother and I should reconsider giving you such duties if they are over your head and beyond your abilities?" he queried.

Robin sat down without invitation on one of the nearby boulders, a cornerstone for her raised platform. "Let's start again, shall we? Good evening, Mother," he directed his words to Morveena as she leaned back in satisfaction. She loved a good fight between the Goodfellow brothers. Cheap entertainment. Robin stood again, took three steps to the edge of the dais. "I've brought you a gift, my queen. I confess this gift is the reason for today's distraction, but when I saw them, I could only think of you." He smiled. Then, he removed a pouch from his belt and laid it at her feet. Rupert snarled and scowled. The Queen and Robin held one another's gaze until the tense moment passed. Queen Morveena signaled her attendant should pick up the pouch and hand it to her.

Gifts, rare among the goblin people, were not to be taken lightly. Robin kept his features blank as the Queen untied the pouch strings and pulled the leather sac open. Her fingers touched the soft, buttery material inside.

When she pulled the contents out, discovered a pair of fine ladies' boots; she clutched them to her breast. No one could miss the pleasure on her face, least of all Rupert. Her eyes locked with Robin's, as if in a private battle.

Robin spoke in a whisper. "Only you, Mother. I could think only of you when I found them."

Crooking her finger, she beckoned him forward. "Robin, my darling. Ever you are the favorite in my heart," she whispered in his ear.

Though she whispered, Rupert heard. He slammed his hand against the stone archway, stalking off, growling. Anyone with sense moved, not to be found in his pathway, should his arm snake out to take out his misguided anger on them.

Robin left the Queen on her throne, trying on her new butter-soft black leather boots. He shifted away from the Queen's end of the cavern as the name Faith, Faith, Faith rang out through his head. Somehow, he would think of a way to make the theft up to the girl he met today. Guilt lay heavy on him for taking Faith's boots, but the value of peace it bought him outweighed his remorse. The opportunity to acquire a pair of boots or shoes didn't present itself often. The footwear provided a type of coin to buy his mother's goodwill, however short-lived.

Robin hurried up the steep mineshaft. The sounds of the Spring Feast preparations grew fainter with each long stride he took toward the open night air. He needed to speak with his lifelong friend Caz, who was up top on guard duty, watching the entrance to the old mine housing the clan.

CAZZIDY BEAUMONT TOUCHSTONE had been Robin's best friend ever since they were wee lads. Happier days, those. He and Robin first took notice of one another as classmates. Master Cornerstone was their assigned scholar. Having Robin and Caz under his tutelage, he found himself saddled with not just one, but two 'class clowns.' Worse, those two spent years trying to outdo the other's last jest! Both Robin and Caz drank in the laughter like applause from their classmates. It was an elixir they never got enough of. Both boys discovered they rather enjoyed laughing at the other's tricks, almost as much as getting the laughs and attention from one of their own jests.

Merriment became the basis for their lifelong friendship, not to mention the bane of Master Cornerstone's long years of endurance. Secretly, the scholar enjoyed their shenanigans. The boys were kindhearted. But it wouldn't do for him to play anything but the role of a stern master.

For a Greater Goblin, Cazzidy was tall and had a solid, barrel-like build. He was broad-shouldered and well-muscled. Robin and Caz were friendly competitors in bodybuilding and weapons training. There were no tricks or jokes between any of them when it came to weapons, only fierce dedication to being the best at everything. A strong jawline and chiseled, sharp cheekbones made Caz's intense eyes stand out. The Touchstone kin had shiny black eyes and thick brown hair. Caz wore his waist-long tangles tied with a leather string, making a thick tail down his back. Cazzidy and Robin were well-matched in physical girth to hone their skills with many types of weapons. Practice was daily, regardless of weather or circumstances, another bond between them.

Respected among the other goblins who served in the Goblin Queen's militia, Caz held a reputation among the clan for treating everyone as an equal. Greater and lesser goblins, male and female alike. It came naturally to him to defend anyone who was a victim of any kind of discrimination. There were plenty of lads and lasses he and Robin had gone to school with who attempted to preserve the unspoken barrier between 'Greater' and 'Lesser'. There was no good reason to perpetuate the lie. Those referred to as Lesser had smaller bodies, a lighter complexion, and paler hair. They were just as smart as any clan member called Greater, yet the internal discrimination remained as strong as ever.

It always made him feel uncomfortable when he witnessed the hatred between the Fae, the goblins, and the human races, much less the discrimination within his own race and clan. He was a fierce fighter, near to earning the coveted title, Master of Weapons. Testing for the designation would take place at this year's Summer Games. He intended to walk away from those tournaments with a 'Queen's Ransom'. A full weapon set, custom-made and monogrammed after presentment for each winner. When the day comes naming Cazzidy Beaumont Touchstone a Master of

Weapons, he will have achieved his longest-held dream. Standing at his post over the last couple of months, he considered potential new goals to pursue while on duty, since he felt he was close to finishing the only one that had been his focus for years. A small pebble hit his nose, interrupting his thoughts.

He loosed a growl, dropped to a crouch, sword at the ready. But saw no one there. Alert, he listened, hearing breathing behind him at the cave's entrance.

"Psssst." Ah, Caz surmised, Robin then, hiding in the shadows. Caz feigned a stretch, strolled to the cave opening, and leaned against the wall.

Hidden behind the cave's arch, Robin didn't want anyone to see the two of them together. He whispered to Caz, "A few of the lads told me today Rupert's looking to make trouble again. I don't want him to send it your way. Aside from weapons practice, stay away from me and spend time with the others. Try not to draw his attention until we find out what's going on. My brother is doing a lot of whispering in the Queen's ear. Now is not the time to endanger your chances of winning at the Summer Games. I don't want him to harm you trying to get at me."

Caz scratched his ass and rolled his shoulders, in case anyone was watching, and responded in his raspy whisper, "I am *not* afraid of Rupert."

"Course not," Robin agreed. "I know you're not, so I don't want to give him any excuse. You can investigate from the inside. Talk to the lads and the lasses. See if there's been any gossip. I know he's going to pull something to mess us up. In the meantime, we'll just act as though our friendship has cooled off. Keep him at arm's length until our tests are over, yeah?"

Caz sighed and said, "All right, laddie, if that's how you want to play it. I'll resign myself to the harsh job of keeping more company with the lasses to see if I can ferret out any secrets concerning a certain shithead brother of yours." Caz stooped down, appearing to adjust his boot. "I bet you'll be round the lasses yourself at tonight's Spring Feast!"

"No, my friend," said Robin, shaking his head. "Don't think I will. I saw a very beautiful girl today. She may just have stolen my heart. It may be hard to win her over though, as I stole her boots to present as a gift for the Queen."

"What's this, Robin?" Caz demanded, only to find empty silence behind him.

No one was the wiser they had talked, nary a witness to see, hear, or report to Rupert. Caz looked up at the sky, judging he had another hour of duty before his shift ended. The Touchstone passed the time lifting heavy stones up and down, working his biceps and chuckling about his friend's confession. It wasn't the first time Robin had professed to be in love. His infatuations rarely lasted. He wondered which of the lasses had caught Robin's eye this time. He meant to keep a keen watch out during the dancing tonight.

REAPPEARING AMONG THE clan, Robin moved in and out amidst the feast preparations. He helped clear the center of the hall for dancing and gave the lads a hand setting up the food tables for the feast. It wasn't long before the steaming platters and bowls were coming out of the kitchen cavern. Freshly cooked bounty filled the room with mouth-watering aromas, attracting a crowd.

The younger Goodfellow gathered a group of lads around him. His mother sat upon her dais, Rupert at her side. Clapping her hands, she announced, "Let the Spring Feast Celebration begin!" Robin and his mates struck up a merry tune with drums, fiddle, and flute, while the food was served. They broke off to join the last of those in line. Robin saw Caz come in from guard duty when the shift changed.

Filling his plate with steamed snails in watercress broth. Zeeka added an extra dollop of butter to his wild asparagus. He forked a thick cut of venison steak, topping it with a pile of butter-sautéed mushrooms and wild ramps. A young lass named Saffron came round with a pitcher and filled his flagon with fresh beer. He settled in at a table with the lads, looked around, caught his mother's eye, raised his cup to her in salute, and attacked his meal with gusto. Rupert glared at him, but Robin paid him no mind. After seconds, then thirds, with his beer topped off twice, he took his flute up again and played a ditty. The other musicians gathered around, and the dancing began. There were at least a dozen talented music makers jamming together. Robin lost himself in music-making.

Caz was not a musician, but he loved to turn out on the dance floor. There were plenty of eager lasses to turn about with. After all, Robin had made it his duty to mingle with as many of the girls as he could. As the night wore on, in between dancing, Caz was dicing with the lads. Today had been Equinox payday, and the rattling dice called to Caz like a lover. He had a passion for games of chance. A love of winning. The Touchstone had magic in his long, strong fingers when he threw the dice. The music makers, dancers, gamblers, and lovers enjoyed as merry a Spring Feast as they'd had in years.

Paying little attention to who was playing, Caz put his attention on the dice. Players came and went. Some found their pockets a little heavier for the play; others with no coins left to jingle. It was a long way away from the next solstice pay. On the last throw of the current game, he whooped, jumped up to claim his win, and found himself face to face with Rupert's scowl. A hush fell over the crowd of gamblers as he shrugged, scraped up his winnings, putting the coins in his pouch, now bulging with half a year's salary. As he turned to walk away, Rupert grabbed his shoulder. Cazzidy growled at the touch.

Rupert, eyes darting around the crowd, challenged Caz. "You can't walk away now, Touchstone. I say it's high time you gave the lads a chance to win back some of their hard-earned money. Right, laddies?" The lads grumbled and growled, though all knew Caz had won fair and square.

"No worries. I'm off to get a fresh beer and have another dance with a lass. I'll be back, Rupert. The night is young," Caz said as he brushed the bully's hand off his shoulder. Rupert moved to stand in Caz's way. The Goblin Prince snapped his fingers. Saffron appeared with a pitcher of beer.

"Fill his cup." Rupert commanded.

Robin and the musicians finished the song they were playing and tensed at the scene. Saffron swallowed and looked up under her lashes at Caz, hoping she would not find herself in the middle of punches thrown. Caz met her gaze, held out his mug.

Saffron topped off the tankard with a good foam head and curtsied. "I'd been hoping for just the right moment to catch your eye, Caz." Playing coy, she smiled at him and went on. "Seems I remember you promising me a dance or two last week. My shift will be over in half an hour. Could a pretty face convince you to leave off gaming by then? Perhaps you could give me a few turns around the dance floor?" She winked at him, flirting. "Can I count on you to make good on your word, laddie?"

Caz looked her in the eye, glanced round at the lads, then at Rupert. The tension was thick. Caz let his left hand drop from his weapon belt, raised his beer mug in salute to Saffron and said, "Aye, my lady, you have my word. Wouldn't want you to think I didn't keep my promises." He winked at her. "I'll finish my dicing while you finish your shift. Then I'll find you on the dance floor." He took a long pull of his beer and rattled the dice in his hand. The music started back up, so Saffron moved on through the crowd.

Rupert's face held a smug smile as he stepped away from the gamblers. He felt as though he'd just won, although he hadn't taken part in the game. Though Rupert was none the wiser, it wasn't the first time Cazzidy Beaumont Touchstone just allowed the fool to live. He'd been a hair's breadth from killing the clan heir, consequences be damned. Moments before, Saffron had saved the bloody prince's throat from being slit. Truth be told, she saved Caz's neck as well. Killing the Goblin Prince would not have gone well. No matter how popular one was with the clan. Their crazy queen would have had him strung up so she could peel his skin off. A shiver ran across his flesh at the thought.

The dice rolled for another thirty minutes.

SAFFRON HAD EMPTIED her beer pitcher, spent ten minutes washing her face, smoothing her wild, curly red hair back with a colorful band tied at the base of her neck. She crushed some berries, dipped her fingertips in the juice, rubbing fresh red over her full lips. Her apron came off, and she fluffed up her bold red and gold striped skirt, strutted out onto the center of the dance floor in her bare feet. She crossed her arms and tapped her foot, dramatizing her wait for the Touchstone in front of the audience.

Robin smiled at Saffron, nodded, indicating, "Well done." She acknowledged him but turned away, eyes searching for Caz.

The Beaumont, as the lads sometimes called him, had taken a few moments to spruce himself up. He strolled onto the dance floor after talking with one fiddler, putting in his request, and turned to bow before the lovely Saffron. She curtsied. Caz pulled a trout lily from his pouch and fastened it behind her ear. The throng let out a collective "Ooooh". The floor cleared for the two.

A fiddler plucked three strings. The musicians knew the song, so they struck up the tune. The crowd began to clap and stomp around the room in time with the beat of the music. Other dancers formed up into six circles. The first circle all moving round to the left. Second, all circling round to the right. Third to the left, fourth to the right, and so on. The dance looked like a living kaleidoscope, with Caz and Saffron in the center. Their singular dance began. It was mesmerizing. The couple found themselves caught up in the melody, caught up in each other. Ending the dance, Caz swung Saffron up and around in a dramatic flourish, the crowd roaring their approval.

Rupert brought his mother down for a dance so she could show off her lovely new boots. She thought them perfect for dancing. Of course, the queen was the *only* goblin wearing boots. All other goblins, male, or female, greater or lesser, went barefoot. Morveena had quite a collection of shoes and boots, all stolen for her over the years. Most by Robin. She valued them above all else. A fact that didn't escape Rupert. Loathing the sight of her ugly goblin feet, the Queen was obsessed with keeping them covered. Her fixation was so strong, she applied her queenly powers by passing a law decreeing only the queen could own and wear shoes or boots among the goblin people.

Robin left the musician's circle. He found Zeeka, took her dancing round the floor for a few songs, as he'd promised. Feeling duty-bound, he made his way to the dais to find his mother to ask her to dance, but she'd already gone down to her chambers. So instead, he moved through the room, drinking and talking with the people. He hadn't seen Caz leave, but Robin knew it was Saffron's quick thinking that had avoided bloodshed or worse at Spring Feast. Tomorrow, he planned to make a point of finding the lass to let her know how much he appreciated her quick thinking in diffusing the situation.

Often the last to leave a party, Robin sat down by the fire and pulled a flask from his vest. He sipped fine bourbon while brooding over several things he was tracking in his head. Issues that looked to be a greater sum of trouble in the future, pondering what he might do about them. But if his father taught him one thing, it was patience. You didn't want to rush in without all the facts. He had already decided that gathering more information would become his focus until he had enough intel to formulate a plan. The fire burned down, coals glowing, and the night passed into a new day.

His last thoughts of the evening rang out in his head like a mantra.

Faith. Faith. Faith.

He smiled as he took one last sip from his flask and capped it.

SAFFRON HAD INVITED The Beaumont to sneak off and meet her in secret a half hour after the last dance. For their tryst, she had suggested a small, little-used and lesser-known cavern room off the kitchens that was down two levels. They parted ways after their memorable twirl, so as not to be seen leaving together. Saffron liked to maintain her neutral appearance of having nothing to do with Robin or his friends. It allowed her greater freedom to gather information for Robin, which she'd been doing for years.

Attracting the older Goodfellow's attention was never a good thing. It could be very dangerous to one's general health and well-being in the best of circumstances. She hoped her actions tonight hadn't drawn Rupert's notice. She'd have to wait and see. It was too late to retract the diffusion tactic between Rupert and Caz she'd employed earlier. With any luck, Rupert only remembered he'd snapped his fingers and someone beneath his notice had appeared at his command to refill Caz's mug. She prayed he did not recall how her words gave Caz the chance to stand down, with Rupert feeling like he'd won something.

The redhead hurried through the cave tunnel, her bare feet making no sound, thoughts in turmoil as she focused on the incident with Rupert. Her sixth sense broke through her chaotic replay of the scene between Caz and Rupert, causing her to stop dead in her tracks. She was just a few feet from the entrance to the room she sought. Instinct drew her body tight as a bowstring as she recognized a voice coming from the room she had intended to enter. Not just any voice. Rupert's voice!

Her body responded to the immediate inclination to hide. Saffron pressed her body against the shadowed wall of the cave hallway. The stone welcomed her goblin form, surrounding her, camouflaging her physique as part of the wall. The terror of a second entanglement with Rupert in one night kept her every nerve on high alert. She tuned in to Rupert's voice, worrying that Caz had come down early to meet her. She feared it was the Beaumont with whom Rupert was talking. *Had Rupert or someone else overheard their plans to meet down here?* Reigning in her fears, she decided the tone of Rupert's speech wouldn't have been the one he would have used with Caz.

Rupert's voice echoed out of the chamber. Even though he was whispering, in a manner not typical for him, *Saffron listened.* "A wonderful spring feast, my love, don't you think?" Saffron couldn't quite catch the response. *My love? Who could Rupert be talking to? Most all the Goblin people hated him!*

"You looked ravishing tonight!" Rupert exclaimed. "Your beauty outshone every other female at the feast. No, no, don't be coy. You know you did. Come close for one last kiss, darling. Our private time is so limited, so dangerous. We must be away and soon, before the kitchens become active again." Then there were some squelchy, wet, sucking sounds. *Must be kissing, Saffron thought.*

Rupert spoke again. "What, my dear?"

...whispering that Saffron could barely make out, but even with Goblin-enhanced hearing, she just couldn't catch the words...

"Don't be silly, my dear. I would do anything for you. Oh my, oh, I do so love your body and the way you respond to my touch. Let me worship you." Several long minutes of bodily noises, and then a rousing female response of combined growling and a last scream. Next...heavy breathing and movements to the beat of a drum, Rupert's own climax, as he growled out, "You. Are. Mine. Only mine. Swear it. Swear it to me!" he demanded. His partner responded, laughing. Then his release, a deafening roar.

A moment or two passed. Saffron felt ill, thought about ripping her body from the stone wall she was hiding in and running for her life. She panicked at the thought of being discovered. Had she waited too long to get away? Especially now. You could hear a pin drop.

"Tell me again," he growled. "Tell me you'll have both those worthless bastards killed and see me crowned, rid ourselves of Robin and Caz! Then...then, we can be together and not have to hide our love. What? No, no, my dear. We'll make it right. Death to any who dare to deny us our love! You should go back to your chambers through the kitchen. I'll go out through the secret door in here."

Next, Saffron heard a series of grunts and groans of pain. "Stop! You know I meant nothing by it. You're hurting me!" Rupert wailed. "Yes, yes. I apologize. Of course, you make all the decisions. I exist to serve your desires. It was only playful lovers' talk. Ouch! Please, I beg your forgiveness. Humph!" Coughing and retching echoed in the hallway. Footsteps came close to the doorway.

Closing her eyes, she held still and hoped her fear wasn't coming through the pores in her body as an odor. Goblins had a very intense sense of smell, and Saffron was terrified of being caught. Saffron's only hope was that Rupert's lover's own odor from their coupling would overwhelm whoever was coming out of the room. She felt disgust wash over her at the idea of anyone mating with Rupert. Saffron couldn't in her wildest dreams imagine who would lie with him! *What was all that bloody violence she heard?*

The door opened and closed inside the room. Saffron picked up the sound of soft footsteps coming toward her. *Please, please, thought Saffron, don't let Caz show up now!* The quiet footfalls came through the doorway and into the hall, then...stopped. Heart thudding in her chest, her anxiety peaking, Saffron thought her heart would burst out of her chest any second. Then she heard the person rush back into the room, only a moment later reenter the hallway and begin moving toward the stairs leading up to the kitchen.

Fear. Terror. Then she decided, torture be damned! She had to know.

Saffron couldn't help but open her eyes, even if it would expose her hiding place if someone looked directly at the space she occupied, hidden in the wall. Unabashed curiosity washed over her common sense. Her quick glance caught the figure heading up the steps. The face was already out of sight, but she saw a flash of red hair and, worse; leather-booted feet as they faded out of sight, climbing the stairway. Only one other female goblin in this clan besides herself had red hair.

And there was definitely only one person who would have boots on.

Remaining hidden, wrapped in the safety of the cave wall, she was stunned into stillness. Her thoughts were like churning mud, unable to coalesce into any conclusion. One thought came floating to the forefront.

I'm dead. Rupert will find me out. He's bound to learn I was down here spying on them.

Then another thought pushed through her shock.

Oh, my stars! Rupert and the Queen are lovers! Bloody hell! A mother and her son. Yuck! Disgusting!

Her mind reared its ugly head.

That bitch and that bastard are planning to kill...what was it Rupert said? Bloody hell. His exact words were, "Tell me you'll have both those worthless bastards killed and see me crowned." That last thought caused Saffron's body to pop out of the wall. She shook her head and looked down at her ugly, bare, bootless goblin feet. In a panic, she turned to run and slammed smack into Caz!

"Sorry I'm late," he stammered. "You're not running away mad, are you?" he asked, half-joking. She clung to him. Caz held her, realizing she was trembling. "Here now, lass," he clasped her upper arms, holding her away so he could see her face. The terror in her eyes was clear as day. "Saffron!" he said and shook her. "Get hold of yourself! What's got you in such an uproar?"

Looking around, eyes wild, "Shhhhh!" she commanded. "We can't talk here. Caz, you're coming with me right now to find a secure place where we can talk. I'm dead! I just know it."

He scratched his head in confusion, saying nothing.

"Quiet!" she hissed at him. He took a step back, surprised, as he hadn't said a word. Saffron grabbed his hand and pulled him toward the stairs leading up to the kitchen. Caz set his feet apart in a deadweight stance. "Hold on, lass," he stated. "We can talk in the room down here. If I recall, you promised me earlier a private kiss or two. At least, that was the impression you gave." He smiled at her, waggled his eyebrows.

Saffron realized he would not budge until she made some sense, gave him some kind of explanation. Taking a deep, calming breath, she cupped his cheek in her palm and pulled his head close. But instead of the kiss he expected, her lips were by his ear whispering, "Cazzidy Beaumont Touchstone, hear me now. It. Is. Not. Safe. For. Us. To. Talk. Here." She pulled back, looking him in the eyes, then closer again to whisper more, "I've just overheard a plot to kill both you and Robin Goodfellow. I am scared witless, and all my senses are telling me to run like the wind from here. So please humor me until we can find a place to talk where there is no chance...none whatsoever...for anyone to overhear what I've got to tell you. Agreed?"

Pushing back from him again, she met his incredulous look eye to eye. He could tell she was serious and terrified. He nodded his acquiescence. Saffron grabbed his hand and started again toward the stairs. She stopped after two steps, turned back to him, swearing under her breath.

Eyes heavenward, she whispered, "By the gods, if I am going to die, I should at least have that kiss!"

She wrapped her arms around Caz's broad shoulders, pressed her soft but muscular body hard against his, covering his mouth with her own.

Time stopped in her brain. There was only this. Only now. All else be damned.

Caz returned her kiss with ardor, and their bodies sang together. When they broke the embrace, they broke the spell. Saffron let her breath out, hissing, "Oh gods." Then, she grabbed his hand and raced up the stairs.

CHAPTER 3: Her Own Little Ritual

(SEVEN YEARS EARLIER)

Dancing round the Faerie Ring;
Magic makes our hearts sing.
Wildflowers in our hair;
Colored dresses for us to wear.
When you have a silver ring;
Perhaps a prince will become your king.
Until that day, we have each other;
And all the magic from your mother.
The secret is part me; part you.
If you join your hand with mine;
The power we wield
Will be combined.

The long rope stopped turning and went slack. Faith and her best friend Val had been singing the rhyme in a cadence, jumping the rope, keeping the beat. They burst into laughter. "Come on now," Val's sister Carlisse prodded, "you both promised that Delainey and I could jump next. You said you'd swing the rope for us."

"We did promise, Carlisse. All right; I'll take your end. Val," Faith pointed at Delainey, "take Lainey's. Let's give them a turn." Everyone got into place, and just as they got the momentum going on the jumping rope, Carlisse rocked back and forth on the balls of her feet, ready to jump in. She matched the twirling rhythm of the rope as it swung up over her head, hit the ground, and then up again. Then, spoiling her turn, the schoolmaster rang the bell, signaling that recess was over.

Faith and Val dropped the rope.

"That's not fair!" Carlisse complained.

"You can go first next time," Val tried to console her older sister. "Promise." She kissed two fingers and pressed them to her sister's cheek.

Recess over, the Scholar clapped his hands to get everyone settled in their seats, energy still running at peak from their morning recess. "All right, all right. Time to buckle down and get our minds back to our work. Your next assignment this morning is to write an essay about your life and your family. I want you to tie all that history up with a view of what you hope for your future. Establish the details you believe influenced you to be the person you are today. I want you to describe the dreams and wishes you have for when you grow up. Finish the essay with a list of ideas of what you can do today, tomorrow, next month, or next year to work at making those dreams come true." The scholar took hold of the hourglass on his desk and declared, "Neatness counts. You have one hour to complete the assignment. Remember, the things you write today about your aspirations are likely to remain with you for the rest of your life. You are the only person who can make your dreams come true. No one else can do that for you. In fact, no other person will do that for you. Choose your words judiciously. Make your considerations with care." Scholar Wilcox turned the glass over, grains of sand falling to count the time. "Begin."

Faith could hardly believe it when an hour had passed, and the Scholar had called for their papers to be passed up front to him. They broke for lunch after arithmetic. The group took their satchels and went out under the oak trees. The students made food swaps: apples for pears, or cheese for meat pies. Then it was quiet while they ate. Carlisse looked around and, with a wide grin, produced a flour sack with a dozen sugar cookies, passing one out to everyone. She took a bite, adding a sound of delight as she let the sugar melt in her mouth. "There'll be hell to pay with Mam when I get home," she giggled. "But she ought to know better than to bake cookies in the morning. I couldn't resist."

Everyone enjoyed the treat. One boy licked his fingers, remarking, "I'm going to the town square with my Da tomorrow to help with the decorations for the Festival of Ostara. Any of you lot going?"

Val spoke up. "All the Purehearts will be there."

"Why do they still call it the Festival of Ostara?" Garrett asked no one in particular. "Isn't that related to an ancient god that no one worships anymore?" He stuffed the last piece of cookie into his mouth. "My Da gave me the day off in the stables, traded for two days after school next week. He's rounded up a group of lads to help him set up the Maypole for dancing."

"One of my Da's cousins, who lives a day's ride from here, was visiting a few weeks ago," Garrett continued. "He said we might see some gobs at this year's festival. A big clan moved into the caves south of his village. They've been coming in to trade, looking to make some connections, get to know some folks."

"Don't call them gobs, Garrett. That's slang. They're goblins. I doubt they appreciate people making them seem like they are less than us, yeah?" Val didn't hide her anger at the slight.

"Sorry, Val, I meant nothing by it. I've heard lots of folks refer to them that way," he told her. "I didn't mean to be disrespectful."

"Well, I heard my mam talking with a neighbor a few weeks ago. They said the spring equinox festival revolved around the old ways. Pagan celebrations had themes of balance, renewal, and rebirth. The symbols of Ostara are spring flowers, fairies, butterflies, rabbits, and eggs. The colors used to represent Ostara are pastels. Yellow, orange, lavender, and green. That's why all the decorations are traditionally in those hues. All the girls' dresses feature those colors as well." Aliah added. She turned and looked at Carlisse, "Don't expect me to take any blame because you helped yourself to a dozen of Mam's cookies without permission," she told her sister as she finished the last two bites of the sweet Carlisse had shared with her.

"Fairies?" Lainey asked. "I'd love to know more about them. There are lots of Fae families that live in town. Da says they own the docks. Sir Robert does regular business with them. Faith, did you know folk whisper about the old nurse and your Lady Reatha being Fae?" She looked around at the group. "There's an old prophecy that Mam was telling Estelle and Andrew I overheard."

"Overheard? More like you hid behind the bushes to eavesdrop, Delainey," Aliah tsked.

Faith leaned closer, touched Delainey's shoulder, "What was the prophecy?"

Ignoring Aliah's comment, Delainey continued. "The Foresight revolves around a girl who doesn't know she's a princess. Mam said the Princess will discover a great secret that will change our lives. It also mentions some kind of attack or invasion that's supposed to kill us or enslave us or something like that. The girl in the prophecy becomes a princess of us all. Saves all the citizens of Sharas." Delainey shrugged her shoulders. "Anyway, it's probably just a bedtime story the old nurse brought with her when she moved here." Everyone laughed.

The scholar rang his brass bell again, interrupting the gossip, calling them in out of the sunshine. He announced they would each take a turn standing in front of the class to read the essays they had written earlier. Faith felt a flush run up her neck and warm her cheeks. She wasn't especially fond of getting up in front of the entire group, much less sharing her dreams with everyone. What if her classmates thought her dreams were dumb and laughed at her?

A third student was called to read her essay. Faith wiped her clammy hands down the front of her tunic and walked to the front of the room. She kept her eyes on the words she'd written and avoided eye contact with her classmates. Her voice had calmed by the time she was almost finished with her presentation.

"One activity I enjoy," she swallowed hard, "some people might consider frivolous, others magical. I like to draw. My dream would be to travel all over Sharas, even beyond. I would create illustrations of people and places. Becoming an artist is my dream. I especially enjoy drawing portraits, capturing facial features, mannerisms, and character, like a mirror."

"What could I be doing tomorrow, next week, next month, or next year to work toward my dream, my goal? I will seek books about places and create a firm itinerary of where I would like to travel. In addition, I'll continue drawing and sketching as often as I can each week to improve my artistic skills and techniques."

Faith raised her eyes to peek up at her fellow students, afraid she would see smirking faces looking back at her. It pleased her to find her classmates smiling. Anxiety drained away. Scholar Wilcox thanked her for her presentation, then called the name of the next student. Faith returned to her seat, relieved that the pressure of speaking in front of everyone was over. Most of the time, she thought of herself as all alone in the world. Grateful for her adoptive family and her close friends. She'd never been able to get over the feeling she harbored—that something set her apart from everyone. It just felt like she was a piece of a puzzle that didn't quite fit into the entire picture. Today, as she listened to each of her classmates read an essay about their own dreams, it was the closest she'd felt to being just like everyone else. It left her with a warm feeling inside.

The idea had never occurred to her to ask her friends about their dreams, their hopes. Focusing on each speaker, she listened as they took center-stage revealing their private thoughts. She learned Garrett loved horses, but wasn't sure if he wanted to be a stable master like his da or if he would pursue breeding and trading horses for a living when he grew up.

Val had natural speaking skills. She looked up as she spoke and met the eyes of her schoolmates. Her voice had a natural rhythm. Using her hands for emphasis as she presented, Val walked back and forth in front of the room. Gesturing throughout her speech, Faith was amazed that Val never once looked at the written essay she held. Val revealed she wanted to put on plays and act out character parts. She talked about how she loved to help people. A blush ran up her neck and colored her cheeks when she read the part in her essay where she wondered if women could be involved in leadership or government. Plans for accomplishing her dreams included traveling to the capital of Sharas one day to learn more about how politics worked. There were a few sniggers in the back of the room, but overall, there was a good acceptance of her future ideas.

A WEEK LATER, A SMALL group of goblins showed up at that year's annual Festival of Ostara. There were seven lads and three lasses. The newcomers were popular at once. The girls presented two big pans of scalloped tubers for the potluck. It didn't hurt that the lads had arrived with two kegs of ale strapped to their backs. Taking the barrels down to the docks, they set the bottoms of the vats in a foot of icy river water to keep the ale cool, then hooked a clever pump on top of one keg to draw a mug.

Faith and Val had wandered over to the display booths, as they'd heard one lady in town was offering tastes of her famous pickles. Standing in line for a free sample, they listened to the gossip from the two women in front of them.

"My grandmother told me that the old prophecy says a witch with magic is the one who'll lead us to win against the enemy," the tall one said.

"Not a witch, silly. A Fae princess," her companion corrected.

"Fae or a witch? It's all the same, isn't it? One never knows if their Fae magic will pass along through the blood to their children. Gran told me magic can only be inherited from her mother if she was a witch."

"You should stop using the description 'witch'. The change could happen to your daughter in a few years, with Fae blood in your family line. Heard it comes with the menses. Besides, a little magic could make life sweeter, yeah?"

Faith and Val's eyes grew big as saucers. They moved a little closer to see if the ladies revealed any other information. The women reached the table, busied themselves tasting various types of pickles; the conversation changed to focus on the pickler's skill.

Val had permission to spend the night with Faith when they got back to Robert's fortress after the festival. Later that night, the two girls were in Faith's room, with a cozy fire burning to take off the chill. Val asked, "Do you think we might be Fae? Have magical powers?"

"Doubtful. I mean, I guess it's possible, but we don't even know who our birth mothers are, much less have any knowledge of whether our mums had the touch. Some of the older girls in town say menses come around the age of twelve or thirteen. Since we're only nine, I don't think we have to worry about it for a few more years." Faith lay on her side, elbow propped on the floor, hand cradling her head. She had a dreamy look in her eyes. "Didn't you love the Maypole dancing? I can't wait until we turn twelve so we can join in. I've already decided my first dance dress is going to be lavender. How about you?" They talked long into the night, as Val rarely got permission to stay over.

Faith's birthday was a week after the Festival of Ostara. Occurring so soon following all the celebration activities, it was a pretty quiet affair. Cook always made her favorite cake. Evy put a vase of fresh-cut flowers on her dressing table every year. Reatha presented a wrapped package that contained a new dress she had sewn.

On the day she turned nine, Garratt approached her, sitting on the back steps outside the kitchen, where she was enjoying a piece of her birthday cake. She went in and asked Cook for a second plate to share the treat with Garrett. Garth and Mara's son had a wicked sweet tooth, so he appreciated her generosity.

"Happy birthday," he told her around a mouthful of sugary goodness.

She laughed as he shoveled another bite in. "Careful, Garrett. Evy always says too much sugar will give you bad dreams."

"Ha! She just tells you that to keep you from taking a second piece of cake, I'll wager."

"I don't need sugar to give me nightmares."

He lowered his spoon and swallowed. "You have nightmares?"

"Sometimes. It is always the same one."

"About what?"

She looked around, then in a low voice told him, "I have a recurring dream. I'm alone and lost. It scares me. My heart is always racing when I wake up."

Garrett watched her for a minute to make sure she wasn't pulling his leg. He decided she wasn't when he saw her shiver just thinking about the bad dream.

"Hey," he said to take her mind off it, "I made you a birthday present." He stuck his hand in his pocket and pulled out a small wooden star he had carved, handing it to her. "Tell you what, let's make a pact. If you're ever alone and lost, find the North Star. I'll always find you there," he winked. "Got to get back to my chores, lass. See you in the morning for our walk to school, yeah? Happy birthday, Faith."

Faith spent the rest of the day sketching in her book by the fireplace. Reatha and Evy nearby, rocking in their chairs, sewing.

MONTHS LATER, FAITH was staying overnight at the Purehearts'. It was a warm evening. The sky was ablaze with stars as Val, Faith, Aliah, Carlisse, and Delainey lay atop a small knoll, stargazing.

"There's one!" Carlisse called out. "That's seven shooters for me."

"Another," Val declared. "I've got you by two, Carlisse."

"I love stargazing," Aliah sighed. "Mam told me you could make a secret wish every time you see a shooting star."

"Have you tried it?" Delainey asked.

"Yes, but Mam also said you can't tell anyone your wish or it won't come true."

"Star wishes. Fortune telling. Nursie claims it's all a bunch of hooey." Faith said. "Oh, there's one."

"That old biddy likes nothing that could be mystical," Val declared.

THE YEARS PASSED. FAITH and her friends were always involved in helping with the Festival of Ostara. Now they were among the many who danced the dances under the Maypole.

The goblins had stopped coming to the town festival several years before. Occasional fights had broken out at past events. Goblins and even some of the townspeople exchanged insults. The troubles were just starting back then, but it put an end to the goblins mixing in at the festivals. Faith and Val felt sad that the goblins didn't feel welcome at the event. It was supposed to be a time of celebration for the entire community. The observance of Ostara should have fostered unity among the people, not exclusion.

Garrett made an annual tradition of giving Faith a star he carved for her birthday, along with the same promise each time. "If you're ever alone and lost, go to the North Star. I'll always find you there." Faith made sure just the two of them shared her special birthday cake.

Later, when Val became a best friend, the trio did almost everything together and were all but inseparable. Garrett kept up that private birthday custom, and Faith continued to only share her cake with the stable master's son. It was something special just between the two of them. That made it one of the few things Val felt jealous of. She never spoke to either of them about it. Her Mam referred to those feelings as the green-eyed monster.

Each year, Faith had Andrew drill a small hole in every carved star Garrett had ever given her. She strung them onto a leather thong and wore it like a necklace. When she was fourteen, she lost the string of stars. She moped about it for weeks. It felt like she'd lost a great treasure and a part of herself. Garrett told her not to worry about it.

On her fifteenth birthday, he proffered a new star and gave her the promise, as always. The star she carried in a little pouch hooked to her belt. She nestled it in with her other favorite things: a handful of loose pearls, a lucky rabbit's foot she won at the festival one year, and a partridge feather she'd found in the woods when mushrooming four years before. She had a few new stars now, but never again saw the necklace with all of Garrett's previous gifts.

It was unlikely she ever would. Val kept the precious necklace buried deep at the bottom of a chest. A cache where she kept things she wanted to keep private from her sisters. Two years before, on the day before Faith's birthday, Val arrived home one day sick with guilt, pulling Faith's necklace from her pocket. The two girls had stripped down to swim in the river. Val still couldn't explain to herself why she'd grabbed it when she'd emerged from the water first and tucked it into the pocket of her tunic. Her best friend looked up and down the riverbank, frantic to find the treasure, but had to give up, never dreaming one of her best friends had snatched it. Val had feigned helping to look for the string of stars. But once she'd stolen the necklace, Val couldn't think of any good way to return it without confessing her selfish act. It wasn't just admitting to the theft she feared, but that she was sure it would ruin the trust her best friend had in her as well. Worst of all, she would have to reveal the horrible feelings of jealousy she'd hidden about Faith and Garrett's special annual tradition all these years. The only thing they excluded her from.

Once the dirty deed was done, Val couldn't see how to undo it. So, she'd kept the necklet, placed it in a small drawstring silk pouch she'd sewn to hide it in. Once a year, while Faith and Garrett did their private cake sharing and carved star tradition on Faith's birthday, Val would sneak off alone, pull the stars from their protective pouch and just look at them. Wondering what it would be like to have someone so close—a friend, one who would make you a gift like this year after year without fail, and give it along with a pledge.

With regret written across her face, she would put the necklet of stars away, hiding them deep within her trunk, and then would forget they were there until the following year. Her own lonely little ritual.

CHAPTER 4: Too Good to Be True

Morveena, Queen of the Goblins, sat at her vanity, hairbrush in hand, staring into the mirror. Her image appeared clouded. The looking glass was ancient, silver worn away, making streaks across the surface. Her thoughts drifted back to another time and place as she studied her reflection.

The first mirror Morveena had ever seen was in the Faerie Queen's palace on the northern shores of Sharas. It wasn't as if she hadn't seen her own image before, but only by gazing into a lake or pond. A mirror seemed almost magical.

The opportunity occurred while traveling with her father, Munro Montestrell. They had been guests, the two of them invited to stay at the Fae palace when she was young. Back then, hatred had not spread so deeply and so far between the races. She remembered the day as fair when they had arrived at the Fae court. A sky so blue it touched her heart. When the sun broke through the Fae Queen's balcony doors, it reflected in an arc from the dressing-table mirror. The beveled edge made rainbows that shimmered all across the wall. The Queen saw Morveena's reaction, her interest piqued, so she invited the young goblin to her personal salon to show her the looking glass. With her first glance in the reflective glass, the girl found herself fascinated with her own image. The Fae Queen approached from behind; both of their faces looked out from the silvered mirror. Feigning disinterest, Morveena quickly left the room. The Queen, disquieted by the odd, harsh rebuke, watched the girl disappear down the hallway.

Morveena Morgan Montestrell was the first and only child of Munro Marcellus Montestrell, a Goblin Envoy. Her father had been acting as an official ambassador between the goblin clans and the Fae kingdom since she was a small girl. Munro told Morveena her mother had left them, but Morveena knew of the secret grave her father kept vigil over. She had followed him on the sly countless times as he stood over her mother's burial place, talking to his dead wife as if she could still hear him. Unfortunately, her father blamed the girl for her mother's death, even though it was dealt by his own hand. He blamed her for everything. Wish as she may, wish as she might, he beat her bloody and bruised at least once a week, just as he had her mother. She often considered that her own fate could end the same way.

Between beatings, as her bruises melted from black and blue to yellow and green, she made up plans in her head. Over time, she learned it didn't matter how good she tried to be, how hard she tried to make everything perfect, because no matter what, Every. Single. Day. he always, always found something to blame her for. The itch for violence got under his skin, setting off his need to control her. Morveena's dreams became a living thing locked away inside. The girl had wants and needs. She had plans, had even promised herself she would one day do *anything* to make them come true. But she couldn't seem to find a way out of the current situation she was trapped in.

As an envoy, Munro Montestrell often had to travel to the Faerie Court to deliver messages from the Goblin King. The summer Morveena turned sixteen, he had asked if she wanted to accompany him first to the Goblin Hold and then on to the Faerie Court.

She was wary of his offer.

Nothing good ever came from her father acting nice. He had never allowed her to accompany him before. Still, she decided it was an opportunity. Conscious of his status, he would never want others to find out she was his punching bag. That would ruin his precious reputation.

Maybe.

So maybe it would be alright, and his fear of anyone discovering his proclivity would protect her.

This invitation seemed too good to be true, but if she declined, he might never offer to take her with him again.

In the end, she decided it was an offer she couldn't resist; she packed her trunk, agreed to be his travel companion. Morveena set her hopes on the chance that things would change, sure she could make her father proud. Maybe this was finally an opportunity to show how much of a help she could be to him. Yes, she resolved. This trip could transform everything between them.

Trunk already down by the front door, her travel clothes laid out for the morning; Morveena sat brushing her hair, ready for bed, too excited to sleep, when her bedroom door crashed open.

He stood, fire in his eyes and liquor on his breath, pointing at her.

"S'yer mother who should travel with me tomorrow. S'yer fault, she won't be."

Morveena stood, backed up, but found herself trapped against the wall. His left fist struck her across the cheek. His right fist was a punch to the gut. She doubled over, falling to the floor. "If ya know what's good for ya, you'll not let a tear leak out or I'll give you something to cry about!" His voice was low, calm, now that he'd unleashed his rage. This tone of voice always scared her more than anything else. He stared at her, waiting to see if tears would betray her. But Morveena had promised herself long ago never to give him the gift of her tears. None came.

He turned to go, calling over his shoulder, "Wear a veil in the morning. We don't want rumors started about how clumsy you are, always hurting yourself by walking into things. Pity you've bruised your lovely face. You ought to be more careful."

BY THE TIME THEY ARRIVED at the Goblin Hold, Morveena's face had healed enough that she could cover the last of the bruising with makeup. She filled her silver washbasin with water so she could see her reflection, allowing her to camouflage the discoloring.

While visiting Lancer Goodfellow's hall, her father treated her with kindness, respect, and even admiration. The Goblin King and his wife, Alora, were expecting their second child. This information intrigued Morveena. She said little, but took to watching Lancer and Alora's young son, Rupert, through dinner and the evening's entertainment. Quiet as a mouse, she listened to all the hall's conversations. There was talk of small grievances between the Goblin Hall and the Faerie Court. The dialogue became intense as her father and Lancer Goodfellow complained about the increasing Gugwe raids, discussing how the clans were losing women and children to slavery.

Several times during the evening, the child required the Goodfellow's attention. Irritation appeared on Munro's face in each instance. Morveena recognized an opportunity. She curtsied before the Goblin King and Queen, asking if she could help by putting young Rupert to bed. Her offer pleased the King. The Queen accepted; being large with child, she especially appreciated the offer. Alora, using the respite to excuse herself to retire, gave Lancer and her father the opportunity to continue their conversation in private. Hoping her father would appreciate her good deed, as she was well aware he abhorred being around children. Her strategy should win her some points.

Rupert went with Morveena, taking the hand she offered. She asked him to lead her first to the library so they could select a bedtime story to read. The boy pushed open the heavy oak door to the library. Morveena turned full circle when she entered, having never seen so many books. Her father had a dozen tomes he didn't allow her to touch.

Bookshelves covered every wall. She dropped Rupert's hand, suggesting the lad look about for a bedtime storybook or two. Morveena took her time walking along the shelves, her forefinger trailing the book spines as she read their titles. Captivated by the wealth of books, she paid little attention when Rupert sat down on the floor. Her charge surrounded himself with children's books. He was used to entertaining himself.

Just as she was about to collect Rupert, the toe of her slipper brushed against the heavy velvet drapes by a window seat, revealing a small bookshelf underneath. Lead glass encased the obscured shelf. It was almost as though the books below were whispering her name. She put a hand on the glass, startled to find the case unlocked. Falling to her knees, sliding the glass open to examine the titles, she read, 'Small Magics Everyone Can Master'; 'Black Magic throughout History'; 'How to Wield the Power of Blood Magic'; 'Death to Your Enemies Using the Power of Your Black Magic'; 'Blood Magic and the Spells to Defeat Your Foes'. She glanced over her shoulder. Rupert was paying her no mind at all.

Suddenly, overwhelmed by the desire to confiscate the small books, Morveena hungered for the knowledge in these small leather-bound works. Power. Magic. A chance like this might never present itself again. She could hardly ask to borrow the books. There would be no way to explain her interest in blood magic, black magic, both prohibited in Sharas. She weighed the risks. There was no question her father would whip her if caught in the theft. The scandal of his daughter stealing from the Goblin Court would embarrass the ambassador. Desire and longing overrode her caution. In the end, she left her thoughts and fears in the space on the shelf created by her removal of the dusty, slim volumes.

Rearranging the remaining books to cover the void, Morveena pulled the velvet drape back to cover the case. Using her crocheted hair covering, she tucked the small books into it, lifted her skirts and bound it to her leg. Clapping her hands to get Rupert's attention, she instructed him to choose only one book and put the rest back in their places. He obeyed at once. Taking her right hand, left clutching his favorite book, he directed her to his bedroom.

Instructing the boy to get ready for bed, she promised she would be right along to read him a bedtime story. Morveena hurried to her guest room, making sure no one was following her.

Slipping in, she removed the slender tomes from under her skirts and hid them beneath the pillows on the bed. The temptation was strong to just start reading and skip the nighttime story pledged to the boy. But she didn't want to take the chance Rupert would tell his mother the next morning; she broke her promise to him.

Back at the child's door moments later, she entered. The youngster surprised her once again with how obedient a child he was. She found him in his nightshirt, nestled in bed, the book waiting on his lap. He smiled a shy smile at her as she sat down next to him. He snuggled close as she opened his book, her voice punctuating the words with emotion, giving each character a distinct voice. Rupert seemed to enjoy it so much, Morveena relented and gave in to a second story. When finished, she told him no more for tonight, tucked him in, wishing him sweet dreams. His eyes were closed, breath coming in soft huffs as she closed his door behind her.

Once ensconced in her room, she passed the rest of the night reading well into the early morning hours. A warm glow rose and filled her as she opened herself to a new world. A world filled with forbidden magic and more possibilities than she ever would have dreamt of.

Munro Marcellus Montestrell did not praise her for the kind gesture as she had expected the next morning. After they'd breakfasted, they found their carriage readied, baggage loaded. Morveena thought of the slim books hidden in her trunk under her small clothes. She didn't think of taking the books as stealing because the topics were taboo. It was doubtful that the Goodfellows would notice the volumes were missing from the thousands of books in their library.

Morveena bid her goodbyes to a few and climbed into the carriage. Her father sat out front with reins in one hand and a whip in the other, which he flourished, sending the horses dancing. They were off, heading for the northern Fae castle. Travel would take up the entire day. She wished she could have spent the travel time learning more about magic, but fear of her father discovering the contraband chased away those desires. As the hours and miles passed, Morveena Morgan Montestrell had the threads of a plan coming together in her head.

WHEN THE MONTESTRELLS stopped at an inn for the night, her father had given her the key to their suite when they checked in. He told her he was going out to see the horses settled and would join her in the dining room shortly. They dined on a simple stew with warm bread. He ordered her an ale and himself a whiskey. Three more times he called for another dram while they ate their meal. Morveena's hands began to tremble. Those many drinks could only lead to one thing. His eyes found hers and glared at her. She could see a monster lurking behind his eyes. To her mortification, she wet herself. Disgusted, he made her clean up the mess and clear their dishes, warning the innkeeper away.

When she finished, he instructed her to head up to their room. Hanging her head, she climbed the steps, her father right on her heels. This was always the worst part for Morveena. The time when she knew he was going to hurt her. The only unknowns were how long and by what method.

When the door closed behind him, he turned the lock and pocketed the key. Her back was still toward him. She swallowed hard, concentrating on controlling her fear.

"Strip. Not a word out of you, not a bloody sound, or I'll take it as yer askin' fer more. You're such a worthless lass. A weight around my neck. A bad luck charm I'm saddled with," he belittled her while she pulled her dress over her head. Her skin broke out in gooseflesh as she stood there in her small clothes.

"Bend," he commanded.

Out of the corner of her eye; she saw. Oh gods! He'd brought the horse crop in from the carriage. Whack! The sting sang through her body. She felt a welt rise on her buttocks. Whack! It was all she could do to keep quiet, to hold her tears at bay.

Don't give him your tears. Don't give him your tears. Don't give him your tears. Never! Her mind screamed. She would never pay the price for tears again. It was too high a cost.

Her hatred grew with each thrash. With every whip-sting, he told her over and over how worthless she was, how disappointing it was to have a daughter like her. Morveena retreated into the safe room she'd built in her mind, separated from what her body was going through.

The following night, at sixteen years old, she decided she would kill him. It was only a matter of time. Of where? Of how?

He would pay. One day, he would pay.

Several sunrises later, traveling in the carriage, a living hell on her welted bottom, they arrived at the Court of the Fae. Her buttocks had healed just enough so she could sit without wincing. Uncomfortable, but able to pull off the ruse her father required. He watched her with a keen eye to be sure she didn't give his secret away.

Morveena took in the opulence of the Faerie stronghold. The King and Queen welcomed them and had planned a dinner in their honor that night. The Fae Queen invited Morveena to come to her sitting room and visit with her attending ladies, while the men discussed business. Everyone was friendly, but the young Goblin girl kept her distance, held her tongue, stuck to listening, absorbing details. She'd never been around Fae.

The first looking-glass she had ever seen was in the Queen's chambers. Later, shown to her guest room, she was delighted to find another mirror attached to the vanity. Morveena promised herself she would have her own looking glass one day. The Queen, sensing the young Goblin's unease, asked if she was alright. But the girl denied any unhappiness.

After dinner, she asked Munro if she could attend his meeting with the King on the morrow, convincing him she could learn from the experience. The Montestrells planned to leave in the next day or two. Morveena wanted to make sure she didn't cause any trouble with her father.

The following day, Montestrell's daughter avoided going to the Queen's salon. The young redhead had just removed her small clothes. She wanted to use the mirror on the vanity in her room to look at the ugly welts and bruises on her backside before she dressed for the day. The door to the room opened. She dragged in a ragged breath, fearing her father had found her vulnerable once again. But it wasn't her father at all. It was the Faerie Queen.

"Oh...I'm so sorry to barge in, Morveena. I, oh...oh my dear," the Queen stammered, seeing the old scars, as well as the new marks the whip had left, the many signs of an abuse victim. All the young goblin girl's behavior fell into place like a puzzle for the Queen. "Morveena," the Queen breathed her name in, "let me help you get away from him."

"Oh, gods," Morveena said, pulling her dress over her head, hurrying to cover the evidence, mortified. The Queen had discovered her secret. No one had ever seen all her marks of worthlessness. All the marks that defined her life. Morveena felt a fierce hatred settle inside for the Fae Queen. Hated her down to her very soul. Abhorred her beautiful life, her fine castle. Detested her lovely face and hair. Who was she to judge Morveena for her lot in life? She wanted the Queen to suffer, to wipe the look of pity off her face. Wanted to stab her eyes, so she couldn't see her damaged body reflected out at her from the Queen's blue orbs.

"Please," she prayed in a breathy voice, "please, for me, pretend you saw nothing. I beg you never to mention it to anyone. Please," Morveena pleaded, "there will be a price to pay if he thinks someone found out. You can't understand. Please..."

"I only want to help you, child," the Queen assured her.

"The best way you can help me is to keep my secret. Forget what you think you saw. Please leave me in peace."

The Queen thought Morveena's face so stricken that she said what she believed Morveena would want to hear. "I won't tell a soul. In exchange, you must promise me that if I can ever help you, you'll ask. Anytime, okay?"

Morveena gave the Queen a curt nod, which the monarch took as acquiescence, but recognized the gesture also served as a dismissal. The girl was embarrassed. And afraid. A genuine fear, so visceral it broke the Queen's heart. She felt compelled to help this poor girl. The abused didn't always know they needed the help of others. They trusted no one and had little self-esteem. Well, the Queen would be discreet. Aleta, deep in her thoughts as she left her guest's room, didn't notice Munro rounding the hallway corner behind her. He stopped, stood stock-still, cocked his head and watched her go, wondering at her hurry.

The door opened again. Morveena's father stood in the doorway, looking at his daughter with suspicion. She stood dressed, offered a short curtsey of the knee. "I am ready to attend your meeting with the King." She held her breath, eyes on the floor.

"What did the Fae Queen want?" he asked in a quiet voice.

"Only to invite me to sit with her ladies again this afternoon, father, but I told her I would attend you," she lied, still casting her eyes to the floor. He decided he could make nothing out of the Queen's visit to his daughter's room and had no time to inquire further.

"I've changed my mind. Visiting with the Queen and her ladies is the best way for you to spend the day," he declared.

"But..." she stammered, then pulled back from his dangerous glare. She changed course. "Yes, Father."

"We can compare notes before dinner," he promised. "Imagine how impressed I would be if you were to bring some information of value to me from the lady's gossip," he mocked her. "So far, having you along on this trip has been a complete waste. I should have known you would be worthless to my cause. You know how I hate worthless things, don't you, Morveena? Here's a chance to prove you have some worth, however small." She withered under his glare. He stormed out of her room to meet Lennox Stargazer.

THE DOOR TO QUEEN ALETA'S salon betrayed Morveena's entrance with a tight squeal, turning all the ladies' heads as one to see her peek into the room. Aleta was up at once to gather Morveena under her wing, bringing her into the fold. Montestrell's daughter listened as the afternoon wore away. From what she had heard so far, there was nothing that would help her avoid another beating. Panic welling up inside and she blurted out, "I've heard frightening news about a race called the Gugwe. Talk of them raiding both the Goblin and Fae clans, taking women and children, forcing them into slavery. Are these terrible monsters real?" Morveena held her breath, afraid she'd brought up the topic; her cheeks colored. It was likely that these foolish women could tell her nothing about.

A young noble's wife, Morveena thought her name was Naomi, responded in a hushed voice. "My husband tells me that all along the northwest coast of Sapphire Lake, the beasts have raided this summer and fall. The Gugwe will have to head back to reach the tundra of Adanna, or snow and ice will trap their ships here. If they wait too long to start their trek home, they won't be able to get the slaves they've captured back alive."

"We will have peace for six months. But the spring thaw will come again, and with it, the raids will start. The Gugwe happened upon a mining village two weeks ago and killed every male in the clan. Mining this year had been successful for the clan. They'd hit a vein of silver. The Gugwe will haul all the silver lode with them," Naomi shuddered and looked round the room. "I am afraid for my child, for my people, and for my husband. We are too few to stand against the Gugwe if they come. Too few," she finished in a whisper.

Aleta spoke up. "Bury your fears, and bury them deep. Our husbands do not need us to add to their burden with our foreboding. They are putting all their efforts into trying to figure out how to deal with the Gugwe. I won't sugarcoat it. The beast-men are a formidable foe. It is true they raid, kidnap, rape and kill, but we must stand strong. Goblins and Fae alike. The kings and the nobles will come up with a plan. Our job is to act like warriors' wives," Aleta finished her brave speech, unconsciously caressing her own flat belly. Silence filled the room. The women, unnerved, alone in their thoughts, bent their heads to their needlework.

Morveena readied herself to go back to her own room. Aleta followed her to the door. "Morveena, there is something I would like to show you. Will you come with me for a few moments?" Aleta asked.

Morveena nodded. As if she would dare turn down a request from the Fae Queen.

Aleta Dawn Stargazer held her forefinger to her lips and beckoned the young goblin lass to follow. Two doors down from Morveena's guest room, the Queen opened a door leading into a large linen storage room. Five wardrobes lined the walls, two on each side and one at the back. Aleta strode to the wardrobe on the back wall. Opening the cupboard door, she pushed aside all the hanging tablecloths and bed curtains, moved the stacked folded sheets, and climbed up into the interior. She felt along the right-hand side until she found the hidden release. Pushing it, the back of the cabinet swung out into a dark stone hallway. She beckoned Morveena to climb in. Aleta held the girl's wrist, guiding her fingers to show her the latch. Just inside the secret passageway, the Queen struck a match, lighting a candle. The flame cast eerie shadows along the walls as the two women walked down a stone path. Ten feet into the passage was a staircase. Aleta took the steps down with care, Morveena right behind, until they came to a small room.

Aleta placed the candle in a holder centered on a small table. Morveena could see the room had a rug beneath the table and a single chair. A seat built into the rounded wall looked big enough to lie down on. Piled at one end were several musty blankets. To the left, the stone passage continued, but the Queen stopped. "If you need to hide while you are here...to...to get away from him, you can come down to this room. He will never find you. No one will. Only the King and I know of this entrance, well...and the King and Queen of the Goblin Clans. They sometimes enter our castle this way when we wish to meet in secret. We don't always want the world to know we are holding private summits. A castle warded with magic makes it so others cannot find it unless we allow it to be found. You see, Morveena? I *can* help protect you."

"I don't need your protection," the girl protested.

"Understood. I just wanted to share this secret with you in case you changed your mind. At least while you are here in my castle, you have an option. I want you to feel you have a safe place to go to, should you ever need it," she offered.

"What's down there?" Morveena asks, pointing down the passageway leading away from the small room.

"Nothing to be afraid of. The passage goes on for a mile or so underground, then comes out to a secret doorway inside a small cave. Covered with vines, the cave entrance leads out into the forest. Our hall lies just west of the cave," Aleta shared with her.

"Thank you for your kindness." Morveena curtseyed. "I don't mean to seem ungrateful, but I have no need of a place to hide."

Aleta looked at her with pity.

Pity made hatred fill Morveena once more. Instead, she commented lightly, "After all, Queen Aleta, you have already provided me with such a comfortable guest room. Can we go back now? I was thinking I might have time to rest before dinner."

The two women bantered small talk as they made their way back up the stairs and out of the linen closet. Aleta squeezed the girl's hand in farewell as Morveena let herself into her room.

MORVEENA MORGAN MONTESTRELL was not at all surprised to learn Blood Magic actually required blood. It would be necessary to steal a knife she could conceal from her father. In the meantime, she contented herself with reading 'Small Magics Everyone Can Master'. The book turned out to be true to its title. By the time the sun drifted over the mid-afternoon sky, she had mastered the ability to change her features. Found she could hold a new face in place for at least ten minutes as a disguise. It would take work to build the strength to hold it for a much longer time. As the sun sank, casting orange and pink layers across the horizon, the books revealed how to make herself invisible, leaving only a mere shadow of her essence to betray her presence. It goaded her to do so, but she packed the books back away, hiding them again in the bottom of her trunk. She was sure her father would pay her a visit soon, with dinner not an hour away.

Envoy Montestrell was in an evil mood when he pushed open his daughter's door, stepped in, closed it and turned the key in the lock. Morveena's heart beat hard against her chest. Sweat trickled down her spine, but her face gave nothing away.

"Well, my little angel," he chided her, "tell me. Have I come to be disappointed before dinner? Or do you have anything of value to share with your beloved father?"

Morveena swallowed hard. She curtsied and recited the information she had gleaned from the noble's wife, Naomi. Finished, she stood, eyes cast down at the floor, silence filling the room, anger coming off him in waves. The young goblin girl thought she could actually feel his hatred of her. Swallowing hard, Morveena braced herself. Danger hung heavy in the air between them.

"You idiot. What do you think I have been talking about with the Goblin and Fae Courts for the last few weeks? Gugwe and nothing else. You think because you regurgitate a noble's words repeated by his wife, I would find her gossip of value? Where is the worth of those words? I knew you were too stupid to find any information that would be helpful to me." He took two sweeping steps toward her, and she felt the muscles in her body involuntarily contract.

Her terror disgusted her. She hated being afraid as much as she hated him for causing her fear. She wished with all her heart never to feel this dread again. It was almost a surprise...almost, when he slammed his fist into her gut. She fell to the floor without a sound.

"We don't have the time for any further punishment just now. Mustn't be late for dinner." He held out his arm, expecting she would rise to accompany him to the dining hall to sup with their Fae hosts. It took every ounce of strength she could muster to get up, straighten her skirt, and take his proffered arm. She kept her face blank as he told her perhaps, after all, she was good for something.

Morveena felt Aleta's eyes watching her throughout dinner. Her role-play was flawless, chatting now and then with those on her left and right. Eating just enough not to cause alarm, and then pushing the food around on her plate, the pain in her belly was a constant agony. At one point, she spirited away the sharp knife at her place setting. She spent the rest of the meal trying to make sure she didn't stab herself where she'd hidden it. King Lennox invited the men into the sitting room for a cigar and an after-dinner brandy. Munro announced that he and his daughter would leave in the morning. That gave Morveena an excuse to retire to her room, saying she had to pack.

Arriving at the linen closet door, she looked both ways. With the coast clear, she slipped in. Following the path the Queen had shown her, she took the stairs with confidence and continued past the little room, plunging further along the stone passage, eager to see where the secret entry or exit was located. Finding a heavy metal door at the dead end of the hallway, it looked rusted with disuse. She twisted the handle, pulled with all her might, but couldn't budge the door. Over the next ten minutes, pushing, pulling, working up a sweat, she still could not claim success. Worried, she needed to get back to her room before her father found her missing. There would be no way to explain to the evil bastard where she had been. Remembering something she had read earlier in the 'Small Magics' book, the word popped into her mind and out of her mouth, "Nepo," her hand flat against the door. The door swung open without a sound. The act filled her with a sense of accomplishment. It was dark outside, but the moon lit up the sky like a lamp. Pulling the vines aside, Morveena could see that a small copse of trees hid the cave opening. Looking beyond the grove, she saw a long stretch of sandy hills and a ribbon of road below. Next to the roadside were three boulders she remembered from when they were approaching the Fae Castle days ago. She smiled in satisfaction, backed away from the moonlit night, moved into the stone passage, closing the metal entrance. Hurrying along the worn, flat stones to the small room and up the stairs. Without a sound, she was out of the wardrobe and snuck from the linen closet to her own bedroom door without detection. Tucking away the details in her mind, she relished having a secret from her father.

Lying in bed, eyes wide open, mind racing, Morveena Morgan Montestrell fleshed out her plan. A strategy capable of changing her life.

CHAPTER 5: Secrets

The cool night air hit them when Caz and Saffron reached the mouth of the goblin cave. Out of breath, Saffron looked right, then left. Having made an immediate decision to move, she tugged hard on Caz's hand to follow. "Wait, Saffron!" Caz hissed. "Listen."

They held their breath. Saffron's eyes took on a panicked look when she heard a noise. "I told you!" Like a trapped animal, she dropped his hand, took off at a full-out run. Caz looked down from the entrance. He glanced back in the direction Saff was fast disappearing into the woods, scrambling across the broken rock and shale along the trail. Caz's natural role of being a protector kicked in. He gave up any thought of seeing just who was fast approaching behind them, instead loping after Saff with inhuman speed. He caught up, frightening her when he grabbed her hand and pulled her along faster. Just as they rounded a corner, Caz heard a series of sharp whistles. Saffron glanced up, looking for the source, causing her to run smack into Caz. The force of the collision caused them both to lose their balance, tumbling in a tangle of limbs to the ground.

Saffron growled at Caz as she scrambled back up. Caz grabbed her ankle, pulling her back. "Saff, wait!" he said. "I know the pattern of that whistled tune. It's Robin! Trust me, it's a signal we've used since we were boys."

Her eyes darted around. "Don't you think others know about your signals?" she sobbed. "It's a trick!" She gasps for breath, heart hammering. Caz was up in an instant, cradled her in his arms, pulling her back against the rock face. He ducked down with her behind a huge hemlock.

Keeping her enveloped in his arms, lending his strength to her, Caz whispered in her ear, "Saff. Trust. Me. It's Robin. Shhh. You're safe. Wait. Catch your breath, love."

Saffron gave in, melting against Caz, letting her heart rate slow. Caz let loose a sharp whistle. One came back in response. A moment later, Caz spotted Robin coming along the trail.

The lifelong friends maintained their silence when they made eye contact and flew into a series of hand signals used only by the two of them. Robin nodded, motioning for Caz and Saffron to follow him. They went at a slower, quieter pace, paying sharp attention to their surroundings. Robin scouted ahead before they rounded the next bend or came out from under the cover of trees or bush or boulder, moving forward in silence. Veering off the path, he led his friends down a steep slope, using the scant moonlight to find stable footholds. Even with his superior goblin sight in the dark, he went with care. They came to a huge maple. Robin touched his finger to his lips, a sign for quiet, dark eyes gleaming. He pressed his back against the tree, becoming one with it. Caz held Saffron cradled to his chest, pressed himself against the bark, melting away into the camouflage of the great trunk.

She felt as if she were free-falling. Saffron heard a whoosh just before landing on her feet. Instinct caused her to bend her knees to absorb the shock. Cazzidy released her. She looked around. Her eyes adjusted to the dark, finding herself in a small cave-like area where tree roots entwined around the dirt walls, the floor soft sand. It was minor magic. One that was available to all goblins and similar to how she had hidden in the rock wall below the kitchen earlier.

Robin stood off to the side, smiling as Saffron rushed over to him. He readied himself for a hug. Surprise lit up his face when Saff pummeled her fists against his chest. Anger came through in her voice. "You scared me to death!" she accused. Looking up at his astonished face, she backed away. "Oh, what am I saying? It's not your fault. I'm dead anyway." Her clenched hands stopped their drumming and fell to her sides in defeat. "It's only a matter of time."

Robin, incredulous, looked from Caz to Saffron and demanded, "Would one of you please tell me what is going on?"

The Beaumont leaned against the rooted wall. The tree roots rearranged themselves to form a seat, where he sank in. "I'm as much in the dark as you, Robin. Saffron led me on this mad run to find a place she felt safe, where she'd tell me about whatever had her in fear for her life."

They both fell quiet, looked to Saffron, giving her time to respond. Her eyes were wide; her heart had just calmed to a normal beat. "You're safe,

Fron. No one saw us come. We can't be heard up above," Robin assured her in a soft voice. He spread both his hands wide, palms up, to let Saffron know she had the floor to speak.

Dropping to the soft sand floor, she pulled her knees up to her chest, wrapped her arms around them, laying her head down to rest on her knees. The tree's roots moved and rearranged to create a curved back, supporting her weight. When she had settled in and made herself comfortable, she lifted her head and began her story.

Her voice was soft as she gave an unrushed account while her spiked-up adrenaline drained away. Neither Caz nor Robin made a move or a sound, giving her their full attention as she recounted every word heard earlier from her hiding place in the rock wall. She wound up the telling with her mad dash to escape to safety. Caz noted she left the kiss out of the tale. Saffron stopped and drew a shuddering breath. "Do you understand? I'm dead. Good god. Rupert and his mother." Robin noticed she didn't say, *your mother*. She grimaced. "It's disgusting! Now I'm a witness. Even worse, they were discussing a plan to kill both of you!" Exhausted, Fron leaned back into the comfort of the roots and let them cradle her.

Quietly, Robin turned inward to his private thoughts. He ran the whole of Saffron's story through his head, putting all the pieces of the puzzle together. It was Caz who finally broke the silence. "I think the time has come, Robin," he nudged his friend. "This changes the plan. We can't afford to bide our time any longer." Caz stared at Robin, willing him out of his silent reverie.

Green eyes locked on the Beaumont's black ones; he released a long breath. "I agree, Caz. These new circumstances change the plan. The danger grows, but we still can't take action yet. We have to complete the Summer Tide competition to claim our Queen's Ransom. We need the weapons. Saffron has given us some missing pieces of the puzzle, explaining a lot. But I won't go off half-cocked, bereft of critical information." Caz nodded his understanding, cocked his head toward Saffron, raising his eyebrows in question.

Robin reached over and took her hand in his. "Fron," he said, "we'll get you out. Take you somewhere safe. You've been a great help to us, and I won't leave you in danger."

The lass lifted her head and glared at Robin, snatching her hand away. She turned her stony gaze to Cazzidy. He drew back against the tree roots. When she spoke, her voice was hard with anger. "You arrogant bastards! I've spent the last three years of my life supporting your cause, gathering bits and pieces of information, throwing caution to the wind. God knows I'd do it all again. Oh lads, all know I love you both, but for once, stop thinking with your cocks! I did this for myself. I did this for our good people! Don't you dare try to decide about my welfare without giving me the right to choose what I want to do! We need to stop that evil prick Rupert. End. Of. Story." Saffron sat back and slanted her eyes at them and said, "I think it's time you lads were more forthcoming with me. I'm glad I could provide you with some pieces of the puzzle, but it would seem I am missing parts of the complete picture. It's clear that my discovery about Rupert and the Queen's sorted relationship surprised neither of you. Not from what I could see. If you can't trust me now, then I'm done, and you can hatch your plans and schemes without my help, or that of the lads and lasses of the clan." Saffron sat back and waited.

She smiled, amused at their facial expressions as she watched the two of them having a deep discussion, using the private communication system they'd developed since boyhood. But she could tell that they knew she was serious.

Caz spoke up first. "Saff, we would never presume to decide for you." She rolled her eyes at him as he continued. "It's just that it seemed you lost your senses as we raced here. The pressure was too great...don't be angry, Saff, but you have to admit, you were half mad with fear," he finished in a stammer. She hissed at him in frustration.

Robin felt a smile play across his lips. As soon as he was conscious of it, he twisted his mouth down into a frown. "Of course, Fron was hysterical, Caz," Robin offered. "Any of us would have been after going through such a shocking experience." Caz and Saffron looked at each other and then at Robin; both flipped him the bird.

Robin shook his head. "Rude," he responded to the crude gestures. He decided then, voice soft as he shared his story with Saffron. Cazzidy, who had long known the details, leaned back, closed his eyes, seeing it all play out once again in his mind's eye.

"I won't ask for your pledge, Fron," Robin started. "I know you've already sworn to me and, more importantly, you've sworn to our people." She noticed he said 'our people and not my people,' so she too leaned back, giving him her full attention.

Robin took a deep breath. "This summer solstice, I'll turn eighteen. Almost two years ago, Caz and I finished our education under Master Cornerstone. The year before, quite by accident, much like your experience today, we stumbled upon some information. It changed my life and our people's world, though few know it yet. My father, Lancer Goodfellow, had been missing for many years already. Caz and I were cooking up a little jest in Master Cornerstone's classroom when we heard footsteps in the hallway. It wasn't an instruction day, and no one should have been there. We melded into the rock walls to hide. Imagine our surprise when Rupert came in hot on the heels of Master Cornerstone. As usual, my brother was talking in his snide way to the Master. Threatening him, telling the Master that if he didn't hold Caz and me back for an additional year, he would make the Master's secret public and ruin him. We think Rupert wanted to hold us back so I wouldn't have completed my education on time. Meaning I also couldn't come of age at eighteen to be eligible to compete for the Master of Weapons title and claim my Queen's Ransom. See, a hold-back would have eliminated any possibility I might still have a claim to the throne if my father hasn't returned. If we have no word after thirteen years, they'll declare him dead and the throne will have to pass to another king. My father didn't appoint his heir before he went missing. It's likely Rupert, as the oldest, will be named heir simply because of tradition. Morveena rules in my father's stead. Though her rule is only temporary as Queen Regent under Goblin law until the King returns or a new one crowned, Rupert will be hard pressed to wrest the power away from her."

"Anyway, back to the story. The Master was angry, telling Rupert we were the brightest he'd ever had. He refused to sully his reputation *and ours* by pretending we couldn't conclude our studies by age sixteen. Rupert went ballistic. His face turned beet red, started screaming at the top of his lungs, threatening to reveal the Master's boyhood mistake, that he'd fathered a bastard. The room became deathly silent. The Master bristled with anger. When he finally spoke, his quiet words for Rupert spilt out with unchecked menace to my older brother. 'Have a care, Prince Rupert. Everyone has a skeleton in the closet somewhere. You, more than one. If you seek to destroy my career or harm those boys, I swear I will open all your closet doors and expose every skeleton you have hidden. Do we understand one another?"

"Next thing we knew, Rupert growled and snarled, but didn't utter another word as he stomped out of the room. The Master took a small journal from his coat pocket and placed it inside his top desk drawer. His eyes wandered around the classroom. But he walked out, locking the door behind him. Caz has always thought he knew we were there, and he deliberately left the log for me. Anyhow, we counted one hundred breaths before we came out of the wall. One look at each other and we both knew the journal was too big a temptation to ignore. We forgot about setting up our planned jest and spent the next two hours poring over the contents of the diary."

"The Master's writings disclosed my actual mother, Alora, died giving me life in childbirth. I was never supposed to know. I'll get into more along those lines later. My father remarried for political reasons. According to the Master's journal, he loved his first wife. He was a changed man after Alora's death."

"Not too long after my birth mother died, he married my stepmother, Morveena, and made her queen. That was when she started displaying her true nature. Morveena hailed from the northern reaches. I doubt you've ever come into contact with those Goblin clans?" Saffron shook her head. "They're a warlike clan and have had clashes with the Gugwe, the Beast-Men. You know the stories about them being a constant threat to our people?"

Saff nodded her head in agreement.

"Caz and I believe the Gugwe are a danger to all the people of Sharas. My father, Lancer Goodfellow, banked on his second marriage as a goodwill gesture. He thought it would allow us to call on the support of Morveena's clans. Figured they would be a valuable ally should we need one if the Gugwe tribes decide to move in force against the inhabitants of Sharas."

Robin heaved a sigh and continued, "Anyway, within a year of their union, Queen Morveena was with child. As you know, under our laws, even though my father recognized the marriage as a mistake, he was stuck. Just because the monster inside her reared its ugly head from time to time, once she bore my father's child, he could never put her aside. Instead, he took other precautions."

"Da told me he stole Morveena's babe away after the birth. He passed the baby to a trusted friend, had him spirit my phantom sister away to be fostered in safety, made him promise never to reveal her location to anyone, including himself. Lancer told Morveena that her child had been stillborn. Morveena had the midwife put to death after confirming the baby was dead on arrival. According to the Master, my father wanted to have the child raised away from the influence of my evil stepmother."

Robin stared off into space for a few moments, lost in his own memories of growing up under Morveena's spiteful hatred. Having to learn how to survive with her as a stepmother was how he developed his own coping mechanisms. Robin's mask was always that of the practical joker, with nary a care to any who observed him from day to day. Getting laughs was his way of deflecting her cruelty.

The Goodfellow shook himself, locked eyes with Caz again, who nodded and encouraged him to finish the tale. Robin ran his fingers through his long, dark hair as he exhaled. "The years went by. Rupert learned Morveena would shower him with attention if he performed mean or cruel acts. Over time, she turned him into her twisted creature. Oh, don't get me wrong; she still punished him. But was always dangling a reward in front of him. It wasn't long before Rupert could no longer distinguish what he perceived to be the love she proffered to him, with the violent beatings she doled out. My father was gone from home more and more. He knew about this behavior, but didn't seem to catch her in it. She, of course, threatened us with torture, pain, or mortal death if we ever revealed to anyone her 'motherly' administrations. Even tried to convince us we brought it on ourselves."

"Lancer used to meet in secret with me before he disappeared, making sure she wasn't able to change me, like she had my brother. At the last secret meeting I had with my father, he confessed the action he'd taken years ago about my sister Valvina. Said it was important I grow up to be a powerful man, asked me to swear to find my sister, protect her and our people. What Lancer failed to tell me was where he had hidden her, fostered out to grow up away from her evil mother. He promised to provide that information at a later date. Throughout all the years he was around during my youth, he made me swear again and again in secret to find her one day. When I do find her, I will make it my duty to protect her. My father insisted she was going to be the key to saving the goblin clans. Lancer promised to one day reveal the mystery of why he felt Valvina would be so important to the Goblin race, as well as how and where I would find my sister, but that day never came. My father disappeared not long after."

"As we grew older, Rupert and Morveena conspired together, putting their own plans into play. Right before he left, he told me he was concerned Morveena had discovered his part in secreting Valvina away. He believed she would have killed my sister long ago. Convinced that if he had not acted, Valvina would have been in danger. My guess is Morveena's vanity and jealous nature would brook no competition, even from her own daughter. My sister would be about fifteen or sixteen now. Lancer shared a vision, using the goblin mind swap with me once to show me what she looked like and proclaimed her the future savior of our clans. But the vision was of her as a babe. I do not know what she would look like today at her current age. The only clue we have to go on is that my half-sister is marked." He clarified, "She has a birthmark."

"Helps a lot, doesn't it?" Saffron perked up.

"Not really," Caz retorts. "The mark is a tiny star under her left breast. Unfortunately, the location is not in a place easy to see it, yeah?"

"Maybe my father dreamed of what he could not have," Robin ruminated. "But he made me promise that once Caz and I earned our titles, gained our Queen's Ransom in the summer games, we would bend all our efforts to seek Valvina and build our own army. He wanted us to overthrow Morveena and fight the Gugwe to take back our lands. Morveena's power has grown vast since I swore that promise. In addition, she has Rupert under her control."

"I have to admit, the Master's observation that my father seemed to have lost interest in being the sovereign of the goblin people after my mother, Alora, died, was a fair assessment. We all know Morveena does not have our people's best interests at heart. Her own power and greed are her sole focus. That makes her and Rupert a dangerous combination in my mind. Rupert would be king above all else. It's what drives him. And Morveena? She does not want to give up her power as the ruler of the goblin people. Ever."

"So, Fron, now you know our position. Not a strong one, and fraught with missing information, and no allies. My father was adamant that we must find Valvina, but left no clues where we should search. Then, to top it off, he disappeared himself. The Beaumont and I will make our escape soon after the summer games on a quest bent on searching for my sister." Robin steepled his fingers together and rested his chin on them, raising his eyebrows in question, Saffron staring back at him.

Cazzidy opened his eyes, stood, stretched his long frame up to the top of the tree's roots and said, "Well, lass, now you know our secrets and our quest. You must decide what's best for you. Stay and hope Rupert doesn't discover you were down below the kitchens as a witness to one of his skeletons? Or if you wish, we'll get you away, safe with another clan."

Saffron smiled a sly smile at them both and countered, "My brave laddies, I think I'll take my chances here and continue to be the ears and eyes of your vast network. But know this. When you go, you'll be taking me with you on your quest. I want that clear. I'm in it for the long haul." Her hands moved like lightning in front of them.

Saffron rendered Robin Wilum Goodfellow and Cazzidy Beaumont Touchstone speechless. They watched in stunned silence as Saffron made an oath, swearing to serve Robin, the mysterious Valvina, and the Goblin race, using the boy's own secret hand signals.

CHAPTER 6: The Wardrobe

F aith surveyed the hall, shocked to see all the faces gawking back at her. Bile rose in the back of her throat. Her back was aflame with pain; torn clothing soaked in blood. To top it off, the rock faces in the fireplace appeared again. Her eyes swung up and found Dedo on his perch. He gave her a slight nod. Robert looked stricken with shock. Garrett took two steps back, staring at her in wonder. Recognizing the sympathy in her cousin's eyes, she regained her balance, working around the two huge wings that stretched from her shoulders to her ankles.

Then, as if they had practiced the timing, all of her newfound cousins stood, rolled their shoulders, and popped out their own sets of wings. Fierce, knowing smiles lit their faces.

Horrified, Faith broke and ran from the room, tripping, then catching herself as she tried to figure out how to move her body with the additional weight on her back. She hit the grand staircase. The same stairs she'd come down hours before, excited about Spring Feast, eager to meet the strangers who claimed to be her long-lost family.

Oh gods! She bit down on her lower lip, tears springing to her eyes, and she screamed over her shoulder, "You've mistaken me for someone else. I'm not the princess you're looking for," she took the stairs two at a time, leaving a trail of blood behind her. What had happened to her? How could this be? Surely, she must be dreaming. No, not dreaming, having a nightmare. The need to get away from everyone overwhelmed her. *'Wake up! Wake up!' she screamed to herself in her head.* Her hair flew out behind her as she raced down the hallway from the top of the stairs. With shoulders and back screaming in agony, Faith reached her bedroom door, dodged into the room, slamming it behind her and setting the latch. Panting like a wild animal, her eyes roamed about, trying to see where she could next run, the flight response still strong. Instead, with eyes locked on the full-length standing mirror, she stopped dead in her tracks, horrified at the reflection she saw there.

BACK IN THE HALL, EVERYONE talked at once as they recovered from Faith's change and dramatic exit. The cousins grouped, retracted their own wings and moved as one toward the doors leading out of the room.

"STOP!" a voice commanded. All eyes turned to see Lady Reatha standing by her rocking chair, her mending laid aside. Nursie still sat in her chair, but gave Reatha her full attention.

"You will all stay here. Faith needs time to absorb the change she had no warning about!" Reatha turned and spoke to Val and then to Garrett. "Val, you must be the one to go to her." Val blinked a tear from her eye and turned to leave the room. Reatha added, "Take Garrett. He can stand guard outside her door. Make sure no one," Reatha put a regal stare around to each of the cousins to let them know she meant business, "and I mean no one, tries to get to her until she is ready for company!"

Garrett nodded. As he passed Faith's cousin Brittany, he heard her whisper under her breath to her brother Travis, "Just as I thought. Evidently, our cousin was raised with no instruction that would prepare her to rule. I told you years ago why it was important. I laid the groundwork to lead the Fae. Someone must step up and take responsibility. What? No jokes about my plans now? I was right. I knew it. Admit it. She's unprepared to become the leader of the Fae. Luckily, I am ready," she huffed and crossed her arms.

Garrett caught up with Val as they raced up the steps toward Faith's room.

BRITTANY COCKED HER head toward Reatha and Evy, asking in a snippy voice, "Why wasn't Faith groomed for the change? How could you not tell her she might have inherited the Fae magic? Clearly, you're the one to be found lacking in this case. You can't blame us for your poor decision to keep her heritage from her. It's a disgrace that you didn't even have the decency to tell her she had other family." The rest of the cousins had the good grace to look sheepish at Brittany's dressing down of their

Aunt Reatha. Sitting back down, the group passed the coffee and teapots around. Travis poured a good-sized dollop of bourbon into his coffee cup and handed the flask to Sir Robert. Robert took a direct swig, then another. He didn't hand the flask back, but kept it gripped in his hand. "Robert," Reatha said, "we'll need to talk later. Please pass me that young man's flask."

The old nurse turned a hard gaze on Brittany. "Mind your sharp tongue, Mistress Brittany. You have developed a bad habit of using words like knives. There are circumstances you do not know of, and that are none of your business. There were good reasons things played out the way they have. You will apologize to Lady Reatha. If you don't, I will see you out the door and beyond the fortress gates myself."

Brittany schooled her face, inclined her head to show deference. "I beg your pardon, Lady Reatha. It seems I've made a rude observation without all the facts. Please accept my apologies."

Both Reatha and Nursie took a healthy swig and passed the tarnished flask back to Travis. He turned it upside down and found not a drop left, causing him to let out a loud guffaw.

Immediate crisis in hand, Reatha took up her mending, rocking in time with Evy. The only thing to do now was to wait until Faith sorted out her feelings and accepted her newfound changes. They would be there for her when she was ready. The thought of all the questions she would demand answers to left Reatha feeling like she'd swallowed a rock. A rock that felt like it was now sitting at the bottom of her stomach.

FAITH COULDN'T TEAR her eyes away from the reflection in the mirror. If she faced the looking glass head-on, she could see the opalescent humps peeking out from above her shoulders. The ruined strips of material from her silk dress hung in shreds at her sides. The barest hint of the feather tips peeked out from behind her dance slippers. She craned her neck to see more of the vision the mirror was capturing. She drew in a sharp breath as she got a full view of a wing attached to her back and shoulder. It was beautiful; she had to admit, but she could see blood trickling down between her shoulder blades. *She squeezed her eyes shut, thinking, 'Oh, gods!*

I'm a freak!' Her eyes popped open, turned, compelled to look at the other side.

Clenching her teeth, she watched in horror as she lifted her right arm and willed the feathered spines to spread in a full arc, then gazed in awe as she opened its mate.

Someone started pounding on her door, causing both wings to snap back into place. "Go away!" she screamed. She covered her face with her hands, but the pounding continued. "Please," she whispered to herself rather than whoever was at the door, "please just leave me alone." Sinking down to her knees, with wings stretched out behind her, she sobbed.

"She's not answering, and the latch is hooked," Val complained. "I've got to get to her."

Garrett nodded in agreement. He didn't know what to say. He'd never seen such a thing and did not know how to help. Garrett acknowledged that Faith and Val were his best friends. He would do anything for them. Nothing had changed from his perspective. Lady Reatha told him to guard her door, to protect Faith's privacy, and he intended to do that. "Go in the secret way," he whispered to Val. "I'll stay outside the door until you need me or until Faith wants to see me. Tell her...tell her I'm here for her," he nodded.

Val squeezed his arm and said, "I will." She bounced on the tips of her toes, like she always did before she took off on a run and disappeared down the hallway.

Valerie Victoria Pureheart was breathless as she reached the top of the stairs, two floors up. Calming herself, she looked to be sure no one had followed her. Val walked at a brisk clip down the hall to the right of the landing. Two left turns and six doors later, she grabbed the handle on the maple door and slipped into the room.

It was dark. Someone had drawn the heavy velvet drapes over the windows. There was just enough light to see the four-poster bed that occupied most of the room. Val reached up, pulled the cords on the bed curtains, and the platform under the bed swung out, away from the wall. Her stomach was a knot of anxiety as she relived the look on Faith's face over and over when her wings had burst out.

Val entered the hidden passage and twisted an iron ring inside the wall, closing the entrance. Moving through the stone-cold passage, Val moved down the slanted walkway in a circular pattern. She passed additional iron rings that operated other openings into various rooms on these upper floors. But Val only had one door in mind.

Faith, Val, and Garrett had put a secret mark above the doorway when they'd discovered it years ago, identifying it as the wardrobe door that led into Faith's room. The three of them spent hours exploring every inch of the hidden corridors through the fortress. Using chalk, they'd marked symbols at each entrance in the secret passageway so as not to lose their way. She smiled, the memory fond, allowing herself to be comforted by the close friendship the three of them had shared for so many years. She hoped nothing would ever change the special love or the fierce protectiveness they felt for one another. Holding that thought close, Val turned the iron ring on the wall. Crawling through the back of the wardrobe, she pushed Faith's clothes out of her way.

The cupboard door was ajar. Val couldn't see Faith, but she could see her reflection in the mirror. Crawling out, she made her way on all fours over to her best friend, who was still on her knees, opulent wings spread out behind her, body wracked with near-silent sobs.

Val wrapped Faith in her arms and rocked her back and forth, whispering in her ear, "It's all right. I'm here now. It's all right. Your wings...they're stunning. Beautiful! Don't worry, we'll figure this out like we always do. Listen, Garrett's outside your door, guarding your privacy. We're both here for you. Whatever you need." Rocking, rocking, until finally her best friend's tears ceased.

Faith looked up and met Val's eyes. "You don't think I'm a freak? A...a monster?" she asked, looking at her best friend with red-rimmed eyes, snot running out of her nose.

"No. Never. I think you're my beautiful friend," Val told her.

They held each other's hands and stood. Val handed her a handkerchief. "Here, let me look," she said, turning Faith around in a circle in front of the mirror. "Wow. Fabulous! Just fabulous!" Val huffed in hushed reverence. "Can we let Garrett in now?"

Faith felt tears sting her eyes again. "No. Val, I can't face anyone. You say I'm not a freak. You can't mean it. Is there anyone else you know who has sprouted wings?" Her question was sarcastic. "I didn't hide this. I don't know how this happened! It's a nightmare. I don't know what this means. Oh God, how can I get back to normal? All the people who've known me all my life will shun me. What must Sir Robert and Lady Reatha think? And Nursie! She raised me." Faith's body shook again, sobbing in Val's arms.

"Did you see your cousins before you fled the hall?" Val coaxed.

"I saw. Yes, they all revealed they could sprout hidden wings as well. I don't care! I don't even know them. Do you think they did this to me? Cast some spell on me to further convince everyone in this hold that I am related to them? You've known me all my life, and I couldn't have hidden this from you! All I know is that I've got to get away from here. I have to break this spell so I can come back to live a normal life with my friends and family. If I cannot remove the spell, maybe I can find a healer to cut them off." Faith's eyes had a wild look as they darted around her room. She looked at the fireplace. Dedo was not there in his usual place. Lenny and Lester had the decency to remain stone-still.

Val took Faith's chin, turning her friend's face back to hers. "You. Are. Not. A. Freak," she said with authority. "You are not alone, and you don't need to flee your home."

A single tear fell from Faith's bright blue right eye. Val wiped it away with her thumb. "Easy for you to say," Faith responded.

Val squeezed her hands. "Faith, you are my best friend and always will be. You're like my sister. No matter what happens, I will always love you! Do you believe me?"

"Yes," Faith whispered.

"Do you feel the same about me?" Val inquired.

Faith squeezed her friend's hands, staring into her eyes. "You know I do, Valarie Victoria Pureheart," her words solemn. "You are family to me. Aside from finding out that Reatha is actually my aunt, a fact she withheld from me, all those people downstairs claiming to be my family? They're just strangers. You are my genuine family. I will always love you as my best friend and sister."

Val's eyes teared. "Promise? No matter what, nothing will ever come between us?"

"Yes, always," Faith confirmed.

Val stood up, silent tears slid down her own cheeks. Without a word, she removed her shawl and bared her soul to her best friend and named sister. "I'm sorry I hid this from you."

Faith gasped, hand flying to cover her mouth, as she witnessed glistening, sparkling, gossamer wings open on Val's back. Wings that were black as midnight. Faith blinked several times. Her first thought was that she would like to trade her opalescent-colored wings for Val's black wings, but tucked away the jealous desire and whispered, "Val, what does this mean? How long? Why is this happening to us? Why didn't you tell me? Oh God, oh God...what is Garrett going to think? Does anyone else know you have wings too?" Faith's voice climbed in pitch with every question, her eyes going wild again.

Val grabbed her hand and shouted. "Faith!" pulling Faith to her feet, Val turned them both toward the floor-length mirror, their reflections looking back at them. "You're beautiful," they both whispered in unison.

Val cleared her throat. "No one knows but you. It happened to me about six weeks ago. I was doing chores in Da's barn by myself. The idea of telling Da or Mam or any of my sisters or you scared me. Now that I think about it, Carlisse would have giggled. Delainey would have shrugged and gone back to her books. Aliah would have asked how she could get a pair of wings. I was afraid to tell you or Garrett for the same reasons you're feeling. There I was. A freak. Just like you, I expected you and Garrett and everyone would reject me, shun me. Then I figured out I could retract them, hide my wings. The last six weeks have been hell, living in fear of being discovered. Afraid I would lose you and Garrett forever, and I just couldn't bear it." Val took a deep, shuddering breath and finished. "I don't know why this happened. I don't know what it means. But we're in this together, and we have each other." Faith nodded her acquiescence, reminded once again Val had foster parents and sisters who cared, while she felt alone in the world, betrayed by her foster mother and likely Nursie, too.

"Now," Val said with a calmness she didn't feel, "let's see if I can help you retract your wings. Close your eyes and tense your shoulders. I know they're sore right now, but visualize the wings gone and your back smooth. Command your body to do as you wish it to do."

There was an audible snap in the room. A second one followed, and Faith opened her eyes. The mirror reflected the two girls as they'd always been. Small, shy smiles started at the corners of their mouths. They hugged and let out relieved sighs, and then nervous giggles. Those turned into uncontrollable laughter.

After they got their hysterics under control, Val suggested, "Whatever is happening, we'll figure it out together, just like always, right?" Her friend nodded in agreement. "For now," Val continued, "let's just keep my change secret until we know more. Agreed?" Faith nodded again.

"I'm not ready to deal with my sisters when they find out."

Val had Faith sit at her vanity. Filling the washbasin with water, using a soft cloth, she washed away the blood from the tender skin. After she finished, Val went to the wardrobe and tossed Faith her leather leggings. They worked in silence as Val took one of Faith's favorite tops from her dresser, measured, then cut two slits in the back and stitched the edges so they wouldn't fray. "There," she said as she helped her friend slip the altered blouse over her head, throwing the shredded gown on the floor, "that will work. We can cut and sew some of your other shirts later. You're all fixed up, so..." Val said as she leaned forward, touching her forehead to Faith's. "Can we let Garrett in now?"

CHAPTER 7: Rock and Roll

Dedo surveyed the hall, noting how every person reacted when Faith's wings had burst out of her back. Locking eyes with Evy, the old nurse nodded once. The gargoyle disappeared from its spot atop a flat rock in the hall's fireplace.

His essence spun through the dark, using his links to all the stone fireplaces throughout the fortress. Finally, he coalesced into a dark gray shadow on the lowest level of Robert's stronghold. Landing on his wide, flat feet inside a large circle of carved symbols, his quintessence still hazy. Dedo reached out his small hand, touched a symbol shaped like Sapphire Lake. His form dissipated, reappearing among the piles of stones on the shoreline as the lake's waves crashed against the beach. Bursts of color from wet agates flashed in the moonlight each time the waves receded. Dedo closed his eyes, reveling in the rushing waves. He let the familiarity of the water washing back and forth among the silent ones soothe his soul. A loud pop, a whoosh, and the waves sucked his embodiment down, down, down. When Dedo opened his eyes, he breathed in, exhaled, ending in a satisfied sigh.

"You seem to enjoy a certain contentment when returning to your homeland," a voice echoed through the cave he'd landed in. Perched on a boulder, Dedo looked at a reflection pool. Somewhere in the background, a clear drip, drip, drip sounded.

"Do me the courtesy of showing yourself, so I might look upon your face once more." Dedo's gravelly voice choked.

There was a soft shimmer of light across the surface of the pool. A beautiful face appeared as a reflection in the water. "Your need must be great, my friend," the voice seemed to float in the air surrounding Dedo. "I wasn't expecting you to visit me for another month. What has caused you to cast off your vigilant watch over your charge, Prince Dedo?"

"The change forced itself upon her today. Unfortunately, it happened before the eyes of a hall full of people. Some who had only made a recent appearance at Sir Robert's fortress, claiming to be her cousins. All of whom revealed their true nature right after she changed."

Light glimmered from the pool as the voice embodied the underwater cave. "So, her cousins have come, and all of them winged, whether with good intentions or bad. What about her friends?"

"I cannot tell yet, my lady. Young Garrett does not seem to have the gift, but maybe he has hidden it well. That or the change has not yet taken him. As for Valerie Victoria Pureheart, she's a secretive little thing. I cannot tell whether any change has come over her yet. The three of them are thick as thieves."

"You would do well to keep a closer watch now, Dedo," the voice instructed. "Faith's mind will be busy thinking up questions. She will put all her will toward finding answers. Surely her cousins will try to get her to leave the fortress. We know that will be necessary, but she must learn of the prophecy first before she goes off with them on a whim."

Dedo nodded, deep in thought. After a moment, he put in, "Then, I must try to direct her actions without her thinking I am doing so." His face twisted into a grimace. "She takes any suggestions from me these days as a covert effort to control her. The girl has adopted a stubborn stand for her freedom and her privacy!" he exclaimed with frustration.

Gentle laughter, music to Dedo's ears he had missed for so long, echoed through the cavern, and the light sparkled with it. The voice, merry now, said, "Old memories, my friend. I felt much the same as a young girl when your task was to watch over me. You must be as patient and clever as you were in the past."

Dedo smiled at his own fond memories. "Yes, Queen Aleta. I see your point, though I doubt I will ever understand young ladies and their emotions."

"You must return Dedo. Increase your efforts. Stay vigilant on your watch to protect our princess. I cannot help being trapped in this prison as I am. Faith is the future of Sharas' people. You must do everything in your power to make sure she does not fall into the enemy's hands. The war is coming. I fear the enemy is growing stronger," the voice sighed.

"Still no knowledge of where they hold you prisoner?"

She shook her head.

"Do they cause you pain, my lady?"

"Not more than I can bear. I will continue to endure for my people and yours until my death is necessary. It is my magic they seek to gain. They have not broken me yet in all these years. Tell me," she begged, "do you have any word of my beloved?"

He heard the catch in her voice and wished he could tell her the news she longed to hear. Briefly, Dedo considered lying to her, just to leave her with false hope. A moment's joy. But he respected her too much and cast the fib away. "No word. Not a hint. Nary a whisper about him from all the corners of the land. Your sorrow is mine." Dedo bowed his head in sadness.

Near silence filled with the never-ending drip, drip, drip, her daily companion, or the edge of her madness. Pasting a grim smile on her face, she responded, "Well then, there is always hope. Hope is what we live for, is it not?"

"Indeed," Dedo agreed. A slight smile began at the corners of his mouth as she reminded him once again of her courage and optimism. Attributes he admired about her.

"So, off with you then. You've been gone far too long to bring me this news. I am grateful to you, Dedo. You have always remained my faithful friend." His shoulders tightened at her words. "Go now and watch over my daughter. I think a quest to see the Dream Weaver may be wise."

"Yes, I had the same thought," he agreed.

"Farewell then, Dedo. Give my regards to Evy. Stay safe," the voice bid him.

Dedo turned his short, squat, stone body to make his way back to the cavern mouth, stilled when she called out, "Wait! I must know, Dedo...what color were Faith's wings?" Her voice rang out with a sharp edge of desperation he'd not heard from her before.

The Gargoyle turned to face the pool again, and said, "Opalescence. I knew they would be. Just. Like. Yours. A lovely, shimmering, gossamer opalescence, my queen." He formed a vision and conveyed it from his mind to hers, so she could hold it in her mind's eye. A small gift to keep her strong against the pain and suffering she would have to abide in the long days to come. He felt her embrace the memory, making it her own.

She whispered, "My thanks," as he strode out of the cavern.

His body passed through the archway. He touched the fortress symbol on the floor from inside the compass where he had arrived a short time before. There was a pop, a whoosh. An icy wave washed over him. Dedo's spirit was swept up. Had anyone been watching, he was gone when the wave receded from the beach. Nothing remained of his clandestine visit. Waves washed away his footprints, leaving only stone and agates bursting with color as the moon shone full upon the shore of Sapphire Lake.

CHAPTER 8: Surprise, Surprise, Surprise

Several hours had passed with Garrett standing guard outside Faith's door. He couldn't hear any noise from within. He stretched and yawned. Guard duty sounded grand, but in reality, it comprised waiting and more waiting. His back ached from standing on the stone floor.

Two hours ago, Faith's cousin, Brittany, wandered by, asking if she could check on her cousin. She came bearing gifts, handing him a basket covered with a linen napkin. Looking under the cloth, he found two thick slices of bread, still warm from the oven. There was a wedge of cheese, three apples, and a flagon of beer. Garrett conveyed his thanks. He sent her on her way with a mouth full of cheese, telling her no one would get in to see Faith until she declared she was ready for visitors. He clarified that, 'no' she could not wait there to keep him company. Brittany smiled, shrugged her shoulders, left him with the basket, disappearing down the hallway.

In a matter of minutes, Garrett had eaten the contents of the basket. Waiting was hungry work after all. He was just finishing the last apple when he heard a click at the door behind him. A hand snaked out, grabbed his shoulder, making him start, pulling him into the room. The door slammed. He heard the snap of the latch, securing the entrance behind him.

Val stood before him with red-rimmed eyes, holding a forefinger to her lips. Grabbing his hand, pulling him into the room after her, she relocked the door behind them.

Faith was sitting on the bed, working her hands one against the other, worry lining her brow.

"Tell her," Val commanded Garrett.

"What?" Garrett said, alarmed, unclear what Val was demanding of him.

Val blew the air out of her lungs in exasperation. "Oh, for heaven's sake! What do you think she needs to hear from you? From us? Do I need to provide you with a script, Garrett Emmon Gladheart?" She stamped her foot.

Garrett looked at Faith, her face so sad. Her countenance slumped, defeated. Going straight to her, he pulled her up by her hands, wrapping her in his arms. Val joined them in a group hug. Garrett lifted Faith's chin with his finger and tilted her head so he could look into her eyes, and whispered without stammering, "Nothing has changed between us." The three friends stood looking at each other. He continued, "Between all of us. It's no different from yesterday. Um, well, it is, but not between us. Um, well..." he always stammered when the girls frustrated him. Both his friends giggled, and Val held up a hand. "Stop. Don't say another word and mess up this moment, Garrett!"

"We need to make a plan," Faith told them. "I need to figure this out! I'm counting on both of you to help me." She looked from one to the other.

"You can count on me," Garrett assured her.

"Me too," Val echoed.

"What do you have in mind?" Garrett asked. "Your cousins are already prowling and waiting to pounce."

"Yes," a deep, gravelly voice called out from above, "what kind of plan do you have in mind?"

All three heads turned, eyes running up the rocks in the fireplace. Garrett's mouth fell open as Dedo hopped down the rock face, landed on the mantel, tapped his left foot, waiting for an answer. Val glared at the intruder.

Eyes bulging, Faith walked over to him. "Now Dedo? Now, of all times?" she hissed. "You decide to show up and reveal yourself to my friends now for the first time?" her voice winding up with each word.

"Well," he huffed, "seems today is one for revealing secrets among friends," he snapped back. Lenny and Lester cringed, dripping hot wax onto the mantel. Dedo made it a point to stare at Val.

Val said nothing, glaring right back at the gargoyle, giving it a dirty look. Faith followed Dedo's gaze and turned to look at Val with raised eyebrows. "What?" Val defended. "I've guessed about him. Noticed him or thought I did once in a while, but always chalked it off as a trick of my mind."

"Ha!" Dedo retorted. "There's more to you than meets the eye, Valerie Victoria Pureheart!"

Garrett's mouth still hung open as he stared at the small stone figure on the mantel.

"You dirty little sneak!" Val screamed. She lunged toward him, violence in her eyes. "Been sitting up there spying on us all this time, have you?" she shouted. "You saw my wings! Who are you a spy for?" Val jumped up to grab him as he leaped several rocks higher, out of her grasp.

"Ung..." said Garrett.

"Don't think that will keep you safe, you ugly little snoop," Val spat at him. Lenny and Lester clung to each other, their faces terrified, then fell into hysterics, candle wax thrown across the mantel surface.

Val snapped her wings open and leaped up. "I've had six weeks to figure out how to make these wings work for me!" she shouted at Dedo, springing for him, wings pumping hard to lift her weight.

Poof! He disappeared.

Garrett blinked his eyes. Faith found her own wings had snapped out, almost as if in response to Val's. Beating her wings twice, she lifted into the air and pulled Val down. "So much for keeping your wings secret for now," Faith scolded.

"I couldn't avoid it. Ugly little monster has been spying on us!" Val shrieked back at her.

"No," Faith said with authority, "no Val. Listen, Dedo's been with me my whole life. I don't know why revealed himself to both of you now, but he's a guardian of sorts. He's not a spy. Ever since I was a babe, he has been here at the fortress watching over me," she finished.

Cowed, Val said, "Oh. Sorry. Guess I overreacted. But I still don't like him. And I certainly don't trust him."

"Er..." said Garrett. Both girls rolled their eyes at him.

"That's a pretty big secret to keep from us all these years," Val pouted.

Garrett pointed at the mantel. His finger traced an invisible line up the rock fireplace and stopped where he'd seen Dedo disappear. "Ah..." he remarked.

Faith let out a deep breath, sat down on the floor, putting her head in her hands. "From the time I started talking, Dedo made me promise I would always keep him a secret. He said others couldn't see him unless he willed it, which seemed to be true. So, I grew up with him. My own little enigma and never talked about him or to him, for that matter, unless we were alone. The behavior was ingrained years before we ever built our friendship. I didn't mean to keep anything from you. It was, well...just the way it always was," Faith finished her explanation in a quiet, defeated voice.

"Whatever the reason, your little sentinel has shown himself to us now, so we'll have to keep the secret with you," Val said matter-of-factly.

Garrett found his voice. "Does anyone else know about your secret guardian?"

"Nursie. Somehow she knows. I don't think anyone else does," Faith ventured. "They seem to agree on how to make my life miserable by watching and directing my every move. More so than ever in the last two years," she shook her head.

"Evy, the old nurse? How curious!" was all Val added.

"Where does he go when he disappears into thin air?" Garrett asked.

"I don't know," Faith admitted. "He can travel using the rocks. I see him throughout the house at different fireplaces, hearths, sometimes at the kitchen ovens, even out and about the grounds from time to time. He is a creature made of stone with a brilliant mind. Dedo's a Gargoyle, a citizen of the People of the Rocks," she said.

"Let's get back to the bigger issue." Garrett suggested, "Since he has shown himself to us, we'll assume he knows we're on your side and we'd do anything we could to protect you, just as he would. Right?"

Garrett turned, pointed at Val. "So...you have wings too?"

Her cheeks colored.

"No. More. Secrets. I want it to be an understanding between us. I won't accept less. Swear it. Both of you," Garrett held out his right hand, and the two girls stood and bumped knuckles with him. Val took out her belt knife and cut a lock of her hair off, then handed the knife to Faith. She cut a chunk of her hair, passed the blade to Garrett, who followed suit. Flipping the blade to his fingers, catching it, he held the handle out to Val. She sheathed it. The three friends threw the snippets of hair into the fire, saying in unison, "Promises bind us together until the end." The flames sizzled, the smell of burned hair wafting into the room.

"How touching. Now, since we're all friends," said the deep, gravelly voice above, "let's talk about your next step." As one, three heads turned to look up at Dedo, who once again perched on his usual rock in the fireplace. "What?" he glared down at them. "I can help."

"We've talked about this, Dedo. I want to make my own decisions," Faith reminded him.

"You're not suggesting that I am trying to decide for you, Lady Faith?" Dedo said, blinking his eyes, trying to look innocent. Val squinted at him with suspicion. "No, no. I have already learned that you are all grown up and quite capable of making up your own mind. I will just offer suggestions and ideas while the three of you make the actual plan. Agreed?" he queried.

"Fine," Faith replied, "but at the first hint of you dictating what *you* think I must do, you're out. Understood?"

"Oh yes, milady, I understand. I just want to help. I won't tell you how to handle your newfound cousins. All Fae, by the way, as I'm sure you noticed. Nor will I suggest how you might go about finding out the whole truth of why they are here. You must be curious about the circumstances that caused them to show up now? Do they pose any new dangers for you and your self-declared Fae sister?" he asked, raising his eyebrows. Val shot daggers at him with her eyes, but Dedo continued, "It is you who must decide what to say to your foster parents. Oh, a thousand pardons. I mean your aunt and uncle," he corrected snidely, "since wings have sprouted from your back. A missing princess, the claim asserted by your cousins? Whatever do you think it means? What next? Thank the gods you're smart enough not to do something stupid, like sneaking off to find the Dream Weaver to have your future told by the seer. Nursie would have apoplexy over such careless behavior! No. My confidence lies in the fact that you are a bright, careful young lady who will seek her counsel from experienced minds. Perhaps, Sir Robert? Well, while the three of you work on forming your strategy, I must see what is happening in the hall. Keeping track of all these cousins is a challenge. I promise I'll be back before the next hour to hear your scheme and offer you my thoughts on your plans."

Poof! Dedo was gone again.

The three friends stood and stared at each other for a few moments in complete silence. The fire crackled. Logs fell against the grate. Lenny and Lester turned to face each other. Both winked, then faced forward again, wax dripping onto the mantel.

Garrett watched in amazement and could see the thoughts forming behind the girl's eyes. He knew the look. They both jumped into motion, rushed to Faith's wardrobe and began pulling out travel clothes and cloaks. "Oh no," Garrett said. "Please tell me you are not thinking of doing something stupid that Dedo just praised you for being smart enough not to do? Are you serious?" Garrett stamped his foot. They turned to look at him. "Let's just take a moment to go over the facts we already know! We've all heard the stories. The Dream Weaver is dangerous. Rumor has it that some people never come back when they go to seek her visions. Even the two of you would have to admit the idea is stupid and irresponsible!"

Val walked up to him and tapped his chest hard with her forefinger, backing him up a step. "We have less than an hour before that controlling, busybody gets back. If Faith thinks it's a perfect idea to visit the Dream Weaver to seek a vision, you and I promised to support her. Who else in all of Sharas can tell us what's going on? Explain why we've turned Fae, and no one ever told us we would? How else can we solve the mystery of what happened to Faith's father? Her mother? Confirm with her whether this wild story presented by her so-called cousins is true? Are they related to her? She was adopted! If it proves true, what should she do now? I'm going with her if that's what Faith thinks she needs to do. You can come, or you can stay, but don't stop us. Faith's little spy or guardian, or whatever he is, will soon be back, and this is our only chance to sneak out. Decide. Now, Garrett," Val demanded. Faith had continued to move about her room throughout Val's lecture, shoving items into a leather satchel.

"We don't even know how to find the Dream Weaver!" Garrett said in exasperation.

"We will figure it out like we always do," Val retorted. "Are you with us?"

Faith pulled open the wardrobe door, ready to escape through their secret way. "We'll find her, Garrett. We all know the stories, have heard them our whole lives. I feel a pull to go now. This must be the right course of action! I'm going with my gut feeling about this. Answers are the only thing that is going to help me decide what to do about my cousin's tale or my surprise wings. What does it mean to be Fae? Tell me you understand, Garrett. I just need to find answers," she breathed. "Most of all, I need the two of you by my side. Even though I said that, you should know, whether you stay or choose to come, you'll always be my friend."

Faith turned to the wardrobe, crawled through, her hanging velvets and silks brushing her cheeks, Val right behind her.

Garrett growled low in his chest and clenched his fists in frustration. He let out a strangled yell, punching the wall.

Before crawling into the wardrobe, he grabbed the basket Brittany had given him hours ago, closing the closet doors behind him. He secured and latched the secret door at the back of the massive piece of furniture, racing down the dark corridor after his best friends.

Several sets of stairs down, the hallway came out at a small door at the back of the kitchen pantry. "Wait!" Garrett whispered to the girls. They turned, attentive.

"It will be dark by now, but it's a full moon, so there should be some light. We don't know how far we'll be going or how long. Give me half an hour and meet me at the north entrance of the barn. I need to gather some travel supplies. If you can, wait here a bit. We'll need some food. Here's a basket. See what you can find that will keep for several days. I can hunt when we're on the road, but it won't do us any good to start off hungry." They nodded their acquiescence.

He moved in front of them, opened the pantry door, peeking out. Seeing no one about, he slipped through the warm kitchen and out the back door. Sticking to the shadows, Garrett made his way to the horse barns. His da and mam would have heard all the goings-on of the day from other household staff. They wouldn't be worried about him, at least not right away. He was sure Lady Reatha would have sent word that she'd set Garrett to guard Faith's door.

Garrett's father, Garth, was Robert's stablemaster, which was the reason Garrett was acquainted with caring for the horses and such. He kept a wooden trunk inside the stable, a place he stored his treasures as a young boy. As he grew older, it became a space for his extra work clothes and a young man's necessities. Sometimes the weather kept him in the stables for the night, rather than taking the road home when the weather was bad. Mara, Garrett's mother, was Lady Reatha's House Mistress. Both his parents would have long been home by this hour.

The horses nickered at him when he entered the barn. He made soothing noises back at them. Heading straight to his trunk, Garrett threw open the lid. He propped a thick stick in the corner between the lid and the frame, so it would stay open as he rummaged through it. He pulled out some extra clothes and stuffed them into an empty grain bag. Next, he added a length of good rope and his hunting knife. Grabbing the metal can that he kept his fishing line and hooks in, he sorted through it, pulling out what he needed, then closed the trunk. Pulling his coat and hat from the peg on the wall, Garrett turned to go.

Moonlight outlined Garth's muscled silhouette as he stood in the barn doorway.

"Da," Garrett stammered. "I, er, I..."

His father, a large, hulking man, moved towards his son. "Garrett Emmon Gladheart," his father said with rough emotion, "no son of mine will go out on the road without a proper weapon." Garth leaned forward, his arms extended, holding out a bow and a quiver of arrows.

"Da...your best bow?" Garrett questioned.

"Son," Garth answered, "No time to discuss it now. The hour is before you. Your mother is hovering over the guests in the house to keep them all busy, so they don't discover you and the girls leaving. You must be off. Evy bade me saddle and ready three horses. You'll find them at the north door. Come back if ever you can, but take care of those girls. Your mother asked me to tell you she loves you." Garth grabbed Garrett in a crushing bear hug and pushed him away. "Hurry now! I don't know why, but you must. I feel it in my bones, boy."

Garrett hugged his da one last time and ran off into the shadows to the north barn door. His thoughts raced ahead of him. *How could it be that there were horses waiting at the very place he'd told the girls to meet him?* He shook his head and hurried on. Garrett heard the horses' nicker ahead, just as his senses picked up the sound of a stick snapping and the rustle of leaves underfoot ahead. He froze.

FAITH AND VAL HAD COUNTED to fifty after Garrett left, just like in their younger days of playing games. They heard no movement beyond the door. When they peeked into the warm kitchen, there wasn't a soul there. Pushing the tiny pantry door the rest of the way open, the two of them came out from behind the pickle barrels. The girls closed the door with care.

Val looked up at the linked cured sausages hanging above them and pulled her knife, cutting down three sets, putting them in the basket. Faith peered further out into the kitchen, saw the oven fire banked, coals glowing. There was peace in the kitchen only a few hours each night, before the early morning baking began. She tilted her head to let Val know it was clear. Val grabbed a small wheel of cheese from the shelf and several handfuls of apples from a barrel on her way out. Faith added two loaves of bread left over from the Spring Feast to the basket. The two girls tip-toed down the stairs and out the kitchen door. Just before Val tucked the linen cloth around their haul, she added a tin of tea and a small pot.

"Wait," Faith whispered. "Stay here a moment." Val crouched down. Faith took a deep breath and raced across the commons to the well, where some water bladders hung. To her ears, it felt she was making enough noise for twenty people as she lowered the two bladders down the well. It seemed to take forever, letting them fill. She pulled them back up over the lip of the well, stoppered them with corks, and hung them over her shoulder. Faith hurried back to where she had left her sister-friend. The two of them moved forward together, well hidden in the night's shadows, wearing their black leathers and soft boots. If either of them had turned back to look right at that moment, they would have seen the old nurse's silhouette in the upper-level window looking out at them. But, like an apparition, she was gone in a flash.

Garrett was waiting for them at the north barn door with three saddled horses. "Garrett! We can't take Robert's horses." Faith exclaimed.

"Shhh!" Garrett and Val hissed back at her. Garrett explained his father had met him moments ago and told him Evy had asked Garth to ready the horses. No time to second-guess things now. Val secured the basket behind her saddle with leather straps. Faith hooked the water bladders, one on each side, from her horse's saddle horn. Garrett led them at a walk out of the barn, keeping to the shadows.

Down the road, a mile away from Val's house, they stopped by the river and let the horses drink their fill. "This is the strangest day I've ever had in my life," Garrett muttered to himself.

"I'm sure that statement applies to all of us. I can say with certainty it pertains to me," Faith said, touching his arm.

"Well," Val whispered, "the important thing now is that we keep moving. I think we want to be well away before morning. I doubt your cousins can be fooled for much longer."

"We don't even know which way to go," Garrett lamented.

"I know what to do," Val announced with confidence. "There's a map my da keeps in his study that could help us. My sisters visited the Dream Weaver once, but they wouldn't tell me a thing about their adventure, only that the Weaver lived in the Edgewood Forest. It's got to be on the map. You two wait here with the horses. I'll go to my house, get the map, and collect a few travel things. Stay put. I promise not to be long."

Faith and Garrett nodded. To their surprise, Val snapped her wings out and flew toward her house.

"It's going to take me a while to get used to that," Faith whispered.

LANDING, VAL RETRACTED her wings. With years of practice, she opened the front door without a sound and tip-toed through the house into her father's study. Hanging on the wall was the map she sought, depicted on cured sheepskin. Val lifted it down, rolled it up, putting it under her arm. She scrawled a note to her mam and da, leaving it on the desk, using his favorite paperweight to hold it down. Next, she made her way to her own room. Passing by her parents' bedroom, Val could hear her da snoring.

Val shared a room with her sisters. A glance showed her the shapes of the three older girls, a tangle of long hair, sheets, and blankets. Careful to be quiet, she pulled some clothes and personal things from her baskets and pegs. Bundling them up, along with her Da's map, in a pillowcase, the youngest Pureheart sister remembered at the last minute to grab her hooded cloak. She turned to go, then stopped, felt her throat tighten up as she looked back at her sleeping sisters, Aliah, Carlisse, and Delainey. She wanted to hug them goodbye, but dismissed the idea as foolish. That impulsive act of love would only increase the chance of getting caught. It wouldn't take much to wake the entire household. She blew each sleeping shape a kiss and stole away under the cover of darkness.

Clutching her bundle against her chest, Val hurried across the yard to the barn. The wooden door creaked a little when she pulled it open. Holding one hand aloft, she whispered, "Lumos." A soft yellow ball of light balanced in her palm, lighting up the barn interior. Making her way to the tack room, she pulled her saddlebags down from the peg and dumped her schoolbooks out on a wooden chest. She stuffed the bags with the things she'd gotten from the house. Prying open the chest, reaching in her hand touched a soft pouch that lay at the bottom. She left it where it lay and set her schoolbooks in, putting a burlap bag over the top of them. Val slung the saddlebags over her shoulders and extinguished her light. She turned on the ball of her foot to make her final getaway, preparing to take flight.

The black-winged Fae girl about fainted dead away, heart hammering in her chest, when right there in front of her, barring her way out, stood her three sisters.

"Going somewhere, Val?" Aliah asked in a soft voice.

"It's not what you think," Val answered. The three sisters looked at one another and then back at Val.

"It looks to me like she's going somewhere," said Carlisse. "What does it look like to you, Delainey?"

Delainey walked over to Val and pulled on a scrap of material hanging out of Val's saddlebags with a flourish. "It looks to me like she's going somewhere with one of my favorite dresses!" Delainey declared.

The three sisters rounded on Val, boxing her backwards into the corner of the tack room. "I didn't mean to take your dress, Delainey. It was dark, and I thought it was mine. I can't explain everything to you right now, but I promise to tell you everything later," Val tried to defend herself.

The three older girls' eyes widened as big as their mam's teacups as Val popped open her powerful wings. She flapped the appendages once, twice, three times and was up above them, headed towards the open barn door. "I love you all! Tell Mam and Da I'll be back as soon as I can. I promise to explain when I come home," she shouted behind her. Out the door, she disappeared, flying as fast as she dared, leaving her three sisters standing in the barn, casting their silhouettes among the moon's shadows.

"Did you see that? She has wings? Do we just let her go?" wondered Aliah out loud.

"You can if you want to, Aliah, but she's got my favorite hair ties and your warmest socks!"

Carlisse smiled at Aliah and Delainey, snapped open her own wings and was speeding away in flight, chasing after Val. The other two grabbed each other's hands and leaped into the cool night air, working their wings so fast they were a blur. The plow horses swished their tails, paying them no mind at all.

Val was making a beeline back to the river, counting on her sisters to remain in shock at seeing her with wings and flying away. Soon, she thought, she'd be too far away for them to find her. Val felt her body knocked to the side, making her lose her balance. In a panic and inexperienced, her wings snapped shut. Val faltered, began to fall.

It was her turn to have large saucer eyes. Her three sisters crisscrossed their hands beneath her and caught her mid-fall. Three sets of wings beating in perfect symmetry brought them all safely to the ground.

When her feet touched down, Val backed away from her sisters as if they were strangers.

"Cat got your tongue, Val?" said Delainey.

"Don't tease her," Aliah admonished her sister.

"She's right." Carlisse agreed. "Remember how you felt."

"You, you..." Val stammered.

Aliah held her arms out. "Val, it's all right. Come here. We love you, and now there are no secrets between us anymore."

"I can't believe it," Val whispered. "I thought I was a freak in our family. And, and...then Faith tonight and now all three of you!" She shook her head in disbelief and dropped to her knees. Her mind screamed. Sensory overload gave her a headache. *This was just too much in one day for a person to deal with. How could anyone handle all this at once?*

She felt herself enveloped, with all their arms wrapped around her. Val's sisters created pacifying noises to calm her, making her feel safe, as they'd done her whole life.

"Okay, all good now?" Carlisse remarked as she grabbed Val's saddlebags. "Give me my hair ties back while you tell us where you're sneaking off to."

Val broke into a smile and started laughing. The next thing, the four of them were giggling out of control. Once the bout subsided, Val knew she couldn't keep the truth from them.

They sat in a circle on the grass in the meadow beyond the house. Soft moonlight shone all around them, lightning bugs blinking on and off in the treetops at the edge of the field.

Val's face crumpled again. "How could you keep such a secret from me? All three of you have wings? Why didn't you warn me, tell me what to expect? I've thought of myself as a freak for a few weeks now."

"We should have told you." Aliah cupped Val's face with her palm. "Except we weren't sure you would blossom from caterpillar to butterfly? If you weren't Fae, we didn't want to scare you."

"Plus," Carlisse put in, "we didn't want you moping around jealous because we have wings."

"Carlisse!" Aliah hissed. "You're not helping!"

Val blinked a few times, considering why they would have withheld such information from her. "Never mind, we can argue about it later," Val suggested. She launched into the details about the day's events, leaving out the part about Dedo. He was Faith's secret. Finishing the tale, she stood, brushed herself off, and picked up her saddlebags. Val told the three girls that she had to hurry. Faith and Garrett would be worried sick. She told them how important it was for the three of them to get as far away as possible before sunrise because of Faith's cousins. She confessed Faith intended to seek guidance before she could decide whether to trust the strangers claiming to be related to her, much less believing she was a long-lost princess. There didn't seem to be a way around it, so Val divulged the plan to find the Dream Weaver.

"Hey, a couple of years ago, you three said you went to get your fortunes told by the Dream Weaver. Remember? It was the year you all got those weird, choppy short haircuts." Val's three sisters all unconsciously touched their hair, smoothing it down. "Since you've already visited the fortune teller, do you have any advice for us? Maybe some guidance on how and where to find her? The rumors always say the Weaver lives in the Edgewood Forest." Val took in the look of fear as it rippled across the faces of her sisters at the mention of the name.

"Well," said Aliah, unconsciously running her fingers through her long tresses, "it's a good thing you came home first to collect some things, isn't it, girls?" Carlisse and Delainey both nodded.

Delainey pushed the dress she'd pulled earlier from Val's saddlebags toward Val.

Carlisse opened Val's hand and put her favorite hair ties in Val's palm, closing Val's fingers over them.

Aliah said, "You can keep my socks."

Val felt tears sting the corners of her eyes. "I have so many questions, but I guess those will have to wait until I get back," Val told them. The group stood up and brushed themselves off. Val scrubbed her eyes with her sleeve. The three sisters nodded at one another. "I'll think of you often," Val promised.

"We know you will, Valerie Victoria Pureheart," said Carlisse. With a fierce grin, she told her sister, "It would be hard for you not to think of us, because we're going with you."

Val's anger returned in a surge, and she stamped her foot, saying, "Don't be ridiculous! Mam and Da need you here. You can't come. Faith, Garrett, and I don't even know where we are going or how long it will take us to find the Dream Weaver! Who knows what the future will be? The three of you haven't been forthcoming with any useful information." She wanted to take each one of them and shake sense into them.

"Calm yourself, Val," Aliah said with authority. "That was my point."

"What's the point, Aliah?" Val asked in a disgusted tone.

"We know how to find the Dream Weaver. We can save you time by leading you there. At least in theory. Plus, Mam and Da would have our hides if we allowed you to run off on such an adventure without our protection," Aliah stated. Val swallowed hard as she saw the shadow of fear reflected in the moonlight on each of her sisters' faces.

FAITH AND GARRETT WERE arguing about whether they should go to Val's house to see if her parents had caught her. Just then, Val held her wings in a tight formation, allowing her to glide down to them. "No, not my parents." Val said in a heavy voice, responding to their argument. "My older sisters caught me leaving," she clarified, just as Aliah, Carlisse, and Delainey floated in behind her.

Faith realized her mouth was open in shock and clamped it shut. Eyes glued to the Pureheart sisters in front of her, she reached over, put her hand under Garrett's chin, pushed up, closing his gaping maw. "All three of you have wings," Faith stated the obvious.

Aliah smiled at Faith and Garrett. "I'm sure we all have 100 questions for each other, but the night is growing old. Val said you were in a hurry. Already, you've lost more than an hour. I'll ride double behind Garrett. Carlisse, you ride with Val. Delainey, you're with Faith."

"Ung," Garrett said. The three girls snapped their wings tight, making them disappear. Val noticed they each had a pack on their backs and shook her head. She couldn't believe her sisters had somehow been prepared to travel.

Faith searched Val's face. Val shrugged her shoulders and responded, "They know how to find the Dream Weaver." Mounting her horse, she extended her hand down to Carlisse.

Everyone mounted up. Faith gripped the reins, and her horse danced around in a circle. "Which way?"

"North," three voices chimed in harmony.

Their own moon shadows raced to catch them as they rode through the night.

CHAPTER 9: Lifelong Dreams

Guard duty had Cazzidy Beaumont Touchstone recalling old lessons taught by Master Cornerstone. The scholar shared a history that shaped the current way of life for the clan. These days, goblin people spend a great deal of time and effort trying not to come into contact with the other races. Their clans spread all over the fair land of Sharas, even beyond its borders to the north. Fewer lived in small villages these days. The clans had taken to living in caves and caverns. They were out during the daylight hours, but most still loved the night best. The Master said their people had interacted with both the Fae and humans for years. Mixed communities where they worked and lived in harmony.

The adage 'history repeats itself' was used to draw attention to the fact that there was always some new affliction, resulting in attempts to take what others had. They knew that over the last thirty years, the Gugwe had raided in Sharas. Butchering, burning, killing, and taking slaves on and off. In the last two decades, the Gugwe established a strong foothold on the shores of Sapphire Lake. Raiders drove the northern Fae from their homes. With the Faerie King and Queen gone missing, thousands of the Fae people were slain or enslaved. Rumors said Lancer Goodfellow, King of the Goblins, had gotten involved to put a stop to the Gugwe invasions and halt the slaughter of the Fae. Lancer disappeared as well.

Insatiable, the Gugwes' recent conquests, seemed all but forgotten. The monsters ever thirsted for more. More land. More natural resources to despoil. More blood and death. More slaves. In the past year alone, there had been talk of small parties of Gugwe roving the lower peninsula of Sharas, scouting to see what additional resources might be available.

Shaking his head, Caz brought his thoughts to the present.

Robin had established a clandestine network of eyes and ears over the last three years throughout the clans across Sharas. He received regular clandestine reports. None he'd had contact with of late had heard of any recent sightings of the Fae in the northern reaches. Caz knew that the news concerned Robin. Whispers said the Fae were dead, enslaved, or were better at hiding than even the Goblin clans.

Passionate, the Goodfellow, expressed his belief that all the races living in Sharas would have to band together to defeat the invading Gugwe. Doing his best to convince the Queen only seemed to pit Morveena and Rupert against him. The duo hid behind the argument of waiting until King Lancer returned to the clans before taking any action. Robin argued Lancer had been gone so long now it was unlikely he would return, that the clans couldn't afford to turn a blind eye any longer, couldn't continue to let the violence go unchecked. Lands held by the Gugwe were increasing at an alarming pace. All his research said the Gugwe had a propensity for greed, ever on the lookout for their next conquest.

Robin and Caz didn't like the odds of the goblin population becoming the next target of the invaders. Unable to deter him, Morveena and Rupert assigned Robin the job of organizing and providing training to the lads. He was teaching them how to use various weapons, practicing defense maneuvers. It was clear they hoped the responsibility would keep him busy and serve as a tool to keep his nose out of their business.

When his watch was over, Caz went in for a meal and a drink. The two friends continued to maintain their status quo of ignoring one another in front of others. It seemed wise to keep up the ruse of pretending a mutual attraction to Saffron as the cause of strife between the childhood friends. She played her part by flirting with both. Her dual role allowed them to exchange information without chancing to meet one another in front of anyone. Saffron was their mouthpiece and secret messenger.

Robin couldn't get rid of the nagging feeling Rupert was going to mess with them. Saffron had more or less told them there was a sketchy plan to get rid of Robin and Caz. No word had leaked out about how Rupert would accomplish such a feat.

So they kept their distance.

The two friends only sparred in weapons practice together when told to and made sure not to give Rupert a reason to take notice of them.

The strategy seemed to work. It also helped that Rupert was busy with the preparations for the guest clans who would attend the special summer festivities. Rupert would want the other clans to be sure to notice the authority and power Morveena entrusted him with. Robin's brother had already envisioned himself filling their missing father's shoes on the road to kingship.

STRIKING A CASUAL POSE at the mouth of the cave as the duty guards went down for dinner, Robin disappeared into the woods as soon as the last lad on watch passed by. The next sentries wouldn't be up for another ten minutes.

While on duty, Robin had spotted a secret mark meant for him. He'd backtracked to where he'd seen the message, pushed against the tree trunk, blending, disappearing. Robin dropped onto the soft sand below. He reached out his hand and clasped arms with an old friend.

"Badger Bartholomew Brogan. Good to see you, mate." Robin nodded at Badger's companion. "Tula." Both had been waiting for him in the 'tree cellar'. "Good to see you again, lass." Tula nodded in response.

"Likewise, Robin," Badger replies. "Can't stay long, but we needed to get word to you. Things aren't looking good in the northern reaches."

"I'm not surprised. Your last report told of increased attacks. Word is that several clans have moved south to escape more trouble. They brought rumors with them that the Fae had glamoured their camps to hide them. Meanwhile, I hear the humans are building wooden walls to keep the attackers out. A method that does not work. Have you been able to get any intel on the Gugwe numbers? Their movements?"

"Tula and I are heading back up when we leave here. I should have more information for you on the next trip down. You asked me to look into your missing father. Sorry to report there's been no sign or word about Lancer. I know the end of the year marks a full eleven years he's been missing, and your stepmother will force acknowledgement of her rule or name Rupert as heir. We'll keep looking, count on it. The Fae castle remains abandoned. Well...abandoned by the Fae, anyway. Lots of squatters. Wondered if you could provide us with some food and a few supplies?"

Tula's eyes flashed up with a look of hope.

"Been expecting you for the last three weeks. Caz and I have been putting aside some things for you whenever we had the chance. You'll find the cache in the usual cave, a mile or so from here. Extra clothes, rope, cook pot, dried fruit, jerky, salt, tea, and herbs. There's a little something special for Tula," Robin winked at her. She blushed and fiddled with her hair. Though their clothing looked worn, it was clean, and both looked healthy. Badger had been taking care of Tula for the last ten years since he'd reported the first Gugwe raids. Robin had yet to hear the girl say anything. He hoped Tula liked the hairpins Saffron had fashioned in the shapes of butterflies he'd left for her.

Robin clasped Badger's forearm again. "Keep safe. Till next time, then. I can't thank you enough for the job you're doing, Badger. Tula, keep him on the straight and narrow, yeah?" He smiled and flipped her a piece of rock candy as he disappeared through the bark.

HAVING BURIED HER FEAR, Saffron spent long hours hidden, infused, in the cavern walls below the kitchen when she was off duty. She was hoping to overhear any plans the Queen and Rupert might make on the off chance of finding them together again. So far, she'd had no success. But her clandestine activities paid off one day when Rupert met with a lad in the small room.

Hurrying down the back steps from the kitchen, Rupert peered into the little-used room. Heart hammering in her chest, Saffron froze in her rock hiding place. She could feel the irritation rolling off the goblin prince when he found no one there to meet him.

Expecting Morveena to appear, it surprised Saffron when, instead, Rolland rounded the corner a few moments later. Saffron, Rolland, and the lads had been schoolmates.

"You're late!" Rupert accosted him at the doorway. "I told you noon. Not five minutes before. Not five minutes after. Noon!" he growled, looming over Rolland. "Never keep me waiting again. Am I clear?"

Rolland blinked his eyes several times at Prince Rupert, but said nothing. In fact, it was rare for Rolland to say anything. Saffron knew his secret. She had told no one else that Rolland's uncle had abused him ever since he was a child.

Rolland met any attempt by anyone else to bully him with stoic indifference.

Outwardly.

Rupert seemed to sense he had taken the wrong tack with this boy without understanding why. He perceived it was in his own best interest to correct his error. "Rolland," he crooned in a soothing tone, "I'm afraid I laced my earlier words with a venom not meant for you. It's been a trying day. I lashed out at you in anger meant for another. Let's start over, shall we? What do you say?" Rupert reached out and clapped him on the shoulder.

Rolland turned those words over in his head. He knew something wasn't right. Prince Rupert extending apologies to him? He decided it was best to play along. "Alright. The same has happened to me now and again when I felt angry at someone, another enduring my anger by chance," Rolland acknowledged.

Rupert swallowed down his disgust for the ugly goblin and put on his best 'friendly face', saying, "Thank you, Rolland. I appreciate your granting me a second chance. Friends?" Rupert queries, extending his hand out to Rolland.

Rolland's hair stood up on the back of his neck. Experience had taught him that things always would end in a bad way when someone offered pretended kindness or friendship. More likely, it would turn to brutal anger. So, he followed his instincts, took Rupert's offered hand, and shook it. His senses shifted to high alert.

"Now then, Rolland, my man," Rupert began, "let's talk business."

Rupert laid out the job he was offering Rolland. He took the time to explain how he needed 'his man' to come up with a secret way to sabotage at least one event each for Caz and Robin in the Summer Games. The prince made it clear Rolland wasn't to tell another soul about this. In particular, Rupert's name could never, ever be associated with a plan to keep his younger brother and his friend from gaining the Weapons Master titles. He assured the burly lad that there was nothing sinister afoot. A mother's love was involved. Rolland looked at the prince sideways at that statement.

Why, Rupert continued, surely Rolland must understand how distraught Queen Morveena must be with her youngest son coming of age, soon to leave home. The best way to keep him near was to keep his best friend close to home as well. He assured Rolland that there was nothing to worry about. Rupert himself would see that the two boys could compete in the Summer Games again next year, with no one the wiser and no harm done. Rolland would help his Queen to adjust to her beloved youngest son's transition to adulthood. Rupert insisted that surely Rolland had heard that the Queen had lost her only daughter years ago, yes? The poor woman had even lost her husband; he reminded his perceived stooge.

The prince changed tactics midstream. Rupert attempted to stroke Rolland's pride by saying he had heard from more than a few from the clan who claimed Rolland was brilliant. In fact, it was why he had sought him out for this special, secret assignment. Rupert said he didn't need to know what clever plan Rolland would use. He had complete confidence in the lad's abilities, based on all the good things he'd heard about him.

Rolland examined the prince's statements. He found lies within. Even he knew there were no second chances to test for the Weapons Master title if you failed. And there was no one in the clan that would have put Rolland and brilliant in the same sentence.

Rupert continued talking, but Rolland's mind drifted back ten years to his boyhood days in school. A day when Cazzidy Beaumont Touchstone's prank made Rolland out to be the laughingstock of the class. Hurt feelings and embarrassment stuck with him for the rest of the school year. Rolland analyzed his reaction over the years. Acknowledging that he himself had laughed along with the class at others who had been the butt of Caz's jests and Robin's jokes. He knew in his heart that the two jesters didn't mean to hurt anyone. Their jokes were done in mirth, not with malice. But with Rolland's home-life problems, the jest at his expense had stung him hard. He'd never forgotten it.

Caz and Robin sensed over time they had overstepped in the jest with Rolland and never pranked him again. From then on, they were always kind when he saw them, but they never became his *friends*. No one did. Rolland couldn't afford to let anyone get close. No one could ever learn the humiliation he suffered under his uncle's cruel hands.

Rolland came back from his musings to find Rupert staring at him. Silence pressed down between them in the doorway to the room they'd never even entered. Rolland realized he'd lost track of what Rupert was saying. To cover for his lapse of attention, he stayed silent so the powerful prince in front of him wouldn't know he hadn't been listening. Rolland just stared back, lips pressed together in a grim line.

Rupert broke the standoff. "Humph. I'd hoped the opportunity to please your queen would be enough," he says with an intended bite to his words. "Very well. If that's the way you want to play it. I came prepared to sweeten the deal. Swear you'll speak of this to anyone. Ever." Rolland did not miss the fact that Rupert had spiked each word with menace. "Swear you'll take care of me, and this pouch of gold is yours. I'd wager it is more than you could earn in ten years. Keep those two clowns from participating in the games if you can't sabotage an event. Make sure you do whatever is necessary. I should mention that the price of failure could be unpleasant. You follow?" Rupert snapped his fingers. "Give me your answer. I've other matters to attend to, and we won't be speaking of this again. Besides, you wouldn't want me to let your Uncle Narrol know you displeased the Queen, would you?" Rupert threatened.

Rolland felt a wave of dizziness crash over him. Auras of light faded in and out in his peripheral vision. He looked up at Rupert, gave a start when he hallucinated his uncle's face in place of the prince's. Then, quick as a flash, it was only Prince Rupert again.

Rolland went down on one knee and chose his words with care, so later Rupert couldn't accuse him of not meeting the terms of their bargain. If he was swearing something, the big smith needed to protect himself by saying the *right* words, since he *would* be bound to them. "I swear to...*take care of you, Prince.*" He reached up, snatched the gold-filled pouch from Rupert's hand, and bowed to the prince.

Rupert patted him on the top of his head. "There's a good lad," he said over his shoulder as he strode down the hallway, never looking back.

"Oh yes, Prince Rupert, I will *take care of you.*" Rolland whispered under his breath, his hatred of the man settling at the bottom of his stomach like a stone.

AS SOON AS ROLLAND had left the area, Saffron released herself from the rock wall. Shaking, she tried to gather her composure. Blast Rupert! Her anger bubbled up. Using poor Rolland in such a way. She wouldn't put it past him to have a plan to put all the blame on the lad after the deed was done. This problem would require some deep thought. The Summer Games were just two weeks away. How was she going to solve this problem without hurting Rolland in the process? She grabbed a basket, filled it with potatoes, and headed up to the kitchen. She saw Zeeka pressing a loaf of bread and a crock of cheese into Rolland's beefy hands as he walked away from the kitchen cavern.

Saffron's mother always told her that peeling potatoes was one of the best activities for serious thinking. The feisty redhead wouldn't be able to talk with Caz or Robin until she was off kitchen duty and at her night job tending bar. Fron's mind began churning, sorting through the details, noting the goblins involved, lining up all the threads in the weave, willing her mind to produce solutions. She peeled potatoes in a frenzy. Zeeka glanced at Saffron from time to time and shook her head.

Potatoes peeled, Saffron seasoned them, and pushed the pan of spuds deep into the warm oven. Her stomach growled as the aroma of roasting venison met her nose. Her earlier activities had made her miss breakfast. Back at the kitchen block, she tumbled out a dozen onions from the sling pocket she'd made using her apron. Letting the corners of the smock go from her hands, the onions rolled on the wooden surface and, like Fron's thoughts, tumbled through her head. She had to figure out a plan to keep Rolland safe, as well as to make sure there was no sabotage to affect Caz's or Robin's performance in the Summer Games. They would have to win on their own merits, but by all the elder goblins, Fron thought, no one deserved to be sabotaged in a competition.

Saffron shook herself out of her reverie and found the butcher block in front of her filled with a pile of chopped onion. Tears wet her eyes as she scraped the diced pieces off into a large earthen bowl and set it aside. Saff just knew there had to be a plan to protect everyone.

The redhead went back down the steps to the lower level, rummaged through the burlap bags delivered from trading in the mid-lands yesterday. Using her apron to hold several bunches of carrots and a generous pile of mushrooms, she hurried back up to the cutting board.

Zeeka met her at the top, her wooden stirring spoon in her hand, which she also used as a tool in conversation. "You, lass, are going to take a break," Zeeka said, pointing the large spoon at Saffron, "sit and eat some soup."

Zeeka directed the red-headed lass over to the sideboard, using her wooden spoon as a baton, as if she were conducting musicians. Saffron found a stool, a steaming bowl of soup, a large slice of warm bread with a thick pat of butter melting atop, along with a cool mug of watered wine. Her eyes teared up. "Zeeka," her voice trailed off in emotion.

"It's no trouble, girl. You look peevish. Besides, you're drowning in your thoughts and troubles. I just wanted to thank you for all your hard work, day in and day out. Never a complaint from you," Zeeka smiled, showing some gaps where teeth were missing. "I've always believed food is good for the thoughts. Now, eat up, lass, every bit before you jump back to your work, mind you."

Zeeka went back to her big iron cookstove. When the clan traveled or moved their location, Zeeka always carted the stove along. The cook turned back on her heel, shaking her kitchen spoon at Saffron and ordered, "And no more thinking on your troubles until you finish your meal! Clear your mind, lass, and I'm sure all the threads of your thoughts will come together to let the pattern settle." Zeeka winked, and Fron gave her a grateful smile.

Saffron ate, felt warmed by the meal, but more so by Zeeka's kindness. She stopped all her meditation on the problems she needed to solve, looked over at Zeeka and thought about how much she missed her mother. It had been three years now since she'd lost her mam. She still felt a vast emptiness inside; sure, nothing could ever fill it. She pushed a little of Zeeka's kindness into that space.

Finished, she licked her lips, hopped down off the stool, and carried her dishes over to the washtubs. She noted the piles of pots and pans waiting for her when she finished chopping up the carrots and mushrooms. As she passed by the stove, she leaned in, held both Zeeka's bony shoulders, squeezing the old cook in a tight hug. Cheek pressed against the other woman's, she whispered, "You're the best, Zeeka." Then, the redhead hustled back to the block, chopping carrots with a fury, diving right back into her whirlpool of brainstorming.

An hour later, Zeeka was dumping a bowl of mushrooms into the kettle on the stovetop. Saffron dropped the heavy pan she was washing and declared, just loud enough for Zeeka to hear, "The pattern." Her eyes glazed over as if she were seeing something very far away.

Zeeka whispered under her breath, stirring the big pot of stew, "Yes, lass, the pattern of the weave. Now you have it."

Saffron turned to Zeeka, asking, "Did you say something, mistress?"

"Why, no, child? Not a word." The wooden spoon never stopped its circular pattern, round and round the bottom of the pan.

Fron wiped her hands on the front of her apron and untied its strings. "Your food for thought did wonders, you lovely thing!" she grinned at Zeeka. "Sorry, but I must be off. There is just enough time for me to get myself cleaned up. I'm tending the bar room tonight for Bedwer, and, and..." Fron beamed at Zeeka. "I think everything is going to be okay!"

The cook looked over at the washtubs. Why, the lass had cleaned every dish and pan except the last one she'd dropped from her hands when all the pieces of the puzzle came together for her. "Off with you then," Zeeka declared, using her wooden spoon like a paddle to show the red-haired ball of energy she should go. "Hazzel will be along soon. She can finish the washing. Mind, you keep those boys on their toes and guessing 'bout your intentions, lassie." Zeeka chuckled to herself, turned back to her stove and oven, waving Fron off. The solace of the kitchen returned to fill Zeeka with peace. She stirred the stew with a knowing smile on her lips.

Saffron Melody Swallowtail hurried to a little-used hall, down the uneven solid rock floor leading deep into the cave system. She slowed her pace as she reached her destination.

Smoothing her skirt, she stood outside Rolland's workshop.

Peeking round the doorway, the girl could see Rolland's large hands working the bellows, bringing hot coals to a searing red, smoke flowing up and out of a natural chimney in the grotto. He wore a heavy leather apron, his shirt off in the heat, muscles taut as he put the large bellows down and leaned over to pick up his heavy hammer next to the forge. Fron watched as

Rolland hesitated, looked around, his skin prickling. Saffron pulled back, holding her breath.

Rolland grabbed the heavy rod of iron, now red-hot, and let his hammer and muscles make the iron sing. He worked with a natural rhythm, beating the iron, shaping it, letting his mind and muscle force it into a long, thin blade. Rolland held the piece up, examining the work. Satisfied with its shaping, he walked over to a large vat and plunged the blade into the water. The metal sizzled, steam rose, coating the big man in slick sweat. Fron stared in amazement as Rolland took the blade over to his stone wheel and began pumping the large floor pedal, pressing the blade's edge to the stone. Sparks flew, burning small spots where they hit the skin on his arms and neck as he made the edge sharp as a razor, smooth as glass. He drew the blade's edge across his forefinger. Blood welled up. Smiling at the result, he sucked the blood from his finger and took his creation to the workbench.

Laying down the iron blade, Rolland picked up two or three pieces of worked iron he'd shaped into handles the day before. Holding each to the top of the new blade, judging which would be the perfect finish for the weapon.

Saffron pulled her slim body around the corner into the hot workroom. "I like the middle one best, don't you?" she commented. "Not that I know anything about making weapons, but those pieces seem to have a certain symmetry together."

Rolland turned, taking in the red-headed lass with a timid smile on her face. He grunted his acknowledgement of her question, took the handle she'd suggested, returning to the forge. Rolland placed the end of the blade on the hot coals. He gave the bellows four or five pumps to bring the heat to a shimmering red that reflected off the wall and made Saffron's hair seem as if it were on fire. Rolland turned, her fiery-red locks catching his eye, then averted his eyes down toward his feet.

"Hello Rolland," Saffron said in her quiet way.

Rolland looked up, blinked at her several times. She smiled. That smile transported him back to the horrible day at school when everyone had laughed at him.

Everyone but Saffron.

She had followed him out into the woods, calling his name, and offered him the same smile. He was sitting with his back against a tree, mulling over the humiliation he felt, sure it would be with him all the days to come. There she was, with the sun shining on a head full of red curls, reaching her hand out to him. Saffron sat down, held his hand, comfortable in the silence, and leaned her head against his shoulder. After a while, she stood up and brushed off her leggings. Touching her palm to his cheek, she said, "Caz didn't mean to hurt your feelings, Rolland," her eyes searching his. "He and Robin just keep trying to outdo each other for a laugh. The jest wasn't personal. I hope you know it's true. The lads aren't cruel, just jokesters. There's something lacking in their lives that makes them crave constant attention, you know?" She pulled her soft hand away and turned to go back inside the school.

But Rolland couldn't make himself return to class. He felt ashamed. Instead, he struck out for home. What his schoolmates and even Saffron didn't know was that when he got home, his Uncle Narrol was there. Narrol was supposed to have been gone for several days. The sight of the boy coming home midday from school put the lad's uncle in an ugly mood. Narrol, already angry because the trade he had gone to make had not worked out, added to Rolland's misfortune. His arrival home was just bad timing. His uncle would take the rage he had built up out on his nephew. It started with verbal abuse: screaming, telling the lad how stupid he was, how stupid he would continue to be if he didn't attend school. The barrage went on and on and on. Babbling about how the boy would damage Narrol's reputation if the lout didn't buck up. Throughout the rant, beating the boy with his wide leather belt until he was a cowering mess. Rolland rolled into a fetal position on the barn floor, the belt flaying into his skin beneath his shredded shirt. Narrol's wrath subsided; nevertheless, he kicked Rolland in the back a few times for good measure.

"Best find some work to occupy you, boy. You'll not be going anywhere until the bruises you've forced me to give you are gone. You brought this on yourself, as always, right?"

Narrol waited. He kicked Rolland again, then repeated, "Right?"

His uncle smiled when the boy whimpered back in a whisper, "Yes, sir. I brought it on myself."

Rolland heard his Uncle Narrol's footsteps retreat from the barn, locking the door behind him. Not moving, he lay there watching the dust motes, visible in the small slits between the barn wood that allowed sunlight in. They fluttered and sparkled, drifting downward, as he remained curled in a heap on the barn floor.

This was the memory Rolland always connected with Caz's jest that day.

A gentle touch on his shoulder from Saffron's hand roused him from his thoughts. He realized he was still at his forge. "Hello Saffron," Rolland responded. "Do you need something? I'm kind of busy. I have a deadline for getting the weapons made for the Queen's Ransom." He fidgeted with the heavy leather glove he wore, used for handling the hot iron.

"Yes, Rolland, I do. You. I need your help," she told him.

His eyes opened wide in surprise. Thoughts of his uncle appearing made him glance back at the pile of iron near the forge, and he stammered, "I can't help you right now, Saffron. I can't!" he sounded panicked. "I've got work I need to finish today."

"Of course you do, lad. Important work, by the looks of it. I've got more work myself. But nothing as special as what you create. You're the only one in all our clan with this talent, you know." She smiled again. He almost smiled back. "No, you mustn't worry. I would never ask you to drop everything for me," Fron assured him.

"But, I would Saffron...if I could, I mean, but..." Rolland trailed off, not knowing what to say, eyes darting to the archway, worried his uncle would appear.

"Well, I only stopped by to ask you to join me for a beer after my bar shift tonight, so I could talk to you about something I need help with. I'm off at moonrise. Will you come?" Saffron chewed on her bottom lip, worried he would say no. The big man looked down at his feet again as they shuffled in place. "Course. Sure," he stammered, "but you don't have to have a beer with me," he told her.

"No, Rolland, I don't have to. But you know what? I *want* to," she beamed at him, turned, waved back, calling out over her shoulder, "I'll see you at moonrise, laddie."

Making her way along the sloping cavern hall, Saffron heard the iron singing under Rolland's hammer all the way up the ramp-way.

HOT AND SWEATY WHEN she reached the main level of the cave system, Saffron hurried to the cavern pool where she bathed. She donned a clean, black leather top shaped like a triangle. It tied at the neck and in back below her shoulder blades, showing off the tattoos decorating her arms and the nape of her neck. Next, she pulled on leather leggings, legs still damp, making it a struggle. Pinning up her hair, she focused on rubbing some coal on her eyelids and under her lower lashes. Last, Saffron stuck a finger in a small earthenware bowl on the shelf and rubbed some soft beeswax on her lips to give them a shine.

There was just enough time to get up to Bedwer's bar as the lads and lasses came in from their day's work. Fron may not have had the artistic flair Rolland had, but she had a special talent for making people feel good, feel welcome. Bedwer, the barkeep, knew his customers looked forward to Saffron's ready smile and clever banter. She had a way of making each person feel special. Grabbing her apron from the hook behind the bar, she tied it on. Greeting the first few of the clan who came in, she directed them to tables with a pitcher of Bedwer's best brew and a tray of mugs. She noticed Robin coming through the door. She stamped her foot, getting most everyone's attention, topped off a mug with frothing foam, and pushed it into Robin's hand. Hopping up on the bar, walking along the edge with a vivacious smile for the crowd, Saffron shouted, "Well now, Robin, this crowd is ready for some music! Yo, lads, and lassies, show the Goodfellow his talent is just what we want!"

The crowd banged their mugs on the tabletops and shouted their approval. Saffron picked up the corners of her apron and did a little dance down to the end of the bar. As a finale, she jumped to the floor, where Bedwer waited, and handed her two fresh pitchers of beer. With a big grin, she was off, working her way around the tables. There were hoots and howls as a large group of Lesser Goblins came in, filling up the side seats.

Robin gave her a grateful nod, took his mug and headed over to the musician's cove. Picking up his flute, the music flowed. He fell into his own small world, where there was nothing for him but his music. A few moments passed, then one of the Lesser Goblin lads came over and joined him on the drums. Two others entered the cove, taking up fiddles, all jamming to Robin's melody.

That was all it took for the dancing to start.

Hot and thirsty patrons drank lots of beer. Fron worked the crowd. Just when the drinking was taking some tempers over the edge, she clapped her hands. That signaled the kitchen staff to come out with pots of venison stew. Stew that had the potatoes, carrots, onions, and mushrooms Fron herself had chopped that afternoon. The other barmaids stepped into a line, each carrying a breadboard in both hands. They tapped a dance out onto the hall floor, delivering a warm loaf to each table. There was a flourish of clapping; the crowd enjoyed the performance. The customers from the clan began lining up with their bowls at the stew pots.

It pleased Saffron; her new idea for the lasses to dance the bread out to the tables seemed a success. She noticed Bedwer grinning at her and shaking his head. She was always surprising him. The barmaids continued serving Bedwer's brew as the customers filled their bellies with Zeeka's venison stew and warm bread. As soon as the patrons finished their meals, the dancing started up again. Saffron headed back to the bar to refill her pitchers.

Her back was to the hall when she felt herself whirled around, only to discover the charming smile of Cazzidy Beaumont Touchstone directed at her. He took the empty pitchers out of her hands, set them on the bar, pulling her out to the dance floor. Other dancers formed two lines opposite one another. Saffron and Caz did a complicated tap dance down the peopled corridor to the beat of clapping hands. The next two dancers at the head of the corridor came through right behind them to tap their way down the makeshift aisle.

Fron waved Caz off, mouthing, 'Back to work for me', heading to collect her pitchers. Before she could claim them, Fron felt herself pulled by her left arm, only to find Robin looking into her eyes. His own eyes danced with mischief. He dragged her back to the front of the line, began a favorite dance between the rows of patrons, all laughing and clapping to the beat of the music.

Not to be outdone by Caz, Robin began a series of hand claps in partnership with Saffron as their feet stamped down with the dance steps. The other dancers mimicked the stomping pattern as they waited in lines, forming the aisle. Robin and Saffron did everything in harmony with the musicians' beat. One fiddler followed the partners, dancing along as he played. A flute player worked his way up from the opposite end, trapping Saffron and Robin in the middle. Robin, sensing he had the crowd's attention, stopped, held up a finger to Saffron. She stopped. The music stopped. The crowd quieted. Robin pointed both his forefingers at the fiddler and the flutist. They pushed a musical beat back to Robin, who stamped out a dance pattern, then with a big smile at the crowd as he turned in a circle and stopped, pointed at Saffron. The musicians started the melody again, and Saff tapped out the same steps, copying what Robin had done. The crowd roared. Two more rounds took place, but this time when Saffron finished, she held up her finger and stopped. The music stopped. The crowd quieted. She held out her two forefingers at the flutist and fiddler, winked at them, and as the music piped up once more, Saffron danced a merry jig down the row. Her feet were moving so rapidly that the crowd struggled to keep up, stomping to her beat. As she pushed the fiddler down the row while he played, she danced, a hand on his chest as she moved him backwards. When they reached the end of the line, two lads nearby grabbed her hands, lifting her onto a tabletop, where her feet danced so fast they were a blur. Her finale was a backflip off the table where Bedwer waited with a smile, once again handing her two full pitchers. The crowd's applause was deafening as the other dancers continued. Saffron bowed her head to Robin, a smile on her lips, disappearing into the crowd to sell more beer. Robin threw up his hands, shrugged his shoulders, and got a round of laughs. He made a show of making his way back to the musician's cove, picked up a flute, joining in the melody once again. The crowd noticed as Robin and Caz stared at one another for several minutes. Robin played his flute, and Caz ate his stew from opposite ends of the room.

The next hour saw the customers thin out. The music slowed. Saffron and the other barmaids wiped up the tables and filled the mugs of those left at the late hour. Bedwer sent the girls off to get their own bowls of stew. The lasses showed Saffron the extra tips they'd gotten because of the new routine she'd come up with and asked if they could try something new every week. She nodded. A slight movement caught her eye, and she noticed Rolland sitting back in the corner, hidden in the shadows. It looked as though he'd been there for a while. Closing time was nearing, and Bedwer shouted, "Last call!" The barmaids made one last round with their pitchers. Someone called out for a song, and others took up the chant. Saffron looked to Bedwer, and he nodded his permission back to her.

The room became quiet. Saffron took off her apron and tossed it onto the nearest chair. She unpinned her hair and shook out her long red tresses, then leaned up against a stalagmite and took a long, calming breath. Her deep, full voice filled the hall, and she held those of her clan in the rapture of an angel's voice. She sang a ballad telling the story of the Goblin people in the old language. Her voice hung in every crevice, echoing throughout the hall. Rolland closed his eyes and let her beauty wash over him. In the background, the drummer added a soft beat. A zither's strings plucked in harmony with her voice, giving her performance an ethereal quality.

The fires burn and burn and burn,
Forever awaiting our return
To home; to hearth;
And all along the road
Our people walk in search of self;
In search of family lost, too high the cost.
The fires burn and burn and burn,
Forever awaiting our return.
Home is where we long to be—on Northern Shores along the sea.
Free to wander long, to sing our songs,
Haunted by forgotten ghosts — our history erased by evil hosts.
The fires burn and burn and burn,
Forever awaiting our return.
Forgotten war and rage
Have brought us to the center stage.
But we have not lost memory
Of those we loved.

Only lost the key; the door closed fast;
Our dreams a nightly reverie.
Some sweet day,
One shall come, one to lead us
Back the way we've come;
Our tears will never build the bridge,
The span we need to cross,
A path we must travel to find the history lost.
The fires burn and burn and burn
Forever awaiting our return.
The clans forgotten,
Then reborn,
Cursed to travel from dusk till dawn.
The souls we mourn, the ones we lost;
Will find their way;
A foretold leader takes our hands
And guides us back to our homeland.
Until that day;
The fires burn and burn and burn
Forever awaiting our return.

WHEN SHE FINISHED, she bowed her head, drained. Bedwer's patrons filed out quietly, emotional, affected, looking inward. Some touched her face as they walked by or squeezed her hand. Saffron had a way of affecting the toughened souls of the Goblin people. Robin sat in quiet introspection, thinking of how powerful Saffron's talent was. She claimed these people as clan, but in truth, she had come from another. That clan had cast her and her mother out. When the two of them came to Robin's father's clan, Saffron's mother asked if they could earn their place with the people. Her mother once had the same talent for singing, but she had died after years of work and loyalty to this clan. Now Saffron was alone. Had been alone for years. He hadn't ever focused on her situation. He looked up, saw Bedwer hand the lass a cold mug of beer, and she took a deep draught to quench her thirst and soothe her throat. It surprised Robin to see her walk over to a shadowed table in the back corner and sit down with her ale in the company of someone he could not quite make out. A tall, muscled lad. Robin glanced across the room to see Caz leaning against the wall, his lidded eyes following the redhead. Caz turned, met Robin's eyes, and held for a moment.

Robin bent down to gather the musical instruments with his mates to stow them away. As he went through the usual motions, he noted how odd it seemed not to have Saff nearby teasing the musicians. She liked to talk about the night's entertainment after she finished her shift.

Bedwer swept the floor. The tables and chairs were pushed back so he could mop away the stickiness after everyone had left. The last of the late-night crew headed out the door. Robin could see Saffron still sitting at the corner table, her mug empty. Long red hair hung down around her shoulders, the dim light casting a strange glow on her cheerful face.

Zeeka came in through the kitchen door. Bedwer had full mugs ready for the two of them. They sat down at a table in the distance between the two lads.

Zeeka shook her head and called out, so only Robin, Caz, and Bedwer could hear. "You lads better go over and give your regards to our Saffron for the lovely ballad she tugged at all our hearts with tonight." Zeeka winked at them. "Sides, unless you're going to mop the floor for Bedwer, you've run out of reasons to stick around so you can discover who the lass is sitting with." Bedwer chuckled. He and Zeeka clinked their mugs and took a drink.

Caz and Robin shrugged their shoulders and worked their way over to the corner table. As they got closer, they realized the large, muscled lad sitting with Saffron was Rolland. They looked at one another in disbelief as they approached the table.

"Oh, good." Saffron said, smiling, "You're both here. You remember Rolland from school, right? It's been a few years, but we all need to talk about a plan I've come up with. Rolland here has agreed to help us." She beamed at Rolland and squeezed his large ham of a hand in gratitude.

"Rolland," Caz nodded his head to him.

"Hello, Rolland," Robin gave him a grin.

Rolland nodded back at them. Robin turned to face Saffron with a questioning look written on his face. "So, Fron," Robin used his affectionate name for her, "what plan are you talking about?"

"Yeah, Saff," says Caz, using his favorite nickname for her, "What's Rolland agreed to help us with?"

Rolland squirmed. His confidence waned as he realized Robin and Caz didn't know about this plan at all. Anxiety filled him. Maybe Saffron was leading him into some kind of embarrassing situation with these two lads again after all these years. She wouldn't, would she?

Saffron sensed Rolland's tenseness and patted his leg to comfort him. An action not missed by either Caz or Robin.

"Oh, lads, sit down and join us. Rolland is critical to my plan."

"Oh?" Caz questioned.

"He is," Saffron insisted. "Rolland is going to help us sneak out on a mission to find the Dream Weaver."

Caz and Robin were stunned. Saffron enjoyed the look on their faces, smiled at Rolland and whispered under her breath to herself, "All the threads pulled into a pattern, a weave, a strategy."

She nodded to herself in deep satisfaction, unraveling her scheme to the three boys. They huddled together. Now and then, they nodded their heads. Zeeka watched from across the room, content to enjoy her beer after a very long day.

CHAPTER 10: Forks in the Road

Faith, Garrett, Val, Aliah, Delainey, and Carlisse kept a brisk pace under the moonlight, walking the horses. Now and then they stopped to rest their mounts or let them drink their fill at any small creek or stream they came to. The collective group stopped to rest themselves close to dawn.

Garrett offered to take the first watch. They all agreed and unsaddled the horses in a small grove. Val and Faith pulled blankets from their packs and dropped to the ground. Exhaustion overcame both girls. They used the saddle to rest their heads on and fell asleep back-to-back. Aliah smiled at her other sisters. "I'll help Garrett with the horses," she told Carlisse. "You and Delainey get some rest, too. We'll want to be sharp when we get to the Edgewood." For once, they didn't argue.

Aliah walked over to the creek bank and pulled up several handfuls of sweet grass. Garrett hobbled the horses near a small patch of grass after leading each down to the creek for a long drink. It surprised him when Aliah began rubbing down the horse she'd shared with him, using a big handful of grass in place of a curry brush. The horse nuzzled her as she continued her work.

"Well, that's a trick I've not seen in a while," Garrett said. Following her lead, he grabbed a couple of handfuls of the grass himself, setting to work on another of the horses.

"Yes," Aliah agreed, "on the farm we get used to having tools on hand, but with the rush to get away, no one thought to bring a brush for the horses. I don't plan on sharing mine!"

Garrett blushed, unseen in the shadows. He'd spent most of his life taking care of horses and hadn't even thought of grabbing a brush from the barn for their care. Then he remembered the tools he carried in the pouch at his waist, pulled out the small metal hook, and coaxed the hoof up of the horse he was working on. He cleaned out the dirt and small stones packed in around the bottom of the hoof, working his way around all four. Aliah smiled at him, moved on to rub down the last horse, Garrett checking the other horse's hooves. Work finished, they went to the creek's edge to wash their hands and faces. Picking a spot on a small hill above where the girls were fast asleep, the two took up the first watch. There was a huge white pine at the top, where they sat with their backs resting against the tree in companionable silence. The view from the hilltop was decent to the north, the south, and in the direction they'd come from. The woods were silent except for the gentle breeze that moved through the tree canopy.

"I can tell you love horses, Aliah."

She nodded. "You too."

"All my life. They're not complicated. You just have to make sure they have food, water, basic care, and that they're content. Easy to please," he observed.

"Not like girls at all," Aliah responded.

"No," Garrett absent-mindedly answered. "Wait! What? We weren't talking about girls," he objected, embarrassed.

"I'm just teasing you, Garrett," Aliah assured him.

He changed the subject. "It must be nice to have all your sisters. I have never had siblings. Seems like Val and Faith have always been like sisters to me," Garrett commented after thinking it over. "Won't your parents be worried when they find all of you gone?" he asked.

"I left a note," Aliah confessed. "They would have been more worried if Val had disappeared without the rest of us. Da can get two neighbor's sons to pitch in and help while we're gone."

The wind stirred the leaves. An owl hooted. Somewhere in the distance, a woodpecker began drilling into a tree. Peaceful early morning sounds, though the sky was still dark.

Uncertainly, Garrett looked over at Aliah. "Uh...er, ung..." he swallowed hard, trying to work up his courage.

Aliah smiled, put her hand on his shoulder, "Garrett Emmon Gladheart, you are a wonder. You go about your business every day with all the confidence in the world. But your tongue gets twisted when you want to ask a question you think is important. My guess is you're fretting it might be none of your business? Am I right?" Garrett's cheeks flushed, now obvious from the sun rising low in the sky. "Well, lad," Aliah pointed a finger at his chest, "put your fears aside. I'm a believer in always coming right out and saying what you need to. Form opinions and voice those sentiments if you think it's important. You shouldn't worry about what others think of your views. Oh, that's not to say you shouldn't keep an open mind and listen to others' viewpoints. But you've got to respect the fact that everyone has a mind of their own. You never know when someone else might present a good idea you can use, or one that may change your thinking if they win you over to their side of an argument. If what you ask about isn't your business, I assure you, people will tell you plainly. There are times you have to be mindful of circumstances and people's feelings. There's a right and wrong time to bring something up. But you strike me as a bright, strong young man with some worthwhile ideas. You shouldn't worry about what anyone will think when you express them."

Aliah winked at him and settled back to wait for her words to sink in, hoping the question on his mind would work its way out of his mouth.

She didn't have to wait long. Garrett took a deep breath and asked without apology, "I'd like to know when you, Carlisse, and Delainey's wings popped out? What is going on? Faith and Val have wings now too, and so did all her mysterious cousins, who showed up out of nowhere. Has our whole fortress gone crazy? Does everyone have wings except me? I mean, I've never heard or seen such a thing and..."

"Stop!" Aliah commanded. She put a finger to his lips. A soft laugh escaped her. "Well, once you decide to ask your questions, it's like a spring flood!" Garrett laughed with her.

"Listen, laddie, since the night has gone by and the sun's come out, I'll ease your mind a bit." Aliah glanced over to see all the girls sleeping. "You've heard of the Fae? The Faerie People? There are several families who live in the town. One owns the docks."

Garrett said in a hushed voice, "Of course I know of them, Miss Aliah."

She clicked her tongue at him. "Just Aliah. You can call my mam a Miss. Besides, I'm only a year older than you, Garrett Gladheart! What about the goblin clans? I'm sure you're aware of their living nearby?" she queried.

A slight shadow passed over his face. "Goblins, yes. Years ago, they used to come to the Festival of Ostara. Remember?"

"Yes, yes," Aliah cut him off. "Though it is rare to see them, the goblins still live among us," she encouraged him.

"I guess so," Garrett thought about it.

"It's true," Aliah tells him with authority. "The goblins, the Fae, selkies, humans, and many other races live all around us, even if *you* never see them. Large groups of Fae are almost never spotted these days. They keep to themselves. Magic protects their borders, keeping their village veiled from us. Rumors say they've left Sharas. My sisters and I believe many stay hidden. Not wanting to call attention to themselves, they use glamours or disguises." She let out a quiet sigh.

"My sisters and I were all orphans. Da found us alone in the woods on his way back from buying a wagonload of seed potatoes to plant. He wrapped us in blankets and gave us each an apple to eat. For the rest of the ride, he described how happy his wife was going to be when he got us all home. And he was right. MaeElla welcomed us with open arms." Aliah stared off, reliving her memories while watching the morning mist burn off in the new sunlight.

"We couldn't have had more loving parents, even if I could remember who our real father and mother were or where we came from."

Aliah took a deep breath and continued her story. "Being adopted, no one could have known we were Fae. I know how Faith felt. My own wings snapped out without warning. At least I was alone, with no witnesses. But I was beside myself with worry. I didn't know what I was going to do. How could I face my family like some kind of mutant? All I could think was I have to run away before anyone finds out! I put some things in a burlap bag to make my getaway. The sun had gone down. I was just waiting for it to get dark so I could sneak off. What a fool I was! Of course, Mam noticed I hadn't come in from chores. It surprised me when the barn door opened, the last dusky light pouring through, highlighting my silhouetted wings."

"Aliah," Mam called to me.

I covered my face with my hands, so ashamed of this bizarre change to my body, and sobbed. "I'm sorry, Mam, so sorry."

MaeElla Pureheart walked over, took my hands in hers, clinging to them. She reached up with her right hand and wiped the tears from my face with her calloused fingers. Without a word, she turned me around a full circle, my cheeks burning red crimson from embarrassment. "Aliah Bethany Pureheart, you are beautiful!" She tipped my chin up with two fingers and kissed me. "Don't you ever feel ashamed of anything that is part of you! Never. Understand?"

"Garrett, my mother gave me a wonderful gift that day. She gave me myself and told me I was good. *Every* part of me. Well, Mam is a wise woman. She got to thinking later it was possible my sisters might also one day experience this same change, so she and I talked about it, but kept my secret. We watched for signs. If the change came for them, we didn't want them to feel abnormal, as I had. Although we each had our own experience when the transformation came over us, my sisters had love and support. Mam encouraged us to find out what we could do with our wings, so we've practiced and experimented for several years out in the barn. Val's wings must have opened in the past few weeks. She kept it hidden from everyone, which is so like Val! Now her secret is out and, as a bonus, she found out her best friend has wings, too."

Aliah stood and brushed off her hands. "Listen, Garrett, I need to get some rest. Wake one of the other girls in an hour or two so you can sleep some. We've got a long way to travel over the next couple of days. I'd like to be off again by noon." Aliah smiled at him over her shoulder as she walked down the hillock, leaving Garrett alone with his thoughts.

THE FORTRESS WAS A beehive of activity the morning following Spring Feast. Faith's cousins had gone to bed in the wee hours of the night, giving up hope Faith was going to appear. The lack of sleep did nothing to deter their single-mindedness when the sun came up.

Brittany made her way down the hall at first light. The household staff was already bustling around, readying breakfast. Shaun rounded the corner toward the stairway, mumbling "morning". The cousins huddled together over a fresh pot of coffee. Brittany let them know she'd already checked, and the staff denied they'd seen any sign of Faith yet today. Her morning report also included the fact that Garrett was no longer staked out in front of Faith's door. She'd tried the door, but found it locked.

Travis came in, rubbing the night's sleep from his eyes. It was obvious he hadn't even bothered to wash his face. He grumbled to the group, words unintelligible. Grabbing a cup, Travis held it out, expecting someone to fill it for him. Brittany complied, rolling her eyes at her half-awake brother. He took his cup away from the crowd, settled on a bench to wake up in peace on the other end of the room by the fireplace. Two of Sir Robert's hounds were curled up in front of the hearth.

Moments later, Lady Reatha swept into the room. Her nieces and nephews swarmed the woman, each shouting out their questions about when they could see their cousin Faith. Their lack of manners appalled Reatha. She pushed them back to give herself space. That's when Mariella and Kristian appeared.

Mariella stamped her foot, clapped her hands, coming over to steer Lady Reatha from the barrage of questions from her aggressive cousins. "Get back, all of you! How rude. Here, Aunt Reatha, let me get you a chair. Britt, please get a cup of coffee for the Lady. Good heavens! The sun has only just risen. Must I remind you we are all guests of this house and you are making the Lady sorry you are here?" There were low mumbles of apology as Brittany placed a cup of steaming morning brew in front of Reatha. The Lady smiled at Mariella, who came and sat next to Reatha with a cup of her own.

"Besides," Mariella continues, "there is no reason to badger Reatha. It seems Faith left the fortress in the middle of the night. No one knows where she's gone." Mariella sipped her coffee and patted the seat beside her, suggesting Kristian should sit down.

The reaction took only a moment or two. Mariella let all the cacophony of demands and questions fall about her unanswered as she sipped her coffee. They knew her well, these cousins of hers. Knew she would not respond until they calmed and behaved in a civilized manner. A few moments passed as Brittany stalked around the room, fuming. Stopping in front of her cousin, she took a deep breath and asked sweetly, "Please, dear cuz, tell us how *you* found out Faith has disappeared? I should also like to know why you didn't rouse all of us at once so we could speak with her before she left?" Sweet words, but laced with anger. Brittany began stirring her coffee with a spoon, watching Shaun as he eyed the kitchen staff bringing out breakfast. When they finished putting out the food, Shaun headed straight over to check out the fare, stomach growling.

Mariella refilled Reatha's cup, who raised her brow and waited as the pretty girl topped off her own. "I didn't rouse all of you because I did not learn of it until I woke this morning. Kristian and I share the nurses' room. It was she who told me Faith had stolen away sometime last night. Our cousin left no word with anyone about where she was going or why. No message about when she intends to return." Silence hung in the hall.

"Well," Lady Reatha said aloud to no one in particular, "this was unexpected. I must find Robert. Faith had never been away from the fortress before. I'm worried," Reatha fretted as she hurried from the room.

One by one, the cousins went to the sideboard with little appetite and filled a plate. Brittany spoke up. "Looks like we are back to square one."

Travis got up and went to the serving table, threw a piece of bacon to each dog, and loaded up a plate. "Don't be so glum," he smiled around at his cousins. "We're not back at square one."

"How do you figure, brother?" Brittany pouted.

"Easy! We found Faith, didn't we? Our timing was just off. Obviously, no one prepared her for her heritage. The wings coming out scared her. We just have to find her again to help her come to terms with her new discovery. We can teach her what it means to be Fae, yeah?"

"Oh yes," Shaun taunted, "easy as pie. No idea where she's run off to. We don't know her. She doesn't know us, and she doesn't trust us. We've not a clue how she thinks or would react in a desperate situation. Yeah, easy as pie, brother."

"We'll just have to talk with everyone around here and see what we can find out. But we'll have to make it quick. If she left last night, we don't want the trail to get too cold. Besides, you have the best tracker in the mid-lands with you." Travis pointed his thumb at his chest. "Auntie Reatha is worried and needs our help to find Faith," Travis smiled.

"Sure, Trav," Brittany retorted. "You can be the one to tell our aunt how we want to take Faith on a dangerous journey to the northern shores. Oh, and by the way, we do not know if she'll be safe, how the quest will turn out, or how long we'll be gone."

"Such a negative attitude," Travis responded. "Too much detail for Auntie Reatha. First, we just need to find our cousin again. Then we'll worry about the finer points. Anyone want to take 3 to 1 odds I can track and find her within a week?" His eyes twinkled with the thrill of beating the odds.

"I'll take 5 to 1 odds with the bet you won't be the one to find her at all!" Kristian says.

"Kristian!" Mariella reprimanded him.

He quirked a half-smile at her and clinked five silver coins back and forth in his hands.

"Stop, all of you!" Shaun says. "Look, this isn't getting us anywhere. Faith is out there, with plenty of dangers that could cross her path. You heard Aunt Reatha. Faith's never been away from the fortress. She's inexperienced as a traveler. Travis can put his tracking skills to work. The faster we find Faith, the quicker we'll be able to help protect her." He looked around the group and met each of his cousins' and siblings' eyes. "Then we'll tell Faith everything we know. It's important that we let her make her own choices once she has all the facts. Clear?"

Travis threw two more pieces of bacon to the dogs and stuffed two in his mouth. "Britt, you come with me to the Purehearts and see what we can find out from them. Shaun, talk to the stablemaster. Plan to meet back here by noon," he suggested as he grabbed his brown leather hat from the floor.

"Oh," Shaun added, "Mariella, can you ask if the cook would mind putting together some travel food for us? When you and Kris finish packing up and asking the household staff about Faith, would you also thank the kitchen for an excellent breakfast?" Mariella smiled at Shaun, pleased with his politeness.

They all filed out of the hall with their assignments. Brittany punched Travis in the arm as he reacted. "What? I don't know why the dogs are following me!"

When silence filled the room again, Dedo stood and stretched from his position on the rock fireplace, then disappeared.

MARIELLA AND KRISTIAN first went back up to the room they had shared with the old nurse. They tidied up, made the beds, and changed into their travel clothes. Mariella stuffed the last of her things into her saddlebags and took a sweeping look around the room. They turned to leave just as the door opened, finding themselves face to face with Lady Reatha and Nursie.

"Oh, perfect timing." Mariella exclaimed, "We were just coming down to find you."

Nursie scanned the room, noted the packed bags, crossed her arms and said, "Were you now? It looks as though you're making ready to leave us." Her stern gaze made Kris back up two steps.

Reatha touched Evy's shoulder, offering a kind smile to Kris. "Don't worry; her bark is worse than her bite. She's just concerned about Faith. We all are." Her eyes twinkled with a flash of bright blue.

"You're both Fae!" Kris exclaimed.

"Kris!" Mariella chided. "Don't be rude."

"But Mariella, they are. I can see it. Can't you?"

Evy tsked several times. Mariella gave a short curtsy, saying, "I am so sorry. He doesn't mean to be rude; he…"

"Never mind, dear." Reatha took her hand and patted it. "Your brother speaks the truth, however blunt. There's no shame in it. We've had our reasons to keep our natures hidden here." Reatha smiled as Mariella looked between the two of them and took a step back herself.

"I can feel the Fae magic in both of you. It's strong," Kris whispered.

"Shhh," his sister instructed, taking his hand in hers.

"We mean you no harm," Reatha assured Mariella. "We need your help, don't we, Evy? Kristian, you may speak your mind with the two of us," Reatha encouraged him.

Faith's nurse made her way over to the rocking chair in the corner and settled in. "You remind me of her," Nursie said.

"Faith?" Mariella asked.

"No. Well, yes, Faith, but also her mother and, of course, your own mother, Mari," the nurse offered.

"How?" The question came out in a whisper.

"Oh, your facial features and honey-gold hair. Your command of speech. Your polite ways. Even your ability to do what needs to be done under difficult circumstances. A lovely combination for strong women," Evy finished. Reatha nodded in agreement.

Mariella reflected on the statement, felt homesick, missing her mother.

Kris spoke up. "If you are both Fae, why didn't you prepare Faith for what was going to happen to her, considering her heritage and all?" The two women stared at him. Neither responded to his question. Marianna gave him a stern look.

Kris cleared his throat. "We really were coming down to see you. Do you mind if we ask if you have any idea where Faith might have gone? Somewhere nearby? You know, a special place she keeps to herself? Or do you think it is likely she's gone off, afraid of everything that happened between the last sunset and sunrise?" he asked.

"I think you already know the answer, Master Kristian. Am I right?" the old nurse leaned forward, stopping her rocking chair to hold his eyes tight in her gaze.

"I think we both do," Kris challenged.

"Look," Mariella started...

"The boy is a Fae seer, Reatha, like your sister, Mari," Nursie stated it as a fact, unable to be refuted. "That's how they all found their way here. How they located Faith. It wasn't the oldest boy at all, the tracker. It was this young man. That's the truth, isn't it, Kristian?" Nurse pressed.

Kristian felt the power behind the old nurse's words. A headache started at the base of his skull, accompanied by slashes of bright light at the fringes of his peripheral vision. His heart began beating at a frenzied pace. His knees felt weak. Mariella saw him sway, reaching out for him. "Don't touch him, dear," Reatha says. "He'll learn to recover quicker if you let him do it on his own."

Quiet surrounded them. Minutes ticked by. Kristian felt the cold sweat leave him. His heartbeat returned to normal. He nodded to his sister to let her know he was fine. They'd long had a silent communication system between them.

"How did you know?" Mariella broke the silence.

"Mari and Aleta, Faith's mother, are my sisters," Reatha tells them. "We all have some ability with sight, but Mari was the strongest. It made sense when we tried to figure out how you'd found us. Found Faith," she corrected. "All these years of trying so hard to keep her here in safety, in secret," Reatha said, not hiding the regret in her voice.

Kris stared straight at the old nurse and stated, "You're also a seer. A strong one."

She nodded in acquiescence to him. "I am many things."

"You know where she went," Kris blurted out. Evy nodded again, then sent him a visual with her mind. Entranced, he watched as a scene played out and then caught his breath.

"So," Reatha took control of the conversation, "now you know why we came to speak with the two of you. We need your help to keep her safe. I don't know what the intentions are of your other cousins, but I trust the two of you. The others are from Faith's father's side, and I can't speak for him and his family. Perhaps they will earn my trust, but until then I prefer caution. You must leave now. Just the two of you before the rest of your cousins return. We know they'll be busy long enough, following through with their plan to talk to different people around our fortress looking for leads to where Faith might have gone. Talking to *my people*. In *my fortress*. Though they are my niece and nephews, I still don't trust them, at least not yet. But Evy and I have seen into *your* hearts. You mean her no harm. There doesn't seem to be an ulterior motive on your part. I've had provisions packed for the two of you, your horses saddled." Reatha waved her hand at their travel clothes and saddlebags. "You're ready to be off. We know you intended to tell the others some kind of story. Maybe the truth, because of what young Master Kristian had already foreseen. All I'm asking is that you go on without the others and find her. Help her as best you can," Reatha pleaded.

Kristian turned and glanced up at the rock chimney in Nursie's room, eyes finding Dedo. "We will. We promise to send word to you through the rock people when we can," he declared directly to Dedo. The serious gargoyle gave a curt nod of acknowledgement.

"Kristian, where are we going?" Mariella asked, her heart strong, ready to do whatever needed to be done.

Lady Reatha, Evy, and Kristian all answered her question in unison. "To the Dream Weaver."

Mariella protested, "I can tell you right now, our cousins will not be happy about this turn of events, especially if we go off without waiting for them."

"Leave your worries about your cousins' reactions to us, Lady Mariella," Nursie ordered, once more contentedly rocking in her chair. "We will cover for you. Hurry now. The noon tide is coming fast. Go west from the fortress, or you'll run right into your cousins returning from their inquiries at Farmer Johnson's. Ride easy. There will be time. You will meet your cousins again in short order. When you do, all will be well between you." Evy stared forward, seeing only things she could see. The two siblings left the old woman rocking in the room, following their Aunt Reatha down the staircase.

BRITTANY BANTERED BACK and forth with her brother as they rode their horses back toward Robert's fortress. Travis sat on his horse, hat low on his forehead, eyes closed, body moving in time on the saddle with the horse's movements.

"Shouldn't you be looking for their trail or something?" Britt asked her brother.

"Not now, Britt," he replied. "I'm thinking."

"Napping is more like it," his sister grumbled under her breath. A smile spread across his face, so she stopped sniping at him.

"I still say it's strange. According to Valerie's parents, Faith's friend, as well as all three of Val's sisters, left on some last-minute trip this morning. To visit some distant relatives." She deadpanned. "You'd think Val, as Faith's best friend, would stick with her right now, wouldn't you?" Britt sulked. "I just find it suspicious, not to mention too convenient."

Travis sat up straight, stretched, and patted his horse's neck. "Well, you're not happy because we didn't get any new leads on where our cuz disappeared to. We're almost back at the fortress. Let's see what the others found out. We'll be on our way this afternoon. The bonus is, I bet the kitchen will have another excellent meal ready for us." He rubbed his stomach in anticipation.

Brittany rolled her eyes at him. As the two of them turned down the road leading back to Robert and Reatha's home, without warning, Travis snapped his fingers. "I knew there was something important I almost forgot!" Brittany perked up. Travis declared, "I've got to refill my flask before we go!" Brittany threw a disgusted look his way and punched him in the arm.

SHAUN WALKED THROUGH the stables, stopping where their own horses occupied stalls. He pulled an apple from his pocket. The barn was quiet, clean, well-ordered, and cool. He walked the two sides of the shelter, stalls running down the middle and on both ends, but didn't find Master Garth. A young boy, about ten, came running in from the north door. Shaun grabbed him by the collar. "Hey there," Shaun says in a friendly manner. "What's your hurry?"

The boy wriggled; his feet were still moving on the ground. "I've got to get a bucket. Please put me down! The stable master is waiting for me!" he wailed.

"Sure. Lead on. I'm looking for the master myself," Shaun told the boy as he released him. The young lad moved through the barn. He grabbed a bucket, a lead rope, and stuffed two apples in his pockets from a tub on top of a barrel, turned and ran back the way he came. Shaun followed at a slower pace.

A quarter mile down the lane, they came to a large, enclosed ring where the stable master was working a horse on a lead around the corral.

Shaun watched with interest for the next ten minutes. The master staked the horse on a lead rope to keep it in place. He worked his way in a circle around the standing animal, dribbling small stones down its nose, then its hindquarters. Throughout the exercise, he kept the horse holding a formal stance, teaching it to ignore distractions. The master wove back and forth, hands shifting up and down. The stallion held, paying him no mind. Then, the trainer unhooked the lead and worked the animal again, round and round the ring. Garth signaled the boy, who came running with a bucket of water, setting it down to let the horse drink its fill. The boy pointed over at Shaun. Garth shaded his eyes from the sun, looking toward the visitor. He gave instructions to the boy Shaun couldn't hear, then the horse trainer headed over to talk to the young man. Watching as the lad pulled an apple from his pocket and gave it to the waiting horse brought a smile to his face.

"Afternoon," Garth greeted him. "The boy said you were looking for me?"

"I am. My name's Shaun, sir," Shaun replied. "Word is, Lady Faith left the fortress last night, and we thought your son Garrett may have gone with her or would have some idea of where she would go? We wanted to check with you to see if you could tell us where we might find Garrett. Or confirm whether he accompanied the lass and, if so, where they might have gone? Is there any chance Garrett spoke with you or his mam about it?"

Master Garth was looking toward the stable boy and the horse. He shouted out, "Boy! No more apples. The horse must work for them! Keep him in full formal stance until I say otherwise, hear me?" The boy nodded and turned back to mind his charge.

"Now then," Master Garth said, turning back to Shaun, "sorry for the outburst, but you can't spoil a horse before it's trained, or it'll never come right. Say, where are you from?" he asked.

Shaun described his home in the mid-lands. Garth asked about their horses. He knew they had stabled their mounts in his barn, pointed out what fine steeds they had. Inquired where they'd gotten such stock and told them how much he admired fine horseflesh. The discussion turned to horse breeding, then to the best equestrian training techniques, as well as the choice of diet for keeping a horse fit. Of a sudden, the horse the boy had been working in the ring rounded on the lad, rearing up. Garth threw up his hands, shouted over his shoulder as he rushed toward the boy and horse, "Sorry, son, got to get back to work. Nice visiting with you." When Garth reached the horse, his voice was all soothing and calm. The man talked his way through the process of gathering up the lead rope the boy had dropped, and began working the spook out of the animal on the lunge line.

Shaun walked back toward the barn, stating the obvious to himself. "He didn't answer my questions or give me any information at all, and I didn't notice until now. That man is a master at manipulating a conversation."

Shaun stopped in his tracks. "Likely, if I went back to ask again, I am pretty sure the conversation would flow, but I'd still come away knowing just as much as I do now." The sun blazed overhead. He decided it would be best to get himself back to the manor and see if any of the others had better luck.

He found his brother and sister waiting for him in the hall. There was another fresh spread laid out on the sideboard for the noon meal.

Both of Robert's hounds stuck close to Travis as he filled his plate. The cook had put out serving dishes with cooked sausages, roasted potatoes, and sweet squash. Travis tossed a sausage to each of the dogs before he sat down to eat. Brittany threw him a dirty look.

They shared their collective tale. Brittany hissed in frustration. "What a troublesome cousin Faith has turned out to be. We're no closer to a lead in finding out where she may have gone. I'm no closer to taking the queenship!"

An elbow poked into Brittany's ribs. She turned an angry glare on Shaun. "Quiet," he whispered, pointing to the other side of the room.

Shaun noticed the old nurse had entered through the far door of the hall and settled herself into one of the rocking chairs by the hearth, mending piled up in her lap. "Good afternoon, Evy," Shaun broached her. "Have you seen our youngest cousins this morning? Kristian and Mariella were supposed to look for you, Lady Reatha and Sir Robert, hoping one of you could give us guidance in finding Faith."

Evy's hands came idle. She blinked up at Shaun, says, "Oh, of course dear. Why, the lovely young lady and her brother were packing up their travel bags after tidying the room they shared with me. Such well-mannered guests. I told them Robert had ridden south at dawn on an errand to the docks in town to pick up a shipment he was expecting before you all arrived. I mentioned he should be back tomorrow, but they said they couldn't wait so long to speak with Robert. So, they set off on horseback to see if they could catch him up." The rocking resumed, as did her needle.

Brittany heard the exchange and came over to Shaun's side. "Evy, isn't it? Are you telling us Mariella and Kris have left? Took their things? Without a word to any of us?" she exclaimed, her voice rising with each question.

Just then, Lady Reatha returned. "Miss Brittany, there's nothing to get upset about. Half the fortress is out looking for my Faith. I'm sure she is just maintaining her privacy somewhere until she comes to terms with her new circumstances. You are all welcome to stay here for as long as you like. I'm sure she'll come to her senses soon and return," Reatha told them, wringing her hands together. "Oh, I almost forgot in my distress." Reatha dabbed at her eyes with a lace-edged handkerchief, reached into her pocket to pull out a folded paper. She proffered it to Brittany, saying, "Mariella asked me to give you this note before the two of them rode after Robert."

Brittany took the note with grace, nodded to the Lady, asking, "How long ago did they leave, do you think?"

Lady Reatha looked to the Evy. "My thoughts are all jumbled up with all the activity in the last twenty-four hours, but would you agree, Evy, maybe two bells past seeing them on their way?" The old nurse nodded in affirmation as she rocked.

"Auntie Reatha," Travis asked, "does Robert have any maps we could look at?"

"Of course, Travis. I'll show you as soon as you've finished your meal. The cook will have the travel food you requested ready, but again, I invite you all to stay here until Faith returns, if you'd rather," she added.

Travis let out a hearty laugh and set his empty plate down. "My thanks for another fine meal, Auntie Reatha, but I think we've taken enough advantage of your generous hosting. I hope we haven't overstayed our welcome? We're all glad we had the chance to meet you and Uncle Robert! If we could just look at Robert's maps, we'll be on our way."

Travis held out his arm toward the archway, asking Lady Reatha to lead him to Robert's library. Calling over his shoulder, he asked Britt to get their bags as he followed his aunt. He asked his brother to request a stable boy to bring up their horses. After studying the maps available in Robert's library, Travis took the liberty of filling his flask from the crystal brandy decanter on their uncle's desk.

Reaching the foyer, Andrew came around the corner, Estelle right behind him, their arms loaded with two large baskets of food. "Perfect timing, Estelle," Lady Reatha thanked them. "Our guests are in a hurry to be off. Andrew, can you help them gather their things and get their saddlebags loaded?"

"Of course, mistress," Andrew bowed, off to meet her request.

Brittany followed Andrew out into the courtyard and set to checking the bags when the horses came up from the stables, saddled.

They thanked their Aunt Reatha for the hospitality and asked her to convey their gratitude to their uncle as well. It was late afternoon, hours later than they had intended to be on the road. Ready to leave, they had no more knowledge of where their cousin might have gone than when they started.

Once they passed through the gate, they stopped in the middle of the road to confer. Lady Reatha, the old nurse, Andrew, and Estella all waved farewell to them from the manor doorway.

"I got a good look at the map, but no bright ideas about which way to go. Does anyone have input?" Travis queried.

Pulling on her leather riding gloves, Shaun said, "Based on Mariella's note, it was as helpful as the rest of our information gathering. Short, sweet, with a statement, the two of them were following Robert on his way to the bay docks, hurrying to catch up to him. They signed off, promising they would find us later, and added a comforting line telling us we were not to worry about them."

"Ha!" Brittany exclaimed, startling her brothers. "Odd and odder. I say we go south to town. Agreed?"

They turned as one, taking the fork in the road south.

Lady Reatha and the old nurse watched until the dust had settled, then closed the door. "Summon Dedo, Evy," Reatha commanded the nurse. "We need to talk. I'll meet the two of you in Faith's chambers." Reatha turned to climb the grand winding staircase, her thoughts spinning in a dozen different directions.

THE NOON SUN WAS BLAZING as Garrett led the saddled horses down to the creek for a drink before the girls mounted up. They'd gathered the last of their things from camp. Delainey had a large pine bough and was sweeping it across the ground anywhere they had slept or walked. The six of them had eaten a quick meal of apples and stale bread. Faith watched Delainey with interest. "Whatever are you doing, Lainey?"

Surprised at the question, Delainey answered, "Just leaving things the way we found them. I'm making sure there are no traces of our passing for others to find. Just in case anyone is looking," she smiled at Faith. "I guess you have had little experience at running from people you don't want to find you?"

Faith blushed. Delainey patted Faith's shoulder as she passed by, careful to lay the pine-needled branch back under the tree where she'd found it.

They mounted the horses with the same riding partners as the previous night—Aliah with Garrett, Carlisse with Val, and Delainey with Faith.

"Garrett," Aliah said, "let's go down by the creek."

"No need, Aliah," he bantered back. "I already watered the horses and topped off our water bags."

"Humor me," she whispered in his ear. So, he pressed his knees against the horse's shoulders, and the animal moved down the bank. "Into the water, please," Aliah requested. "Turn left, walk down the middle of the stream."

Garrett twisted around to look at her face. He didn't want to embarrass her in front of her sisters. "Ung, ah…"

"Out with it!" Aliah demanded, exasperated by his tied tongue. He lowered his voice so that only she could hear him. "But Aliah, left will take us south, and you said we were to go north last night."

Her gentle laughter was like tinkling bells. "Of course, silly," she agreed. "We'll only travel south, walking in the stream for a mile or so, then turn north to go upland on the other side."

Garrett stared at her. Aliah leaned forward and whispered, "It might throw anyone tracking us off our trail. At least for a while," she suggested.

"Oh, of course," he stammered.

"What's the hold-up?" Val shouted as the others had ridden up, all standing at a stop, bunched together behind Garrett and Aliah's horse.

"Nothing," Aliah waved her off. Garrett moved his horse forward midstream, turning left. "Garrett just had a great idea to put anyone off our track by heading south a while through the water before we turn north toward our destination."

The small group of travelers kept their voices low. Their conversations were quiet with their riding partners as the horses splashed down the center thread of the waterway. When they climbed up the opposite side of the river, there was a road. Without discussion, they took the fork north.

CHAPTER 11: An Unexpected Bonus

Narrol led the way up the ramp, his cane clicking on the smooth cavern stone in sync with his hurried steps. Built like an ox, even Rolland struggled the last fifty yards uphill, hauling a load behind him like a beast of burden. Two thick leather straps crisscrossed his chest, running back across his broad shoulders, connecting to a large wheeled cart. Two hours earlier, he and Narrol had loaded the haul above the sideboards, covered the contents with dirty canvas to keep things from falling out.

Sweat dripped down his nephew's face, neck, shoulders, and chest. The leather straps rubbed his skin raw. Narrol assaulted him with a stream of vulgar comments. His uncle dabbed his own forehead with a clean, soft cloth as though he were doing the sweaty work.

"Hurry, you oaf, you're taking too long."

"What a worthless piece of shit you are!"

"Move it, you lazy dog. I'm going to be late for my meeting with the Queen and the Prince."

"I could pull the cart twice as fast as you, you clumsy oaf."

"Careful! You clod! You're going to tip the cart over!"

"I don't know why I'm saddled with such a worthless sod like you."

His uncle's diatribe went on and on. Rolland had long ago learned to shut out Narrol's voice. He used his imagination to block out the constant rant. Focused his thoughts on shaping a special long knife design as he put one foot in front of the other, pushing his muscles to their limit to reach their destination.

Narrol stopped his diarrhea of commentary about ten yards from the Queen's dais at the top of the steep cavern. No point in letting the Queen and Prince Rupert know what a moron his sister had left him with.

As they reached the edge of the platform, Narrol went down on one knee. He pulled his cane around, smacking the back of Rolland's calves. "Kneel before your queen, you idiot!" Narrol hissed in outrage. The pain took Rolland by surprise after the strenuous climb. He fell to his knees on the hard rock floor, the cart rocking against the force of his weight and the sudden change in his stance.

Rupert kept his face stony, showing no expression. The Queen smiled behind her red silk fan. "Come now, Narrol. Was that necessary?" Morveena secretly hoped to see the cane used again in her presence.

Rolland looked up, settling an impassive gaze on his queen. She leveled her gaze at him, her fan close, covering her face except for the eyes. *My, my,* thought Morveena, *what a strapping specimen of a young male goblin.* She licked her lips behind the fan.

Rupert put his hand on her shoulder, cleared his throat with a growl. She slanted her eyes at Rupert and gave him a knowing smile. Only he could see behind her red fan.

"Ah hem," Narrol rose, using his cane as a tool. The Queen's red fan snapped shut. She struck her palm with it. "Stay where you are, Narrol. I do so *love* to see men on their knees before me." She batted her eyelashes; her beady black eyes fastened on him. Narrol flushed, anger coursing through his blood, but he kept his face plain, showing her nothing of the rage roiling inside. Rolland's heart thudded in his chest, knowing he would be the one to pay the price later for the Queen embarrassing his uncle.

Prince Rupert stepped forward, took Narrol's hands, and lifted him to his feet. "Our queen has a unique sense of humor." Rupert glanced in disgust at Rolland, snapped his fingers, "Up, boy. Time to show the wares you've lugged all the way up here." Rolland set the handbrake on the cart and undid the buckled straps of the harness he wore.

Narrol's voice took on the character of a proud peacock as he spoke. Snapping his fingers, imitating Rupert, drawing his nephew's name out condescendingly, "Hurry, Roooll-land, get the canvas off so I can show off my weapons to the queen and prince," he commanded.

Rolland's large, meaty hands clenched when Narrol said 'my weapons', but he held his silence, doing as he was told.

A fire blazed in the fireplace, smoke curling up the natural rock chimney behind the Queen's chair. Throwing the canvas off revealed the wagon's cache—hundreds of shining steel weapons stacked in the cart, catching the light, the metal sending shimmers across the cavern ceiling and walls.

Queen Morveena squealed with delight. Narrol bowed from the waist, saying, "Behold my Queen, look at what I've made for you. There are many more weapons here than necessary to make up this year's five Queen's Ransoms. I thought perhaps you might like to purchase extras for the Clan's Guard?" Narrol beamed with pride at the queen and prince.

Rupert wore his usual scowl.

The Queen uncrossed her soft, leather-booted feet. She stood with her hands on her hips against her tight-fitting red dress, glaring at Narrol. "You've made?" Morveena screeched. "You've made?" she repeated, taking three steps to the edge of the dais, her face turning dark red, the firelight enhancing her angry features. Queen Morveena squatted down and stared into Narrol's eyes. Her voice gravelly, spittle spraying from her mouth as she growled, "You've made nothing, *Master Narrol*. But it appears you seek to ride on the shoulders of Rolland's talent. You do not amuse me, lickspittle," she almost whispered the last as her words came out in a hiss.

"My Queen...my Queen," Rupert said. "Come now, let Narrol's nephew show us what he has brought." He touched her shoulder, pulling her back. Morveena sat back again on her cavern throne chair, chest heaving. Then she crossed her leather boots at the ankles, snapping open her red silk fan, fluttering it in front of her face. She nodded to Rolland, giving him permission to display the weapons.

Rolland didn't nod or bow, but in his own straightforward way, started by laying all the short-bladed knives across the dais in a row. Rolland had blackened some weapons. They shimmered with a blue glaze. Others were shining steel. The handles varied, using clever, decorative designs, or were plain with wrapped leather grips. Rolland displayed half a dozen blades of various lengths and widths, as well as sheaths for the weapons. Then, he set out maces, hatchets, quarterstaffs, bows, arrows, crossbows, slingshots, making up row upon row of weapons exhibited for their perusal.

Maintaining his silence, the young smith continued to display the fine leather-worked sheaths, longbows, and short bows. All the weapons are unique in design, weight, shape, and size. Last, he presented them with saddles; the leatherwork decorated in hand-stamped designs fit for a king. When all the arms lay on the dais before the Queen, the cart empty,

Rolland stepped back, stood with his feet apart, hands behind his back, eyes downcast. Morveena recognized that stance. It made her blood boil.

Narrol took this opportunity to spread his arms wide, palms up and open, as if he had created a miracle for the goblin queen and the prince, but dared not say a word.

The red fan closed with a snap. She leaned forward in her chair, staring into Narrol's eyes but speaking to Rolland. "I hope your uncle recognizes the impressive talent you have, Rolland. This is fine work. Clearly, you are a master of your art. As a reward, I want you to keep one of your own blades for yourself and wear it with pride. Rupert will pay for all these fine weapons you've made. The Queen's Ransoms, as well as all the extras."

Narrol's smile widened.

"Rupert," she called over her shoulder, still staring Narrol down, "pay *Rolland* and add a generous amount for the extra weapons."

"Ah, my Queen," Narrol ventured, clearing his throat, "if you don't mind, I handle the funds in our family."

The Queen grimaced. "Rupert, my instructions stand. *Pay Rolland* for the beautiful weapons he has created. Rolland, *you* may pay your uncle the traditional one quarter for marketing, but only if you feel he deserves the cut. Oh, and I would like you to consider coming on as part of the royal staff. Chief Weapons Maker, perhaps? You'd like that title, wouldn't you? Take a few weeks off. Think about it, Rolland. If you decide to accept the offer, the Court will take over the cost of your current workroom and provide you with private living quarters. In addition, the Crown will provide the materials you need, as well as a generous wage. You'll consider my offer, yes?" she demanded with a hiss, eyes never leaving Narrol's.

"Yes, yes, of course, my Queen," Narrol stammered, backing away.

"Rolland?" He nodded his acquiescence to her. She smiled in return.

"Rupert," she crooned in a comely voice.

"Yes, my Queen?" Rupert inquired.

"Have you heard the delicious rumors about Narrol? The ones that say he likes to beat the shit out of his talented nephew because he enjoys it. Likes how it makes him feel he's a powerful man," she sneered.

"Yes, my queen. I have heard Narrol goes all in for violence. Also, whispers say he uses different cruel methods and tools, looking for ways to cause the lad the most pain."

Rolland's face flushed with shame. He kept his eyes averted, staring at the ground.

Rupert snapped his fingers. "Oh, Morveena, I almost forgot. I have it from a reliable source. Narrol takes particular delight in belittling his victims. I know how you detest such behavior, yes?" Rupert turned, offering Narrol a crazed grin, eyes wide.

"Leave all your fine work here, Rolland. Rupert dear, be a darling and give Rolland his pay. If there is a discrepancy's just let us know. We can make up the difference in a day or two, yes?" she promised Rolland.

"Narrol, may I inspect your cane?" she asked. "It looks like a quality piece." Rolland's uncle handed his cane up to the Queen's waiting hand. She turned it around, scrutinizing the workmanship, then handed it to Rupert.

Rupert laid three heavy pouches of coins in the palm of Narrol's nephew, his uncle's eyes bulging at the insult.

The Queen spoke again to the smith. "We thank you for your fine work, Rolland. You're dismissed. You've earned some time to rest. Off with you now!" she shooed him away with her hands.

Narrol was sweating, straining to be sure he heard each word, his face red with rage as he witnessed his nephew pocket the payment. He was still analyzing what the Queen's words might mean for him when, of a sudden, she shouted, "CANE HIM, RUPERT!" her hideous, bright red lips forming a wicked grin.

Rolland, ten steps in retreat, stumbled away in fear down the cavern slope. He covered his ears as he heard the first "thwack" against Narrol's ribs. The screams ripping from his uncle's throat haunted his nephew's desperate flight down the cavern hallway.

REATHA HAD A ROARING fire going in Faith's chamber when Evy arrived. "The old codger is nowhere to be found," the nurse grumbled.

"He'll come, Evy. You put out a word for him?" Reatha asked.

"Course," the old nurse nodded, "but you know as well as I do, Dedo will come when *he* deems it time and not a minute before," she complained to Reatha.

Lenny and Lester winked at one another on the mantel, dripping wax onto the wood.

"Never mind, Evy. We can make our own plan," Reatha suggested. Pulling two rocking chairs over by the fire, she handed Evy her sewing basket. Then, settled her own basket in her lap. Reatha always said sewing helped her think and sort things out, 'one stitch at a time'.

"Where do you think Faith has gone off to?" Reatha asked as she rocked.

"Hard to say," Evy replied. She heaved a heavy sigh. "It's been a long time since I dealt with a young girl old enough to make her own rash decisions. There's a possibility some of her cousins may not have our girl's best interests at heart. Time will tell."

Reatha rose from her chair and walked around Faith's room, fingers placing light touches on some of the girl's keepsakes. She could see Faith's vanity top covered with a collection of small rocks, dried flowers, and hair ribbons. Things she'd long outgrown. Reatha peeked in the drawers and noticed Faith's drawing paper and pencils were gone. "I can't even tell if she took a dress or two," Reatha commented.

"I doubt dresses were at the top of her packing list when she rushed to get away, Madam," said a sarcastic, deep voice from the rocks in the fireplace.

Reatha started. Nursie didn't even look up, continuing on with her rocking and mending.

"Nice of you to join us," Evy said, acknowledging Dedo's presence.

"Ho hum," a deep baritone voice rumbled from one of the huge rocks in the center of the chimney. "I can tell you everything Lady Faith took with her, including her friends, Valerie Pureheart, and Garrett Gladheart." The large boulder yawned a great, wide yawn, and the rocks in the fireplace grated against one another.

"Traitor!" accused a small, deep-green rock.

"Hush, both of you!" Dedo commanded.

Lenny and Lester snickered, each with a hand in front of their mouths, dripping wax down their fronts, then turning forward. The duo became stoic again.

Reatha leaned forward with urgency, asking, "Dedo, give us details. Should we be doing anything? She's never even been off Robert's land, for goodness' sake! Everything seemed to happen of a sudden," Reatha complained.

"The time for planning is long past. It would have been better if you had prepared the girl for her heritage. Then she would have expected the changes that happened to her," he accused.

"Ha," Nursie bantered back at him. "You're a fine one to talk about planning and guidance. Got a natural knack for it, eh? You should have learned from your last charge you can't do should've, could've, would've!" Angrily, she poked her thumb with the needle she was using, a bright spot of red blooming on the shirt in her hand.

"Evy," Reatha said, "we won't get very far by pointing fingers. That goes for you too, Dedo. Now," she said, settling again in the rocker next to her old friend, "tell us what you know. And I mean everything! My sister, Aleta, had a hand in this, no doubt?"

Dedo raised his eyebrows in surprise. "Faith and entourage are on their way to find the Dream Weaver. Our princess convinced herself that looking for insight about what her next step should be was the best course of action."

"Told you," the nurse gloated.

"Oh, dear." Reatha moaned. "She's so young. Dealing with the Dream Weaver can be dangerous."

"The time had come. Time for her to find out the truth, the dangers, the past, and most of all, it is time she found out the prophecy," Dedo announced.

A single teardrop fell from Reatha's eye as she accepted the fact that she would no longer be a large part of her ward's life. The light of her life passing out of her care. And it all happened in the blink of her eye.

ROLLAND HURRIED, CHOOSING the left fork in the road. The significant weight he carried on his back was double-wrapped in heavy canvas to make sure there were no accidental injuries. The road was an overgrown two-track, little used. He marched toward his destination, weeds tugging at his boots, blackberry bushes scratching his arms.

Saffron had told him to meet her at the oxbow in the river where he liked to fish when he had the chance to take an afternoon to himself, when his uncle traveled. The quiet spot was about five miles from the clan's cavern. He calculated that he still had about a mile to go.

Sweat trickled down his face. Rolland shifted the load, bringing the ache in his shoulders to the forefront of his thoughts again. His uncle Narrol's screams plagued him. He spent all night worrying about what Narrol would do to him when he returned from the queen and prince. But his uncle hadn't come back. Paralyzed with fear far into the hours before dawn, he came up with an idea. Once the notion took shape, details consumed his thoughts. The sun rose, golden pink stretching across the horizon. He had sprung into action, worried, hoping he hadn't waited too long before Narrol could be upon him. He knew his uncle would blame him for Prince Rupert's beating and the Queen's words, as if Rolland had planted them in her mouth.

Collecting a rough canvas off a shelf where he'd stored it under an overhang, he'd wrapped the weapons in layers to keep them from clanging against one another. Rushing around the shop, the smith grabbed his heavy leather gloves, his large, and small smithing hammers, and his tongs. The last weapon he'd made still sat on the workbench. Rolland picked it up, along with the leather sheath he had tooled to fit it, strapped the sheath on his belt, and slid the knife home. After all, he reasoned, the Queen commanded him to take a knife for himself and told him he deserved it. His uncle had never allowed him to carry or own a weapon. It felt strange on his belt. But, good. Very good.

He grabbed the slim piece he had laid aside. A weapon designed for a special purpose. Rolland slipped it down inside a tight pocket in his left boot. He snatched an extra shirt from a peg and laid it across the canvas items to keep the contents from rattling. Pulling several thick leather thongs hanging from the nails along the workbench, his eye caught on the leather forge apron hanging by the door. He reasoned it would be useful in keeping the package from coming apart while he carried it. Securing the heavy leather over the canvas, binding it, he used the rest of the thongs he'd laid out to finish fastening the load.

From the two tool belts on the workbench, he removed the small leather stamping tools, putting them in a pouch. He wrapped the belts around each end of his parcel. Hoisting the entire pack onto his back, he slipped his arms through the straps. When the weight had settled against his body, he used another strap to connect the two shoulder straps across his chest. That would hold the load against his broad, beefy shoulders so he wouldn't have to use his hands to hold the straps. Last, Rolland took up the pouches filled with coins Rupert had paid him, stared at them, the clock ticking. In a rash decision, he pocketed all three. There would be no marketing percentage left for Narrol.

Quiet as a mouse, he left the shop. It surprised Rolland to find a small cloth bag outside the entrance containing a fresh loaf of bread, still warm, a block of cheese, and three apples. His eyes sprung a leak. He felt Zeeka's love touch his hardened heart.

Leaving by the back cavern entrance, thinking it was a miracle his good luck had held, allowing him to make his getaway before his uncle returned. He didn't see or pass another soul from the clan as he made his way out of the cavern and into the woods. A mile down the road, he relaxed. As his heavy boots crunched through the dense forest, he devoured an apple and let the memory of Saffron's singing carry him on his way.

ROBIN AND CAZ SAT ON the riverbank at the oxbow, leaning against a large boulder. The sun was shining. Insects buzzed around their heads. An occasional fish would jump out of the water to snatch at one. Saffron couldn't sit still. She wandered back and forth along the shore, poking at things with a quarterstaff. The thick rod, a weapon she knew how to wield, also doubled as her walking stick.

"Saff," Caz sighed, "you're wound up like a fiddle string on a Saturday night. Come sit. You'll be wishing for rest soon enough."

"I sat on pins and needles all night, Caz. The waiting is making me crackers," she huffed.

Robin jumped into the fray. "Fron, there's no sense wasting energy on your worries. Rolland will show up," he assured her.

Saffron stamped her foot in frustration. "Of course, Rolland will show up. That isn't even a question for me, Robin. Zeeka said not to worry. She assured me she could handle the kitchen for a few days. But I am worried because Hazzel is so lazy. I don't want to add to Zeeka's workload. She works too hard already," she lamented. "Bedwer was ever so understanding when I asked for time off. The other barmaids have never been on their own in the tavern before. I just hope they can keep up with the customers without my help," she fretted. "Or worse yet, everything goes so smoothly while I'm gone, they'll discover they don't need me at all! I feel all twisted inside."

Caz and Robin looked at one another and rolled their eyes.

"There's not a person in the clan who would ever think they didn't need you, Saffron," Rolland's deep voice rumbled as he walked up to the group sitting by the river's edge. She turned to gift him her best smile.

Shy, Rolland said, "Hello Saffron."

"Hello Rolland," Saffron answered.

Rolland saw Caz and Robin getting to their feet and nodded to them. "Caz. Robin."

"Rolland," Robin acknowledged, "glad you could make it. All went well with your uncle in getting some time off, yeah?" he asked.

"As well as it could," Rolland responded. "I guess you could say timing worked out. I've been putting in a lot of extra hours these past months. We delivered all five of the Queen's Ransom weapon caches to your mother and brother yesterday, plus some extra pieces for the guards. It will be fine with me if I don't work for a while," Rolland finished in a near whisper.

"You alright, lad?" Caz asked with concern. "Hey, Rolland, let me help you take your load off." Caz reached under the wrapped satchel to help lift it off Rolland's shoulders, saying, "Whoa, this is quite a burden, laddie! Did you bring your anvil with you?" he joked.

"Need help?" Robin offered.

Saffron came up behind Rolland and rubbed his shoulders. "What's what?" she whispered to him.

Much as he didn't want her to stop rubbing his sore muscles, he turned and clasped one of her hands, feeling as if she was keeping him grounded. "I need to tell you all some things before we go. It's only fair, you know. I don't want to bring trouble to anyone else, but I've decided, and there's no going back. Nothing's going to make me change my mind." Rolland swallowed. His mouth was dry as dust. He'd never said so many words to anyone at one time.

"Rolland," Robin ventured, "tell us what you need to do. We'll help."

"I don't need your help," Rolland insisted.

"Trust? Friendship? People you can count on?" Saffron asked. "We can share all those things with you, Rolland. The way it works, though, is that you have to share them back. Those are the best things in life," she finished, twirling her boot toe in circles in the dirt, hands clasped behind her back. She raised her large hazel eyes from the ground and held his gaze, a question in her eyes.

Robin and Caz stood nearby. One horse they had tethered in a grassy patch nickered, breaking the silence. Rolland cracked a half-smile.

"Caz," Rolland started, "I didn't bring my anvil." Robin raised his eyebrows, and Rolland continued, "But I brought a lot of my favorite smith and leather-working tools. See...the thing is, I...I'm going to help you on your quest just as Saffron asked, but I'm not coming back here after. I haven't thought through where I'm going, but I plan to start a new life somewhere and ply my trade." He looked them all square in the eye, worried, daring them to challenge his decision.

Robin stepped forward and clapped Rolland on the shoulder. "Again, we're glad you are here, lad. You can tell us more about what brought you to this decision when we're on the road. Maybe we can help by talking about destination ideas after we complete our task. Let's be off. We need to make the best use of the daylight. Looks a heavy load for the mount we brought for you. Can we re-pack it? Divide things up so we can share the load between the horses?" Robin suggested. "I brought a well-muscled horse for you, but not that big!" Robin laughed, and they all joined in, the tension broken.

"Glad you asked," Rolland shot back as he disassembled the belts and his leather shop apron. He untied the leather straps from around the canvas wrappings and rolled out the contents. The enormous hands took a piece of tarp and gathered his personal things. He placed his smith and leather-working tools, heavy forge gloves, and apron on it.

Caz let out a long, shrill whistle, expressing how impressed he was, looking at the contents of Rolland's parcel. Saffron held both her hands over her mouth in surprise. Robin dropped to his knees and drew his hand along the detailed handle of a sheathed sword. Rolland had decorated the leather scabbard with a pattern all around the edges. Robin looked closer and saw the stamped leather was a design of stylized letters repeated over and over. RWG.

"I made it special for you," Rolland told Robin, his heart hammering against his ribs.

Robin looked up at him, then back down, waving his hand across the cache of weapons, saying, "What's this all about, Rolland? Your work is exquisite," he said with wonder. Robin picked up one, then another, another and another, while shaking his head at seeing his initials on each of the weapons he examined. Caz dropped alongside him and began exploring the cache as well. Saffron studied the beautiful metalwork, handles, and leather sheaths. She was the first to register that there were two different leather-stamped designs, the second one using three different letters. CBT.

"Rolland?" The lilt of her voice formed a question mark. "These are Queen's Ransoms, aren't they? Two full sets?" she looked into his eyes.

"They are," he confirmed.

"You've personalized them?" She stated her questions matter-of-factly. Rolland nodded in affirmation.

Of a sudden, realization bloomed on both Robin's and Caz's faces!

"Rolland, I...I don't know what to say." Caz stuttered. "You've got a lot of confidence in both of us to have already put our initials on the weapons. We haven't even competed in the Summer Games to win them yet."

"They're beautiful, Rolland. Works of art." Robin complimented the smith as he pulled the sword from its scabbard and tested the weight and balance. "It's perfect," Robin told Rolland. "Not only have you marked each sheath with my and Caz's initials, but you've put them on every weapon handle," he noted with wonder. Then, as an idea struck him, Robin choked, "But, Rolland, you've done so much specialized work here." Robin locked eyes with the smith. "What if I'm not one of the Queen's Ransom winners? You said you delivered the five Queen's Ransoms to Morveena yesterday. We've got to get these back before they're missed," Robin sounded panicked. His brother, Rupert, could become violent over something like this. "The Summer Games begin next month. If Caz and I don't win, we won't deserve to get the Ransoms' and you'll have so much extra work to do, just to remove our initials from everything," he worried.

"No, I won't," Rolland told them firmly. "Remember what I told you? I'm not going back to the clan." He looked from one to the other. "I delivered five Queen Ransoms yesterday, all still in the hands of your brother Rupert." Rolland let them absorb the fact.

"But Rolland," Caz reasoned, "there are only five winners every year, so you've made two sets too many." He said, thinking of how much work this must have been.

"They're yours." Rolland declared. "I didn't get money from the Queen for these. No one but you three know about them. I was careful. My uncle never saw them," he finished.

"How will we get them presented after the Summer Games?" Caz asked, "if you've brought them to us already?"

"You two can't take part in the games," Rolland declared. "There is no doubt both of you would win if you were to compete, so you would have earned the prizes. Everyone knows it. I simply made them for you as a gift. You shouldn't have to be denied what would have been yours just because your brother means you harm." His face sheepish, he looked to the ground.

Saffron enjoyed the moment. There were so few when those two lads found themselves speechless!

"Wait a minute, mate," Robin paused. "Did you just say we can't be in the games?" His voice rose as he posed the question. "Please explain what you mean."

Having lost some of his confidence, he looked to the ground and began dragging his toe through the dirt in counterclockwise circles.

"Well?" Caz coaxed. "Come on, manno. You know I've been working towards winning the Summer Games for years, Rolland. What's what?"

"Push off, Caz," Saffron said in Rolland's defense. "He's going to tell you. Aren't you Rolland?" Saffron took his hand in hers to encourage him to continue.

Robin recognized Rolland's distress, remembering he had brief contact with the clan on a day-to-day basis. He'd heard things about Narrol, Rolland's uncle. Unpleasant things he'd paid no attention to, never investigated. He hadn't been a very good friend. Both he and Caz had played a prank or two where Rolland had been the butt of their jokes back in their school days. They'd meant no harm, but maybe he hadn't taken their jests as a joke.

Robin spoke up. "Rolland will tell us when he's ready, Caz. In the meantime, we've been here for longer than we should and need to get some way up the road to the north before nightfall, yeah? Let's redistribute the load, pack up, and be off." He smiled at Rolland, offering reassurance.

"Rolland," Robin said sincerely, "this is the best gift I've ever received in my whole life. You're a master of your craft. Ah..." Robin looked down at the sword and asked, "Is it alright if we wear some of our new weapons and pack the rest?" His eyes sparkled in question.

"It would honor me if you would," Rolland beamed.

Saffron squeezed Rolland's hand. Engrossed in sorting their caches, the boys decided which weapons they would carry on their persons. Throughout the process, they kept exclaiming about the fine workmanship. Praising Rolland for his designs, the perfect weights, and balance of the weaponry.

Rolland attached his old slingshot to his belt with a leather thong, along with a pouch of stones. Saffron dropped his hand and started towards her horse. Rolland followed, reaching for her hand again. He felt the blood rush up his neck to his cheeks. She tensed with a question in her eyes. "Saffron," Rolland whispered, looking over his shoulder to be sure Robin and Caz weren't paying attention, "I...I have something I made special for you. I mean, just in case you ever need it. I..." he stammered.

Saffron grinned. "Something for me? What is it, Rolland?"

Rolland bent at the waist and pulled the special weapon he had hidden in his boot back at the shop. "You're a brave girl, Saffron, but there are a lot of bad people out in the world. You never know when you'll need some teeth." He proffered an elegant stiletto, the hilt inlaid with silver and black obsidian, polished to a sheen. "Look," he showed her, "it fits in the lining of your boot. Hidden until needed."

"You made this for me, Rolland?" she breathed.

"I did. Just for you, Saffron."

She beamed a smile at him that acted as a balm to his soul. They went back to where Robin and Caz were re-wrapping the rest of the weapons. Double-checking the load on each of the horses, making sure the weight was equal on both sides. Roland repackaged his tools. The big man used his smith's apron again to enclose the canvassed load. His extra shirt, his meal knife, cup, and bowl, he placed in the saddlebags for easy access.

The party of four mounted. Caz took off, with Robin racing after him. Rolland waited for Saffron to move in front of him so he could take up the rear to protect her.

BEGINNING ITS WESTERN traverse, the pending sunset produced a heavy sigh from Brittany. They'd ridden down to the harbor in search of Mariella and Kristian, only to find the two had left hours ago. Robert, still busy loading his wagons with goods that had arrived by ship, told them he had no additional news about Faith. As far as he knew, she was still up in her chambers. Faith's cousins dismounted. Brittany led the horses over to a water trough. The boys made quick work of getting the rest of Robert's goods loaded. He thanked them, pointing in the direction he'd noticed their younger cousins had ridden when they'd left the docks. Robert asked if they planned on coming back to his fortress, suggesting they might want to seek advice from his wife about Faith. Shaun explained they'd just left Reatha to come and find him. Travis told Robert that he was not coming back until they found Faith.

The group thanked Robert again for his hospitality. He assured them they would always be welcome to visit. Horses watered, the three of them climbed into their saddles and turned west. "Hold up!" Robert shouted. Three heads turned at once. "Those look like my two dogs at your heels, son," he queried Travis.

Travis nodded and laughed. "They are. I can't get them to stop following me, sir," he complained.

"Well, if they don't leave off when you pass the manor again on your way west, you'll have to promise me you'll take good care of them. Special breed," Robert told him.

"Oh yes, sir," Travis tipped his hat. "I'll leave them at the gate if I can. If that doesn't work out, I promise I'll take care of them like my own. We'll send word if we find Faith's whereabouts."

He led the group away from the dock, with the two dogs following. When they reached the end of the main street in the small town, they took the left fork in the road. Travis whistled at the dogs and tossed out two pieces of bacon. The two canines snapped the treats clean out of the air, tails wagging, running alongside his horse.

"STOP."

Mariella almost didn't hear the command, as Kris had whispered it. Her horse had drifted ahead. She turned back with a curious look at her brother. Kris sat in his saddle, the horse under him shifting its weight from side to side. His eyes had a glazed look, just staring into space, not moving or speaking.

Two crows swooped along the road, calling out, "Caw, caw." Kris shook his head to clear away cobwebs.

"What is it?" Mariella asked.

"We have to hurry," the words rushed out of him. "It won't be long before Faith arrives at the Dream Weaver's. I...I...there's something I can't see, but I have a bad feeling. We have to go faster," he repeated, moving his horse forward on the road at a trot, then a canter. Mariella raced behind, the afternoon shadows lengthening in the waning light. They took the fork in the road to the north, the wind chafing their cheeks.

CHAPTER 12: The Edgewood

Dusky light crept in along the treeline, driving out the daylight as though a door had been closed. Three horses stood in a row at the edge of a meadow. Six somber faces sat staring at the edge of a dark forest that appeared to have no discernible end as far as the eye could see. The dense trees made the sudden dusk seem like midday.

"I don't like the looks of it," Val said to herself. Her horse nickered in agreement.

"This forest is known as the Edgewood. The Dream Weaver lives here," said Aliah, "in the heart of the great wood. It's a long way in." She shivered.

"A long way in and a long way out," Carlisse added, goosebumps breaking out across her arms. "Sometimes the forest plays tricks on you." No one could think of a response to that statement.

"Maybe we should make camp in the meadow for the night and start tomorrow at daylight?" Garrett suggested.

"It doesn't look like daylight will make much of a difference inside those woods," Val commented, peering into the trees. "What do you say, Faith? It's your decision." The group all turned to look at Faith.

It was odd, Faith thought. There were no sounds at all, except those being made by their small entourage. Just as the sun had set, dusky light surrounded them. That's when she noticed that no birds, no small creatures moved through the meadow. The trees were like giant sentinels. There wasn't even a breeze to stir the leaves. Even the insects seemed to have disappeared.

"I agree. We should camp here and start fresh with full daylight," Faith told her friends. "Let's make a hot meal. We've been pushing the horses hard. They could use a night's rest. Besides," Faith said, "I'm the one who's seeking the Weaver. The rest of you can just wait here. We don't all of us need to go into the forest. I can just venture in first thing in the morning, find her, and be back here before nightfall." She swallowed as she suggested going in alone.

"No," Val countered. "Absolutely not. We started this together. We'll go all the way together. Not negotiable." She rounded on Faith and looked her in the eye.

"Okay, okay. Don't get all bent out of shape about it." Faith held her hands up to ward off any argument with Val. But relief washed over her.

"Uh...er..." Garrett struggled as he became tongue-tied.

"Garrett?" Aliah asked. "Something to say? Out with it!" she stomped her foot with impatience.

"I have a question," he started, but then nothing more came out of his mouth as he felt ten female eyes turn in his direction, causing his mouth and throat to go dry.

"Cat got your tongue?" Lainey teased him.

"Lainey!" Aliah chastised. "You, of all people, should be ashamed to tease someone else about being nervous about speaking up!"

Delainey's face crumbled. She looked at the ground. "You're right, Aliah. It took me years to find my voice." She went to Garrett, took his hand in hers, stood on her tiptoes and whispered in his ear, "Sorry, Garrett. I'll stay right here while you ask your question and support you." Garrett offered a shy smile to Delainey. Aliah nodded in approval. Carlisse came and took Garrett's other hand, lending him her support as well. Val tapped her foot in irritation at her sister's antics. Faith tried to hide her smile. She had been a victim of the Pureheart sisters and their tender manipulations before. Garrett was in over his head here.

"Well, okay," he started. "Thank you for your support," he told them.

"What did you want to ask, Garrett?" Carlisse urged.

"I've been thinking all day while we've been riding," Garrett said. Val rolled her eyes. "When we began our travels together," he licked his lips and cleared his throat. Delainey squeezed his hand for encouragement. "You three girls said we should head north to find the Dream Weaver. You seemed to know the way to get here. Well, here we are, almost at our destination." They all nodded in agreement. "What I want to know is why the three of you came here in the first place? What did the Dream Weaver tell you? Why do you keep hinting about how scary and dangerous this is going to be?"

Delainey and Carlisse dropped Garrett's hands like hot potatoes. Aliah found her mouth hanging open in surprise and shut it. She rearranged her shawl. Delainey and Carlisse came to stand next to her.

"None," Delainey said, her arms crossed. "Of. Your." Carlisse continued. "Damn. Business." Aliah finished for them. They turned as one and stalked off to the forest edge and began gathering wood to start a fire. Val shook her head and followed her sisters to help.

Faith took a cook-pot from her saddlebag and began filling it with water from one of the water bladders to make tea once they had the fire going. She sympathized with him. "I wondered the same thing," she confided to him. "Figured they would have told us if they wanted us to know when they first confessed to already having come here."

"Faith, I'm confused," Garrett admitted. "They encourage me to speak up, ask questions, and share my thoughts and ideas. But when I do, they ignore me or look at me like I've got two heads or like I suggested some foolish idea. Then they tell me to mind my own business. I just don't get it!" he said, completely at a loss.

"It means they like you!" Faith told him, and he looked at her as if she had two heads.

Garrett decided the less he said now, the better. He pulled the bow and quiver of arrows from his saddle. Walking back out toward the meadow in the opposite direction of the Pureheart sisters, he announced to Faith, "I'll go see if I can find some meat for the pot."

When Garrett returned to camp, the campfire was going. He found the horses cared for, hobbled nearby, grazing. The girls had chopped wild parsnips and mushrooms they had found. Water was boiling in the cook-pot. He laid two fat rabbits, already gutted and skinned, on a makeshift table, the surface of a downed tree trunk. Aliah made quick work of quartering the hares and put them in the pot. Val opened a small pouch on her belt and crushed some dried leaves into the water. Faith took out a small vial she kept safe in her waist pouch, measured out a teaspoon of the contents using her palm and added it. Then she took great care in securing the cork stopper so as not to lose a grain of precious salt. Carlisse and Delainey finished brushing the dirt off some handfuls of wild leeks they'd dug a few yards inside the tree line and added them to the boil.

It was quiet while they waited for the rabbits to cook. Lainey and Carlisse played a game of stones. Garrett and Val cleaned and sharpened their knives. Faith and Aliah sat apart from the others in a private conversation. The aromas coming from the cook-pot set everyone's mouths to watering. Lainey came over and gave the pot a stir, then added the mushrooms and parsnips after fishing out most of the rabbit bones from the broth with a slotted wooden spoon. She put a smaller pot of water on for tea after the meal. Val cut up the last loaf of bread they'd brought, though it was quite hard. They filled wooden bowls with rabbit soup. The stale, crusty bread was perfect for dipping in the broth.

Wistfully, Lainey told the group, "A few potatoes would have been nice to thicken it."

"All the same, the rabbit is excellent," Aliah commented.

"Everyone's contributions made it into a fine meal," Garrett smiled. Gentle laughter went around. The mood of the camp eased from the earlier tension.

When they had finished every drop in the pot, Garrett took the pan and rubbed it with handfuls of sand until it was smooth and clean again, packing it away.

Faith handed him a mug of tea. Garrett joined the girls by the fire, sitting next to Faith. He noticed she had her sketchbook and pencils out and could see the outline of the foreboding forest taking shape under her talented hand.

The night sky was ablaze, studded with shiny stars. Aliah raised her voice in reverence. Garrett pulled a small zither out of his saddlebag and played in accompaniment. Delainey and Carlisse rolled the hollow log they'd been leaning on, took up some sticks, adding a drumbeat to the mix. Val and Faith sat shoulder to shoulder, blending their voices in some background harmony to Aliah's deep, haunting song. She danced with grace, sang under the moonlight, the open meadow her stage.

Though they'd risked a fire for the hot meal, they agreed to let the flames die out to coals. They cleaned up their camp, stowed the gear, and everyone wrapped up in a blanket. Delainey and Carlisse took the first watch, the moon moving across the night sky.

ROLLAND'S EYES TRACKED the moon's arc across the skyline, clouds floating in and out, blocking the starlight. His companions dozed below in a small clearing he could see from the hillock he perched on, keeping watch. The moonlight caught Saffron's hair, a wild mass of shimmering red, spread out in a fanlike fashion. Rolland averted his eyes. *Best not to dream of things that would never be,* he thought. His hands began moving again, honing his knife across a sharpening stone. The repetitive slide gave him a sense a calm. He let his hands idle, eyes drifting over the sleeping redhead who held his heart. No sense in denying himself the pleasure of her beauty as long as he stayed honest with himself. No one would ever have to find out how he felt about Saffron. He'd spent a lifetime hiding his feelings. His uncle had taught him well.

Rolland put his sharpening stone back in his pocket, pulled out a soft cloth, and began polishing the gleaming blade. Without looking up, he said in a hushed voice, "Can't sleep, Caz? Are you in a hurry to take the next watch?"

Caz came around from the back of the large boulder that Rolland leaned up against, responding, "No lad, I had to take a piss. I keep tossing and turning, thinking about everything you told us," Caz toed the ground. "I mean, I knew Prince Rupert didn't like us, but I never dreamed he'd try to sabotage his own brother. There are other weird things going on in the clan, too. Don't know what to think is all. Since I can't stop thinking, thought maybe you should try to catch some shut-eye. Robin will be up and about early, eager to move on, yeah?"

Rolland sheathed his knife and used his quarterstaff to push himself to his feet. "Thanks, Caz. I'll take advantage of your offer. I've been short of sleep myself the last few weeks." For such a large man, he made no noise as he made his way down the mound, pulled a blanket from his pack, rolled up in it, and lay down across from Saffron. He gave a quick salute to Caz, watching from above.

The night stretched out in front of the Beaumont. He ran Rolland and Saffron's stories over and over in his mind, trying to make sense of it all. An owl hooted nearby. Moments later, another answered. The birds continued this exchange for five minutes, then the nearest owl took flight, soaring over the meadow opposite their camp. If it had not been for the owl, he never would have noticed the figures moving on the opposite side, right near the border of the Edgewood Forest. Some people called it the Black Edgewood. From up here, it had a sinister look to it. Try as he might, even with his enhanced goblin sight, he couldn't see the end of the forest treeline. There were plenty of rumors about the forest. None good. Most of them are bloody terrifying. For now, he would ignore the dreaded woods. They'd head into the dense canopy soon enough. He brought his attention back to the silhouettes he'd spotted, blinking until he could focus on them again. They were at least half a mile off, if not more.

A few clouds clustered together. A large one passed in front of the moon, blocking the light, causing him to lose sight of the profiles he'd been watching. Caz continued to strain, trying to see out across the darkness. The cloud moved on, and the moonlight broke open over the meadow once more. Surveying all along the Edgewood tree line, he suddenly jerked up. His sixth sense made him hit the ground flat on his stomach. He used his arms to pull his body along in a belly crawl to the edge of the hilltop, tall grasses hiding his position.

Blinking his eyes to focus again, he wanted to be sure of what he was seeing. Bloody hell. This was bad. He waffled about whether he should wake Robin right away. No, Caz thought, better to wait, to have all the details before waking the Goodfellow. He settled in to see if he could make sense of what was going on.

From the south, there looked to be a small gang of goblin lads moving along the rim of the trees. They headed right toward the small camp, where earlier he had seen the silhouettes. What mystified him was the hulking size of the leader, who appeared to be driving the lads from behind. He couldn't make out what it was. Whatever it was, it was big. Bigger than any goblin he'd ever met. It was hard to decide if the goblins were running from it, trying to get away, or if the big thing was driving them forward.

The moon disappeared behind a cloud curtain again, seconds ticking by while Caz's heart pounded in his chest. He wondered why he could still see outlines of the figures with the moonlight blocked? What he'd taken for large boulders in the meadow moved. With just enough light to see, he noted the imagined boulders were horses hobbled; he counted three.

He smacked his hand against his forehead in disbelief. Now he could make out the embers of a banked fire, two bodies standing up, looking south, listening. The hair on the back of Caz's neck stood up. The firelight lit the bodies up enough so Caz could see the long hair and slim figures. Females. He couldn't believe anyone would be stupid enough to have a fire right next to the Edgewood Forest. Didn't they know where they were, what lived there?

Their beacon had reached a roaming gang of lads. There looked to be at least twelve, maybe fifteen of them, plus the hulking leader. He could tell this was going to be more than a bad dream for those stupid girls! Just as he decided he was going to rouse Robin, he saw wings snap open on the backs of both the girls' shadows. Fae. The pair shot up into the night sky, shouting as they launched. Several other heads came up around their fire at the commotion. Now Caz could make out the horses as they began to prance and whinny, eyes rolling back, mouths frothing from fear, the smell of goblins in their nostrils.

Caz barreled down the hill. When he reached Robin, he clamped his hand on Robin's shoulder. In a flash, he found a knife at his throat. "Robin, it's me, Caz! Wake up! Get your bloody knife away from me, you chump!" Caz growled.

"What's what, you fool?" Robin growled back, shoving Caz away. "Never wake me like that. I could have hurt you!"

Saffron and Rolland were already on their feet. Caz shot back an angry retort at Robin. "It's what the watch does, mate. When the watch sees something, they come wake their mates up!" he continued, not bothering to disguise the irritation in his voice. "There's a nightmare about to go down. I thought you might want to know, since it involves some goblin lads. We've spent the last six months trying to keep any violence down, to keep peace with the other races. Just a minor issue among our other bigger concerns, yeah?" his words laced with sarcasm.

"Okay, okay," Robin held his hands up in acquiescence. "Sorry. Being startled awake while near the Edgewood, I thought we were being attacked.

Now slow down and tell us what's what?" Robin said in a calm voice to defuse the situation.

Caz gave them a rundown of what he guessed was about to happen, estimating they had about ten minutes before a bad clash started. He strapped on his weapons and gathered up his stuff while he talked. Robin followed Caz's lead. Pulling his gear and weapons together, he called out, "Rolland. Saff! You with us on this?"

Saffron caught the quarterstaff Caz tossed to her. Rolland directed his own heavy stick forward. "Lead on. We're right behind you."

"Rolland," Saffron pointed at the large pack by the tree, "your smithy tools."

"I'll have to come back for them. No good in a fight. I need to move without being hindered by the weight of a pack." He grabbed her hand, and they raced across the meadow after Caz and Robin, leaving their horses tethered in camp.

VALERIE VICTORIA PUREHEART sat next to her best friend, their backs against the biggest tree they had ever seen. Faith and Val had just relieved Carlisse and Delainey for the second watch. She saw Lainey throw a couple of logs on the coals. "Lainey," Val scolded, "we were letting the fire go out!"

"Just those two logs, Val. I'm cold, and it's been quiet all night, not a creature stirring," Delainey yawned, rolled up in her blanket near the stoked-up fire, turning her back on her sister.

The horses nickered. The two friends turned, looked at their own reflections in each other's eyes, jumped up, staring south, straining to hear. "What the bloody hell was that?" Faith whispered. Val kicked sand over the fire, reducing it back to coals.

Moments later, there was no mistaking the deep goblin voices. It sounded like they were a ways away yet, but moving closer. The girl's wings snapped out in reaction to their immediate fear. With the footfalls they could hear, it sounded like there were a lot of goblins headed this way, coming on fast.

Val flew out into the meadow about a hundred feet, her black wings acting as a natural camouflage against the night sky, where she could see the approaching band. The sight of a dozen goblins was reason enough to put a fire under her innate instinct of flight over fight. But the gigantic monster driving the group from behind looked bloody terrifying.

She'd never seen or even imagined a creature like it. Val noted the thing was at least nine feet tall. It had huge, powerful-looking thighs. A bipedal digitigrade, Val remembered from their science classes. Its leg from the knee angled back behind it, connecting to an ankle, where it formed the top of a huge, muscled foot. The thing looked capable of making high, springing jumps. She noted the torso was a mass of muscles. Its enormous arms bulged with brute force and ended in hands large enough to crush her skull, and appeared to be finished in long, lethal claws. Some type of armor covered the thing, the beast's body overlaid with shaggy hair. The massive head had a sweeping mane running from the top of the head down the back between the shoulder blades. It must have been four times the size of Garrett, maybe five. The face was a horror, mouth filled with long, pointed, razor-sharp teeth. But the bloody eyes. It was the thing's eyes that froze her where she stood. Red glowing orbs, which seemed to have some power over her, held her in limbo, when in reality, the creature hadn't seen her yet.

Val took in all those details in a matter of seconds before the monster let out a bloodcurdling roar that made the ground shake. The pack of goblins sped up in a frenzy.

Faith flew to her sister-friend, pulling her away from the oncoming horror. Both began screaming at the others in the camp to get up. The horses were panicking. Garrett came to a stand from a sound sleep, his bow nocked with an arrow. He pushed Val's three sisters behind him toward the horses, not understanding what the danger even was.

"Get to the horses!" Val screamed.

"Run! Run! Hurry! Get into the woods to hide!" Faith yelled.

Delainey got to a horse first, held the reins fast as she took the hobbles off it and threw herself in the saddle. Aliah pushed Carlisse up into the saddle of another, handed her the reins, released the horse, slapping it on the rump as if it needed encouragement to run like hell. The two girls disappeared into the thicket, leaping over deadfall, branches slapping them in the face as they galloped into the dense woods.

Aliah freed the last horse, mounted, and grabbed Garrett's hand. He swung up behind her while keeping his bow pointed south. Aliah shouted, "Ha!" slapping the reins left and right. The horse leaped into action, charging into the Black Edgewood, just as a dozen goblins rounded the treeline where they had camped.

The monster, a Gugwe, was driving the goblins forward at a pace almost impossible for their legs to maintain. Spotting prey, the Gugwe roared again, giving the group an extra surge of energy. Energy fueled their terror.

"Faith! Val!" Aliah screamed, her voice fading into the woods. The two fairy girls flew haphazardly through the dense tree branches, trying to follow the others. They soon lost track of their companions. Faith had only practiced flying a few times with Val and her sisters while they traveled. Her back was still sore where the wings had split it open just days before. She wasn't confident in the control she had when flying, yet. The two girls found the woods growing darker the deeper they went. They flew in a zigzag pattern, losing their sense of direction. Faith landed high on the branch of an ancient, massive white pine. She gasped, trying to catch her breath. Panic fueled her adrenaline.

Val saw her land, changed direction, going back to join her. Surveying the ground below, they registered a carpet of trillium, Dutchman's breeches, and wild leeks. Their eyes scanned in a frantic search for their pursuers. Faith couldn't stop quivering, feeling like her heart was going to burst. Val came down on the branch next to her, trying to gain her balance from a shaky landing. The two girls clutched each other in a hug.

A small rock sailed like a missile through the tree branches, hitting Val mid-forehead. The blow stunned her, knocking her from the tree limb they perched on. Val's wings snapped closed as she fell unconscious twenty-feet below. Her body landed with a thud on the mounds of leaf litter and pine needles built up over the years, knocking the air from her lungs. Faith spun around, looked down just in time to see four goblins hooting and howling, racing toward Val. In a flash, Faith thought she was hallucinating when she spotted a mop of red hair out of the corner of her eye as someone scooped up Val's limp body.

The two figures vanished before her eyes. Faith blinked. Blinked again. Val was gone. She'd disappeared. "Val!" the scream ripped from her throat. The goblins looked up and danced around the base of the tree she was sheltering in.

Of a sudden, the goblins stopped, standing stock-still beneath her. All noises ceased. Faith felt like dread, corruption, and death encased her. The stench of rot and putrid decay overwhelmed her senses. She hung her head to the side and puked. When she finished retching, got a closeup look at the monster as it arrived at the base of the tree. Dead red eyes looked up to behold her. It released an ear-piercing screech, a sound like nothing she had ever heard in her brief life. The beast grabbed the trunk of the behemoth of a tree she sheltered in and shook it in fury. For a moment, Faith lost her footing, her balance off, but she grabbed the branch above her and held on for dear life.

She concentrated, which was a miracle, because the stench of this creature made her want to hurl again. Then, at her command, she felt her wings snap out. Pushing off the branch with her toes, the young Fae took flight just as the hairy monster ripped the roots of the tree right out of the ground. Faith raced away, just fast enough to out-fly the falling, ancient white pine. The uprooted tree took down several other trees with its fall, branches locking and grabbing. It twisted into a mess of destruction, a crash that made a thundering noise as it hit the ground. The tearing of limbs and cracking tree trunks made it seem as though the world was ending for a few brief moments.

The angry Gugwe shook his fist at the fleeing Faerie's opalescent wings. In a fit of rage, it grabbed the closest goblin, crushing him until his body exploded into a mass of blood and guts that spattered across the forest floor. The other goblins seemed to come to their senses, scattering in a panic as the Gugwe searched about for something more to assuage its anger on. Goblins ran in every direction. The monster roared and roared, smashing its foot down on one unlucky lad. It grabbed another by the ankle, beating him against a tree until there was nothing left but a bloody heap of broken bones. And still the Gugwe raged on.

This was the state of things Rolland, Robin, and Caz found the Gugwe in when they reached the destruction. The big smith had lost track of

Saffron in their race to save the girls Caz had seen from the watch hill. Crazed with fear for her, Rolland rushed ahead of Robin and Caz, searching for the redhead.

"Rolland, wait!" Caz called out too late, as the big smith sprinted toward the monster. Robin and Caz locked eyes. Caz ripped open his shirt and began unwinding a rope he carried wrapped around his torso. Tossing an end to Robin, Caz went left, Robin right, just as Rolland used his quarterstaff to vault himself into the air, his knife at the ready. Rolland's body flew upwards. His hand stabbed down, right into the Gugwe's left eye. He hadn't taken the time to think about his trajectory coming back down. Hitting the ground hard, he rolled, moving just before the monster's enormous foot came down in a stomp where his head had been only a second before. Robin's crew wasn't even aware that Faith flew back and forth above them, looking for a sign of Val.

A dozen of the goblins ran through the woods towards Faith. The faerie flew away, a narrow escape, avoiding crashing into tree limbs, her body operating on high-octane fear. She was sure they were pursuing her. Her only thoughts became consumed with getting away before they caught her. In truth, the lads were only trying to get away from the Gugwe who had been driving them. But there was no way for her to know that.

Robin and Caz continued to run right-to-left and left-to-right. Round and round they moved, while the Gugwe raged at its ruined eye. The creature reached up, split the air with an ear-piercing howl, pulled the knife from the eye socket, throwing it to the ground. Oddly, the weapon landed about three feet from where Rolland lay hidden behind the downed white pine. Blood gushed down the monster's face while it struggled to track Robin and Caz with its good eye, reaching out, grabbing at them as they ran in circles.

Then, the Gugwe spotted Rolland, and became incensed all over again. The big smith curled up and repeated his lifelong mantra to himself, "Don't see me. Don't see me. Don't see me."

The crazed creature took a step toward Rolland, who reached out, reclaiming his knife. Rolland Rafael Brown decided if he was about to die, he was going to die fighting. He hoped only to inflict as much damage as he could before his life was over. That was the best he could do for Saffron and his friends in his last moments. He jumped up, ready to charge. To his great surprise, the Gugwe wavered back and forth, back and forth, then toppled like a falling tree. When the monster fell, a jagged tree limb from the pine it had ripped out by the roots impaled the hairy beast. A cloud of stench ballooned into the air when it pierced through its stomach, right out of its backside. The innards of the dead brute caused the gag reflex in all three of the clan companions to puke at the same time.

Rolland couldn't believe he still lived, wiping his mouth with the back of his hand. He surveyed the carnage. Now he understood what had just happened. The boys had run round and round in circles. In doing so, had tied up the giant's legs with a long, slender rope between the two of them. The Touchstone always kept a rope wound around his midsection, under his shirt for access. In a way, rope also served as a kind of body armor.

Caz and Robin, giddy with relief, slapped one another on their shoulders. Manic laughter followed until Rolland's somber question brought them back out of it. "Where's Saffron?" he worried.

"We thought she was with you," Robin responded.

All their faces took on a look of worry and concern. Each called out her name as they were wont to do. "Saffron!" Rolland bellowed.

"Saff, where are you?" Robin yelled for her.

"Fron, come out, lass! Fron!" Caz hollered, close to panic.

"Here, you bloody fools!" Saffron called back. She pushed her way out of the back of an old oak and turned, reaching back in to help someone out behind her.

The three lads stood gaping as she pulled Val up and out of the oak tree. Though her wings were closed, Caz recognized her from his sighting back on the hilltop. He let out a slow whistle. "Fron, you saved them," he said with a certain admiration.

"Them?" Saffron looked confused.

"Well, lass, I guess we were in such a hurry to get here. We didn't talk about it. There were at least five fairies I saw on my watch. The monster was driving the lads right to their camp. You saved them all, yeah?" he fisted her shoulder.

Val hung her head in apparent grief.

"Oh. Oh no, sorry," Caz stammered, "I didn't think. I..."

"Yeah, I guess you didn't think, laddie," Fron said to him.

"Where's Rolland?" Saffron asks, looking around with concern.

"Here, Saffron. I'm here behind you, lass," Rolland answered. She turned and threw her arms around his neck. "What you did was one of the bloody bravest things I've ever seen, Rolland," she told him. He looked away, embarrassed. Caz and Robin exchanged a look.

"Robin," Saffron pointed her thumb to the big oak she and Val had taken refuge in, "we captured a couple of those lads. They're tied up down below. Thought you might like to talk to them. Find out what's what. They aren't from our clan," Saffron took Rolland's hand and walked a few feet away to tell him her part in the action.

Robin jumped down from the oak. Caz stood looking at Val, who'd sat down on the forest floor, resting with her back against the oak tree.

"Hey," Caz asked her, "you alright? What's your name?"

Val wiped her hands off on her leather pants, stood and held a hand out to him. "Val. Um, Valerie Victoria Pureheart, you?"

"Caz. I mean, Cazzidy Beaumont Touchstone." He toed the dirt, pushing leaves around with his boot.

"You're quite clever, you and your mate...Robin, is it? The rope and all. I thought I was dead for sure. Then, the next thing I know, Red slides in, wraps me in her arms, and we disappear into the tree. Right down to its roots. A little hidey-hole. Never knew of such a thing." She finished this brief speech with wonder in her voice, but falling silent, her grief settled back over her like a shroud. He saw her countenance sag under the weight of her sadness.

Val swallowed hard and brought her eyes up to meet his. "You said you saw five fairies?" He nodded. She pushed on. "You don't know what happened to the other four or to Garrett?" she asked with little hope. He shook his head. "They had horses. Maybe they got away." Her voice trailed off.

"We'll help you search," Caz committed without his companions' agreement.

"You don't have to," Val told him. "I think we're supposed to be enemies, right? Goblins and Faeries. Sworn enemies. I...I know little about the history between our races. I haven't lived among the Fae. It's been years since I've seen a goblin. Goblins used to come to the town to celebrate the spring equinox. You know. Ostara." Her voice soft, she continued, "I guess I've lived a sheltered life. You don't feel like my enemy. Anyway, I don't want you to feel obligated to help me. I'm grateful for everything you and your friends have done already. Besides, if my sisters and friends are all alive, I have a general idea of where they would go." Val toed the dirt with her boot.

When she looked up again, she saw a smile tugging at the corners of Caz's face. "You don't seem like an enemy to me, either. Where do you think your friends would head? I don't like the idea of leaving you alone anywhere near this forest. What do you know about the Black Edgewood?" he prodded.

Before she could answer, Robin burst from the oak, holding the two lads by the scruffs of their necks. He glanced at Val and told Caz in a gruff voice, "Things have worsened since the clan left the far north."

"How so?" Caz asked.

"These lads are from a northern clan. The Gugwe have been raiding, breaking up the clans and forcing them to help the Gugwe track down Faerie kin. This changes everything and all our plans." Robin softened his voice, dropped the two smaller goblins and turned to Val, asking, "Do your kin know about this?"

"You mean these monsters? What did you call them? Gugwe?" Her voice rose with each word. "No. We'd never heard of them until a couple of days ago. I didn't know they existed until some of Faith's cousins showed up and were telling us about them. Do you know why they would hunt Fae?" she demanded.

"Calm down, lass. I'm just trying to gather information to decide what to do next."

"Robin," Caz said, "this is Val. Um...Valerie Victoria Pureheart. She told me they don't live among the kin. Think, man. That creature almost killed her and her friends tonight. Her friends are missing. I, um, told her we'd help her search for them," he finished and waited for the Goodfellow to say the right thing.

Robin turned and met Val's eyes, surprised to see defiance and determination reflected at him. She reminded him of someone, but he couldn't put his finger on who it was. "Of course, we'll help you search, and if we can't find your friends..."

"My sisters and a friend," she corrected.

"Well, if we can't find your sisters and your friend, we'll see you safe to wherever you were going," Robin assured her.

Val felt laughter bubble up inside and couldn't hold it in. "Oh, that's rich." She laughed and laughed until tears ran down her cheeks, leaving Caz and Robin at a loss for what to do next. Robin wondered if the big goose egg on Val's forehead had given her a concussion. Caz started the unpleasant job of reclaiming his rope, all twisted around the dead monster's legs. He muttered to himself that the smell would never come out of the cord.

Saffron and Rolland strolled back over to see what was going on. Recognizing Val's laughter as a loss of emotional control, Saffron put her arm around Val's shoulders. "Are you all right?" She whispered to the beautiful girl. Val fanned her hand in front of her face and took some deep, calming breaths.

"Look," Robin announced to the group, "we told Val here we'd help her search for her sisters and her friend."

Saffron and Rolland both nodded as if it had never even been a question.

"If we can't find any trace of them, Val can come with us to finish our quest, then we'll see her safe wherever she wants to go before we head north."

"North?" Caz exploded. "Wait! Aren't we going back to the clan to confront your brother about the Summer Games?"

"Well, I'm not going back, Caz. You and Saffron can do as you wish, but what's the sense in it? My brother plotted against us. Rolland can't go back after what happened with his uncle. Plus, he's already gifted us with the Queen's Ransom weapon caches he made. Rolland told us Rupert hired him for gold to sabotage us at the games. If not Rolland, Rupert would just hire someone else to stop us from winning. Besides, what's there to win? Our pride? A title? If Rupert has his way, our pride will be the death of us."

Caz punched the nearest tree, regretting the thoughtless action, rubbing his knuckles. The goal he had worked toward for years, stolen right out from under him, even though Rolland had gifted him with a Queen's Ransom.

"Besides, the two lads I just interrogated gave me a piece of news that worries me more than anything," Robin admitted, concern lacing his words.

"What's what?" Caz asked.

"Hey!" Saffron looked around in alarm. "They're gone, Robin! The lads have escaped."

"No matter, Saff. I told them to go back home or to another clan. The Gugwe has a kind of mind-control ability. It messed some lads up." Then Robin dropped a little news bomb. "They also told me rumors are everywhere that the Gugwe are working with Prince Rupert and Queen Morveena." Walking away, he called over his shoulder. "That's not all. Word is, the Gugwe are searching for a Faerie queen or princess or something. Morveena's paying them to do it."

Val's face turned a pale shade of gray.

"Rolland," Robin called out, "you and Saff go back to where we camped and collect your smithy tools, our horses, and the rest of our gear, yeah?" Rolland nodded. "Meet us back at the edge of the forest where Val and her companions camped. We'll start there to gather up anything they left behind and see if we can't find a trail to track them. They had horses, so we should be able to pick up traces of their escape." He put heavy emphasis on the last word for Val. Robin's eyes conveyed sympathy when he caught the Fae girl's sideways glance.

Everyone moved. Val called out, "Red! Wait!" Four sets of eyes turned to her. She reached out and touched Saffron's hand. "I...I just wanted to thank you. Thank you for saving my life, Red. Thank you all for helping me and my friends, even if I am supposed to be your enemy."

"I don't know what you grew up believing, Val, but we don't think of you as our enemy. I admit some of the goblin race may think so, but we don't," Robin offered.

Saffron gave Val's hand a gentle squeeze, then she and Rolland headed back toward their camp.

Val turned in a full circle. The woods looked the same in every direction. "I don't even know which way is back to my camp. My sense of direction is all turned around," she confessed.

"If you like, I'd be happy to teach you some woodcraft while we search for your sisters," Caz offered.

"So, you're headed north after we search?" Val asked as they walked through the woods.

"Well, not straight off," Robin answered. "We have a short quest we need to finish first. If we'd gotten there sooner, maybe we could have avoided all this," Robin reflected.

"Or maybe we were where we needed to be at the right time," Caz suggested.

"Where were you headed?" Val wondered aloud.

"Val," Robin said, "where we're going could be dangerous. Maybe you and Saff could set up camp and wait for us outside the Edgewood Forest, so you're not in any further danger?" he suggested.

"But we already encountered danger outside of Edgewood," she argued. A smile bloomed on her face. "I'd sure like to see you sell that idea to Red," Val laughed. "Danger seems to be the path I'm walking right now. Can't be much worse than today, yeah?"

"It could be," Caz stated.

"For heaven's sake! Just tell me where you are going and let me decide for myself if I think it's too risky?" she demanded.

The two lifelong friends looked at one another, their hands moving in some kind of communication Val had never seen. Then they nodded in silent agreement.

"Val, we were on our way to find someone called the Dream Weaver. Ever heard of her?" Caz asked.

Val lapsed into mad laughter again. Robin and Caz didn't understand this girl at all. Val put her hands on her legs above her knees, letting the laughter die out, bending over and taking several deep breaths. "Yeah, I've heard of the Dream Weaver. In fact, that's why we're out here, on a quest looking for the Weaver as well. Coincidence? Doubtful. We're in the Edgewood Forest. Her realm. Bet the bitch has been messing with us already." She heaved a heavy sigh, then continued, "Faith was so set on this plan of action. I hope she doesn't get there before I do. All I can do now is search for them and keep my fingers crossed that they're all safe." Her words, like a prayer, drifted into the wind.

Hearing the name, Robin kept silent as the name Faith. Faith. Faith echoed through his brain like a drumbeat.

KRISTIAN AND MARIELLA kept a steady pace north. Every hour, they dismounted and walked the horses for fifteen minutes to conserve the animals' strength. Twice they came upon small flowing creeks, allowing the horses to drink their fill. Kris would fall silent, eyes glazing over, and then he'd come out of the trance a few minutes later saying, "I still can't see the outcome. Let's keep moving." Miles defined the day until at last, from high above, in the distance, they could see the great Edgewood Forest spread out before them.

"We're within a day's reach of the forest's edge," Mariana declared. "Let's find a place nearby to camp for the night, so we're fresh in the morning."

Surprised, Kris said, "I think we should keep going."

"No," his sister tells him in a firm tone. "We've had no sleep for three days. We're riding blind into something you can't see. People make mistakes when exhaustion sets in, and we don't want to ride our horses into the ground."

Kris stared off at the distant border of the great Dark Edgewood, then responded, "There's a shallow cave a couple of miles just west of here. We can camp there," he tells his sister, resignation in his voice. She said nothing, urging her horse to the west as the sun dipped below the tree line.

TRAVIS SURVEYED THE ground in a crouch, rubbed some dirt between his fingers, and looked up, eyes scanning the area in front of him. He stood. Both of Robert's hounds waited at his side, tails wagging. Absent-mindedly, he reached down with both hands and scratched the tops of their heads. The dogs leaned into him.

"Well?" Brittany rode up.

Horse reins in hand, Travis answered his sister, "It's odd, but they turned due north from here after all those miles traveling west. Let's go. They're hours ahead. I don't want the trail to grow any colder. Hey," he called to his sister, "isn't that Mariella's scarf you're wearing?"

"I didn't take it without asking," Brittany tells him defensively. "Mariella let me borrow it a few days ago." She adjusted the silk material around her neck.

"It wasn't an accusation, sis," Travis laughed. "Jeez, girls and clothes." He shook his head in disbelief. "Can I see the scarf for a minute?" He held his hand out.

Suspiciously, Britt narrowed her eyes at him, but untied the colorful material and handed it over. Travis reached down to the dog on his left, scarf in hand. The hound burrowed its muzzle into the material. When the canine pulled away, a long piece of drool was swinging between the soft material and its mouth, tail wagging. Travis repeated the process with the dog on his right side. When the second dog was done, Travis commanded, "Seek!" Both dogs took off at a run, heading straight north. "Excellent," he commented, mounting up.

Travis held the scarf out to his sister, the string of dog saliva swinging in the wind from the corner of the wrap. Brittany turned cool eyes on her brother, held up her right hand, middle finger extended, trotting her horse past him, catching up to Shaun.

"What?" Travis called after his sister.

ALIAH SLOWED THE HORSE she and Garrett were riding to a walk. They both turned their heads, scanning the woods in all directions. Struggling to see through all the trees and branches, straining to listen, but neither could hear any sounds of the other girls or horses.

"I hate to admit it," Garrett said in a soft voice, "But, I do not know what direction we came from. As usual, when you get lost in the woods, everything looks the same no matter which way you turn," he told her, defeated.

"We're not lost," Aliah said. "Our plan was to be in the Edgewood Forest seeking the Dream Weaver. All we have to do now is find my sisters and Faith, or find the Dream Weaver's house. If we don't find the girls first, that is where they'll all head," she said with positivity.

CARLISSE AND DELAINEY were off their horses, leading them at a slow walk. "I hope we can find the others soon," Delainey whispered.

"Why are you whispering?" Carlisse asked her.

"Because we're in the Edgewood, silly," Lainey retorted. "You know. The Dream Weaver's realm?"

Carlisse shuddered at the memory of the last time they had found the Dream Weaver. "Can't we stop and rest for a while, Lainey? I'm so tired," Carlisse complained.

"No!" Delainey chided. "The last thing we want to do in these woods is fall asleep, Carlisse. You know what it could lead to! Sleep. Dreams. This is a dangerous place to dream." Carlisse nodded her agreement. "We'll just keep moving and try to find the Weaver's house again, because it's where everyone will go. If they're all right, that is. And if they don't show up there, then and only then, will we take the chance of sleeping. That will be a last resort—to find ourselves at the mercy of the Dream Weaver, asking what happened to the others. We are only going to go that route if we have to! Personally, I think the price is too high for the Dream Weaver's services," Delainey finished in a whisper to herself. She turned, looking all around them because she felt as if they were being watched.

Carlisse stumbled on a tree root, her eyes fluttering. Delainey hooked her sister's arm in hers. "Carlisse, did I ever tell you the story about how Da rescued me from the rowboat in the middle of the lake where I'd lost a paddle?" Delainey's quiet voice stayed between the two sisters as they walked on, leading their horses, letting the forest choose their path for them.

CHAPTER 13: The Dream Weaver

Faith remembered it was a Friday and the 13th day of the moonrise that month. March in high spring.

She had lost the goblins who were chasing her and attributed it to the luck she always thought came to her on a Friday the 13th. The problem was not only had she lost her pursuers, she'd lost everyone else, too. The woods were dark. Little sunshine filtered its way through the thick, leafy canopy. Her back and shoulders ached. She'd never flown for so long or over such a distance before. Her muscles felt strained, not conditioned for this. She slowed, touching down both feet onto a thick limb of an oak tree. Her wings snapped shut without her giving a thought to the action. She winced in pain.

Faith brushed her loose hair back from her flushed face and wiped the sweat from her forehead. She pulled the water bag slung cross-body over her shoulder and took a deep drink. All the while scanning the ground below, on her guard. It took her only a few moments to realize she had no sense of the direction their camp had been located. Since she'd opted to fly to make her getaway, she wouldn't have left any signs for her friends to follow so they could find her. Val and all her sisters' faces flashed through her mind. Picturing Garrett protecting them brought a quick smile amid her grim situation. *What had happened to Val? She couldn't have disappeared. So, who was the person with the red hair she'd glimpsed?* Her skin pebbled, and a shiver ran down her spine as she pictured the creature's face—all those razor shape teeth, the drool, the stench of decay and corruption erupted in memory. *Where did that thing come from? Why was it here? Why was a giant monster driving a group of goblins in front of it? Was that thing the monster her cousins had described as northern invaders? What had they gotten themselves into?* Her thoughts were on the verge of wallowing in self-pity. Questions swirled in, then out of Faith's thoughts. Anxiety level rising, her heart beat a steady hammering against her chest.

She stamped her boot down on the tree limb, refusing to give in to a self-pity party, where she was the only attendee. Instead, Faith gathered all those broken thoughts, closed them up in an imaginary box in her mind, locking them away to be dissected and solved later. *No point in using up energy on why, why, why's. You can't do could've, should've, would've. Be here. Be now. Do what you need to do to move forward. Move through your situation; don't let fear paralyze you!* She rolled her eyes. Then a small smile played across her lips as she concluded she was giving herself a 'Val lecture'! Her spirits rose instantly.

Taking a deep breath, skimming the ground below, then sweeping her eyes up to the treetops, then back down. Faith worked a pattern, keeping watch as she puzzled out her best options. Resting with her back against the tree trunk, legs stretched out on the limb, she pulled her sketchpad and pencils out. Her hand moved deftly over the paper. She drew the forest from a bird's-eye view. Her muscles relaxed as her paper filled with hundreds of details. When she was done, she noticed a massive white pine that seemed to be the focal point of the drawing among the vast sea of green. She packed up her art supplies. Strands of blond hair tickled her cheeks in the breeze, the beads in her braids clicking together as she studied the landscape. One hundred yards straight out from her perch rose the biggest white pine tree she'd ever seen. There were many grand pines in these woods, but nothing so far bested this one. It was at least a third taller than all the rest and had to be well over a hundred years old. *Best of all*, she thought, *it was so tall it looked to reach way above the rest of the treetops. All she had to do was climb it, giving her access to a natural lookout tower. From up there, she should be able to get some sense of where she was and which way she needed to go.*

Opalescent wings snapped out. Focusing, she pushed off the tree limb using the balls of her feet. With a new focus, all her aches and exhaustion melted away, forgotten. She flew across the forest, seeking the mammoth white pine. Faith landed on the tree's limb thirty feet from the ground. Putting a new strategy into play, she flew in brief spurts, moving up as far as she could without catching her wings in the thick needled branches, until she had to snap her wings closed and just climb. Her hands became tacky with sap as she reached a point where she could stick her head above the overstory. Faith found herself blinded after so long in the dark woods. She spent a few moments blinking to adjust her eyes to the bright light. When she surveyed her location, her body swayed, vertigo making her stomach roil. Turning in a complete circle, she named herself a fool when she realized a sea of green surrounded her as far as she could see. There was nothing up here to help her get her inner compass in line for a destination. She felt her throat choke up, a renewed sense of helplessness overwhelming her. One thought consumed her.

She was alone.

The declaration echoed through her mind, but she swallowed it down. Instead, she reflected on things she was grateful for, like *enjoying the light breeze and sunshine From there, her list grew. 1) she was alive, she'd survived the attack from the awful monster; 2) there were no monsters in her immediate view; 3) she still had water; 4) she could keep looking for her friends; and, 5) she had a good idea where she might find them. As long as they all found the Dream Weaver somewhere here in the Edgewood Forest.*

There. She felt better. Purposeful thought was very satisfying. *Oh, she remembered as she opened a pouch on her belt; 6) I have jerky.* She pulled a strip of jerky off with her teeth and chewed while her eyes did a sweeping radius of the treetops. It was an impressive perspective.

Faith stopped munching. Raising up on her tiptoes, the branch supporting her. Straining, shading her eyes with her free hand, focusing across the green expanse. *Was...? Yes! It was!* She could see smoke rising way out in the foliage. She crammed the last piece of jerky into her mouth, dropped to a crouch, scrutinizing the tree trunks under the canopy tops. Lining up the direction below with where she could see the smoke from above, syncing it. In minutes, she climbed far enough down the white pine until she could use her wings again.

Her back still ached, but she had a new destination. A plan. Flying through the trees, looking for where the smoke was coming from. It had to be Garrett and the girls signaling to find her. She reminded herself that it would be smart to be cautious, vowing not to make any stupid decisions without checking things out first. Before she took any action, she would think everything through. *Shut up, Val!* She thought, with a grin plastered across her face.

Faith knew she was close now, the smell of wood smoke hitting her olfactory sensors. She slowed her approach, drifting to ground level, where she closed and folded her wings so they didn't show. Sticking to her commitment of caution, she stepped onto the ground, keeping to the shadows from tree to tree until she saw a small clearing. Instead of finding her friends at a campfire, what she saw was a small log cottage.

Peeking round the tree she hid behind, she spotted smoke curling out of a stone chimney, wafting up into the treetops. There didn't appear to be any windows in the house, except some triangular-shaped ones at the very top, near the roofline. The place looked old, but appeared to be a very solid structure. Whoever lived here had stacked firewood in a small woodshed to the right of the dwelling. Next to the shed was a huge stump, an axe blade planted in the middle of it. The door looked solid, made of thick, dark wood and hung on tarnished brass hinges, with a large knob set in the center.

The entrance opened. Faith pulled her face back behind the tree trunk, heartbeat ticking up. She made herself take a few calming breaths, then peeked out from behind the tree. A woman emerged carrying a large basket. Faith watched the stranger walk over by the woodshed, where she set the basket on the stump by the axe. Pulling a dress from the basket, deft hands pinned it to a clothesline. The rope ran from the corner of the shed, secured at the other end to a large pine about forty paces away.

Well, thought Faith, *this scenario looks safe enough. She could ask this woman for help. Maybe the woman could give her directions out of the forest or tell her how to find the Dream Weaver.* 'Think it through,' she heard Val say in her mind. Faith watched for a few minutes longer as the woman hung out her laundry. There didn't appear to be any men's clothing being hung on the line. The female was rather small. She seemed to have long legs and a short torso. Her hair was shiny black, pulled back from her face in a severe knot at the nape. Faith noted she wore a short black tunic, shiny black leather leggings similar to her own. Her feet were shod in clumpy, worn black boots. Over her clothes, she wore an old black cloak marked with two faded round red stains on the back. The hem swirled around her ankles as she walked.

Faith startled when something touched her leg. She looked down to find it was only a tabby cat rubbing against her. Reaching toward it, she ran her hand along the sleek body as it walked back and forth, rubbing her legs and purring.

With the last of the laundry hung, the lady picked up her basket, heading toward the house. She turned in a half circle calling out, "Here kitty, kitty, kitty." The cat's ears pricked up, but continued rubbing Faith's legs. Making a quick decision, she bent, grabbed the feline, and strode forward from behind the tree. The woman gasped, dropped her basket, and held her hands to her chest in surprise.

"Hullo," Faith called out. "Sorry if I frightened you, but your tabby was next to me, rubbing my legs. I...I was trying to work up the courage to come and ask for help. I'm lost." Setting the feline down, the cat ran toward the woman and jumped into the laundry basket. They both laughed.

"You gave me quite a scare, young lady!" the woman scolded.

"I'm sorry," Faith apologized. "My name...my name is Val. Er, Valerie. Um, Pureheart." As soon as the lie left her lips, she regretted it. She had no idea why she had presented the falsehood, but there was something about the woman that was putting her on edge. Now that she'd given the fake name, she didn't see how she could explain the false invention and so had to live with the fib.

The woman looked her over and could see the dirt stains of travel and the girl's bedraggled state. She offered a warm smile, reaching out her hand to Faith. "I'm called Persid. Welcome. Let's go put on the kettle for a cup of tea, and you can tell me how you came to be lost. You look a fright. There's water you can wash up with." The woman looked down at the cat curled in her laundry basket, saying, "Come along, Ginger." Ginger jumped out of the basket as Persid grabbed the handles, leading the way to the door.

Persid pumped water from the sink into a kettle, putting it on the cast-iron stove to heat. She added a log to the fire within. Then, busied herself with putting out things for tea. Faith stood just inside the door, surprised to see how sparse the house was. She noted the dust particles floating in the air, exposed by the sunlight coming from the open doorway. She could see cobwebs covering all the ceiling corners. The floor was dirt, hard-packed from years of Persid's footsteps. There seemed a light coating of dust on the few pieces of furniture. Cooking inside and dust sticking to a layer of grease had caused a film to build up on the few windows in the room. The kitchen area to her right had a table with three mismatched chairs. To her left stood a small washstand holding a pitcher and a bowl. A clouded mirror, the silver worn, hung above. Along the same wall, Faith could see shelves holding Persid's boots and shoes. Next to the entrance, pegs held a coat and a shawl. The wall opposite the front door featured a soot-stained fireplace. On each side of the hearth, a door, both closed. Persid had an old copper boiler by the fireplace; she had laid up with kindling and logs. There was a moth-eaten blanket folded on the stone hearth where Ginger now rested, licking a paw, washing whiskers and face. Arranged in front of the fireplace stood a small bench and two hardwood chairs. Off to the side sat a small spinning wheel with a large basket of colorful yarn next to it.

"Bring me the pitcher on the washstand, dear. I'll give you some warm water to use in the washbowl," Persid directed her. Faith obeyed, feeling shamed she was judging Persid's housekeeping skills when the woman had only shown her kindness. Opposite the small kitchen, Faith picked up the pitcher and brought it to Persid. Pouring off some of the water from the kettle, Persid used a dirty rag wrapped around the handle to protect her hand from the heat. She handed the girl a clean rag, shooing her toward the washstand. "The late afternoon air is cooling, but we'll be toasty warm with the fire built up," Persid told her as she closed the door to the cottage. Absent the afternoon sunlight from the doorway, the room darkened considerably. Faith startled at the abrupt change. Persid's eyes had a slight shine to them. "There's a brush on the shelf, next to the washstand you're welcome to use," the woman offered as she measured tea leaves out of a grubby-looking jar.

The washstand stood in front of the only window on this side of the small cottage. Faith could see the forest surrounding Persid's home. She drank in the view, the forest floor carpeted in spring wildflowers. *It must be peaceful to live here,* she thought. Pressing the warm, water-soaked cloth to her face, breathing in the steam, wiping away the dirt. To remove the pine sap, she had to scrub. She drew a sharp breath and jumped, brushing away a spider that had dropped onto her shoulder. Shivering, involuntary goosebumps popped out on her skin.

"Tea's almost ready," Persid called in a singsong voice across the room.

Face and hands washed, Faith moved away from the dirty corner.

"If you'd like to take off your shirt, I'd rinse it out for you and hang it with the other laundry to dry while we have our tea. The breeze will dry it in no time. There's a spare tunic hanging on the peg behind the bedroom door. You can change in there while I finish getting our tea ready, dear," Persid offered.

Faith walked over to the door, reaching for the handle when Persid shouted, "No!"

The sharp rebuke caused the girl to jump back. Persid chuckled with embarrassment, saying, "Not in there, dear. The other room. I know my housekeeping isn't the best, but that space is a mess. I use it for storage. Some would say I'm a bit of a pack rat."

Faith's eyes roamed over the sparse living area and couldn't imagine what Persid thought the term 'pack rat' meant. She shrugged her shoulders, smiled at her benefactress, crossed over to the other door, letting herself in and closing it behind her. The room contained only a straw bed and a cracked mirror hung on the wall. Above it, a tiny window was near the ceiling, framed with crisscrossing wooden slats. The opening emitted a small amount of the fading sunshine. It provided just enough light to see by. Faith couldn't help but notice the glass, covered in spiderwebs and grime. She pulled off her top, a shiver running over her skin as she donned the borrowed tunic from its peg. Closing the door, she handed the soiled material to Persid, who held out her hand, saying, "Here, dear, give it to me. Before I wash it, let me sew up these two tears in the back."

Faith made no comment about her torn shirt. She could always rip out the stitching later to accommodate her wings, but she didn't want to mention them now.

She sat down at the table across from Persid, as the hostess pulled needle and thread from a basket on the floor near the table. "Oh, Persid, you didn't need to do all this," Faith told her, staring at the table.

Persid had set out two small porcelain cups and saucers, with the teapot between them. On her table were a pot of honey, small plates, and butter knives at each place. Off to the side was a chipped vase holding a wilting Jack-in-the-pulpit. She'd placed a bowl of fresh butter and a basket of thick-sliced bread out for her guest.

"Don't tell me you're not hungry, dear?" The woman's plain face and dark, shiny eyes locked on her guest. She nodded to the teapot, asking, "Will you pour for us?" She pulled the material close to her face, biting off the thread from the needle. Persid was quick to tie the loose ends of the thread into a knot, having finished sewing. "Help yourself, Valerie. Share your story with me about how you came to be lost in my woods, while I just wash this out," Persid encouraged.

Faith poured the tea and found it had a sharp aroma, so she added a couple of dollops of honey to her cup. "Put some butter on your bread. No need to skimp; I've plenty. I just baked that loaf this morning. Tell you what, I'll be right back. It'll just take a minute to hang this on the line, dear. Besides, you can't start your story with a mouth full of bread," she laughed good-naturedly as she went outside to the clothesline.

Faith slathered butter onto a thick slice of crusty bread and crammed a bite into her mouth. Nothing had ever tasted so good. She chewed and swallowed, chewed and swallowed. Taking another large bite, her eyes trailed around the kitchen, taking in the details. Aside from the table, chairs, and the small wood stove, the rest of the kitchen comprised a wooden counter with a dry sink. The far end of the countertop featured an enameled washtub with a water pump. There were curtains hung across the front of the counter, reaching to the floor to hide the area under the sink. A small chopping block fitted into the corner, with a sharp cleaver hanging above it on a nail. Utensils poked out of a large ceramic jar on the shelf. There were various mismatched dishes. Bunches of herbs, tied at the stems, hung upside down, tacked to the bottom of the shelf to dry. Two pots, one large and one small, hung on nails near the wood stove above a small stack of wood in a copper bin. A dingy, dark green paint covered the cabin walls. Faith was popping the last bite of her bread into her mouth when the door opened. Persid came back in, closing the door behind her.

"The wind this afternoon carries a chill. I'm ready for my tea!" she exclaimed, rubbing her chafed hands together. "Now then," Persid said as she settled in, taking a sip from her teacup, "help yourself to more, dear; you're so thin."

Faith took another thick slice of bread from the basket and spread a generous pat of butter on it. "Do you live alone, Persid? No husband? No children?" Curious, Faith asked as she wiped the last of the butter from the knife on the crusty edge.

"Oh no, dear. I don't live alone," she smiled. "Ginger lives with me," she said, pointing at the cat. "My husbands have all passed on. Well," she corrected, "except for the one who left me."

Faith blanched. "I'm so sorry to dredge up your grief, Persid. How...how many husbands have you had?" she inquired as she took another bite, creamy butter coating her mouth.

"Oh, not so many, dear. Just five," Persid answered. "Oh my, look at your beautiful, long hair! Why it's all snarled, full of needles and leaves. Let me brush it for you when we've finished our tea, hmmm? Now, tell me how you got lost. Drink your tea before it gets cold, dearie," she said, taking another gulp of her own. "You've hardly touched it yet. It's my special herbal blend," Persid winked at her guest.

Faith took up her teacup, sipping the tincture, trying to keep a grimace from her face at the stringent flavor, barely hidden by the honey she'd doctored it with. Not wanting to appear rude or ungrateful to her host, she took three generous drinks before setting the cup down again. Persid watched her closely.

"You've got a lovely face. I must say, you remind me of someone, but I can't think for all the world who it might be," Persid commented.

Faith blushed, looked down at her lap, taking a moment to consider where she should start her story and how much of it to tell. She stalled by taking another drink of Persid's horrid tea, now tepid, making it fouler, if that was possible. It coated her tongue as she began her story. She left out all the parts about her and Val's wings, as well as Val's sisters being faeries. Faith gave a general background about growing up with her friends, not knowing who her parents were, having been adopted. She described her recent surprise at finding out she had cousins recounting their unexpected arrival. Faith shared with Persid how she, Val (inserting her own name for her best friend's) and Garrett snuck out of the manor. Explaining the unexpected visit from strangers, having no reason to trust them, was the reason she and her friends came up with a plan to find the fabled Dream Weaver. Confessing her hope that the Weaver could tell her what to do and whom she could trust. Somewhere in her telling, careful to keep the story straight, pretending to be Val, Ginger had jumped into her lap. The cat curled up, producing a steady purr that rumbled under Faith's hand as she absently stroked the feline.

"Here, dear," Persid said in a sympathetic voice, "wet your whistle with another cup of tea before you go on," as she poured them both a full cup, draining the pot. Faith cringed inside, careful not to let it show on her face. Persid pushed the honey toward Faith, who stirred in the sticky sweetness, resigned not to hurt her hostess' feelings. Taking a deep draught while picturing the next part of her story, reliving it. Shaking herself, Faith sipped the bitter tea again and told Persid about the goblin raid on their camp. Horror rode across her face as she described the terrifying giant she'd seen driving the goblins on before it. Skin pebbling with goosebumps, her telling recalled those long, razor-sharp teeth, the smell of rot and decay emanating from the creature. She felt quite sick to her stomach. The room tilted. Faith closed her eyes, willing control back to herself. Murmuring about how everyone had gotten split up to get away from the monster. Sharing how the goblins had chased her through the woods until she found herself lost. Persid's hand rested atop hers, offering comfort.

Faith sighed. "I climbed a huge white pine. That's when I saw the smoke rising above the tree canopy that must have come from your wood stove, and well, here I am," she shrugged. "I hope you can give me directions. You've already done so much to help me," she declared, feeling great relief getting the story out and sharing it with someone else. "I'm sorry, Persid, but I don't feel well. I'm a little dizzy and sick to my stomach."

"Nonsense, dear," Persid patted her hand. "You dredged up details of what must have been a traumatic experience. Your memories are causing a sour stomach, that's all. Now, put the cat down and bring a chair over to the washstand, so I can brush the rat's nest of snarls from your lovely hair." Faith was thinking it was just what Nursie used to do when she was little and needed to calm down. A comforting thought, bringing a small smile to her face. She deposited Ginger on the floor, where the cat gave her an insulted look. The tabby raised a paw, licked it a few times and waved her off with a swish of her tail, taking up her perch on the hearth, turning her back to them both.

Faith dragged a chair over to the stand and sat down. Persid took up the brush, starting at the bottom to work out the tangles. She worked at the knots with patience. "So, goblins are coming out in violent gangs again?" the woman stated matter-of-factly. "Not good news. What's more worrying is the giant monster you described. Sounds like it might be a Gugwe from the far north. Do you think it was tracking you?"

Faith winced as a difficult snarl ripped some hair from her scalp, fighting the brush Persid was wielding. "I don't see how. We didn't even know we were coming to the Black Edgewood until a couple of days ago. Besides, I've never even heard of a Gugwe until just a few days ago. I've only seen a goblin a handful of times in my life. Years ago, they used to come to Ostara festivals in the spring. It had to be a coincidence. What could a gugwe want with me or my friends?" she questioned.

"Perhaps those who showed up claiming to be your cousins have something to do with the attack?" Persid suggested.

"Maybe, but I doubt it," Faith told her. "That's why I wanted to consult with the Dream Weaver. They say she can tell you the future, as well as the past. I don't seem to know much about either. You sound like you're familiar with them. Just what is a Gugwe, Persid?"

Faith looked out the dirty window as she sat in front of the washstand, Persid working on her snarls. She could see that the sun was dropping below the treeline. Shining spikes of yellow and deep orange filtered through the tree branches. "Oh," she said, "it's going to be dark soon," her voice worried.

Persid glanced at the colors shimmering through the woods, her dark eyes reflecting the rich palette. Almost finished with the last of the untangling, hands working with the brush, she asked her guest, "Are you feeling better now, dear?" Persid looked into Faith's eyes reflected in the mirror.

"Yes, a little," she yawned, but it felt like she couldn't quite get enough air. Her eyes fluttered. "My stomach hasn't quite settled yet. I think I ate too fast. I'm so tired, Persid," she admitted, holding her hand to her forehead, swaying a bit in the chair.

"That settles it, young lady." Persid told her in a 'Nursie' kind of commanding voice. "The very least I can do is keep you warm and wrapped up here for the night, my dear." Persid wet her finger with saliva and pressed down several flyaway strands along the part in Faith's hair. We'll talk tomorrow about how I can help to find your way out of the Edgewood. Soon it will be nightfall. You can't go on your way now. Not in the dark. I insist you sleep here tonight, warm and dry. I won't take no for an answer. With what you've told me, there are dangerous things in this forest right now.

The young Fae's focus faltered as she looked in the mirror at her caretaker. The girl blinked several times. Persid's face seemed to change in the light and then came back into focus again. A slight shiver went down her spine.

"Oh, you're cold!" Persid exclaimed. The severe-looking woman went to the cookstove and added two small logs. She took an oil lantern down from the kitchen shelf, placed it on the table, removed the glass shade, struck a match, lit the wick, and replaced the shade. Next, Persid moved to the fireplace, repeating the procedure with the lantern on the mantel. Before putting the glass shade on the lit lantern, she took a small stick from her pile of kindling, lighting the end from the lamp wick. Then she touched the twig to the kindling and logs already laid in the fireplace mouth. The firelight cast flickering shadows on the walls. Opening the door to the left, Persid disappeared behind it into the chamber she had referred to as a storage room. Faith struggled to hold herself steady in the chair, dizziness overtaking her. Gripping the seat, her knuckles whitened. She could hear Persid tossing things about in the other room, muttering to herself. After a heavy thud or two, Persid reappeared with a woven straw mat and a moth-eaten wool blanket. She laid both on the floor, pushing the bench back that sat in front of the hearth. Coming to Faith, Persid helped her to the makeshift sleeping place. When the girl was sitting, Persid assisted, pulling off the borrowed tunic, bunching it up for a pillow.

"Sit here, dear, while I go out and get the laundry off the line. Then we'll bundle you in your own clean shirt and settle you in to sleep."

Crossing the room, Persid pulled her cloak from its peg, threw it over her shoulders, and opened the door. She let it slam shut behind her, causing a gust of cool air to push across Faith's exposed skin. Goosebumps popped out across her shoulders and arms. She thought she might be sick right there. Wanting to take her mind off her sour stomach, she stood up and took three quick steps over to the storage room door, hand hovering over the doorknob. The cat watched her from the hearth, tail flicking back and forth. Faith turned back once, looking toward the front door, and then decided. It was a choice that went against all Val's advice for thinking things through...she opened the door to satisfy her curiosity. What she saw made her draw in a sharp breath, and her stomach roiled. The room was filthy, as was everything in it. The floor was littered with broken pieces of furniture, old clothes, and books thrown askew. Along the ceiling, she could see rows of herbs tied in bunches drying, but they were all linked with thousands of cobwebs. It horrified her to see that every corner of the ceiling held masses of spider eggs spun over in silk nests, round and suspended in webs. What was wrong with Persid, allowing all these horrible spiders to live in her spare room? Spiders were among Faith's biggest phobias. The grimy window in the room featured several webbed patterns. She could see all kinds of insects, winged and otherwise, trapped in the window webs. A few exoskeletons were attached, all with the inner bodies sucked dry. Several captives struggled in vain against the sticky hold of the web that held them. She wanted to get away from here and out of this house, but another wave of dizziness crashed through her. Faith heard the crunch of Persid's footsteps approaching from outside. Pulling the door closed, she lay down on the mat again, broke out in a cold sweat, body racked with shivers, not only from the cold.

Persid brought in her laundry basket, setting it on the kitchen table. Removing her cloak, she hung it on a peg. Shaking out Faith's silk shirt, came over to help her slip it on. "There now. You'll warm up in no time." The girl pulled her knees up to her chest, curling up into a fetal position, arms closing around her legs. Persid pulled the musty wool blanket up around her, tucking it in behind where the girl's back faced the door. The older woman snapped her fingers. Ginger came over, snuggled up against

Faith. The feline started kneading its paws against the girl's sore shoulders, purring.

"Now then, a good night's sleep will do wonders for you. I'm just going to do a bit of evening spinning while you drift off. Won't bother you, will it?" She asked without waiting for an answer. "It's so nice to have company. Rest now. Things will look different in the morning, then we'll see what's in store for you."

Persid seated herself next to the fireplace at her spinning wheel. It seemed to Faith that she was hallucinating. She thought Persid was pulling out the hair caught in the brush used on her snarls. The pile of golden strands was almost as big as a skein of yarn in Persid's basket. She let her eyes flutter shut. The gentle whirring of the wheel lulled her into a deep sleep. Ginger's purr keeping time with the spinning wheel, firelight flickering, shadows dancing.

FAITH WOKE WITH A JERK. She panicked as she felt a tickle on her face. Her eyes snapped open, only to find a spider dangling on a web above her forehead. She let out a strangled scream, tried to pull her hand up to swipe the creature away, but found she couldn't move her arms. Eyes opening wider, she could see hundreds of spiders swinging down on long strings of webbing toward her. She struggled to move, her terror of spiders overtaking her senses. Partially raising her head, Faith looked down her body, finding herself wrapped in a thick, sticky, silk cocoon, unable to move. *This must be a bad dream*, she thought. Adrenaline surging, she found she could roll as three spiders landed on her face, heart hammering. In her panic, she hit her head against the bench.

Hands clapped behind her. She heard Persid's voice scolding, "Not now, children! Back to the nest until you are called!" Her hands clapped again. The tiny spiders climbed up their webbed ladders and scurried across the ceiling. Using a small crack between the storage room door and the door frame, they disappeared from Faith's view. She lay shuddering. Concentrating, she tried to force her body into action, but couldn't move a limb, couldn't feel her fingers or toes, much less her legs and arms.

"Persid, help me!" she cried, still confused, thrashing about on the floor. Persid had put the lamps out at night. The fire had burned down to coals, providing a small glow from the last of the embers.

"Of course, dear. I'm just about finished with my night's spinning, then I'll help. Once the spinning has begun, I can't stop until I incorporate the last of the gold into the weave," she informed Faith in a light voice. "You understand. We must see tasks through to the end. It would surprise me to find that you hadn't been raised with the same concept. Ah, there now. What a fine thread your hair has made. I can't wait to see what I can weave it into," she exclaimed. "Can you?"

Faith stilled. Her struggles stopped. She ran Persid's words through her mind. Dizziness swept over her, head spinning. Squeezing her eyes closed, then opening them wide, all the pieces of the puzzle fell into place. "It's you. You're the Dream Weaver," Faith announced, shaken.

"Yes, dear. What a clever girl! So, you've found just what you were looking for, yes?" Persid said with a hiss.

Faith kept her eyes shut, fighting another bout of nausea. She heard Persid climb off the spinning wheel seat, her skein of spun fiber in hand, coming to stand over her captive. When Faith forced herself to open her eyes, they went wide. She gasped, taking in the giant spider straddling her. Persid's shiny black body had a bulbous abdomen marked with two red ovals shaped like an hourglass. Bristles stuck out all along its legs, and two pincer-like appendages were dripping with a substance smelling very much like the tea she'd served earlier.

"You've poisoned me," Faith voiced her realization. "I'm paralyzed," she hissed out. "You dirty bitch!" Faith yelled.

"Now, now," Persid chastised, "and to think we were such good friends just a few short hours ago." The spider waggled its front left leg at Faith. "No need to be rude. You're only partially paralyzed. I wanted to talk with you before I finish the process," she taunted, showing her fangs. "Just guessing, but I don't think you told me the whole truth, dear," beady black eyes glared down at her captive.

Faith's anger flared. "I told you I was looking for the Dream Weaver and why," she hissed. Her legs, still pulled up against her stomach, arms, and hands, lay against her thighs in the same fetal position as when she'd fallen asleep. They felt numb. Faith could just move the fingers under the gauzy, sticky wrapping on her left hand. If only she could reach for the small knife she kept in her boot. Her mind focused on the task as the spider hovered above her. The girl's body didn't move while trying to work some feeling back into her fingers. Stalling for time with the only tactic she could think of, she began asking questions to keep the giant arachnid engaged.

"You're a Black Widow. Hence the five dead husbands," Faith told Persid. Rubbing two fingers together caused sharp, needle-like tingles to erupt from her nerves. The same pain you feel when your appendages 'fall asleep' and you get the blood flowing to them again. She gritted her teeth against feeling nauseous. It passed.

"Only four dead husbands, dear," Persid corrected. "One left me, remember? Doesn't my special blend of tea agree with your system, dearie?" Persid asked in a mocking tone, bringing her head and fangs closer to her captive's face.

Faith wrinkled her nose and spat back, "Your poison, you mean?" Her body became rigid, racked with cramps, a painful groan emanating from deep within. "What do you want from me?" Faith groaned at the arachnid.

"My children are hungry, dear." The spider spat venom as she shook with anger. "But first I want the truth," her eyes glittering. "I think you're more than meets the eye," Persid accused. "What do I want with you?" Persid repeated her hostage's question back to her, raising her back legs to stand on Faith's hips, her face pointing straight at Faith. "You've told stories of goblins and Gugwe, but you're not the human you pretend to be! Fill in the blank spaces you left out!" Persid demanded. "What do you offer me?" the spider asked as she rubbed her silk spinners together, secreting a sticky saliva over a patch on Faith's neck. The spider blended it with her silk, the bristles on her legs rubbing together to spread the mixture. Faith tried to twist her head away, but still couldn't move it.

"Stop!" Faith screamed, but Persid only laughed.

"Alright," Faith told the shape-shifter, "I left out some details in the story!"

Persid stopped spinning the sticky silk, waiting to hear more.

"I'm just coming to terms with it myself." A single tear rolled down her cheek. The spider reached its mouth down, sucked it up, eyes bright.

Faith had her forefinger unnumbed and was working on her thumb. "I...I had wings burst out of my back five days ago, and did not know what was happening to me. All I could think was that I was some kind of freak," she choked out.

"I only just learned I am Fae. A...a faerie." The words rushed out of her, interrupted as severe cramps wracked her body again, the Black Widow's venom coursing through her system. She used the involuntary action to stretch her arm toward her boot, but still couldn't reach the knife she carried.

"I don't believe you," Persid pouted. "I want to see those wings!" she demanded. The long, spindly legs gripped the girl's stricken, trapped body, rolling her hostage over. Then, she used her pincers to cut away the silken binding across Faith's shoulder blades. She poked a sharp mandible between her blades. To Faith's shock, her wings snapped out, unbidden, ripping open the tears in the material Persid had sewn closed earlier on her top. Then the wings snapped right back in, this time at her own angry mental command.

The wings displayed long enough for Persid to see their opalescence shimmer. "Ah," the spider considered, her memory came crashing back. "Now I remember who you remind me of," she spat.

"What? Who are you talking about?" Faith demanded.

The giant black widow moved off her prey. She was still clutching the golden skein she'd spent the evening spinning. Persid paused. "I suspect you remind me of your mother, dear. Aleta Dawn Stargazer," Persid told her captive with relish at the look of panic in the girl's eyes.

"My mother?" Faith exclaimed, "I don't know what you're talking about. I told you I was adopted. If I ever saw my actual mother, I would have been a baby and wouldn't have been able to remember what she looked like. She's dead. I told you, my aunt and uncle raised me. My name...my family name is Pureheart."

"Yes. That is exactly what you said." Persid accused. "Well, whatever your name, the Fae bloodline owes me! Now I finally have an opportunity that will allow me to claim a small piece of my revenge," she informed her hostage, shaking with rage.

"Revenge for what?" Faith swallowed as she asked, fear spiking through her.

"Why," the spider stated, "revenge for the murder of hundreds of my children, of course." Persid announced, "Retribution for turning me into the monster I am!"

"Did...did you kill Aleta Dawn Stargazer?" Faith choked out, fear gripping her heart.

"I wish I had, dear. If that were true, there would be no reason for me to impose my revenge on you, would there? Bloody, sneaking faerie, your mum," Persid spat. "Well, you'll do in her stead. She's dead, you say?" Persid asked as if she were talking about today's weather.

"I don't understand," Faith told the Weaver.

"Before I give you any explanation," the spider said, "since you've told me who you are, I must say I am curious to see what dreams your weave will present, even if you won't be around to realize them."

She jumped back onto her prisoner's body. Without warning, the spider sank its two fangs deep into the girl's neck. Her embrace was intimate, holding the girl against her abdomen as she injected venom. When Persid was done, the spider released her victim, letting her fall to the floor again. The widow sat still until Faith's eyes dulled. The Fae brat twitched twice as the venom coursed through her bloodstream at a full dose.

Colors swirled like a tornado through her mind as Faith's eyes glazed over. Hundreds of sketches she'd drawn over her brief life rippled through her memory like pages flipped through in a book. Snippets of conversations cascaded through her thoughts, but sounded far, far away. A memory of Dedo reprimanding her about an unpicked trillium; Nursie cupping her face, telling her to get hold of herself; Val lecturing to think things through; Garrett stammering 'oh no' when he realized she and Val were going to make him up like a girl for their play; Uncle Robert's kind words as she showed him a pair of princess moths she'd found lying in the grass one day; the Fortress Scholar praising her school work; Estella and Andrew telling her of their escape from a band of goblins; her cousins, all their wings snapping out at once and Brittany saying, 'See, I told you we got here just in time.'; Mariella revealed to her that she was their Faerie princess; and the shadow of her mother's face lifted away from hers as she had kissed her forehead, the only memory she had of Aleta Dawn Stargazer. Last, the horror of the screeching howl the Gugwe let loose before she raced away on her wings deep into the Edgewood Forest.

A heavy darkness took her under.

While these scenes flashed through Faith's memory, Persid busied herself weaving with the skein of golden thread she'd spun from the Fae girl's hair. Hair the spider had salvaged from the brush on the washstand.

KRISTIAN SAT BOLT UPRIGHT from a deep sleep, a soundless scream ripping from him.

Mariella was right there, taking him into her arms, rocking him back and forth, murmuring soothing sounds into his ear. Shushing him, telling him all would be well. His body went limp, and he whimpered.

"Tell me when you're ready," she whispered to him.

He shed silent tears as he came back to himself.

"It's Faith," he shivered. "She's in terrible danger. The Dream Weaver is holding her prisoner and plans to kill her." He shuddered once more, trying to shed the terrible vision.

After they boiled water, had a hot cup of tea and a crust of bread at Mariella's insistence, the siblings saddled their horses and broke camp. Mariella checked twice, making sure their small fire was out before they rode north, the sun rising in the east.

THE FIREPLACE HAD GONE cold, with dead ashes. Faith woke with a blinding headache, still lying on the plaited straw mat. As she came out of her muzzy haze, that her left hand gripped the small knife from her boot, registered. She tightened her grip on the weapon.

The Dream Weaver hovered up in the corner above the storage room door. Her eyes stared at the vast web she had woven across the length of the room, while Faith lay dreaming under the spell of spider poison.

The young Fae found she could raise her head just enough to see the sun shining through the window by the washstand. The rays highlighted the gossamer, opalescent design that hung across the room. Frightened as she was, she had to admit it was beautiful.

Exhausted from the ordeal, still sick with the effects of the venom, she dropped her head back down onto the bunched tunic serving as her pillow. That effort sapped all the strength she'd built up. She could only wonder what came next, trying to think how her hidden knife might help her, though she could not move.

"Persid," she said softly, "I don't know what wrongs you suffered in the past, but I did not come here to inflict more on you. Please," Faith begged, "tell me what I can do to convince you to let me go?"

"Do you wish to know what your future holds?" the arachnid queried. "After all, you said you were seeking a fortune from the Dream Weaver, hmmm? It's all right here before you," she waved her spidery leg, showcasing the sparkling web design.

"I'm told you don't provide weaves for free. What's the price?" Faith ventured.

"Your hair," the spider tells her, "I want all of it. It won't feed my children, but I have a use for it. Considering the exchange for your life, it would be a tiny price to pay," Persid assured her.

"And what of your revenge?" Faith asked. "If I let you cut off my hair, does the fee come with the promise you no longer plan to kill me?" She laughed inwardly at the hope Persid would change her mind about ending her life for a pile of hair.

The Black Widow did not deign to answer. She reached out with her front leg and touched the web. The entire design quivered in response. A tiny insect flew across the room and became caught at the lower end of the dream weave. Faith watched in horror and fascination as the gigantic spider skittered at a speed Faith didn't know was possible. Made its way across her lace creation and punctured the insect with its fangs, injecting it with venom. The spider spun, encasing the prey in its sticky silk after coating it in its saliva.

"Do we have an agreement, princess?" the spider eyed her with distrust.

Faith startled at the word 'princess.' Had she talked in her sleep? "I'm no princess, Persid. I don't know where you came up with the idea. Very well, it's a deal," Faith lied, "but not until you tell me the weave's fortune." She leveled a stare at the evil creature.

"What a talented liar you are! I will give you the weave of the Princess of them all, Valerie Pureheart." She spat the name out as though it had left a nasty taste in her mouth. Persid shape-shifted before her eyes, once more wearing the form of the woman Faith had first spotted coming out of the cottage across the clearing. That woman now sported dark circles under her eyes. Wisps of hair had broken loose from her tight bun. The young girl gripped her hidden knife, but the woman walked to a kitchen chair and sat down, exhausted.

Faith worked her knife back and forth behind her as she listened to the Dream Weaver's voice reveal the woven fortune.

Persid chanted, her eyes glazed over, lost in the telling of the words she'd weaved.

> *"All for one and one for all, leads the Princess of them all.*
>
> *This weave takes in all the races; all their history interlaces. There's no escape; nowhere to hide; hate's been woven in with pride. The races hate and hate and hate. It's you must find a way to soothe, to patch, and to remake before the Gugwe charge through Shara's gate.*
>
> *Behold! A daughter of a queen, a long-awaited princess, heretofore unseen; a princess of the land of Sharas, found just when need falls upon us. Gugwe come to purge the land, to make us slaves; 'tis you must keep us from our graves.*
>
> *This is the foretold prophecy of the princess of the Fae, the Goblins, the Gargoyles and those who live within our woods; all those blessed with magic, both evil and good. It is a weave for all to understand; you'll only find safety, united, under one ruling hand.*
>
> *Listen! Can you hear the sand falling through the hourglass? A clock ticking as eras pass? Your compass points to the northern shore.*

Fear holds you tight within its grasp; but only you can give fear power. Only you can save the hour.

All for one and one for all, leads the Princess of them all.

Heed my words and heed them well. Those few you trust, like coins, have different sides. Eventually, you'll discover all the secrets that they hide. The long-lost secret, when exposed, shall make you weep; our world betrayed by those who hid it deep. The secret knowledge changes everything. Still, you must deal a cruel blow; take a life, claim a death, blood stains your hands, and steals your breath.

The clock will strike to mark the time; that fated hour, so long awaited, will find you filled with all the power you need to win; your mother's song upon the wind. When the clock has made that sound; blindfolds all fall to the ground; all eyes will see; bindings will be loosed, men will be set free, you're more than meets the eye, you see.

All for one and one for all, leads the Princess of them all.

What if you fail? You ask? Worry not. Few will notice; because the Gugwe will have smote us."

Persid let out an exhausted sigh, dragged in a deep breath. Then she turned her beady eyes to Faith's blue. "The fortune says you will not, but I want you to swear to me you won't harm or kill my children if I let you go..."

Faith felt the silk cocoon loosening at her back, sawing at the binding on her legs. Persid got up from the chair, pulled scissors from the ceramic jar above the dry sink, and turned back toward Faith. "Promise you will just leave after I take your payment. Once you are free, promise you won't hurt my children," she demanded.

"Your own weave confirms I won't harm your children," Faith reminded the Weaver. "But I have no qualms in assuring you of that truth. I have no wish to hurt them, Persid," Faith told the shifter honestly.

The woman came toward her, ready to hack off her golden tresses for a payment she felt was too small. A payment not able to quench her hate for the Fae; her hate for the Faerie Queen. She had no love for any but her own kind. The memory of the fire the Fae Queen had started when she tried to get away from Persid years ago made her burn with hatred. The smoke and char brought her previous home to ruin, and she relived her anguish in finding all her children dead in the ash of their nests. She looked again at the gossamer weave; the fortune told and decided to hell with letting this girl survive. To hell with the prophecy. Persid didn't owe anyone anything. It was she who was owed! To hell with the bloody weave's predictions and saving Sharas! She would stab the life out of this Fae and harvest the golden hair all the same.

Persid grabbed a handful of Faith's golden mane, bringing her scissors down, hacking off a chunk. Faith ripped her knees apart from where she had used her knife to slice the binding. The silk shredded apart. Reaching around, grabbing Persid by the neck with her left hand, she plunged her knife into the woman's abdomen with her right. Persid released an anguished screech, drew back her hand, and tried to stab Faith with the scissors. Before she could, the homely woman's body went limp, a gurgle loosed from her lips. She dropped to her knees, her shape shifting back to its spider form, convulsing on the floor.

Faith struggled to finish liberating herself from the sticky silk clinging to parts of her body. Her legs wobbled as she stood for the first time in twenty-four hours. Adrenaline coursed through her as she heard chittering, what sounded like hundreds of skittering legs, moving in the storage room. She grabbed her cloak and pouch belt from the peg by the door, a wave of nausea rolling over her. Flinging the door open to the clearing surrounding the cottage, she heard a last wish pass through Persid's lips: "Avenge me, children!"

The faerie puked to the side of the doorway.

Faith's head came back up as she wiped her mouth with the back of her hand. Looking left, then right, to see which way she should run. Over her shoulder, she could see hundreds of small spiderlings pouring through the crack in the door by the fireplace. A fleeting thought crossed her mind as Persid's children rushed to their mother. Faith turned back, took five strides to the Dream Weaver's web depicting her fortune, and memorized it. Then, waving her hand through the mess, she destroyed the pattern. Sticky silk covered her hand up to her elbow. She bolted from the house towards the woods, panic kicking in.

Just as she reached the edge of the forest surrounding the spider's home, she heard wild chittering following on her heels. Her movements were still jerky, her muscles stiff from the venom paralysis, as well as being trapped in the same position for hours and hours. The toe of her boot caught on a tree root. She flew face-first to the ground. In seconds, before she could get up, hundreds and hundreds of spiderlings raced up from behind, swarmed over her leather leggings, working their way up her torso. Faith felt the spiderlings bite her back, arms, and chest. In a frenzy, she waved her arms and hands, crazed. Panicking, she tried to brush them off. She hated spiders! But the hundreds of small doses of baby Black Widow venom added to their mother's previous doses shut down her system once again. Cheek against the ground, Faith's eyes stared ahead at the beautiful carpet of white trillium gracing the forest floor. Dedo's voice echoed in her memory... "You were about to pick a Trillium when you thought no one else was watching, were you not? Even though we've warned you of the danger."

"I...I," she had stammered. Dedo lifted a finger from his knee and pointed at her. "You. Were. Going. To. Pick. A. Wake. Robin." Her head swam with the memory as the spiderlings swarmed, covering her body.

The last semiconscious effort she managed was watching her arm stretch out. Let her fingers run down the stem of a trillium, just to the sweet spot of picking. Then, she pinched the stem between her forefinger and thumb; the flower came away in her hand. With an effort, she dragged the flower to her heart, the name "Robin" passing through her lips as a whispered prayer before she blacked out.

CHAPTER 14: Wake Robin

R obin clutched his chest, a painful groan escaping his lips. Caz whipped his head around to look at Robin and could see the agony written across his face. "Robin!" Caz shouted in alarm. "What's wrong?"

Cazzidy, Valerie, Rolland, and Saffron all started toward him at the same time. "A Wake Robin," he wheezed out. "She's picked a bloody trillium and called my name." His face turned pale. Lights sparkled at the edge of his vision.

"Who Robin? Who summoned you?" Caz demanded, not even sure Robin could hear him. They were almost to him now. Robin had told him long ago about what he called the trillium curse. Sure that his best friend was about to be transported right under their noses, he broke into a run. Caz didn't think it would matter, but if he could just touch Robin and hold on-maybe, just maybe, his own body would transport along with Robin's. He would have his friend's back, whatever was about to happen.

Robin coughed, stammering, "Faith. Faith has called me." Her name beat through his head like a drum.

Caz dived at Robin, arms extended, just as the Goodfellow vanished. The muscled warrior crashed to the ground, knocking the air from his lungs. He tried to suck in a breath, but he couldn't seem to. Val was behind him in seconds. She wrapped her arms around his chest, pulling him against her, then flipped him onto his back, pushed his chin back, and plugged his nose. She took a deep breath and pressed her mouth against his. Pushing air into his lungs, she came up for breath after breath until Caz's chest heaved. He coughed, gasping in draughts of air.

Saffron and Rolland stood looking on, stunned, her hand clutched in his, squeezing through the tenseness. Cazzidy blinked his eyes, pulled himself up on his elbows, looking around. "He's gone, yeah?" he asked no one in particular.

Val, still on her knees next to him, reached out her hand and put it on his shoulder. "He is gone, but where? I don't understand what just happened? How can I help?"

The Beaumont rubbed a hand over his face. He could smell a hint of honey on the dark-haired girl next to him. Shaking the cobwebs from his head, licking his lips and tasting honey, he pulled himself up to stand, reaching his hand out to this strange lass. She gripped his palm, and he brought her to her feet.

His companions stood staring, waiting for him to explain. Dragging his fingers through his dreadlocks, he told them what he knew. Not enough, that's for sure, he groused to himself. "It's an old wives' tale. You know, folklore, a fairy tale." He cringed, turned a guilty glance at Val. "Sorry, I meant no offence," he said.

"None taken," Val replied, smirking. Boys could be so inconsiderate, she thought to herself.

"Anyway, I know little about it. Robin claims someone put a spell on him when he was a young lad. The old tale said if a maiden picks a trillium, the tale actually refers to the flower as a 'wake-robin,'" he clarified. "Anyway, if she invokes Robin's name when picking the flower, the spell pulls his entire essence to where the maiden is. He's compelled to save her or protect her, or some such. We don't know how long it lasts or how he gets released. He can't remember when or how or even who put this curse on him," Caz finished his explanation. Then, a thought smacked him between the eyes. "Val, didn't you say your friend's name is Faith? I'm positive Faith is the name he said right before he vanished when I crashed into the space he disappeared from. Yes!" he exclaimed, snapping his fingers as the memory became clearer. "I recall I was yelling at him, asking him who summoned him, and he blurted out, 'Faith. Faith called me.'" With expectant looks, three heads turned to stare at Val.

"Yes," Val answered, a little breathless, "Faith is one of my companions. She's like a sister to me. We were together when the Gugwe attacked, and the two of us got separated from the rest of our group. Then, she just went missing after Red rescued me. I've got to find her, my three sisters, and Garrett. But Faith doesn't know anyone named Robin. I'm sure of it. Look, we were on a quest to find the Dream Weaver. I'm confident my sisters would all try to find their way to the Weaver since we got split up. Faith would also try to find the Dream Weaver, as long as those goblins didn't capture or kill her!" she said. Then, with shocked, saucer-wide eyes, she walked back her statement. "Sorry. I didn't mean for it to sound that way. But you have to admit, they seemed crazed with that horrible giant driving them on." She blinked her long eyelashes, looking for forgiveness from the three goblins who stood gawking at her.

"Yeah, well," Caz said, brushing his hands one against the other, "we get it. Don't we, Fron and Rolland?" He turned his chin in their direction. "No harm done. No hard feelings, yeah?" Caz's words were for Val, but his eyes locked on Saffron and Rolland's clasped hands, lingering there. He let his eyes drift up to Fron's. Instead of dropping Rolland's hand, she squeezed it tighter, moved a little closer to the big smith.

Caz released a deep sigh, turning back to Val. "Get your things. Let's all go find the Dream Weaver. See if it leads us to Robin and your friends, yeah?" He gave Val a small smile of encouragement.

CHAPTER 15: Unexpected Alliances

A little over an hour after Kris and Mariella left their camp, Travis and the two hounds were examining the same ground. The dogs moved through the area, sniffing everywhere, excited hind ends wriggling, tails wagging. His brother and sister caught up moments later.

"Our cousins can't be more than an hour ahead," he informed them. "It looks like they left in a hurry. That worries me." He stroked the goatee on his chin, a wide-brimmed hat shading his eyes from the sun.

Brittany had dismounted, walking about, studying the story that could be read from the ground and surroundings. The dogs came to her. She patted them both on their heads, scratched around their ears, as she praised them for their good tracking work. The canines' tracking skills had gained them almost an hour. The only explanation she could think of for the younger cousins going off without the rest of them would be if Kris had some vision that seemed urgent. Both hounds sat at her feet, tails brushing back and forth in the dirt. Glancing over her shoulder, she could see Travis and Shaun stretching their legs. Using covert movements, Brittney pulled a linen napkin out of her pocket. Folding it back, she took out one of the last pieces of bacon she'd spirited from the breakfast table at Aunt Reatha's. Breaking it in half, the hounds gobbled it down.

Travis whistled for the dogs. He wanted to rub Mariella's scarf over their muzzles to remind them of her scent again. He turned to look back at Brittany, puzzled over the dogs remaining at her side. The third time he whistled for them, they ran to him. Travis stared at his sister questioningly. She shrugged her shoulders, suggesting it was a mystery to her why the dogs hadn't responded to Travis's command. After reminding them of the scent he wanted them to seek, the dogs hurried ahead, working north.

ROBIN GOODFELLOW COALESCED at the base of an ancient white pine growing on the very edge where the forest encircled a cabin clearing.

He shook his head, trying to cast out the muddled sensation he had that left him feeling like his brains were underwater.

His eyes spotted a female form, body lying still on the ground just a few feet in front of him. He blinked to be sure he wasn't hallucinating. *Wait*, he thought, *she was moving*.

No, it couldn't be! He came a few steps closer and recognized the girl. He couldn't believe this was the very girl he had been pining over since he had first caught sight of her mushrooming. "Hey! Hey, Faith," he yelled, hoping hearing her name would shake her out of her trance. No response. When he got within inches, he discovered the girl wasn't moving at all, but something *was moving* all over her! "What the?" Robin sucked in a breath.

Taking several steps back toward the white pine, Robin grabbed a hefty dead branch from the ground, needles still intact. He rushed forward, using the branch and its needles to brush away the spiders he could see swarming over the body, working in a frenzy to remove them. A black mass hurried away, heading toward the log cabin in the clearing.

Casting the pine needle broom behind him, he kneeled beside the girl, brushed away a stray spiderling here and there with his rough hands. He picked leaves and sticks out of her hair, then touched everywhere on her body in a gentlemanly way, checking to see if she had any broken limbs or wounds. When he finished his initial injury examination, he put his hand on her forehead and could feel a fever raging under her soft skin. Hundreds of spider bites covered her face, each welt an angry red. Robin cast about, surveying the surrounding grounds, then, reaching his fingers out, plucked up a spider he must have killed when he was sweeping them off their victim. He looked at the arachnid's features: a shiny black body with bristly legs and two large red spots in the shape of an hourglass on the abdomen. Bloody hell, Black Widow, he confirmed to himself, tossing the dead spider over his shoulder.

The Goodfellow bent down, putting his ear to her lips to see if he could hear her breathing. Right in his line of sight, he saw her hand clutching a trillium to her heart. He realized the widow's poison had paralyzed her. Robin looked over at the cottage in the clearing. He knew something bad had happened here. He didn't want to put her in any further danger, so he went to check it out first.

It surprised Robin to find the door standing open. He couldn't hear any movement or see any motion as he stood at the threshold. Robin pushed the door wider. A roving glance allowed him to view the spartan room. Then his eyes settled on the huge black widow with the knife buried to the hilt right in the center of one of the red markings on her abdomen, as if it had hit a bullseye. Yeah. Just like that. There was a pair of scissors on the floor. The Goodfellow made quick work of opening both doors on either side of the fireplace, sticking his head in to check for any other surprises. The room on the left was a junk-filled mess, everything covered in cobwebs. This was where all the spiderlings had retreated to. He closed the door behind him. On second thought, maybe bringing Faith in here was not the best option.

Two long strides brought him to the kitchen area, where he ran a steady eye over the jars on the shelf above the dry sink. Nothing. He pushed the curtains under the sink counter aside and let out a low whistle. Jackpot! Like most poisoners, the spider had a batch of antidote distilling. Poisoners liked to keep an antidote on hand should fortunes change. There may be certain circumstances when the arachnid would need to bring one of its victims back from the brink.

Reaching down, Robin picked up a half-full pint jar and slid another into its place, where it caught the next drop from the still's tube. A hodgepodge of containers littered the floor. He found a lid and screw cap on the drainboard at the sink, putting the cap on the jar to protect the precious antidote from spilling. If he could get her to come back from the brink of the poison's hold, Robin knew it would be best if she didn't wake up where her nightmares had turned real. He grabbed a blanket from the floor and one off the hearth. A cat hissed at him from the corner of the room. On his way out the door, he took the things hanging off the pegs and rushed back out to help the girl who had somehow summoned his soul.

Piling his gathered materials on top of Faith, he pushed the jar deep into his pant pocket and kneeled down to put his arm around her shoulders and under her neck. He used his other arm to gather her under the knees, pulling her against his chest, and rose to a stand. He moved toward the firewood shed. Once there, he discovered a long, low building not visible before, hidden from view behind the woodshed. The ground sloped down, following the course of a small creek. He noted a sliding barn door at the base of the small drop.

Holding fast to his charge, Goodfellow lifted the door latch using his knee. Pushing the slider open revealed a barn full of stale straw. Dust particles floated around like the Milky Way, hanging in the sunlight that filtered through the slats. The building had once served as a shelter for some kind of farm animals, but had long been uninhabited. It had an old, musty smell, but better than the log cabin, he decided. He sensed the clock was ticking and knew he needed to get some antidote down her throat before it was too late.

If it wasn't too late already.

Robin balanced her dead weight against his chest, bringing his knee up to keep his hold on her. Pulling the jar from his pocket, he removed the cap, plugged her nose, and dribbled what he thought would equal two full spoons of the antidote down her throat. She swallowed. He twisted the cap back on the jar.

Two small stalls made up the other side of the barn. He opted to use one of these. Laying her down, Robin rounded the stall wall, found a pitchfork leaning against it, and used the tool to throw off a layer of dirty straw. Next, he spread out the blankets, cloaks, and coats he had confiscated from the spiders' lair. He laid the beautiful lass on the makeshift bed. Well, maybe not so beautiful right this minute. Angry welts covered her face, neck, chest, and shoulders, but he knew beneath those inflictions that she was, in fact, a beauty.

He concentrated all his efforts on the next task, recalling the time he and Caz had seen the procedure. There was a lad who had taken a widow's bite, and they'd gotten him to a healer and stood looking on while he administered an antidote to their mate. Robin needed to dispense small sips of the antidote interspersed with sips of water, but had to be careful he didn't give her too much of the concoction at once. With a gentle hand, he tried to make the lass comfortable. He knew the spider's venom paralyzed her muscles. Robin covered Faith with the remaining wool coat and cloak. Foraging around, he found a long-handled cup hanging on a nail in the opposite corner. Retrieving it, he noticed another door. It looked as if it opened onto a cellar below. He gave a yank on the handle and stepped back in surprise.

A natural spring flowed underneath the door on the floor. He dipped the cup into the water. So, he nodded to himself in satisfaction; this low building was also a springhouse. Delighted with the convenience, he carried the dipper across the floor, spilling only a little. He brought the clear liquid over to Faith and wet her lips and mouth. Then he laid the cup aside and opened the jar of antidote, tipped her head back, plugged her nose and gave her a second dose. She gagged, her body stiff in a rigor mortis imitation. He released the nose pinch when he saw her swallow. He secured the lid and cap on the jar again, setting it aside. Standing, he brushed himself off, went back to the spring door, dipping the cup in twice more to quench his own thirst. He wiped his mouth with the back of his hand and ran his fingers through his thick, twisted hair.

Returning to the log home, Robin rummaged through the kitchen, but found little he would count as suitable food. He sliced the rest of the loaf of bread in the basket on the table. There was a honey pot next to the basket. He grabbed both, along with a quart jar, a bowl, and a linen napkin, and waltzed out, closing the door behind him. As he passed by, he grabbed the woodshed hatchet. Most of his weapons, except the knives he carried on his person, were back with Caz and his horse. Might as well be prepared for surprises, he thought as he tucked the hatchet into his belt.

Back outside, Robin walked along the low building until he came to the creek. He stopped at a young striped maple tree, grabbed two handfuls of leaves, ripping them off the branch. Then he broke off several small twigs to make tea for Faith. Sticking close to the water's edge, he scanned the foliage along the bank. There! He jumped across the small flow of water into a patch of skunk cabbage, one of the first spring flowers. This patch was already producing its large cabbage-like leaves, the ruby-colored, waxy flower gone. He harvested a dozen large leaves from the plant, then took a round, palm-sized rock from the water. Back at the cottage, he fed small kindling into the coals still warm in the woodstove and boiled a kettle of water. Robin noted that in the short time since he had last been in the house, the giant Black Widow's body had been bound in spider silk, cocooned where she lay. He thought it best just to leave her as she was. He noticed a backpack on the floor by the kitchen table and slung it over his shoulder. Wrapping a kitchen rag around the kettle's handle, he went out, closing the door behind him.

Robin filled the quart jar with cold spring water and brought it back to the stall. He nestled in next to Faith, keeping the jar of water, the antidote, the bread, honey, and his weapons close. Once settled, Robin pulled Faith closer, laid her head on his lap, stroking her long hair. He noted an old bucket in the corner. Good. He hoped he would need it later. All he could do now was dose and wait; dose and wait; hoping her body would purge itself of the spider's poison. He vowed to see her through it.

Setting to work on the skunk cabbage leaves, Robin used the bowl and the rock he'd taken from the creek like a mortar and pestle. He began grinding the leaves, beating them, breaking them down with a small amount of water added now and then to make a paste. Happy with the consistency, he kneeled next to Faith and used two fingers to spread the paste all over her face, neck, shoulders, and back. Robin made sure he covered each of the angry red welts the spiderling bites had left across her skin. Skunk cabbage had properties that reduced swelling. The striped maple leaf and twig tea would come later if the antidote worked. Finished, he settled back down, pulled a blanket up over them both, and closed his eyes. Sleep washed over him as the name Faith, Faith, Faith reverberated through his mind like a drumbeat.

The hoot of an owl dragged him from the dregs of sleep. He looked first to the lass, head still resting in his lap, her blanket kicked off and a sheen of sweat along her hairline. She seemed on fire with fever. He thought it was a good sign. Her body was fighting. He dosed her again, followed by water. Robin laid her head on the cloak beneath her.

He rose, stretched his limbs, went to the spring and drank away his thirst. Stale air and dust filled the old building. Moving to the small window by the door, he ran a slow eye, surveying the cottage clearing. From this position, he couldn't see the door of the cottage. The barn sat lower, but nothing was moving. No immediate threats. Dragging his fingers across the top of his head, he loosed a deep breath he didn't realize he was holding, his thoughts random.

Robin felt confident Caz would not give up looking for him. He hoped his friends would find him soon. He trusted Caz with his life. Robin found himself unable to reconcile the fact that he, Caz, Rolland, and Saff had left the clan, much less that they'd set out to consult with the Dream Weaver. How had everything turned upside down over the last few days? Considering the news about Rupert's plan to sabotage the two of them at the Summer Games, coupled with Rupert and Morveena scheming to do away with both him and Caz, he'd be a bloody fool to go back.

To top it all off, making everything that much more bizarre, was Rolland's gift. Robin still couldn't believe both he and Caz now had a Queen's Ransom of weapons. What was he really hoping to gain from a visit to the Dream Weaver? Gods. He raked through his long dreadlocks again. Now he had to worry about a Gugwe here, in the mid-lands! Yeah, and a Gugwe who was driving a gang of lads! He had to do something. Get more information. Investigate north; see what's what. Then he reminded himself that he still had the task of finding his half-sister hanging over his head. Yeah, he had just a few things on his plate at the moment.

Faith interrupted Robin's stream of consciousness by letting out a long, low moan. Robin went to her side and kneeled down. "Are you awake, lass?" he asked. She moaned again, and her body convulsed.

"Well then, lass, it's good. You may not think so until it's over, but your misery is a good sign you're going to live. Don't worry, Faith, I'll be right here. I'll help you get through," he whispered to her.

He refilled the water jars and brought the bucket close by. Taking the steeped maple leaf and twig tea, he filled a cup and brought it over to the poisoned victim. Setting the cooled liquid aside, he tried to be gentle as possible as he wrestled with her body. Her weight was nothing compared to his build, but she was deadweight, limp-limbed. It was like trying to arrange a child's rag doll that weighed ten stone. He held her close between his legs, his knees up for support. Her head against his chest, lying in the crook of his shoulder. He spoke to her in soft tones. "Alright, lass. We just have to get this tea down. It's got an unpleasant flavor, but you need it to rid the rest of the poison out of your system, yeah?" Robin spent the next twenty minutes tipping her head back, cup to her lips. Each time, he looked at the face he'd covered in green paste, plugged her nose and forced her to swallow until the whole cup was gone.

When she'd drunk the last of the tea, he pulled the surrounding blanket, tucking it in here and there. Then, he wrapped his arms around her and rocked her back and forth, humming a peaceful song he remembered from his boyhood, his face buried in her hair. The edge of the window was visible from where he sat, and his eyes reflected the orange glow in the sky as the sun was setting.

About fifteen minutes later, Faith cried out with a painful shudder, her stomach cramping. "I'm here, lass," Robin assured her. "I'll help you through it." Robin grabbed the bucket just in time, guiding Faith above it. He gathered her mass of thick hair, the beaded braids clicking together as violent retching racked her body. She gulped for air, moaning after each involuntary reflex action. Acid burned up her throat. Mumbling soft words of comfort, he kept her hair back from her face, supported her weight, and rocked her between bouts. An hour passed. The compulsory retching began subsiding. That allowed her longer stretches to recuperate before the next fit of the dry heaves took her. Robin used a damp cloth, wiped her mouth, held her head up, and gave her sips of water. Another hour passed, and the nausea abated.

CAZ HAD TO BE CONVINCED to stop when the sun went down and darkness dropped across the forest like a heavy curtain. He felt as though the Edgewood was a living, breathing thing. Somehow, sure it was making them go in circles, he told his companions that the Edgewood was keeping them from finding the Dream Weaver. Saffron declared him cracked, but Rolland looked like he believed Caz, though he wouldn't speak up in opposition to Fron. And Val...well, the lass had a sixth sense. Her dark eyes followed the treeline at the ground, then moved up to the forest's upper story, repeating the pattern again and again. She seemed to talk to herself, but not loud enough that he could make out what she was saying, even with his enhanced hearing ability.

The small group laid out bedrolls in a row, Val using Robin's. Caz and Rolland took the outside spots, with the two lasses lying down between them. Everyone kept their weapons close.

Sleep eluded Caz as he twisted and turned. He planned to be looking for Robin again at first light and couldn't keep his worries at bay. The moon had almost set when he drifted off into a fitful sleep.

MARIELLA AND KRISTIAN dismounted, walking their horses down to a creek. They let the tired animals drink until they quenched their thirst, while filling their own water bags.

"Mariella," Kris said, "I'm sorry. I didn't want to scare you with the vision I had earlier. You would have only been worried about it. But now I need to tell you what I saw."

"I know. It was sweet of you to want to save me anxiety, since there was no changing it. I heard them following us about half an hour ago. They've been on our trail for a while. I figured you must have already seen it coming in a vision because I could tell you knew they were there too, and you didn't seem scared or worried."

"You're the bravest person I know," he told her.

Taking the horses' reins, they led the animals back up from the water's edge. The two siblings stopped in their tracks at the top of the ridge, finding themselves surrounded by a dozen goblins.

TWO HOUNDS TRAMPLED the growth around the creek, tails wagging, baying back and forth to each other. Dogs letting their masters know they had found something.

Travis sprinted up the swell from the creek, Shaun at his heels. They could see Kris and Mariella's tracks where they'd led their horses after watering them. The two brothers looked at each other in surprise, both picking up on the other's prints at the top of the ridge. Brittany came alongside. "Goblin prints," Shaun stated as a fact.

"Sure looks like it," Travis agreed.

"You say that like it's a bad thing," Brittany accused. "Maybe the goblins are helping them. I think you're jumping to stereotypical conclusions," their sister pointed out. "Just because you found goblin tracks intersecting with our cousin's tracks shouldn't automatically make you think they intend harm!" she lectured them. Britt shook her head in disgust. She loathed racism and automatic profiling. That is what she thought was being projected about the goblins at that moment. How she concluded that, with the few words spoken between them, remained a mystery to her two brothers.

"Hey, we said nothing about goblins being bad people," Shaun countered, irritated.

"Just because you don't voice racist remarks and only think them, doesn't absolve you," Brittany snipped as she walked away from them.

"The light's only going to last for another hour. Let's keep going until we can't see the trail. And, Sis," Travis directed to Brittany, "keep your judgements to yourself. We," he pointed around, "we live and let live. I don't think any of us are bigots or racists. So shut it!" Travis turned back to his brother. "Seems Kristian and Mariella have picked up some travel companions—about a dozen goblins. Just another day in paradise," Travis commented.

ROBIN SAT ON A PILE of straw with his back propped against the stall wall. Faith had been sleeping for a couple of hours. He'd cleaned her up, re-wrapped her in the cloaks and blankets and donned his own coat again. When he washed her face, neck, and shoulders with warm water, he removed the poultice he'd put on her, glad to see it had done its job. The welts were all down, the irritated bite marks fading. To kill some time, he sharpened all his knives, as well as the hatchet he'd taken from the wood-splitting stump. Time was wearing on him. He was bored silly. Sitting idle was not one of his strong points. Toying with the thought of going back to the cottage to see if there was something there to keep his mind occupied, he noticed the pack he'd found by the kitchen table.

Moments later, the contents of Faith's backpack lay spread out around him. The rucksack had contained a waterskin, an extra shirt, and some small clothes. Digging deeper, he found a comb, a compass, some rope, and four apples. Well, there were four, but only three remained now. It surprised him to discover a box of pencils, along with several small charcoal pieces. The last item was a bound book, which he held in his hands, slowly turning the pages.

He studied each page in the poor light with a sense of wonder, along with a guilty feeling that he was invading her privacy, yet he couldn't tear himself away. Each sketch came alive off the page in vivid detail. Her artistic talent impressed him. Each piece told him how she saw the world—people, places, things. He decided she could convey her deep connection to nature and the natural world through her eyes and hands.

Robin, startled, looked over to see those deep blue eyes staring straight into his. The girl across from him blinked twice, looked down at her hand to find the crushed trillium stem still tight in her fist. Recognition flashed across her face, and her eyes drifted back up to his. "You came for me," she said in a rough voice.

"Robin Goodfellow at your service." He inclined his head toward her.

She shook her head, struggling to remember. "I can't seem to recall..."

Her voice trailed off, and then, as if a bolt of lightning had shocked her body, her nightmares came alive for her. "Oh my God, Persid! There's a giant spider! Gods and all her children, hundreds, and hundreds of spiderlings!" she shrieked as her last memory caught up with her. She dropped the trillium. A madness came over her, and she started slapping her hands on her arms, shoulders, hair, face, and all about her head. Her mind trapped in the nightmare she had endured. Her body went rigid with the memory, feeling as though spiderlings were crawling all over her again.

Robin put the sketchbook down and went to her. Squatting down behind her, he took her hands in his, wrapping her in his arms as he shushed her and calmed her. "It's all right now. She...Persid, did you call her? She can't hurt you anymore. You put a rather neat knife in the bullseye, so to speak. She's dead. In fact, her children have put her up for the winter larder, I'm afraid. Waste not, want not, yeah?"

Faith turned her head up toward him. He released her and moved away in the blink of an eye, not wanting to frighten her further. In quick motions, he gathered up her things and stuffed them into her pack. He held the pack in one hand, her sketchbook in the other.

"So, you're the type of person who rifles through a girl's pack while she's unconscious after being poisoned? The type that plays with her underwear and has no respect for a person's privacy. I...I...wait!" she screeched. "Are you holding my sketches?" she was incredulous. "Hey! My book is private. Personal. Give. Me. My. Book." Her breath was coming in quick gasps now. He took two steps toward her, placing both the pack and her book in front of her prostrate form.

"I meant nothing by it. Hours of idleness made me curious. There is nothing else to look at in this old building." He stammered, somewhat angry at her reaction. "I thought they were the most talented drawings I've ever seen, by the way. So, I'm not sorry I looked at them because I didn't do it to invade your privacy. Once I got the antidote into your system, your fever broke. Then, we moved on to the maple tree tea. You're weak from puking your insides out for hours. But your body was ridding itself of the poison, and that's when I knew you were going to make it. So, I washed the skunk cabbage poultice off you everywhere I'd applied it while you were visiting la-la land. It worked. The welts and swelling from where the spiderlings had bitten you have gone down. They're fading. You've been asleep for hours now. I found myself bored stiff. You can understand why I poked through your bag, can't you?" he shrugged his shoulders.

Faith gaped at him with an open mouth. "How long?" she asked.

"Two days now," Robin tells her. He crossed his arms and leaned his shoulders against the stall.

"You took care of me through all of that?" she whispered.

"I did," he confirmed.

"Look, I'm sorry," she offered. "It feels like I have large chunks of my memory missing. You've been so kind to me, and I sounded so ungrateful. I..." she winced.

Concerned, Robin prodded, "What's what, lass?"

"Oh, gods, I can't believe I puked for hours in front of a perfect stranger," she hung her head, a hand over her eyes. "What a horrible way for you to meet someone!"

Robin didn't see the need to point out it was the tea he gave her that made her puke for hours. So instead, he offered her a shy smile, saying, "Not such strangers after all. We met mushrooming once." He pointed at her sketches. "I learned a lot about you by looking through your eyes."

She returned his smile. "I guess I learned something about you too," she told him.

"You mean the fact that I rifled through your pack and played with your underwear?" he teased.

Her cheeks colored. "No. No, I learned you're a person who puts himself out there to take care of others with no expectations. I bet you help people all the time just because someone needs it and because it's the right thing to do?" she lifted her long lashes up to look at his handsome, roguish face.

"Well, that sounds nice, but in this case, I kind of had no choice." He pointed at the trillium that had dropped from her hand. The flower was lying on the floor, drooped, limp, and faded.

"I thought it was an old wives' tale. But I wanted it to be true with all my heart when I picked the Wake Robin and called your name. A desperate act that I can't believe worked. But here you are," she said with a little wonder in her voice. "How does it work exactly?" She asked him, raising her eyebrows.

"I don't know myself," he admitted. "The memory is clouded, but I was just a wee boy when someone put the curse on me. In all these years, you're the only one who ever picked the trillium and called my name. I've got to tell you, it was weird. My entire being frizzled out from where I was, then reformed, popping in here where you were," he pointed out towards the woods where he'd found her. "How did you know to pick the trillium?" He asked, filled with curiosity.

Faith sat in serious thought, her forehead crinkled with frown lines. She looked up at Robin, eyes tracing the hard line of his jaw, his full lips, the angle of his nose. Her gaze ended at his serious green eyes. She noted the small gold flecks in his irises catching the light. "I don't know," she answered him. "I mean, I have childhood memories of my caretaker cautioning for years, telling a story over and over while growing up, warning me off picking a wake-robin. A trillium. I don't know why I defied all their years of counsel. Those warnings ran like an echo through my head while the spiderlings were attacking." She took a deep breath, and he offered her a drink of water before she went on. "The fact is, I felt compelled to pick it, as if they had groomed me for the action all those years. It was the last thought I had before I passed out. And here you are. You're not the monster people led me to believe you would be. Frankly," she tilted her head and looked sidelong at him, "you don't seem much different from me," she finished.

"To be fair," Robin tells her, "not all goblins *are* friendly to other races, particularly humans." She started at his remark.

"Are you hungry?" he asked. "I saved some of the bread I found on the table in the cabin. You must be starving after turning your insides out over the last forty-eight hours. You were lucky the spiderlings hadn't developed their venom yet. If they had, you would have been dead before I could give you Persid's antidote," he said.

Faith shivered at the mention of the Dream Weaver's name. "She gave me poisoned tea," she relayed to him as the memory surfaced. "Persid was a shape-shifter who could hold a woman's form. It's how I got tricked into becoming her victim. It seemed like she was just a woman living alone in the woods. I asked her for help because I had gotten lost, separated from my friends," Faith remembered. "Robin, the last handful of days have been a bloody nightmare in my otherwise peaceful, boring life!" she told him with genuine anguish in her voice.

"Why were you and your friends out here in the Edgewood in the first place? Have you never heard of the dark magic of this forest?" he asked.

"We came here so I could find the Dream Weaver. I was hoping she could read my fortune and tell me what I should do. What a naïve fool I was. As if the Dream Weaver would be just like an Ostara Festival fortune teller." She shook her head at the reckless idea and noticed a look of surprise on Robin's face. "What is it?" she whispered.

"Fate has a funny way sometimes," he tells her. "I also came to the Edgewood seeking the Weaver. Maybe we can help each other find our friends, yeah?" His face brightened a little. "We'll look for the Weaver together. I need her insight, her advice," he confessed. "I've got some serious problems to solve for my people."

"Oh, Robin," a shadow of horror passed across her face.

"What's what?" he asked, a serious look on his face.

"Persid," she started, her hands wringing together in worry.

"What about her?" he asked. "I already told you; you don't need to worry about the Widow any longer. She's dead, and her children have wrapped her up in silk to feed on for the winter," he reassured her, took two steps closer and dropped to his knees. He reached over, using his coarse fingertips to lift her chin so he could look into her eyes. But he found only distress there. A question mark settled on the line of his brow.

Those green eyes made her release a bone-deep sigh. "I am so sorry, Robin. It's like I'm responsible for stealing your chance to seek guidance for your own problems," she confessed.

"What do you mean?" he said, confused.

"Persid...Persid was the Dream Weaver," the words flowed out of her, "and I've killed her. There's no one who can help you choose your course now. The last weave she did, she did for me. A weave that left me with more questions than answers and only one solid direction to follow. Nothing but a confusing prophecy. A prophecy that contained no obvious reasons to account for the direction her fortune-telling pointed me to," Faith said with frustration.

Robin stared at her in surprise. "You're not human," he stated. Her eyes flashed. "No human would have been able to kill the Widow without her seeing it before it happened. You must have blocked her sight somehow, which tells me you have some kind of magic. Maybe magic you don't even know how to control yet. Which also gives me an idea to think about. So, are you Fae?" he asked, his voice filled with incredulity as he sat back on his heels, increasing the space between them.

Shakily, she rose, then backed away to lean against the wall for support. "Oh, gods," she worried a silver ring on her finger, turning it round and round. "The Fae and the Goblins. I've always heard they were mortal enemies. Now I've dragged you here against your will and bound you somehow to help me. I swear I knew nothing about the spell put on you," she said, and a great laugh bubbled up from deep inside, and she couldn't hold it down. "Gods! I didn't even know I was a faerie until what? Five or six days ago? My world has been on fire ever since. If I have any magic, I don't have the slightest idea what it is or how to use it." She felt her eyes well up with tears and berated herself. "Oh, yeah, right?" Now she appeared to be talking to herself, rather than to him. "I've, like, beamed Robin Goodfellow's essence to me, puked for hours in front of him as he nursed me back from the brink of that witch's poison and...wait. Did you say you gave me Persid's antidote?" she demanded.

It surprised him to find himself in front of that question. The way she leaped from thought to thought and back again was a little disconcerting.

"Yes," he answered the question. "Poisoners often brew an antidote in case they find a reason to offer it. Usually for their good fortune and definitely not because they've developed sympathy for their victim," he offered.

"I haven't even thanked you for everything you've done for me. I can't tell you how much I appreciate it. You don't have to feel you're bound to do some noble thing when you have issues of your own to resolve! All because someone put a bizarre curse upon you as a child! We have choices!" she assured him. It seemed like she was declaring something about herself too, he thought.

"Would you mind handing me my sketchbook and pencils, please? Drawing sometimes helps me calm down," she smiled shyly.

He met her request. "I have some questions. There are rumors about the Dream Weaver. The usual things, like she's dangerous. But also, that the Weaver asks for crazy types of payment for her services. Still, I've never heard of her trying to kill someone. I won't press for answers just now. You can tell me when you're ready," he assured her, trying to lighten the tension.

"You deserve some explanation, since I've messed things up for you." Faith set about digging her pencils out of her pack. She fussed around arranging the straw to her liking, tucking her cloak around her before opening the book to a fresh page. As her pencil moved over the paper, the words flowed from her mouth.

She shifted from topic to topic, then backtracked like the changing of the seasons. It fascinated him to watch her hands as they worked. Drawing, one moment pressing hard, then switching to lightly rubbing a finger against the lead on the paper, smudging and blending lines. One page filled with memories he couldn't see, denying him the details from where he stood. She flipped the page to start another, told him about strangers showing up where she lived, claiming to be her relatives. That was confusing because she had been told she was an orphan her whole life. The outsiders presented a story about her background she found impossible to believe.

He felt sorry for her when she relayed how embarrassed she was when her Fae wings burst out of her back in front of everyone at their Spring Feast. No one had ever told her about her heritage, so she'd had no warning of what to expect. Admitting that the experience freaked her out, along with what the strangers had suggested, she and her friends sneaked out to find the Dream Weaver for direction. No details were forthcoming about what the mysterious cousins told her, and he didn't press. She skipped anything about Val and her sisters all having wings and didn't want to put Dedo in the narrative. Everything she was saying sounded outlandish, even to her own ears.

He filled her cup with fresh water twice during the telling. She took a deep breath and continued at the point she and Val discovered the horror of the Gugwe driving the band of goblins right at them. Robin snarled at the vision. Her words created a visual for him of how she'd gotten separated from the group. She owned up to the fact that her fear drove her on, thinking the goblins were after her. But the lass confessed that, perhaps; it was a fear of her own making, as the lads never even tried to capture her. And now that she'd had time to reflect on it, she thought it more likely the poor fellows were trying to escape the Gugwe, just as she was. Panic had made her jump to the assumption that they were after her. She surmised that the conclusion was her own fault, panicking after she'd gotten lost, separated from her companions.

It was hard to follow the blow-by-blow description of how she became the spider's captive. Her tale mentioned the Widow hated Faeries, but not the reason the Weaver had attacked, intending to kill her. Her hand moved in a frenzy across the page as she told him the spider had indeed spun a dream weave. The price the spider demanded for the fortune was her hair. The shifter intended to shear her to the skull while trapped in the silk cocoon, but then, before cutting her long mane, attacked instead. Faith didn't reveal a single detail about what the Weaver had predicted.

Her hand came to a stop, pencil stationary on the paper. She rested her hands on the book in her lap. It was as if whatever had driven her to draw had been blown out like a candle's flame when she ran out of words. Blue eyes turned up to meet his, inviting him to ask the questions he had mentioned earlier.

He'd been swirling a stick round and round in a circle on the barn's dirt floor while she had purged some of her memories. It was clear to Robin that there were still holes in her story. Silence enveloped them as he tried to decide which questions he should ask first. His mind landed on, then stayed stuck on the fact that he had some details he thought he should share with her before he started his inquisition. He completed a final circle on the floor and tossed the stick over his shoulder.

"You mentioned one friend with you named Val. I can't tell you about the others, but I can tell you she was alive and well before you brought me here. My friends and I took down the Gugwe that attacked your camp. Val didn't get hurt. It is likely she's still with my mates, looking for us." Robin offered that news and let her absorb it. Hearing it, her relief was visible.

It only seemed fair to provide her with some background, as she'd done him the courtesy. He launched into the story of how his mate, Caz, was on watch. He discovered the Gugwe driving the group of lads toward their camp. Robin and his friends had raced to their aid. She had already flown off before he and Caz reached the camp. He gave credit to Saffron for rescuing Val.

After providing a minimal description of how he'd found himself torn away when she picked the trillium, he confessed he was glad he could offer her at least one bit of comfort about Val. The sun was setting. There was no hurry. Faith was in no condition to travel yet.

She excused herself and left the barn to take care of her personal needs. When she'd closed the door behind her, Robin had lifted the sketchpad to see what all the intense drawing had produced while she had talked.

The last sketch held a complete depiction of the Dream Weaver's fortune as a spider web that appeared to stretch across the room of the

Weaver's cabin. Reading the entire casting, he flipped the book closed, let out a low whistle, and dropped it just before she came back inside.

Robin had some serious thinking to do.

CHAPTER 16: The Lads

Mariella poked at the logs in the fire, waiting for the water in the pot to heat. It came to a rolling boil; she bunched up her tunic, using it to grab the pan's handle, then set the hot pot down on a flat rock. Kris handed her a small, round parcel tied at the top with string. Mariella put the ball into the water, which added color and released an aroma of lavender into their small camp.

Twenty-four black eyes stared at Kris and Mariella as they went through the motions of making tea, but no one spoke. The goblins hadn't said a word since they'd surrounded the siblings back by the creek, but they hadn't tried to harm them either. When they first encircled the Fae siblings, it was obvious two lads within the group had injuries. One unconscious, being carried over the shoulder of another. Kris had offered to put the injured on their horses, willing to walk to help. Two of their companions took the reins and led the horses carrying their wounded. Without comment, the rest crowded around the two siblings, everyone on the move again.

Stopping for the night to rest, they set up a small camp. Mariella came round to each lad, offering hot tea. Kristian went to the two injured goblins and kneeled down next to one. He slid his hands over the lad's frame, looking for broken bones or wounds. Another of the lads jumped up, rushed over, pushing Kristian back. Kris shoved right back at the young goblin, telling him, "I'm only trying to help him!" Turning away, continuing with his triage. Talking out loud to himself, reciting his conclusions, "Two broken ribs, a sprained ankle, multiple contusions on the back of the head. Broken ring finger on right hand, major bruising on the left back shoulder, possible fractured collarbone."

The goblins watched when he moved over to the second lad, but aside from multiple minor cuts and bruises, he could find no major injuries. He rolled the lad onto his stomach and examined the back of the head, finding a large lump at the base of the skull. He turned to the companions and asked, "Has he come awake at all since this injury?" They all traded looks, but gave him no answer. Kristian sighed, frustrated. "Look, I need to know if I am to help him," he pleaded. Silence stretched on.

Mariella stood with an incredulous look on her face and stamped her foot. The group startled. "Stop this foolishness! Can't you see my brother is trying to aid your injured friends?" She bristled with anger. "Tell him what he needs to know," she rounded on each lad and looked them hard in the eyes. "Now!"

One of the younger ones came to his feet and went over to Kristian. He pounded his right fist against his heart, saying, "I am called Lehto."

Kris nodded in acknowledgement. "My name is Kristian. Can you tell me how your friend got hurt? Do you know whether he has regained consciousness since the injury occurred?"

Lehto answered, "He is my brother. His name is Bento. This damage happened to Bento when the Gugwe swung my brother by his left leg and smashed his head into a tree. The Gugwe was venting his anger." Lehto's eyes, filled with worry, came to rest on his brother.

Kristian nodded, swallowing hard. He looked at his sister with a silent question. She nodded back at him; her eyes conveyed the message, 'Be honest'.

"Lehto," Kris looked him in the eyes, "Bento may have a very serious injury. Swelling on his brain. If I don't remove the pressure, he may die."

Lehto nodded his understanding. He turned and looked back at his companions, then again at Kristian. "Can you help him?"

"I don't know. There are no guarantees with something like this. A small incision will need to be made in the swollen area, allowing the fluid causing the pressure to drain out. Sometimes I can see into the future, but I cannot see the outcome for Bento. We can wait through the night to see if he improves before I do anything, but I fear if he has not woken in two days gone, he will not survive without relieving the pressure soon. The other lad's injuries my sister and I can administer to those. He will wake again soon. I know he was awake when you first came upon us, but none of his injuries will heal cleanly unless we tend to them. If you wish me to help, you must grant me permission."

Lehto looked to another lad in the group, who stood and came over. Tears glistened at the corners of his eyes, his voice a husky whisper as he addressed Kris. "I am called Vega. This one," he pointed at the other injured goblin, "this one is called Burda. He is my mate. If you can fix him, I bid you to try. You shall have my gratitude."

Kristian clasped Vega's shoulder and bent down to start his work, calling out to his sister, "I'll need hot water, Mariella, and clean bandages. Oh, and do you think you can find something to make a splint for his broken finger?"

Mariella moved about the small camp to comply with her brother's requests. She had no qualms about giving orders to the other lads to find and bring what she needed. Everyone was involved. Kris removed a wide belt from his waist, where he carried his pouches filled with a variety of healing herbs. Lehto put the palm of his hand against Kristian's chest to get his attention. Kristian looked down at the hand touching him, then up. Lehto's eyes were like ice, hard and unyielding. "After you tend to Burda, you will heal Bento."

Kris stared at Lehto. "I told you, I can only *try* to help Bento. I cannot guarantee Bento will be whole again."

"Bento will be whole," Lehto declared. "Bento will be whole, or your sister's life is forfeit." Lehto threatened.

Mariella walked up behind Lehto and pushed him away from her brother. "Get your hands off my brother! Are you a fool to threaten the one person here who may have the skill to save your sibling?" she asked. "You should be ashamed of yourself! We weren't the ones who caused his injuries, remember? Now, help the others gather wood. If any of you have hunting skills, see if you can bring in some fresh meat for a meal, while we work to help your own," she ordered, leaving no room to argue. Lehto looked down in shame.

The two siblings bent first to attend to Burda. They worked in concert, as they had many times before. Hours passed with the moon overhead while the two patients rested near the fire. The lads circled around, feeling relieved since the immediate danger to their hurt companions had passed. The relief allowed them to find comfort in the crackling fire, their bellies full of rabbit stew. Vega had cooked and served equal shares around. Hopes were high that their friend would recover.

After the meal, Mariella started asking the lads their names. They recited Lehto, Burda, Vega, Bento, Maddo, Perk, Cervil, Drako, Bobbit, Tuck, Weasel, and Zud back to her. She inquired where they were from? Then she presented a question that had been burning bright in her mind since she heard the word spoken, "What in heaven's name is a Gugwe? We've heard they are invaders, but know little about them."

A shadow passed in front of the moon, making the goblin crew shift with discomfort. Vega scraped the last of the stew from the bottom of the pot and licked his fingers. He looked around and decided no one was going to speak of their nightmare. "The lady deserves an answer," Vega stated as he filled the cook-pot with sand and rubbed it round and round to clean the burned bits off.

"Where to start?" Bobbit wondered aloud.

"Always at the beginning," Zud suggested.

Silence deepened, holding the moment in suspension. With a tired sigh, Cervil stood. He recounted the story of how they came to be driven forward in the madness, like a bad dream they couldn't seem to wake from.

Mariella shivered as Cervil described the Gugwe. She took Kris's hand in hers as the stout goblin relayed the tale of their long trip from the north. The Gugwe drove them on and on until it seemed they were almost waking from a long sleep filled with terror, only to find themselves still in the nightmare. Cervil recalled leaving dead companions along the way. He named Murry, Sancho, Tock, Danna, Bello, and Thatch. The Gugwe had killed them in its never-ending rage because their path didn't cross whatever it was looking for. A few others had died when three large greater goblins attacked the Gugwe at the time the group had reached a Faerie's camp. It was there, Cervil recalled, that the monster took the lives of Zip, Cato, Conrad, and Unta. After they escaped and talked about it; they concluded the Beast-man had put them under some kind of powerful mind control. When they reached the Faerie Camp, they didn't know why they found their minds suddenly free of the Gugwe's control. Some greater goblins raced into the camp, and the largest one buried a knife in the Gugwe's eye.

In their shame, he explained, at the abrupt release over their minds, all they could think of was to run. Get away as far and fast as they could. Embarrassed, they never even considered helping the strangers who fought against the monster. Cervil said their disgrace was even greater when they realized they didn't know the names or the clan of the goblins who saved them, and never thanked them. Also, they had not given a single thought to the girls the Gugwe had driven them toward. Their only feeble defense, Cervil claimed, a certain madness had overtaken them all the long days the Gugwe drove them forward. The monster had complete control over their actions. When it no longer had that control, their minds snapped into flight mode, not wanting to come under its control again.

Kris and Mariella asked if they could describe the girls. Cervil rationalized that they didn't notice details. Weeks and weeks traumatized under the Gugwe's power, common sense didn't return. It took them a few days. They still couldn't rid themselves of a ghostly sense of grieving after so many deaths of their companions.

"Wait!" Perk exclaimed, sitting up straighter. "I remember one girl who flew away above us while the 'Greater's' fought the Gugwe! She got separated from her friends when everyone ran helter-skelter to get out of the Gugwe's reach." Perk wrinkled his forehead, thinking hard. "I would estimate she flew above us for at least an hour, maybe two. Rays of sunshine kept coming through the trees now and then, lighting up her golden hair and gossamer wings. I had a vague sense of an angel watching over us. We lost her somewhere along the way. I am sorry, but I remember nothing else." Perk leaned back.

Mariella squeezed her brother's hand. "It may have been Faith," she said, hope blooming in her chest.

A long, low moan came from one lad recovering. Kristian was up in an instant to check on his patients. He found Bento's eyes open, staring up at the star-filled sky. Burda also awoke, eyes blinking like an owl. "How do you feel?" Kris asked.

Lehto pushed Kris out of his way and dropped to his knees. "Bento! You're alive! You're awake!"

Philosophically, Bento tells him, "I think you have to be alive to be awake, Lehto."

"Oh, shut it!" Lehto replied, punching his brother on the shoulder.

Vega had come over to Burda, stood smiling down at his mate; their hands clasped.

"I've woken from a nightmare with a Gugwe, only to find myself looking at an illusion with Faeries," Burda said in wonder. Everyone laughed.

Relieved over their companion's recovery, camaraderie grew as they talked long hours through the night. The goblin clan told the faerie siblings about the terror of the Gugwe attacks in the northern lands. The Fae told the lads they were looking for their cousin. It was possible she might be the same person Cervil described as they were escaping the Gugwe. Mariella also mentioned that they had other cousins who would catch up with them tomorrow.

Drako yawned, suggesting they at least try to get a couple of hours of sleep before sunrise. Bobbit and Zud offered to keep watch. Kris's eyes were already closed, his head on his sister's shoulder. Mariella pulled a blanket around them, laid her own head back to rest against the rock she leaned on.

THE SUN'S RAYS BURST over the horizon too early for everyone in the small camp. They woke to find the fire tended and water boiling for morning tea.

From a small bluff across a vale, Travis tried to make heads or tails of the scene he viewed through his spyglass. "This makes no sense," he told Shaun.

"Can you be more specific?" Shaun retorted, "Let's quit wasting time and get down there to rescue our cousins." He kicked his brother to encourage action.

"That is my point, bro." Travis's words dripped with sarcasm. "Our cousins don't look like they need rescuing."

"Let me see." Brittany grabbed the spyglass from her brother and put it to her eye. "I told you goblins are not all bad." She mounted her horse, started down the ridge toward the goblin camp, with Shaun right behind her. The two siblings pushed their horses into a canter. They came rushing into the camp, surprised when all the lads jumped to their feet, pulling weapons.

"Good morning, cuz!" Brittany called to Mariella. "Please introduce us to your new friends," she requested, dismounting.

"What's for breakfast?" Shaun asked. "Travis was in a hurry to follow your trail. He wouldn't allow us to take time to eat."

Shaun looked around at the baffled faces of the goblin band. "Oh, good morning. My name's Shaun."

Half the lads put their weapons away, but Lehto, Vega, Tuck, Weasel, and Zud kept theirs in hand, anxiety building as Travis rode into camp.

Travis eyed the group with suspicion. Brittany tied off her horse, jumped down, and crossed over to Mariella and Kristian, the dogs at her heels. Grabbing Mariella, Brittany hugged her. "Thank the stars you're both alright. We were so worried." Releasing Mariella, she repeated her gesture with Kristian, pulling him into a bear hug. "You two have some explaining to do."

"The three of you made it just in time for breakfast," Kris said as he disentangled himself from his cousin's embrace. "There's plenty to go around. We've been expecting you." He smiled around at the newcomers.

Brittany smirked. "Of course you were."

Mariella had moved to the other side of the fire and touched Lehto's shoulder. "Peace, Lehto. They'll not harm anyone. These are the cousins I told you about last night."

Lehto nodded at his new friend, trusting. He sheathed his weapon, waved his hand, instructing the other lads to follow suit.

Kristian pointed out each of his cousins, naming them. Reversing course to introduce Lehto, Burda (who could now push up onto an elbow from where he lay), Vega, Bento, Drako, Bobbit, Tuck, Weasel, and Zud. He beamed with pleasure, remembering all their names.

Weasel went at once to Brittany and the dogs. "I've always wanted a dog," he told her, reaching out a tentative hand to touch one of them.

"Let him smell your hand first," she cautioned him. There was wonder in Weasel's eyes after the dog checked his scent and pushed its head under the young goblin's hand, its hind end wagging the tail.

Mariella asked Shaun to get the bag of cooking tools from his horse. Cervil, Zud, and Perk helped her move the big pot of porridge over to a tree stump they used as a makeshift table.

Shaun delivered the burlap bag of kitchen goods. His younger cousin began rummaging through. Perk hovered over her shoulder. She stuffed her head into the big burlap bag and began handing out wooden bowls to Perk. "We'll have to share," she mumbled. Pushing further into the sack, she exclaimed, "Oh!" her voice cheerful. She backed out of the burlap, her hair all askew, cheeks pink, eyes twinkling.

"What'd you find, miss?" Perk asked, his hands juggling the ten bowls and holding them against his chest, using his chin to hold down the topmost.

"Perk, it's our lucky day," Mariella winked at him, holding a bag in each hand. "There are raisins *and* brown sugar to go with our porridge."

Weasel's eyes grew wide as he stroked both dogs. He took a bite of the last piece of jerky he'd been holding off his morning hunger with. Without thinking, broke the jerky in half, offering a taste to each dog, who sat and...oh...so...gently, took the treat from Weasel's fingers. The hounds leaned into Weasel's body, drool escaping from their jowls. Weasel couldn't remember ever being so happy.

When everyone had had porridge, Cervil came, collected the cook-pot, and again filled it with sand to scrub it. Shaun joined him, using the same method to clean the bowls. Travis and Brittany tended to the horses, as Maddo and Tuck looked on, watching them unsaddle the mounts, then rub each horse down. They hobbled the animals to pasture in a grassy patch so they could rest and graze.

Travis and Brittany made the rounds, asking each of the goblin lads where they were from and about their families. Travis wanted to know what it was like living underground. Easy banter went on throughout the camp, everyone taking their measure of the others. Mariella offered hot tea. She'd found another four cups in the cook's bag. The sun rose overhead.

It was Kristian who broke the rhythm of the interaction when he stood on a tree stump. He cleared his throat but failed to get anyone's attention. Brittany noticed, put her fingers to her tongue, and let loose a shrill whistle, making both dogs jump up and come to her, causing the crowd to laugh.

"Kristian wants to tell us something," she announced as she bid both hounds sit. She hunkered down between them with an arm around both, but tilted her head at Weasel, inviting him to come sit by her and the dogs. Without hesitation, Weasel settled down next to one dog and rubbed behind its ears. Both the dog and the goblin boy were in their own kind of heaven.

Not wanting to miss his chance at the lull his cousin had created for him, Kris blurted out, "The lads have a story you need to hear, and I had a vision I need to tell all of you about."

The sun shimmered, moving across the blue sky. Two hours flew by. The lads retold their account of the Gugwe raids in the north, their harrowing trip south under the mind control of a Beast-Man. They wound the story up, describing their escape and how Mariella and Kris had helped their injured mates.

Lehto told the Fae cousins his cohort intended to go north to see if they could find family and friends, to determine what they had left of their clan. They planned to locate other clans along the way, checking in on them.

Shaun spoke on behalf of his Fae cousins and siblings, telling of their own journey to find their long-lost cousin Faith. He expounded on their need to find Faith, thinking she could unite the scattered Fae again to stop the Gugwe from killing off their people or making them into slaves. Both their races now had a common enemy.

Travis winked at Kris, as if he were already in the know. "Come on then, cuz, tell us what vision you saw. It must involve everyone here, or you wouldn't be sharing, right?"

Kris smiled at him, gesturing with his hand in an arc to include the entire group. "Travis is right. The vision I had involved everyone here. Everything is not always crystal clear when I see things. A thousand unknown events or details can change the outcome of a vision in the snap of your fingers."

Drako and Maddo started snapping their fingers to a rhythmic beat. Shaun added a light two-handed drumming on the hollow log he straddled, while Kris laid out one potential future. A future that may come to be. Or not. They would see.

His voice kept in cadence with the background beat. The vision he shared came out in a melodic picture of words. Speech carried a visual to each person in the small company as he painted the Gugwe race in their lands of ice, snow, and tundra; described flooding that was forcing them to resettle their villages further south. His hands moved in symmetry, as though he pushed the images out to each of them, illustrating the Gugwe, destroying both Goblin and Fae alike, as well as humans and other races living in Sharas. The spectacle he shared involved killing, burning, and rounding up women and children to serve as slaves. Slaves sent in chains to the mines, existence pared down to providing their captors with iron ore, gold, silver, copper, and mica. The Gugwe would work their slaves to death, making them suffer from starvation. They would treat their captives as nothing more than pack animals. Forced to live in the harshest conditions.

Kris caused the vision to enlarge, revealing an army led by the Gugwe Emperor across the tundra. There was a mist blocking the image of the entire Gugwe might, but the audience could make out a force large enough to crush all three races.

Shifting the visualization of his audience to a Faerie. He allowed them to see her gathering people; people who would come from every village, every city, mountain, lake, stream, and forest, joining to fight for their freedom; their lands; their homes and families; fighting to preserve their culture and ways of life. Each of the listeners realized the pilgrimage to join the Faerie was not just for the Fae, but included goblins and men by the thousands. The sun was setting. Kris's voice faded away, taking the vision with it.

Shaking his head to clear the cobwebs, Bobbit asked, "Master Kris, you're saying the Gobs and the Fae are going to join forces to fight the Gugwe? That so?"

"My vision is only one probable outcome, Bobbit."

"Well, laddie," Bobbit told Kris, "it would be a fine thing to see, but the reality is decades have held us at odds. I have to say," he looked around at all the Faerie cousins, "I like you a lot. Guess we could learn a thing or two from each other if we travel together for a while. Now you know where I stand. What about you, Lehto?" Bobbit pressed. He figured the rest would fall in if Lehto agreed.

Lehto took his time looking deep into the eyes of each of his comrades. The group of lads nodded once. "Well, Bobbit," Lehto stood, pulling up the pants at his waist, licking his lips. "Not sure how other Gobs will respond with all the hate stacked up like a rock wall between the races. Especially when they see us all friendly, traveling with this faerie lot. Could be trouble, and we've all had a bigger dish of trouble than we could eat of late." The camp held its collective breath. Lehto turned around in a circle. "But chance and change come to those who take them. I'm a believer in choosing my road. I don't hold with hanging on to others' past hate for the sake of piling more hate on the scales. So, we'll commit to traveling as far north as the Copper Peninsula. Then we'll see what's what." Lehto turned back to the cousins. "Too bad," he informed them. "The tradition, when forming a new company, is to drink a toast to our success as we make oaths to one another. Much as I appreciate Lady Mariella's tea, it just doesn't fit the bill. Our word will bind us all the same." Lehto's rough face split into a grin as he offered his hand to shake with Kristian.

"Wait, Lehto," Travis called out. The leader of the small group turned to face him. Travis said, "I think we can follow your tradition." He wiggled his flask, catching the last of the orange and pink sunset rays glancing off the silver flask as he tossed it to Lehto. A cheer when up as they passed the flagon round, exchanging oaths. Kristian imparted a private, silent thanks. When the flask was passed to him, he found his sister had her back turned, so he snuck a swig.

Tonight, they would celebrate. Making a plan could wait until tomorrow.

CHAPTER 17: A Stone House in the Vale

Caz startled awake at the sound of soft sobbing, raising the hair on his neck. Thick fog covered the ground; the air above was a haze of wispy mist, billowing in and out through the trees. He could hear Roland snoring, but couldn't see him six feet away. The crying continued. Cazzidy reached to his right to see if Val was awake, but his hand touched an empty bedroll. He scrambled out of his own bedding to reach further for Saffron, only to find her blankets empty as well.

Cazzidy fumbled for his pack, then began arming himself with every weapon he could carry that wouldn't hamper his ability to move. He toed Rolland with his boot and called his name in a harsh whisper. Rolland came awake, shot up to a full standing position with his knife drawn. Caz couldn't know, but Rolland did not have a pleasant history of being awakened from a sound sleep.

"Easy now, laddie," Caz whispered, "it's only me."

"What's what?" Rolland grumbled. Rubbing the sleep from his eyes, he cocked his head. "Wait. Do I hear crying?" he asked with alarm. "Saffron! Saffron!" Rolland hissed, hands falling on her empty bedroll.

"Quiet," Caz spoke into Rolland's ear, "Arm yourself with all the weapons you can carry and still be able to move freely. Both girls are missing. I'll stash all our stuff under the huge white pine behind the boulder. We can come back for it after we find the girls."

"I have only my long knife," Rolland told Caz in a hush.

"Robin's pack is next to Val's. Take any of his weapons. You know those weapons better than anyone, yeah?" Caz couldn't see Rolland nod in acknowledgement, but felt him move away. Moments later, the big goblin was back at Caz's side.

"Stick close, or we'll lose each other in this damnable mist," Caz swore. Their feet moved with care toward the sobbing.

The ground fog assaulted their senses and did strange things to sound, making it seem the weeping came from all directions. Caz and Rolland stopped, turned full circle, senses heightened. "This way," they said simultaneously, but moved in opposite directions.

"What the..." Rolland breathed out, breath catching in his throat when he heard Saffron's muffled voice call his name. It seemed to him her voice drifted across the mist through the forest. "Caz, Saffron was calling. Did you hear?"

"I heard," Caz answered as he turned again in a circle, squinting his eyes, trying to see through the patchy vapor.

"Caz! Caz! Where are you? Rolland? Saffron? Where..." Val's voice cut short. Caz heard a heavy thump, like a body falling.

Splitting up happened naturally. Caz ran through the haze, his body threading around and between the trees and branches like a professional dancer, his sixth sense honed in on Val's voice. "Caz! Where are you?" she cried.

He was preternaturally fast for a man of his girth. Rolland moved with surprising grace in the opposite direction. His entire soul stretched out to retrieve the person he loved most in the world. Chasing the tremor in her voice as she called for him, "Rolland! Rolland! I'm lost. I need to find my way back to you. Rolland!" Rolland advanced through the woods, but never seemed to get closer to Saffron's voice.

The sun was rising; burning the mist off. Caz moved with caution now. Skin chafed, clothes wet from absorbing the moisture as he pushed through the morning mist. The dew on the ground cover had soaked his boots through. As the last of the haze dissipated, Caz pulled up short, aligned his body with a tree trunk and held still. Moving only his head, eyeing the land in front of him, he could see a clearing far below in a deep valley. There was a small stone house, a barn, and a burbling, rocky creek lined on both sides with cedar trees. He could make out neat rows of crops and a well laid-out orchard. The homestead featured a woodshed, a well-housing with a green roof, a bucket hanging at the ready, reminding Caz of his terrible thirst. He'd loaded himself with weapons, but in his rush, had not thought to grab his canteen. He swallowed his stale spit, watching the homestead, taking in every detail. The Beaumont was sure Val was down there, maybe Saff. Across from his location, the sunlight drifted into the valley, causing dappled sparkles on the flowing stream. Catching the shimmer of sunlight on metal, it winked at him from across the gully on the other side of the ridge where he watched. Squatting at the base of the tree trunk, he waited. Counting to ten, he stuck his head out from behind the tree just enough to look again, sure whoever carried that metal had not seen him.

He focused his vision in, then back out, moving his eyes to take in small sections. Then, repeating the action: focus in, back out, slight move. Focus in, back out, scan forward, in, back...wait. Yes, there was movement. For mere seconds, he saw the body between the trees, letting the breath go he'd been holding in a slow exhale of relief. It was Rolland. Caz pulled himself up and began moving toward his friend. He crossed the top of the ridge; keeping the house below just at the edge of his peripheral view. When Caz judged himself to be about two hundred yards from Rolland, he stopped, straddled a log, and sat to wait.

Moments later, Rolland came up from behind him, tapping him on the shoulder. Caz sprang into the air, drawing two weapons before landing like a cat, eyes fierce. "What the..." Caz shook his head. "How'd you get behind me? I didn't even hear you. Hey! You were coming from the opposite direction," Caz pointed the way he'd been facing.

Rolland looked in the direction Caz had pointed. "Yeah, but sometimes when you go up hills, down vales and across ridges, the woods make you follow the land's contour. You don't walk in a straight line. Especially in this forest," Rolland said the last bit to himself and looked around with suspicion at the Edgewood.

"You realize we've been led here, yeah?" Caz looked at Rolland, arching his brow.

"I figured. I'm worried about the girls. This is where Saffron's voice guided me. Now she's gone silent." Rolland leaned against a tree and heaved a deep sigh.

"Same for me, mate," Caz nodded toward the stone house in the deep vale below. "I've followed Val's voice and the eerie weeping all the way here. Look! Smoke is coming out of the house's chimney. There wasn't before."

They both dropped to the ground and belly-crawled to the ridge rim. Looking out through a veil of tall grasses, they saw a black cat moving with purpose across the yard to the covered porch attached to the stone house. The feline scampered up the steps onto the porch, where they couldn't see it anymore. A moment later, they heard the door open and close, followed by quiet again. Rolland and Caz could hear their own hearts hammering against their chests. Out of the silence grew the sound that tortured them both. The sobbing. Wretched, sad weeping had started again.

Exchanging a look, the two young men stood, bumped fists, and slammed a right-handed fist to their hearts. "Let's go find the girls, yeah?" Caz urged.

"I'm with you," Rolland responded.

Moving fast, working their way down to the stone house, Caz saw the door open. A small, muscular man stepped out, a well-worn quarterstaff in hand. He planted one end on the ground, leaned against the oak staff, jutting his chin out as the two young men approached the house. He spat. "Who are you?" he called out to them from the bottom step of the porch. "Seemed to me like you were coming down to my home aggressively, hey?"

Caz took in the man's stance, the quarterstaff, his oily black hair pulled tight into a tail, fixed with a leather cord. Looked to be in his early twenties. The man's eyes shifted back and forth between the two intruders. He exuded a dangerous aura. "I'll ask again. Who are you? What brings you to my home?" the man demanded.

Rolland stepped forward. "My name is Rolland, sir. This is Caz." He pointed his thumb back at his companion. The Touchstone had schooled his face to a blank calm, instead of the unbridled rage Rolland had seen there a moment before stepping in front of his companion.

Caz side-stepped Rolland, calling on his charm. "Look here, manno, we got off on the wrong foot, yeah? Truth be told, me and my boyo here were traveling with two girls and ah...ah..." Caz stammered.

"Right, two girls. Saffron and Val," Rolland filled in. "We thought maybe you'd seen them or maybe they'd come...uh...here?"

"So, you lost the two girls you were traveling with? Sums it up, hey? Now you're asking me if I'd noticed two lost girls in the Edgewood? Oh, and by chance," he tipped his head sideways, squinting his eyes, "you wondered if they'd found their way here to my home and hearth?" He shifted the quarterstaff to his other hand, leaned to the side, eyes dark and shiny in the dappled sunlight filtering through the trees. He waited for a response. When he got none, a frown crossed his face and his voice lowered, with a drop of menace mixed in. "What brought you to the Edgewood Forest?"

"The truth is, we came here seeking the Dream Weaver, sir. We lost the girls. I know it sounds all messed up. But, is there any way you could help us?" Rolland averted his eyes to the ground when he finished, as he always did when asked for help.

Caz looked from one man to the other, then, of a sudden, the stranger's face crumpled into laughter he couldn't seem to contain. Laughter bubbled out of him. He slapped his knee, shook his head, tears streaming down his cheeks. "Ha!" he shouted. "Ha! I knew it when I saw a rainbow this morning, just after the mist cleared and the sun came out! Ha!"

Rolland's eyes were round as saucers. "Knew what, sir?"

The man took four quick strides, coming nose to nose and eye to eye with Rolland. "Are you pulling my leg, son?"

"No, sir," Rolland shrunk back. A memory of his Uncle Narrol's face fizzed at the edges of his mind.

The man backed off. "Oh, sorry, son, no need to feel threatened. You two have all the weapons, hey? Anyway, my name's Arnid. Ari for short." His shoulders still shook with laughter.

"What's what, manno?" Caz's patience stretched almost to snapping.

Ari collected himself, stood up straight, his face flushed, and announced, "Well, I'm pleased to solve one problem for you!" he informed the boys. "Welcome to my humble home. I'm the one they call 'The Dream Weaver'. The person you said you were seeking." The man reached out with his left hand and pushed up under Rolland's chin to close his gaping maw. "First, let's get you lads a mug. You look as if you're overheated. I've got a fresh batch of ale ready, and you both look parched. There's a well near the woodshed. Wash the dust off. I'll fix us a round."

"I have questions," Caz stated.

"Yes," he said as he turned back around to address Caz, "that's why people seek the Dream Weaver, hey?" Ari chuckled. "We'll wet your whistle so you can ask as many as you like, hey?"

Ari winked at Caz, headed up the steps to the stone house, calling over his shoulder, "After you've washed up, come back to the porch. Then we'll see what we can do about finding your girls, hey?"

"You stay here, Rolland. I'm going to backtrack, collect our gear, and stow it on top of the ridge. I won't be long."

CAZ WAS BACK IN LESS than a quarter of an hour. He found Rolland by the well-house.

"This is strange," Rolland tells Caz in a quiet voice.

"Man gives me the creeps, yeah?" Caz responded.

Rolland lowered the bucket into the well, felt it hit the water, and began turning the crank to bring it back up. He took a tentative drink of water cupped in his hands. Deciding it tasted fine, he began scooping handfuls into his mouth, quenching his initial thirst. Next, he splashed water over his face, then upended the last of the water in the pail over his head. Shaking his hair like a dog, spraying his companion with wet drops. Lowering the container down to the water, he moved out of the way so Caz could take a turn.

When they were both refreshed, Rolland turned to see the black cat looking at them from the porch. The feline jumped down the porch steps, moving toward them. Caz grabbed Rolland by the arm. "Wait." He looked around cautiously, keeping his voice low. "Be on your guard, Manno. I don't like the feeling I've got about the Dream Weaver. I'm worried about the girls; we have seen no signs of them here. This is where we followed their voices. Now we don't hear any crying or anything? Something's not right. I can feel it in my gut. Robin's always harping on trusting your gut feelings, your sixth sense, yeah?"

Rolland grunted in response. They walked back toward the porch at the back of the stone house with a sense that they were being watched. Rolland bent down to stroke the black cat, but it bounded away, disappearing into the porch entryway. They followed.

The veranda held a table and four chairs. Ari had laid out a tray with a pitcher of ale, three mugs, along with a loaf of bread and a large wedge of cheese. He came bustling out of the house, inviting his company to sit as he poured mugs full to the brim. He waved his hand over the food, gesturing that they should help themselves.

They thanked their host and bolted down two pieces of bread, topped with thick slices of the sharp cheese. Ari was quick to top their mugs off for a second round as he asked, "Now, mates, if you're feeling better, mayhap you can tell me why you seek the services of a Dream Weaver, hey?"

Rolland shrugged, which Caz interpreted to mean Rolland wanted Caz to do the talking.

"The Edgewood is a strange forest, Ari."

"You'll get no argument from me on that, lad," Ari agreed, but offered no more on the subject. He took a sip from his mug, waiting for Caz to continue.

"One of our friends was traveling to the Edgewood to find the Dream Weaver." Caz hesitated. Ari said nothing; Caz continued. "Tall, muscular lad named Robin," he prompted.

"I can't say I've met anyone matching his description," Ari commented.

"Well, we got separated in the woods, hoping that if we found the Dream Weaver, we'd find him, since he was making his way here."

"As you can see," Ari says, picking a piece of lint off his black wool coat, "he's not here."

"Then I would venture to say that puts us in need of your services. Can you help us locate the girls and our friend, Robin?" Caz asked in a neutral voice.

"Of course. Of course," Ari chuckled, "at your service, hey?"

Both young men's faces broke out with wide smiles. "What a relief," Rolland said under his breath.

"So, how do we go about this?" Caz asked.

"First, we must agree on the price of my services, hey?" Ari laughed. "You two seem to have a knack for losing your friends in the forest!" He winked at Caz, pouring the last of the ale in the pitcher between their mugs.

"What kind of price are we talking about?" Caz asked with suspicion. The ground tilted under his feet. He blinked his eyes, rubbing his temples to regain his balance.

"I don't feel so good, Caz," Rolland told him with a thick tongue.

"Something wrong, lads?" Ari's face creased with concern.

Caz tried to stand, bumped against the table, sloshing the last of the ale in his mug across the wooden surface. "Hey now, laddie," Ari reached out to steady him. "Maybe you boys should come into the house and gather your wits before we start negotiations. It seems to me you're overwrought about your missing friends, hey?"

They heard the door open, but their eyesight was blurry. They saw only a flash of the black cat's tail disappear through the doorway.

"Caz," Rolland says, his tongue thick, "I don't think we should..."

Just then, they heard a muffled scream from inside. Saffron called Rolland's name. Val screamed, "Get away from me!"

Adrenaline shot through Caz and Rolland's bodies, overriding their maladies. The two lads burst through the door. Momentum caused them to run right smack into the biggest spiderweb they'd ever seen. The two muscled goblins struggled against the sticky silk snare, but couldn't break loose. Dizziness swept over their systems, limbs taking on a stillness they couldn't fight. Behind them, an enormous spider hummed a soft song as it worked at a furious pace, spewing out webbing across the boy's legs and arms. Not long after, they found their entire bodies encased in a tight net, making it impossible for them to move.

Just before Caz passed out, he caught sight of Saffron and Val. Both girls appeared wrapped in cocoons on another part of the same web that trapped him. Rolland puked down his front. The girl's soft sobbing carried him deep down into the darkness of his subconscious.

"I'M STARVING, LAINEY," Carlisse whined to her sister.

Delainey rolled her eyes for the hundredth time in the last half hour.

"Well, I am!" Carlisse reiterated. "Hungry. Cold. Tired. You might as well add angry to the list!" She stamped her foot, refusing to take another step.

Delainey stroked her sister's back between her shoulder blades. "I know, sweetie. We'll just go on for another hour or two..."

Carlisse moaned, "You've said the same thing every hour for the last four." Her lips quivered.

Delainey hugged her sister. "Let's ride the horses for a little then, so you can rest up. I'll tell you another story," she offered.

"The story thing will not work this time." Carlisse said as Delainey saw a series of subtle changes take over her sister's body. Delainey recognized Carlisse's body language as stubbornness, a trait her sibling sometimes adopted. Experience told her nothing could reverse the girl's inflexibility once it settled in. "The horses are tired too," she whined on their behalf. "It's going to be dark again soon. I'm desperate to find a place to sleep. We haven't slept in two days, and it's making me slap-happy," she complained. "Please, Lainey. I can't go on anymore without some shuteye." A solitary tear leaked from the corner of Carlisse's eye, making a track down her dirt-streaked cheek.

Delainey took notice because Carlisse hated to cry. "Okay, okay. I'm tired too. We should at least climb the hill in front of us and see if we can find some shelter where we can rest. We don't want to just camp out in this open field."

Carlisse looked at her sister with dubiety, but Delainey added, "I promise. Just to the top of the hill." Carlisse took Delainey's hand, started forward, because Lainey always kept a promise if she gave one.

They crested the top of the ridge; the horses nickered. Dropping behind a hill, the sun still blazed across the treetops, a brilliant pink against the slate-gray sky.

"Look," Carlisse pointed at a small grove of trees with a grassy undergrowth. Standing at the very back was an ancient white pine.

"Perfect," Delainey squeezed Carlisse's hand. They moved toward it with a last surge of energy.

Hobbling the horses so they could graze, Delainey grabbed their bedrolls. Carlisse climbed the branches of the white pine ahead of her sister. She found a nice, wide limb, sat with her back against the trunk, tucking her blanket around her legs. She blew a kiss to Delainey, who settled on a branch above her. "Sweet dreams, sister."

ALIAH LET HER MIND wander, Garrett leading their horse by the reins down to a river's edge. Three days had passed since they had become separated from her sisters and Faith. She knew they could take care of themselves, but this was the Edgewood. Unexplainable things happened here. The horse she and Garrett escaped on was carrying most of the food in the saddlebags. She knew worrying did no good to those being worried about. And nothing for the one doing the worrying, but logic didn't always win over even the most positive person.

Aliah Bethany Pureheart had magical powers. The attractive Fae had made a practice of never revealing those powers to others, including her sisters. Which meant she couldn't engage in their use with Garrett as her companion. Not unless she took him into her confidence. That was the question she had been brooding over. It had always worried her that if she revealed her powerful talents, someone might turn against her. Or worse, they would see what she was capable of and try to use her against her will. She kept a constant vigil, making sure never to use her abilities when anyone could see. It was a simple matter of protecting herself.

The disputatious other side of this debate was that she felt a natural protectiveness over her sisters, Val in particular. Three days lost in the Edgewood, Aliah didn't know who was with whom, if they were dead, hurt, safe, hungry, or in terrible danger. Time was running out. Anxiety threatened to crush her.

"Garrett," she cleared her throat. "I need to tell you something. Before I do, I want your word, *your promise*. Promise me you'll never reveal what I'm about to say to anyone else. It's essential that I can count on your trust." Nervous, she licked her lips.

"You have my word. Give me your trust," Garrett told her.

"It's just...just, I've never shared this with anyone, not even my sisters. It is important that I be the only one in control of revealing this...ah...information. Important that I alone have the choice of whom, if anyone else, I reveal it to, as well as when, if ever."

"I'll guard your secret and respect your privacy, Aliah," Garrett affirmed, looking her straight in the eye.

"I...I have...certain special abilities. And, I can't live with...well, it's just...it's just that three days is too long not to know where they all are...if they are all safe, so I have to..." she stammered.

Garrett grabbed Aliah's hand. "Have to do what, Aliah?"

She snatched her hand back, took a thick strand of her hair, twisted it round and round, then released it; twisted it up again, released it; over and over...

"Look," Garrett said, "just tell me when it feels right. Nothing you say is going to change the way I feel about you." Garrett's face flushed crimson. "I mean, you know...you're my friend."

She nodded, but the words caught in her throat. They set about the tasks, glad to have something to do with their hands. Garrett came back to the water's edge, where Aliah was kneeling on a sandy patch of ground by a cut-out along the bank. She capped and set aside the canteen she'd just filled.

"I'm wasting precious time," she blurted out, then softened her voice. "I'm a seer," she confessed.

Garrett squinted his eyes. "I thought you were a fairy?" He tried to clarify her statement.

"Yes. A faerie who's a seer. I need to do a ritual to use my sight so I can view my sisters and make sure everyone's okay."

"Why have we waited three days for you to do this?" he asked. "Did you wait because you thought I would reject you as a person for having weird abilities?" His voice was incredulous at the idea.

"Shut it, Garrett," she sliced her hand at him to cut off any further comments.

Aliah sat cross-legged at the side of the stream, chanting a rhythm of words in a language Garrett didn't understand. He could see she held small items in her hand, things belonging to her sisters. Hair ties, a neck chain, a scarf.

He kept watch over their surroundings for any danger while she concentrated, calling on her power. A soft squeak emitted from his mouth as he watched a vision unfold. It was like a picture in a mirror, only it was playing out on the surface of the water below where Aliah sat. The reflection portrayed Carlisse and Delainey sitting on some branches in a huge white pine. Both girls' eyes widened when they heard Aliah's disembodied voice, as a whisper on the wind. "Stay right where you are," she instructed her two sisters. "I've got your location now! Garrett and I are coming to get you."

Aliah passed her hand over the water. The scene flickered to show a flash of Val, seated next to a red-headed girl, both of them wrapped in a silk cocoon, attached to a giant spider web. Aliah pushed a whisper out to Val. "I'm coming to get you, Valerie Victoria Pureheart."

The scene flickered again. Aliah and Garrett both drew sharp breaths. Faith appeared wearing a strange hat, walking with purpose, her pack strapped across her back. She had a companion they didn't recognize. Her fellow traveler was muscular, handsome in a rapscallion kind of way and, oh! Aliah started! Faith was walking with a goblin! The vision winked out. Aliah stood up at once, turning around to face Garrett.

Garrett confesses his admiration. "You're amazing." Then he put two fingers to his lips and mocked, turning a key. Aliah smiled.

Wings snapped out, and Aliah announced, "You get the horse. I am going to fly and direct you from above. I've got Delainey's and Carlisse's location pinned."

"How?"

"Hard to explain, but think of it as a thread of love that I can follow. That's the best way I can describe it for you," Aliah told him. "We'll go get them first, then we've got to get to Val as soon as possible. It looked like she's in danger. We may need all four of us to rescue her. Go, go, go!" She fluttered her hands at him to get moving. Garrett didn't need to be told twice. He grabbed the full canteen and headed for the horse. He watched as Aliah ran a few steps, jumped, pumping hard on her wings, her cheeks flushed with the effort. Garrett cupped his hand over his eyes, shading against the bits of sunlight. Rising, she took flight on an air current. Garrett felt awed. And jealous. Very jealous. The ability to fly was his secret dream.

"Garrett, head north as soon as you're ready," Aliah shouted down at him. "I'm going to scout ahead. I'll be back to guide you, so we stay together."

This pattern played out over the next two hours. Aliah spotted the copse and the white pine that sheltered her two sisters. Landing near the forest treeline, Garrett caught up and dismounted. With shoulders tense, he began surveying the area for any signs of danger. He shot three feet into the air when someone tapped on his shoulder.

Carlisse broke into laughter. "You should have seen how high you jumped just now! Delainey and I heard you approaching from the hillside ten minutes ago."

Aliah grabbed Carlisse, hugging her sister.

"Are you hungry?" Carlisse asked them. "Delainey found a hot spot and gathered a motherlode of white morels and wild leeks," she smiled, motioning with her hand for them to follow. Another round of hugs ensued during the reuniting with Lainey.

Aliah shared how she and Garrett had spent the last three days. Carlisse and Delainey reciprocated. Sharing her vision, Aliah told them she thought Val was in danger. The girls asked how she could produce a vision. They both shrugged their shoulders when she described her ability. Three people knew her secret now. She tamped down her anxiety.

The four discussed strategies. Garrett took over the cook-pot, adding dried thyme, oregano, two precious pinches of salt and extra water. He pulled open a pouch on his belt and tossed in two handfuls of dried wild rice, then added a few sticks to the fire. When he looked up, there were six saucer-wide hazel eyes staring at him.

"I want one," Carlisse said, referring to Garrett. Delainey socked her sister in the shoulder.

"What? He can cook. I want to keep him forever." Delainey declared.

"Stop!" Aliah told them as she laughed at their jesting. "Let's get organized while the food cooks. Then we can set out after Val."

"You know where she is?" Garrett asks.

"From what I can tell, it seems Val is a prisoner of the Dream Weaver," Aliah tells him. "We need to rescue my sister. From previous experience, we know the Dream Weaver can...devious."

The four of them strode to the horses. Garrett mounted, reaching a hand out to help Aliah swing up.

"You can ride double with me, Aliah," Carlisse offered, "until we get Val back."

Aliah looked up at Garrett, took his hand, swinging up using his leverage. "Thanks, sweetie," Aliah smiled, "but Garrett and I have this down now, and we're a good team."

Delainey and Carlisse beamed at each other. They rode off, strung out in single file, with Garrett and Aliah in the lead. Aliah, following an invisible thread of love only she could see, would take them to a stone house in the vale.

CHAPTER 18: Capture

"Can I see what you sketched while you were telling your tale?" Robin asked.

"Maybe later. I've just got this sixth sense, a nagging feeling we need to move out of here, get on the road to look for our friends. I can't explain it, but I don't think sitting around here is helping anything. Something tells me we need to go."

Robin didn't argue. He gathered up Faith's sketchbook and pencils, shoved them in her pack, threw some things onto the blanket she had been sitting on, and bound the ends together. He took two lengths of rope from a nail on the barn wall, threaded them through the knots and finished by hoisting it up, slipping his arms through the rope holds. "I left my pack back...uh...back..." His thumb pointed in a different direction.

Faith's cheeks colored. "Yes, of course, back where you were. With your friends. Before I, um, picked a trillium," she hung her head. "But I didn't mean to mess up your life. Listen," she said earnestly, "as soon as we find your friends, Val and I can go our own way and you can get back to what you were doing. Right?"

"I wasn't sending blame your way, Faith. It's like I told you; I only kept snatches of a memory about the trillium spell put on me. Only a blink of an image. It's the memory of a vision where a beautiful woman is leaning over me. She has long golden hair, sapphire blue, sparkling eyes, a gentle smile as she speaks strange words to me," he reminisced to himself. "But, yeah, okay. We'll find our friends and see what's what. Then we can decide about whether to go our own ways, yeah?" He wanted to ask her about the prophecy the Weaver had foretold for her, but didn't want to admit that he'd looked at her sketchbook again without permission. For now, he resolved to wait until she told him about it herself.

Faith buttoned up the wool coat taken from the hook by Persid's door, slung her pack over her shoulder, ready to go.

Robin grabbed her hand, swept a black leather hat with a wide brim off a barn hook by the door. "Here's a hat. Looks like a good fit for you." He put it on her head, adjusted it to tip to the right, "Perfect fit."

"I don't wear hats." She reached up to take it off. He stopped her.

"You'll want one. Maybe put your hair up. The deep brim will cast a shadow over your eyes." He raised his eyebrows and nodded.

Faith took three steps back, and as he instructed, twisted her hair up, fixing it to stay under the crown, pulling the brim down low. Hat settled, she pulled the doorknob and went out. Her thoughts consumed with the idea, Robin thought she should attempt a...a...disguise. That's what it seemed like to her, anyway. A shiver went through her from shoulders to toes. "You think I need to sneak? To hide? Just what is it about my story that suggests that stratagem to you? I mean, I know little about my cousins, but I don't think they found me just to hurt me. Use me? Maybe, but I'm confident they didn't intend me harm. What are you thinking?"

"Look, lass, I don't know all the circumstances, information, or the people to have a true opinion about it. I just think you shouldn't be so forthcoming in sharing information about your identity. Keep that in mind if we come across other strangers while we're out here. Think about the Dream Weaver's reaction when you said she thought you reminded her of someone. At least until we figure out what's what. Doesn't hurt to blend in, not attract attention, yeah? Come on, this place gives me the creeps. Happy to be leaving here, yeah?" he said as he pulled the door closed behind them.

About three miles away from Persid's house, they came to a deep gully. The terrain was rocky, dotted with tall, spindly pines growing wherever a sparse patch of dirt allowed a seedling to catch hold in the rough landscape. There before them, like an invitation, was a half-mile long swinging bridge. It creaked in the gentle wind, drawing the eye all the way over to the other side, running across the expanse of the gulch. Faith and Robin exchanged a glance.

"Looks safe enough," Robin nodded toward the span.

Without a word, she led the way. The sun beat down on them. Faith had to admit the hat brim shaded her eyes from the bright light. "I don't think I mentioned it, but besides my fear of spiders, I'm also afraid of heights," she confessed in a shaky voice.

"Don't look down," Robin cautioned.

She looked down.

The world tilted; her stomach rolled. Robin steadied her from behind. "Eyes forward. Think about Val. You need to cross to get to her, yeah? Good lass, keep going." Robin kept up the encouraging banter all the way across the wooden boards held together by ropes. The whole contraption swinging in the wind currents that were cutting up from the gorge floor. There was a tense moment when Faith's feet froze. An eagle launched off a tree, screeching at them for disturbing its afternoon. "The raptor's not interested in you, Faith," he told her as she flinched. "See?" Robin pointed. "He's just trying to get away from us. Come on. You're doing great. Keep moving. We're almost across."

Faith could see the flat, rocky ground at the end of the swinging bridge ahead of her. For all its creaking, groaning, and strange noises, the boards felt solid under her feet. She came to a stop, Robin running into the back of her. Leaning against him for support; her hands had a white-knuckled grip on the bridge's side ropes.

"What's what?" Robin asked, a little agitated at *another* fear of heights delay. She adjusted to the right so he could see what waited for them on the other side. His body stiffened.

"Bloody hell. Looks like I picked the wrong direction. Trust me, it's best if you let me handle this. Say nothing. Not. One. Word. Here's what we're going to do now: trade places with me. Real smooth, yeah?" The choreograph took place with seamless footwork. They tuned into each other's movements, switching places on the swinging bridge, so Robin was in front.

Fifty feet ahead at the end of the bridge loomed Robin's brother, Rupert, snarling like a starving dog. "Look what we have here!" Rupert's voice boomed, echoing in the gulch, spittle flying from the corner of his mouth.

Faith could see a woman sitting on a flat wooden platform, carried by six stout goblins using handholds on the sides. "Stop," she commanded. "Put me down."

Behind his stepmother was a host of fifty lads. Robin knew most of them. They kept their eyes free of any expression at seeing their familiar mate.

Morveena clapped her hands, held them in a prayer-like stance, and exclaimed with drama, as though she was performing on stage, "Rupert! You've found him. My missing son. Your darling brother. Robin dear, Mother was so worried! Thank goodness no harm has come to you!" She threw her arms open as though she were expecting a hug.

"Oh, thank the gods," Faith breathed in. "You're related to them. It's your mother and brother? Why didn't you say so? Good news, right?"

Robin shook his head. "I can't describe how *not* good this is, Faith. Get ready to use your wings. You're going to need to fly. Get away. Do not let them capture you under any circumstances. Just get away as fast as you can, as far as you can. Don't worry about me, lass. I can figure things out. I can't stress enough that these are terrible people, Faith. *Bad people.* Cruel goblins. Not Faerie friendly. If I'm putting the pieces of a puzzle together from all that you've told me, throwing in a few good guesses, I'm sure they would mean you harm. You've got to trust me on this." He tried to emphasize how serious he thought their situation had just become.

Rupert started forward on the bridge. "Who's with you, brother?" he growled. "Doesn't look like the Beaumont, your trusty sidekick." Rupert sneered.

"Now, Faith!" Robin yelled over his shoulder as he ran full on at Rupert.

Faith stood frozen, locked in place. What was he doing? Why was Robin going after his brother as if he was going to attack him? Confused thoughts tumbled through her mind, freezing her body from taking any kind of action.

Faith's eyes widened as Morveena strode forward with a hatchet in one hand, snapping her fingers with the other. A gang of goblins stepped up behind her. Morveena used the hatchet to hack away at the rope that secured the bridge to the pillars embedded in the ground. With each strike of the hatchet, the rope split. Fibers unraveled with every whack of the deadly tool. Faith felt the ropes pull taut as the boards under her feet quivered, pressure building against the weight of the bridge. The floorboards shook; the whole bridge groaned. Robin collided with Rupert in a full headbutt, sending the bridge boards dancing with the impact between them.

"Stop screwing around, Rupert!" Morveena screamed at the top of her lungs. "Bring me my wayward son now! He owes me an explanation and an apology." The corners of her bright red lips twisted up in a snarl. "Guards, get whoever his travel companion is. Hurry now before I cut the rope on the other side." She tilted her head to eye the soldiers. "You live to please your queen, yes?" They rushed forward to do her bidding.

Rupert tightened his grip on his cane and brought it down on the back of Robin's head. The muscular lad crumpled like a sack of flour. His brother was down, so Rupert punched his face for good measure and kicked his ribs because he felt like it. "You there," Rupert called out to the first guards hurrying onto the swinging bridge that hung at a dangerous tilt. "Yes, you two! Get my brother off the bridge this instant!" Rupert snapped his fingers at the other lads standing near Morveena. "You three! Grab that other lad, take him prisoner," he ordered, pointing his finger at the figure in the black hat. One guard hefted Robin under his arms; another picked up his legs. They man-handled him off the bridge, grappling with his body weight against the odd angle of the bridge.

Robin's eyes flew open. Struggling and disoriented, he tried to focus, stars dancing in his vision. He could see Faith was still standing on the bridge, three lads rushing towards her. But he couldn't believe his eyes. She hadn't moved an inch, suspended in place. All his bluster for nothing but a knot on the back of his skull! "Move!" he screamed at Faith. The fear in his voice roused her from her state of shock. She shifted her pack, slipped her arms through the straps to carry it across her chest. Her wings snapped out as one of the goblin guards came within four strides, hands outstretched toward her. She pushed off from the bridge, her wings filling with the updraft from the ravine.

Morveena screeched, pointed her twisted, sharp-nailed finger, rings glimmering in the sunlight as she raged with hatred. "Faerie! It's a dirty, stinking fairy! Treason! My son has committed treason! Kill it! Catch it! Rupert, do something!" she thundered.

Faith flew across to the cliff-side, coming in close to the raging goblin queen. She was about to say something when she screwed up her forehead. Wings flapping, the Faerie girl pointed a finger at the Goblin Queen, shouting, "Where did you get those boots?" Her words were more of a demand than a question.

Robin's mouth fell open, incredulous. Why? Why wasn't she racing away to safety?

"I don't think we're meeting under the best conditions." Faith yelled at Morveena. "But you're wearing *my* boots!" she announced, anger flaring.

Morveena glared at Robin, then back at the strange lad with suspicion. The Goblin Queen shot toward Faith, hatchet at the ready, intentions clear. The Fae girl panicked, pumping her wings with every muscle, racing away from the woman brandishing the hatchet.

Racing away from Robin.

Panic drove her thoughts. *What just happened back there? I can't just leave Robin with those horrible people, family or not. They're evil. I've never seen anything like that!*

The faerie touched down on a wide tree branch a mile away, out of sight. She stashed her pack so she could move faster without the extra weight.

Heart pounding hard against her chest, she dropped to the ground, thoughts swimming. *What to do? Gods, he saved me from a terrible death. I owe him. Oh, I wish I weren't alone! Right about now, I could use Val's advice. There was a whole troop of goblins back there. What am I going to do against a whole troop? I need help. But there is no one else to help. Ok. Calm down. Val would tell me to think this out, one piece of the puzzle at a time. Analyze the situation before taking any action. Take a few minutes to look at what's what, as Robin would say. So, 1) bad people. I don't get the mother's behavior at all. The brother is dangerous. Something is wrong between Robin and his brother. 2) Robin saved me. Twice. I have to save him. At least try. 3) There's only me to do this. 4) Only me. So, I will have to be enough. I am enough! 5) Reconnaissance. Yes! Reconnaissance first, then form an action plan based on the gathered information. I need more information. 6) Stealth and sneakiness are among my best abilities. At least according to Val.*

Faith swallowed hard at the thought of Val, missing her friend more than ever, wishing again that she was here.

Mission decided. Reconnaissance. The golden-haired faerie flew low, quietly working her way back to where she'd last seen Robin. When she thought she was close, she landed on a gigantic oak branch. She rearranged her hair, wrapped it with a leather tie, securing it up under the hat again. Gliding to the ground, she stooped, dug down to get some black soil, and rubbed it all over her face and hands. With her black hat, black leathers, and coat, if she moved slowly and stuck to the shadows, she'd be hard to spot.

It didn't take long to catch them up. A large group always moves slower. Especially with his mother being carried about on that ridiculous transport, wasting those men's energy instead of walking herself. Well, that just spoke volumes about her vanity and selfishness, Queen or not, Faith thought.

Keeping her distance, she stuck with them for the next hour. She couldn't see Robin as the crowd moved through the forest, but she knew he had to be with them. Now and then, she'd catch a snatch of sound, able to identify the voice as belonging to Robin's evil brother. The group headed for the base of a small hillock. A brilliant setting sun motivated them to stop and set up camp for the night. The queen shouted for the troops to halt. They lowered her platform. As the Goblin Queen climbed off, the lads flipped the flat structure up.

From her lofty perch in a tree hidden in the foliage, Faith could see that the Queen had trapped Robin beneath the platform, forcing him to carry it on his back. The other lads used handholds running along the sides of the structure. Robin looked terrible. Rupert yanked on a chain hooked to a collar around Robin's neck.

Tugging without mercy, the iron biting into his skin, Rupert fastened Robin's chain, securing it with a crude lock. He left just enough slack for Robin to sit without choking. His face was mottled, filled with bruises and cuts. Robin was sporting a black eye, developing deep purple and green bruising. Another prisoner had also been beneath the platform. Rupert chained him to the same tree. Robin looked at the other captive, but couldn't recognize him. The face appeared swollen. Someone had beaten it to a bloody pulp. The poor soul made quiet, whining noises, his breath wheezing through a broken nose, crusted over with dried blood.

Robin leaned his head against the tree trunk, grateful to have the platform off his sore shoulders and aching back. He played back the scene that had occurred by the swinging bridge, grateful Faith had gotten away. Still, he couldn't believe the girl's crazed return over the boots his stepmother was wearing. A painful smile stole over his cracked lips. Those were the very boots he had picked up from Faith's pile of clothing the day he'd first seen her mushrooming. His smile widened at the memory. He hadn't given too much thought to stealing her boots. It wasn't personal. His only consideration was how a gift of boots for Morveena might buy him some small amount of goodwill. So, he'd taken the black, butter-soft boots. The goodwill those boots had earned him had been spent ten times over by now. Presents didn't hold value for long with Morveena.

Almost as if someone could read his mind, the same boots dropped from above his head, landing between his feet, startling him. Robin tipped his head to the right, squinting his eyes, enabling him to see Morveena from an angle. Not her best side. Red hair fell in waves to her shoulders. Delighted with herself, she dragged her blood-red, sharpened fingernail across his jawline. "It seems you thought a fitting gift for your mother was a used pair of stinking Faerie boots, yes? I should kill you just for that offence alone," she sneered.

Turning to the other prisoner, she crooned, "Narrol would never be stupid enough to give me a used pair of boots once belonging to a stinking Faerie, would you, Narrol?" The slumped body groaned in agony and began to cry. Morveena gave him a vicious kick with the toenails, which she kept sharpened to lethal points. Then, added three hard kicks to the ribs.

Narrol! Robin thought, *good gods. The poor lout chained beside him was Rolland's uncle. He doubted Rolland could even recognize the man now.*

"Tell me, Robin Wilum Goodfellow," she spat his full name out like a rotten piece of meat, "just who was the faerie with you?"

His silence earned him a punch to the jaw from her gnarled fist. "You and your bleeding-heart friends. When will you learn Fae are nothing but sneaky, backstabbing, gold-grubbing worms? You've committed treason by consorting with the enemy! You know the penalty for treason is death," she shrieked. Dragging her knife-like fingernail along his jaw again, she put it under his chin, forcing him to look at her. "I'll have to make a special example of you, my son," Morveena showed him a rictus smile; her facial features bespoke of horrors she had yet to unleash. "There are things I want to know, Robin. If you're a good boy, for each honest answer you give me, Mummy promises to reduce your torture. You hold the key to making the torture you will endure easier. Less painful. You understand?"

On the other side of the tree, Narrol broke out in manic laughter. That earned him a bash on the top of his head with a heavy cane she produced in a flash from a loop on her belt. Robin flinched at the cracking sound the strike made, much to Morveena's pleasure.

"Need water," Robin gasped.

Morveena snapped her fingers. A lad came running with a canteen, placing it uncapped in Robin's chained hands. He knew the lad. Raven. He was a good young man. Had other family in the clan. Raven dared not even glance at his old mate and retreated to the shadows, to wait until he was called upon again to serve Morveena's whims. Young male goblins always made up her retinue. Robin drank. Just as he was about to come up for air, Morveena stepped close and wrapped her hands around Robin's, holding the canteen. She pushed the canteen against his mouth, forcing his head back. He choked on the forced water, couldn't catch his breath, eyes bulging. She let go at the last second before he lost consciousness. Robin coughed, hacked, spat out water, and then puked up more. He tried to draw air into his lungs to get his breathing under control again.

"Oh, I am sorry, darling. I thought you were thirsty," Morveena dragged out the last word with drama. "Too much?" She asks with feigned innocence, batting her eyelashes.

Rupert fumed on the other side of the clearing, directing the troupe in setting up the camp and prepping food to feed the traveling goblin gang. He hated it when Morveena insisted on doing the man-handling and punishing. The lads likely thought him weak, while she ordered everyone around. He lashed out at the closest lad, smacked him upside the head, "No dawdling!" Rolland growled, the boy trotting away. His bad mood continued to play out to the troupe's misfortune the entire time his lover took out her displeasure on the other side of the base.

"Since you're all refreshed, dear, Mummy's got some questions, yes?" Her eyes sparkled in challenge. The fake pleasantness left her voice. She asked with a growl, "I want to know if you have any information about the whereabouts of Narrol's nephew, Rolland Rafael Brown? You will provide the name and details about the faerie lad you had with you. And you *must* tell me, darling, where your false twin, the Touchstone, is hiding, hmmm?" Her beady eyes stared daggers at him. Her teeth ground together, face twisting. "You will explain why you abandoned the clan? Why you choose to ally yourself with the scum of our world? The lowest of the low races!" This last she could barely choke out in her rage. "I can believe many things about you, Robin, but this was not something I foresaw. You know I don't like to be surprised, darling." She released a long breath, calmed. It was the calmness, more than anything else, that scared the shit out of Robin. "I won't ask a second time," she warned in a soft voice.

Morveena slipped a garnet ring out of a small pouch at her waist, holding it out for Robin to see, then forced it onto his forefinger. "You know what power this truth ring has," she stated matter-of-factly.

He did. He hated the ring growing up. The gemstone would flash if he lied while wearing it. Over the years, he had learned you could pick your words with prudence to skirt around the edges of the truth without being discovered. Robin leaned his head back against the tree trunk and heaved a heavy sigh. Concentrating on his words. "I do not know where Rolland Brown is right now, mother," he told the truth. "Cazzidy and I got separated in the Edgewood."

"How?" she demanded.

"There was an attack in the woods. Everything happened so fast." He lifted his head so he could look at her when he told her the next part: "A gang of lads were being driven under some kind of mind control by a Gugwe monster. I'd not seen the beast before, but it is a terrifying foe."

Not a muscle on her face moved; she gave nothing away. "Continue." She lifted her chin at him.

"There was a clusterf...ah...confusing fight, as we tried to save those lads. Caz and I took down the Gugwe," he told her. Morveena's eyes glittered with the rose color of sunset, making her look demonic.

"The Beaumont took off into the woods, chasing after the crazed lads. I've been looking for him ever since we lost each other." Robin felt the thick ring warm around his finger, but there was no damning flash, so he continued. "While I was stumbling around in the woods, I crossed paths with the faerie. *It* was ill, so I helped *it* until *it* became conscious again. Told me *it* was lost, needed help to find a way out of the woods, yeah? So, I was just letting *it* follow me while I kept searching for the Beaumont. No treachery intended, Mother. Nothing in the dark corners. Come now," he implored her.

Morveena considered him and his story. She thought there were large holes in his telling, but she couldn't put her finger on anything specific. Plus, the truth ring hadn't activated, disclosing any lies. Perhaps she had misjudged him.

He continued under her appraising gaze. "You know me, Mother. I *am* loyal to the clan. Are you going to fault me just because I ran into strange circumstances, got caught up in them like a trap, and couldn't get out?"

"I will mull your words over while I have my dinner. Oh," she feigned as though an idea had popped into her head. "Would you like another drink before I go, dear?" words laced with malice, Morveena dangled the canteen by the strap, swung it back and forth. Robin's eyes tracked the movement.

Robin shook his head, then watched. About twenty feet in front of him, she set the canteen down right next to the black leather boots she'd confronted him with. The canteen lay out of his reach. She snatched her garnet ring back. He closed his eyes in a moment of peace, then opened them to watch her swagger across the length of the camp.

Robin did not know what it meant that she had left him alive. At least for the moment. Granted, still chained to the tree, but not dead. The Goodfellow adjusted his head, tried to relax his shoulders so he could begin taking in every detail of the camp. He divided the site into small sections so he could scan them, commit details to memory, and then move to the next small segment. Total focus, then to the next, moving his eyes, never his head. His body remained still. Anyone looking at him would never notice that he was studying the unit. He could see the watch on duty moving in a repeating pattern. Though familiar with the soldiers' maneuvers, he still timed their movements, as well as their guard changes. He needed to be familiar with the surroundings and the routines, in case an opportunity for escape presented itself. When he could hold his eyes open no longer, darkness dragged him down, and he drifted into a deep sleep.

WHILE THE GOBLIN SOLDIERS were busy setting up camp, Faith had flown back to retrieve her pack. By the time she returned, the moon was just a sliver, allowing her slim frame to move undetected in the shadows. Slow. Sure. There was not a sound of her passing. This was a familiar game for Faith. She, Val, and Garrett had practiced the art of sneaking ever since she could remember. The trio created their own game of 'how to be a ghost' in the woods, making no sound, moving like an apparition. Her skill at it had been the best of the three. The young Fae had also been watching the perimeter guards and knew she had three minutes before she had to move away.

Faith put her lips softly against Robin's ear. "Robin," she murmured.

His body stiffened, but he didn't make a sound or a move.

"I can't get you out right now, but I wanted you to know I didn't just slink away and abandon you. I'll always be somewhere nearby. At some point, a chance will present itself to rescue you, and I'll take it. Trust me," she whispered, sincere in her promise. Then, he noted her scent moved away, felt the absence of her warm breath on his ear.

Nice dream, Robin thought to himself.

An owl hooted. Another answered across the way. Robin's body jerked to attention. Coming awake, he heard Faith's quiet voice, "What the...my boots!" she hissed.

"Faith, wait! Don't!" he tried to warn her off.

"These are my boots, and I'm taking them!" she hissed in a hushed voice at him. "We will talk about how they came to be in your mother's possession later!"

A sliver of moonlight gave him just enough luminosity to see her stepping into the boots. As she put a hand out and grabbed hold of them, ropes pulled taut around a thick netting, pulling it closed and springing up off the ground. With the motion whipping Faith off her feet, her body turned upside down, trapped. With a lasso pulled tight around her ankles, closing the net. Her body began swinging back and forth, dangling ten feet off the ground.

"Those boots won't have been worth your capture," Robin shook his head, heart pounding hard against his chest, fearing for her safety.

"Well, well, well," Morveena called out, Rupert two strides behind as they approached. "What have we here?" She loosed her evil laugh, turned, touched Rupert's face, and kissed him hard on the lips. "You are so clever, Rupert, my love," she told him, giddy with anticipation. "Rupert suggested setting up this little trap," she giggled like a young girl. "He thought you seemed awfully attached to your boots. Figured you'd put yourself in danger just to get them back." Morveena clapped her hands in delight. "Brilliant, darling," she beamed at Rupert. "I'm going to enjoy this." Morveena licked her lips, the moonlight exposing the chill in her eyes.

"Get. It. Down." Her voice changed, hard as granite in three words. "Why, I haven't had a dirty, stinking, sneaky faerie to play with in a very long time."

Two lads unwound the rope from around the tree limb and, with little slack, let the net and its contents fall to the ground. Faith landed with a huff, the air knocked out of her lungs. She came up on her hands and knees, gasping for air.

Morveena came from behind and caned Faith's thighs. The girl fell forward in blinding pain, having felt nothing like it in her life. Morveena poked Faith inside the netting. "Skinny thing. It doesn't smell bad. Yet." Poke, poke, poke as the cane pushed at her thighs, buttocks, and ribs. "Take your stupid hat off. Put your head up. You will look at me when I am talking to you!" Morveena screamed, then knocked the hat off with the cane.

Morveena sucked in her breath, spun to look at Robin, and saw his mouth fall open. He appeared to be surprised, as she was when the long, golden hair fell out of the hat in a tangled nest of snarls. Morveena took Robin's response as shock, just discovering this creature was a female. Morveena was pleased he hadn't known.

The Queen had been examining her plans for Robin while resting in her tent. Had concluded his death for treason wasn't in her best interest in the immediate future. She had specific uses for her stepson. The owl's hoots alerted her that Rupert's plan was in play, and she'd rushed to where he waited as the Fae stepped into the trap.

"What a surprise, Robin! The *lad* you were guiding out of the Edgewood Forest isn't a *lad* at all, but appears to be a *lass,* yes?" she said, feeling triumphant. "Rupert!" Morveena called.

"Yes, my queen," Rupert stepped up from behind.

"Bind its wings. Tie its hands and ankles. Gag it. It will not speak until spoken to by me or with my permission. I declare it to be my new pet," she announced. Some lads glanced around at one another, knowing what that likely meant for this lass, faerie or not.

Faith lifted her head, forced herself to stand up to face the Goblin Queen for a moment.

Robin attempted to convey a message using gestures to attract Faith's attention, hoping to dissuade her from saying anything. But the Fae Princess didn't take her eyes off the Queen.

The girl put on a show of bravery, shook out her golden hair, and jutted her chin toward the Goblin Queen. Before Faith said a word, Morveena's entire face went pale as death. A look of disbelief formed on her face.

Morveena whispers to the Fae girl, "Holy hell. It's you."

She clutched Rupert's brocade jacket. "It's her! She exists!" Morveena tells him. Rupert's forehead wrinkled in confusion. The queen walked in a circle around the prisoner. Laughter gurgled up from her throat as she said, "The bloody witch has held out all these years, and here you are. You've fallen right into my hands!" She finished her reverie and leaned against Rupert.

"What bloody witch are you talking about?" Faith hissed out, spoiling for a fight. "And..." she glared at everyone in her view, "let's get something right out on the table, shall we? I. Am. Nobody's. Pet!"

Robin hung his head, pinched the bridge of his nose with his forefingers, hands still chained.

"Morveena," Rupert cooed at her, "what's going on, my dove? Do you know this girl somehow?"

"Look at the hair, Rupert. The blue eyes. See the defiance. Why, she's the spitting image of her mother."

Rupert peered closer at the girl trapped in the netting, sucked in his breath, and lurched backwards. "Aleta's spawn!" Rupert spat.

"Yes," Morveena confirmed. "You see it now, yes?" she chuckled to herself again. "We've got our game piece, haven't we, Rupert? We've got a place at the table." Morveena turned to the guards behind Rupert, saying, "Send two lads back to the clan cave and tell them we must go on an urgent mission north. Tell the clan to stay put until they hear from us, nothing else," she fixed them with her eyes. Eyes promising a hard death should the lads not obey her every command. "Tell no one about this girl's capture. No one!" She shooed the lads, sweeping her hands, to show them she wanted them to go away. They didn't need to be told twice. The entire gang was off in an instant, disappearing like ghosts back into the camp.

"Secure the prisoner, Rupert. Then we must make plans, yes?" she asked in a breathy voice. "Rupert, but make sure she can't get away, darling," she teased him.

Morveena turned her attention back to Robin. "You've done well, Robin. This should tip the scales of justice to weigh in your favor. Tomorrow, I will let you know where you stand for your crimes. Tonight? Tonight, you must contemplate your wrongs against us. But, Robin," Morveena looked over at Faith with reverence, "you've done very well to bring this gift to me. Ta ta for now, darling."

Off she went to her tent to wait for Rupert while he secured the faerie scum to a tree opposite Robin's. The wheels were turning. She had plans to make. Morveena hadn't been this happy since she'd witnessed the mirror image of the same face and hair being locked away fifteen years ago. Queen Aleta. The High Queen of the Fae. Her oldest foe. And now? Now, she had her enemy's daughter right in her hand. They'd never been able to confirm Aleta had given birth to a child, much less a daughter. Trying to find Aleta's babe had been like chasing a whisper in the wind. Her mind had never accepted that her own daughter had been stillborn, as Lancer had informed her.

Rupert swept the tent flap open and found Morveena standing on a bear rug wearing nothing but garnets around her neck, garnets dangling from her ears. Her fingernails and toenails sharpened to knife points, painted blood-red, decorated with as many rings as she wore on her fingers. "My love," he said with reverence.

Morveena crooked her finger at him, beckoning him forward.

"We can talk about details after we celebrate," she coaxed him, her voice husky and inviting. He fell into his role as a worshiping servant. Everyone in the camp tried to keep busy, ignoring the noises coming from within the queen's tent. Apparently, the two no longer felt the need to hide their passion for one another.

CHAPTER 19: Dryocopus Pileatus

Rupert left the tent to check on the prisoners. Morveena lay sated, warm on the bear rug, covered with the blanket he'd laid over her. Seeing the likeness of young Queen Aleta, matched in her new Fae captive, stirred memories she hadn't thought of in years. Drowsy, she allowed her mind to drift back to the visit with her father at the Fae castle as a young girl.

Memories stirred the hatred in her belly. She found she couldn't stomach the pity she had seen reflected in Aleta's eyes so long ago. The day the meddling Fae Queen discovered her bruised, battered body and had the audacity to stand there judging her. Passing judgment on her father. How dare a Fae force her contemptuous sorrow down Morveena's throat, as if Morveena was less because her father was an abusive prick? Only she had the right to judge anything about her own situation. From that moment on, Morveena had hated the Fae witch. There would come a day, she promised herself, when she would teach Aleta a lesson. Morveena Morgan Montestrell vowed never to be defined by suffering a person's pity. Nor would she tolerate another's belittlement.

It all started one bright morning when Morveena and her father left the veiled Fae Court. Riding inside the carriage, back straight, chin high in defiance, proud of herself for having turned down the Queen's pathetic suggestion. The offer for Morveena to stay at their court until Envoy Montestrell returned on his next visit. The emissary's daughter admitted she had relished the Queen's expression when Morveena had declined the offer.

While her father was driving, the goblin girl didn't move a muscle from her proud stance. Only once did she turn her head, glancing up to where she knew the hidden entrance to the Fae castle was. The three large boulders along the road, passing from view. The landmark burned in her mind.

When they stopped at an inn for the night, she didn't utter a word. Munro Marcellus Montestrell hesitated for all of three seconds, though he saw something in his daughter's eyes to give him pause. But couldn't quite put his finger on what it was. Giving in to his baser side, he beat her black and blue as soon as the door to their suite had closed. Through it all, Morveena never made a sound. When he tired of his own violent actions, she rose, gathering her dress about her, turned to look him straight in the eyes, gaze fixed. What he saw there made him flinch. She left his room, closing the door so quietly she might as well have slammed it.

In the morning, she and her father broke their fast, the innkeeper offering her a piteous look as he served her porridge. Walls were thin. There were few secrets between them.

Off again, the carriage bounced down the road, sending sharp pains through her bruised body with every jarring thump and pothole.

On this day, Morveena had risked hiding one of the small tomes on black magic, 'Small Magics Everyone Can Master', in the pocket of her skirt. Confident her father's monster would be sated for a day or two, it was likely he wouldn't stop the carriage again until nightfall. That gave her the day to study the book. She practiced a spell she had already learned, to make a fire with her fingertips, producing a small fireball that didn't burn her skin. Drilling for another hour, she worked on a method to make her face look like a different person.

Another spell offered the ability to bind someone without ropes. Before the sun went down that day, the girl had become adept at moving objects by the command of her voice alone. Small things at first, then larger objects, heavier, using her travel trunk to practice on as she polished her newfound talent. The small book had been tucked away long before the carriage rolled to a stop for the night.

Munro's daughter maintained her silence throughout dinner. But her brain was repeating the spells over and over, memorizing them, perfecting her knack to recall them at a moment's notice. There were other guests in attendance in the common room of the inn as they ate. They enjoyed a wonderful stew, and for the first time in memory; she asked for a second helping. Munro looked at her sideways, but ignored her unusual behavior and ordered another whiskey while she ate it. When the kitchen lass came to clear the table, he ordered an additional shot and told the lass to leave the bottle. Morveena steeled herself, knowing her soon to be drunken father would beat her again tonight after all. A man from a neighboring table struck up a conversation, and her father agreed to play a game of stones. Taking his glass and the bottle over to a small game table in the corner by the fireplace, he acted as if she didn't exist. Silence accompanied Morveena up the stairs to her small room.

By candlelight, she began reading 'How to Wield the Power of Blood Magic'. She jumped at every small noise, ever conscious of her father's pending return, not wanting her abuser to catch her out with the book. The tome warned that each time she used her blood for the power of magic, she gave up some of the essence of her life. It would be years before she realized what that meant, ignoring the advice, only keen on pursuing spells to discover the power she could wield.

That night was the first time she had deliberately cut herself.

Morveena took the knife she had secreted away from the Fae castle and sliced the inside of her forearm high enough up so her dress sleeve would later cover the wound. The sting was unexpected, but she savored the pain, because it was pain of her own making, her secret. She let several drops of blood fall into the washstand bowl. She bound the cut with a strip of material she'd torn off the bottom of her petticoat. Crumbling some dried mint taken from herbs hanging by the inn's kitchen door when she'd gone to use the privy, she mixed it in with the drops of blood. Drawing her forefinger through the mixture, she put three dots of blood on her face while looking at her reflection in the dressing-table mirror. One drop between her eyebrows, one below each eye. Then, applied it across the top and bottom of her lips. She pulled her fingers through the rest of the blood mixture and dragged a line from the tip of her forehead, across the top of her head, through her hair. Morveena could see the candle behind her, its reflection in the mirror. She stared into the looking glass, admiring the placement of the blood markings, her thoughts morose. She sat looking deep into her own eyes reflected in the silvered glass, the candlelight flickering, until she saw what she was looking for. Morveena Morgan Montestrell began chanting in a whisper.

Dryocopus pileatus inside me,
open your wings to fly;
Take me with you.
I'll be watching through
our beady eye.
Black and white our
feathers glisten;
our blood-red crest ablaze
under Luna's bright beam.
When we're done,
our flight complete,
I'll wake from this dark dream.
Then you will see the world
through our blue eyes,
but wait within unseen,
until I call upon you next,
my sweet Picidae.

THE CANDLE FLAME FLUTTERED, shadows jumping across the walls. It felt like the blood spots she'd put on her face burned. The young goblin watched in abject horror and a mixture of intoxicating joy. Morveena witnessed her reflection; every detail of her body's complete shift into a Pileated Woodpecker. She opened her wingspan to eighteen inches, then tucked them tight, preening in the mirror's reflection; turning from side to side, admiring her deep black, shiny feathers, her sharp hawklike bill. Her attention shifted to regard the beautiful, flaming red crest that crowned her head. Intelligent eyes turned toward the door, hearing her father's stumbling footsteps coming up the stairway.

Morveena's heart pounded, and she whispered, "Wake from the dream. Stay with me."

Her image rippled with shapeshifting. After blowing out her candle, she grabbed the book and put it under the mattress. She lay down on the small, stiff bed just as her door crashed open. The Goblin Envoy stepped in, reeking of whiskey, with a madness dancing behind his eyes.

"Bringin' you with me on this trip has been nothin' but ill luck," he slurred at her. Then he closed the door behind him as gently as he could.

It was the gentleness that made her fear for her life. With his cane in hand, he walked toward her. She trembled, trying to separate her mind from her body before he brutalized her. But the Picidae inside her kept making deep-drumming sounds, nudging her with its long, hard bill. Before she knew what she was doing, Morveena raised her hand, palm out, fresh blood running from where she'd just sliced her hand open. In a shaky voice, she commanded, "Bludgeon!"

Her father swayed, blinking his eyes, confused. He saw his daughter's eyes light up and open wide with fascination as a heavy, silver candlestick left the dresser and crashed into the base of her father's skull. His knees sagged. The candlestick struck again. Monro dropped like a stone, bruising his knees, eyes rolling up and back into their sockets. Morveena watched, captivated by her own power, her hand still held in command, her father's blood splattering across the walls, across her face. Power coursed through her body. Her feet rooted where she stood while the candlestick bludgeoned Munro Marcellus Montestrell to death.

Her Piliated signaled her with a high-level kik-kik-kik-kik-kik-kik, rousing her from her trance-like state. She looked at the bloody mass of pulp before her on the floor. A thrill ran through her, similar to an orgasm.

This wasn't what she had planned at all.

However, she reminded herself; if her father had taught her nothing else, he had given her many lessons about always being adaptable.

Morveena Morgan Montestrell was a survivor.

Stooping, she patted the Envoy down, locating his pocket watch. She triggered the latch; the watch popped open, showing the time to be just after midnight. The gold locket preserved a faded picture of her mother inside. She closed the watch and slipped it into her pocket. Next, she located his pocketknife, as well as the blade he used for eating; six gold, four silver, and two copper coins fell as she turned out his pant pocket. She retrieved his tobacco pouch and pipe from the inside pocket of his vest. Struggling with his belt buckle, she wriggled and worked it until she could pull it from under him. Wrapping the belt around her slim waist, she found she had to punch a new hole with the knife so she could buckle it. She stashed all the items she had collected in her own travel bag.

Morveena strode to the balcony and opened the French doors. Cool air flowed against her face. There were no lights showing in any of the other windows of the inn she could see. The stable was visible from her room. Judging everyone to be fast asleep, she leaped into action.

Her father's body lay on the braided rug next to her bed. She pulled the edge up and tugged it across his back, and with her foot, rolled his broken, bloody body, wrapping him in the rug. The moon hid in deep cloud cover. Gritting her teeth, the slip of a girl, all jacked up with adrenaline, dragged the rug across the room, where she rolled him out the French doors onto the balcony. Heaving the rug up on the two-foot molded edge, Morveena pushed him over the side. The body landed sixteen feet below with a heavy thud.

Heart pounding, Morveena stood stock-still in the shadows, waiting to see if anyone had heard his body land below. She listened to ensure no one would come to check out the strange noises. No lights came on. Nothing happened. So, she slipped back inside, grabbing the book from under the mattress last and pushing it into her bag.

Opening the small door between their adjoining rooms, she took her father's bag, then pulled the rug in his room over into hers, so the one missing wouldn't be so obvious in the smaller room. She ran her eyes over his room, noting nothing out of place, and closed the connecting door. Glancing about her own room with a discerning eye, she went about straightening every little thing. Smoothing the bedding down as though no one had used the room at all.

Morveena poured a small amount of water from the pitcher into the bowl and washed the blood from her face and hands. She dried off using one of Munro's shirts from his luggage, then tore off the shirt's sleeve to bandage her hand, using the button on the cuff to secure it. She carried the wash water to the balcony and splashed it out onto the ground. Next came the two carpetbags. After she had stuffed the ruined shirt in, she tipped them out over the balcony curb. They landed a foot away from the body. She scrutinized every surface, every corner. Satisfied that no trace of the patricide was discoverable at the scene, she climbed down the metal scrollwork, careful not to get her feet caught in the ivy vines.

Feet touching the ground, she stooped to grab the two bags. Finding their carriage still parked on the side of the stable, Morveena loaded the bags inside. Dragging the rolled rug, ignoring her bruised, battered body's aches and pains, she forced herself to do what had to be done.

Placing a wide barn board against the open floor of the carriage door, she propped the board at an angle on the ground. Using the last of her strength, she climbed through the door on the opposite side, leaned down and grabbed the edge of the rolled carpet. The spindly girl pulled, pushed, grunted, groaned, making slow progress. She moved the rug-wrapped body up the board an inch at a time into the carriage. Taking the lap blanket on the carriage seat, she draped it over the top of the rug. Risking a few precious moments, she waited for her heart rate to slow while she caught her breath, then climbed out of the cab, closed the door, and went to get the horse.

An old, stable dog kept his head down, but wagged his tail at her. She patted his head. She couldn't take a chance on the old canine rousing anyone before she was away, so she whispered a spell under her breath. Morveena patted his head again, caressing his soft ears, as he sank into a deep sleep. Satisfied that the dog would not bark until morning, she led the horse out of the stall and harnessed it to the carriage. Tearing two of Munro's shirts in half, she covered the horse's hooves to muffle their sound.

Morveena led the mare on foot, her hand holding the halter. Her efforts kept things quiet as possible while leading a horse and carriage in the dark. When she was half a mile down the road, she judged it safe to remove the cloth from the hooves and drag herself up onto the driver's seat. Settling in, she took the reins in hand, clicked her tongue, signaling the mare to move. The cloudy night and the rustling wind helped cover her getaway.

MUNRO'S DAUGHTER STUCK to the main road, didn't take any side tracks that would lead to other roadside inns or small villages. She traveled back the same way they'd come over the last two days. It was dusk when she rounded the bend she'd been watching for. Her heart thrilled when she could see the boulders she sought. Pulling off in the shade of a small grove of oaks, Morveena unharnessed the horse, tethering him to a tree branch. Reaching behind the buckboard seat, she pulled a small pick and shovel, fixed them together with a thin rope, slinging them over her shoulder. She unfastened the carriage door, hooking it open with a strap, and led the horse alongside the carriage. There was a moment or two of high-stepping, the horse's eyes rolling back in its head. The animal balked at the closeness of the carriage and the copper tang of blood it could smell. Morveena tapped its hindquarters with the crop and commanded, "Be still."

She loaded the rug-bound body onto the horse's back. Rigor mortis had set in, making the task difficult. She lashed her father's frame down, using the rope she had stolen from the stable, running the rough cord under the horse's belly and across its back. With her load secured, she led the horse toward the cave's hidden entrance to the Fae castle. When she reached the secret access the queen had revealed days earlier; she went past it, staying alongside the rock wall another fifty yards. Stopping at a patch of grass, she gave the horse its head to graze while she dug a shallow grave. Owls called back and forth as her shovelfuls of dirt grew into a pile. Blisters sprouted on her hands, unused to such work. Loosening the rope, the corpse dropped to the ground like a sack of potatoes. Her arms ached while dragging the rug filled with stinking, rotting flesh to dump into the hole. As her parting gift, Morveena opened the rug just enough to stab her father's heart with the knife from the Fae castle she had stolen five nights prior. Without emotion, she picked up the shovel, filling the dirt back in, covering over her father's unmarked grave.

Back in the direction she'd come from, Morveena took her time traveling home. Every moment, sleeping and waking, she put to use roughing out, then refining the details for a plan of her making. In calculating every step, she made a list of what she would need to achieve the goals. Steps that would provide her with the success she felt she deserved.

SEVERAL DAYS LATER, Montestrell's daughter arrived home, driving her father's carriage. She looked as if she'd been to hell and back. Her fire-red hair was a rat's nest, face bruised, a black eye shone out, circled in blue, green, an ugly yellow around the edges. Dirt streaked across her face, her hands, and crammed under her nails. She stank, dry sweat from her physical labors and her time on the road. She professed to having been lost for days to the manor staff. When she found her way again, she claimed she had been too afraid to stop anywhere to ask for help or directions. The story she put forth was that she feared for her life. Feared the Fae would come after her.

Her theatrical performance for the household staff was stellar. She ranted. Raved. Told them how the Fae had murdered her father and how she had gotten away. The redhead shouted orders to the stable boy to unload the bags and trunks from the carriage, unharness and care for the bedraggled-looking horse. Next, she issued orders for the housemistress to ready a bath for her and set to repacking her bags with clean clothes. Making her voice quiver, she announced her intention to travel at once to the Goblin Hall of King Lancer, to report in her dead father's stead. She wailed with feigned grieving; claiming it was her obligation, her duty, the last service she could give to her beloved father. She maintained that she alone must deliver the message to their king.

Morveena intended to tell King Lancer face to face about the murder of his ambassador, Munro Marcellus Montestrell. A murder, she claimed, left blood on the hands of the Fae royals. The Goblin Court would have no reason to doubt her. The girl looked as though she'd been to hell and back.

Morveena picked up her carpetbag containing her magic books, held up her skirts, hurried up the front steps, and entered her home. *Her home.* The patriarch now dead. All this was hers. The household staff was stunned. The ambassador's daughter almost never uttered a word in their presence. But the staff came around and set about carrying out her orders. If she were mistress of the household, best to start off by pleasing her.

She pointed at a houseboy from the top of the stairs and sent him to the cook, to tell her to prepare some travel food, as she'd be leaving early in the morning. Pointing at another, she bade him go tell the stable master to ready her father's stallion, Black Jack, at dawn. She planned to ride alone to Goblin Hall.

After a steaming bath and a meal, bundled in her floor-length green velvet robe, Munro's daughter went down to her father's office. False tears streamed down her cheeks. She closed the door with instructions that she wasn't to be disturbed. The moment she ensconced herself in the room, her tears dried up. Her slender fingers skimmed along the leather bindings of a long row of books shelved in bookcases. Her father had never allowed her to touch them.

Leafing through his desk papers, digging around in his drawers, put his account books into her hands. Ever a quick study, she skimmed the records, gleaning just where the manor's funds came in and went out; the list of those who owed her father money. She found the key she sought hanging at the back of the desk. Dragging his chair over to the fireplace, Morveena stood upon it. Reaching up, she swung the portrait of her mother away from the chimney on well-oiled hinges, revealing a lockbox on a shelf she had discovered years ago. The key slid into the locking mechanism. With one click, the box opened. For the first time in her life, Morveena Morgan Montestrell found payment for her pain and suffering. Taking up handfuls of small diamonds, letting them trickle back down into the box. Closing the lid, she locked it, covered its hiding place with her mother's smile once more. She caught her own reflection in the window behind his desk. Not a mar or imperfection to be seen since dropping the glamor she had arrived home with. She would have to put the mask back on before she left in the morning, making sure her bruises were heavy with blue, green, yellow, and purple. Before she retreated from Munro's library, *her library*, she cast a binding spell that sealed around her mother's portrait. Now, only she could open it.

Wasting no time, she searched her father's bedroom. In moments, she located his cash, rings, and her mother's jewelry. Dividing the goods into separate soft felt bags, pulling the strings closed after filling each.

Back in her own room, she tucked the bags of jewels away in the bottom of her personal luggage, along with the cash. Keeping a small roll of bills out, Morveena secured the rest in a pouch on the belt she now wore.

She slept very little before the sun rose. Morveena dressed in a black wool split-riding skirt and a black silk shirt she'd taken in at the seams last night. She pulled on her father's gold and silver-threaded brocade vest, having sewn darts and small gatherings at the back of the waistline to make it fit her. The vest now housed Munro's knife, tobacco pouch, and money purse. She'd masked her face with magic once more, presenting bruised and battered flesh. The redhead gave a list of orders between spoonfuls of porridge as she gulped down her breakfast. She made it clear what she expected while gone, as well as upon her return, brooking no questions from the household staff.

She swung a floor-length, heavy green wool cape around her shoulders, then grabbed her small, personal carpetbag. The staff loaded the rest of her luggage and saddlebags last night. The envoy's daughter swept out the door.

Climbing up, she settled herself onto Black Jack's saddle; the stallion reared up, but she held her seat, turned his head with the reins and cantered out of the courtyard.

MORVEENA ARRIVED AT Goblin Hall wearing the same abused face she'd shown to her household. Knowing the rumors would fly, she didn't bother keeping her hood up to hide the abuse.

The stunning chestnut-haired goblin girl entered the gates, galloping in on the stallion Black Jack. She got the horse to rear up once again for her, showing off her horsemanship. When the magnificent animal had calmed, Morveena dismounted, her cape sweeping about her in a flourish. She handed Black Jack's reins off to a stable boy.

Stalking into King Lancer and Queen Alora's throne room, she ran uninvited up the five steps to the dais, falling to one knee before Lancer Goodfellow. Lancer's wife, Alora, was beside him, huge with child.

"I beg Your Majesty's pardon, but I've bad news to report, my liege." She practiced this speech over and over while riding, wanting to deliver a perfect performance, and wrote the whole play. Her part? Star of the show.

The story she had concocted fell from her lips like a professional actress. The girl mixed some little truths with the poisonous lies of how the Fae

King and Queen rejected Lancer's request to join forces; rejected the request to hold pre-war talks or even to take counsel on how to stop the Gugwe Emperor, Thana NukPana.

Tears flowed down her cheeks as she spun her tale, providing the details of her father's murder. She offered the suggestion that perhaps the envoy had pushed too hard trying to change their minds. Morveena told them how Queen Aleta had tried to keep her at the Fae Court, perhaps for a later ransom? Lennox had lost control, smashing Munro Montestrell's head in and stabbing him in the heart.

Lancer balked at Lennox's loss of control. He had known the Fae King for a very long time, but had never seen or heard of such a thing happening. Morveena reacted by backing away from the King of Goblins, her mouth opening, and closing, but no sound coming out. It was here that she gained Queen Alora's sympathy. The pregnant woman struggled to stand and came to put her arm around the distraught girl's shoulders. "Can't you see she's traumatized, Lancer?"

"I...I can prove it, my lord," Morveena said as she panted, panic crashing across her face. "Never would I dare to make up a story like this! What point would there be? I...I watched my father murdered by those Faeries, and I came here to warn *you*. It is my belief they're going to turn against us," her voice quivered, eyes darting back and forth between Lancer and Alora. "I can show you where they've hidden his body, his grave, to prove my story true. Please...you've got to believe me for the good of our people."

That's where she hooked Lancer. The good of the Goblin people was Lancer's highest priority. The King insisted she stay safe with Alora. Lancer had her describe where the unmarked grave was located. He knew the Fae castle well, took a small force of ten, leaving at daybreak. Morveena promised to look after Alora and help with their toddler, Rupert, while the King and his men investigated her story.

That evening, Morveena brought a tray to the fireside table where Alora sat reading. "I put Rupert to bed, tucked him in, and read him a story. Here, my queen, I've brought you some tea."

Alora thanked her, asked if Morveena would join her for tea, but the girl declined, saying she'd had some earlier when Rupert was getting ready for bed. They read in quiet companionship for another hour, when Alora announced she was ready to turn in for the night.

The Queen stood. The room spun.

Wrapping her arms around her waist to protect her pregnant belly, Alora was groaning in pain from hard cramps.

"Queen Alora!" Morveena called with concern. "What is it? What's wrong? How can I help you?"

"Morveena," the Queen grimaced, "find the housemistress and send her for the midwife. I think the baby is coming." Her breaths came in heavy pants through each cramp. Alora's water broke, running down her legs and pooling on the floor. Morveena took hold of the goblin queen's arm, helped her lie down on the floor, tucking a small pillow beneath her head.

"I'll only be gone a few moments, my lady," Morveena assured the Queen in a hush, then ran from the room, closing the door behind her.

Standing on the other side of the closed door, Morveena listened as Alora moaned and groaned, thrashing on the floor. After a few minutes, she could hear no more noise coming from the other side. Opening the door just enough to see through a crack, she deemed it safe and re-entered the room. Using her considerable ability to playact, she rushed to the Queen's side. She feigned huffing and breathlessness as though she'd run all the way to the housemistress and back.

She dropped to her knees, in between the Queen's own, just as the baby's head was crowning. Alora's face was turning purple. She was gasping for air. Mesmerized, Morveena watched the woman she had identified as a stumbling block to all her plans as Alora Fiona Goodfellow died of suffocation. The Queen's throat had closed up from a severe allergic reaction. Morveena remembered her father mentioning the Queen's bane two years before. He told his daughter Alora had a lethal allergy to sumac, which was the type of tea Morveena had brewed and served the Queen just an hour before. Alora's body convulsed, causing the muscles in her cervix to give one last contraction. Her dying body pushed out a squalling baby who would become known as Robin Wilum Goodfellow.

The moment she held the naked babe in her hands, Munro's daughter screamed her head off, bringing the house mistress running. She found a sobbing, inconsolable Morveena, clutching the newborn to her chest, babbling about how Queen Alora had died giving birth.

In the end, the housemistress had to give the girl several shots of Lancer's whiskey to calm her, but Morveena wouldn't let them take the babe from her. The housemistress cut the cord, wrapped a blanket around the girl and the baby. Sitting and rocking her body back and forth, she and the baby fell asleep.

WHEN LANCER GOODFELLOW returned home a week later, he confirmed he had indeed found the shallow grave holding her father's body. It was obvious Munro had suffered a brutal murder. The Goblin King had found one of the Fae castle knives plunged to the hilt in her father's heart. Angry and demanding an answer for this deed, Lancer had ridden to the Fae court proper, confronting the Fae monarchs. They denied any knowledge of the murder vehemently, saying the envoy and his daughter had left alive and well. Queen Aleta had suggested the girl might be unstable because her father abused and beat her. But Munro had protected his secret abuse of his daughter with such skill that not even his own household knew of it. Lancer had questioned a few of the court staff, and they confirmed Morveena's story that the Queen had tried to get the girl to stay on at the castle.

Stricken with grief upon hearing the news of his wife Alora's death in childbirth, Lancer's mind entered a dark place. His wife gone, and with two small boys to raise without her, put him in a deep depression. Months went by as he retreated deeper and deeper into himself.

No one questioned Morveena as she stepped in to care for both children. Others had to take on the day-to-day tasks of running the Goblin clan's business until their king was whole again. Having never been around a baby before, Morveena spent hours each day pretending the child was her own. Rupert resented the new child. His mother was dead; his father was emotionally unavailable. What Rupert knew was that prior to the baby coming into his life, Morveena had paid attention to him. It seemed to Rupert that Morveena was now besotted with his brother. Rupert felt forgotten. The angry thoughts he harbored festered and grew as time went on.

Several more months passed. No one ever noticed all the scars and scabs Morveena had on the insides of her arms. She worked her black magic and blood magic on the staff, the King, the children, and the Goblin clans. The mutilations increased as she was casting her spells, creating her glamours, working toward her next goal.

One night, with the full moon throwing shadows across the land, Morveena stained her lips red and dressed. She donned a shimmering satin gown she had remade from one of Alora's. Altering the dress to give it a low-cut bodice and a tight fit along her curves, which had grown somewhat voluptuous, having plenty to eat and no regular beatings. Her hair shone red-gold in the firelight as she brought a crystal cut-glass decanter full of Lancer's favorite whiskey and poured them each a glass. The fire crackled as she toasted his family; toasted the clans, then filled their glasses again and again, finding more things to toast. The booze flowed. Morveena took advantage of Lancer's grief and loneliness. He was silent when she went down on her knees in front of him, her blood-red lips shining in the firelight as she reached up to touch him, pleased to find him aroused.

She spent the next several hours seducing him until he took her.

Early the next morning, she washed away the symbols she had written in her own blood on the floor of her bedroom. She had discovered a ritual in what was now, by far, her favorite spell book, 'Blood Magic and the Spells to Defeat Your Foes'. The instructions for the invocation required the caster to paint the symbols using her own blood, forming them into a circle large enough so she could lie down within. Inside the circle, she had pleasured herself and, right at the moment of climax, gasped out the words of the spell. After the ritual, she had dressed and gone down to Lancer's library, where he sat brooding night after night, her own wetness, and musk wafting off her.

Lancer didn't say a word to her the day after their lovemaking. He went back to his moping, piling on more guilt for having taken her virginity and adding it to his other miseries. Morveena had been careful to leave evidence for him to find.

Weeks passed. She cared for Rupert and baby Robin. They were both quite attached to her by this time. Another month went by when Lancer noticed Morveena's waist had thickened. A few weeks later, she'd developed the telltale 'bump' in her belly, making no effort to hide it, outlined in her tight gowns. Lancer called her to the library one evening after she'd put the children to bed and asked her, to his shame, if she carried his child?

"I do, my lord. Though I make no claim on you. You were still grieving when our lovemaking took place. It would be unfair to hold you responsible. You must not worry about me. In fact, I think it's high time I got back to my clan and estate before I get too far along. I'm wealthy enough to take care of the child on my own," she suggested.

"That will not do, Morveena," Lancer declared. "You carry a child of the King's blood, another heir to the Goblin kingdom. We must marry Morveena. I know you're young, but Rupert and Robin have already grown attached to you." He paced back and forth in front of the settee she perched on. "We could be a good match. You've a powerful clan to join to mine. You would be the queen of all the goblin clans in Sharas. Though there is no love between us, others have made marriages on less. Will you accept the match, lady?" He turned to look her in the eye.

She offered a coy smile and accepted.

It had only taken her half a year to complete her goal.

HER MEMORIES VANISHED when the tent flap opened. Rupert stood looking inside, puffing on a cigar. "Prisoners are quiet for the night, my love. Come join me for a smoke and a walk." Brazenly, he watched every move she made as she pulled her naked body from under the blanket. She waved him away, told him she would join him as soon as she dressed, and he let the flap of the tent drop.

A twist of fate. How things had changed over the years, she thought. A smile tugged at the corners of her mouth. Now she had a new goal in mind, and nothing kept Morveena Morgan Montestrell Goodfellow from reaching her goals.

CHAPTER 20: A Grand Scheme

"**A**re you alright, lass?" Robin asked Faith.

"So far," she replied. "I'll thank you not to tell me how incredibly stupid I am." She shot an angry look at the boots tossed to the side. "What do you think is going to happen?" She whispered to Robin.

"The Queen kept referring to someone named Aleta. Seemed to think you reminded her of that person. Do you know who Aleta is?" Robin wondered.

Narrol snorted and laughed, his mania taking him again.

"The cousins who appeared at my home told me my mother's name was Aleta," Faith confessed.

"The mother you can't remember because you were an adopted child?" his voice going up an octave.

"I guess so," Faith said, depressed. It seemed Morveena knew something about her mother's disappearance.

"Who was she?" Robin breathed out.

"Aleta Dawn was her name. According to my new relatives, she's the missing Queen of the Faerie." Faith held a hand up to her mouth, too late to stop the words, afraid to feel the weight of their meaning.

Robin stared toward her into the dark, moments ticking by. "So, that means...uh...that means..."

"Yeah," Faith acknowledged. "It means I'm a princess. A Fae princess with a missing mother and a father who I don't remember." Her voice wound up, "A Faerie princess whose people—a people I didn't know I had—seem in mortal danger from a terrifying monster race called the Gugwe. Just another little something new to me in the last day or two, Gugwe monsters." A single tear rolled down her cheek. "And I didn't even find my friends."

Robin let her stew in her own self-pity for a few minutes so he could think. Before he got it all sorted out, he heard Narrol's voice croak, "I wish I had your luck, you scamp. To find and bring in the long searched for Faerie princess? What I wouldn't give..." he pondered. Narrol fell silent again.

Moments later, they could see Rupert strolling away from Morveena's tent, puffing on a hand-rolled cigar. It was clear he headed toward them to check the prisoners once more. Stopping at the tree where he had chained his brother, he kicked Robin in the shins. "Maybe I had you all wrong, brother, but I doubt it. No more talking tonight!" He clenched the cigar in his teeth while he gagged Robin, Narrol, and Faith. They could hear him whistling a tune as he walked back to the other side of the camp.

ROBIN LEANED HIS HEAD against the tree, gagged, *wished for a long, wet drink, wondered what was going through Faith's mind, and then laughed to himself. As if he could guess her thoughts. She surprised him at every turn and seemed to have no fear. Well, he corrected himself, no fear, except of spiders and heights. That much he had learned about her in the short time they'd spent together. She was so different from anyone he'd ever met, yeah?*

Faith's forehead rested against her knees. *Gods, she was so thirsty. Thirsty and alone with her thoughts. What an immature, idiot thing to do in a time of danger, she berated herself. Obsessing about her boots when she was supposed to be helping Robin. She'd messed everything up. He must think I'm a total dumbass, she told herself. She couldn't argue against it, since she was sitting here, wings bound, hands and feet chained to a tree and gagged. She blinked her eyes, determined not to cry. No. No crying. You don't get to cry when you created your own troubles! Val would have said. 'Besides, there's no time for tears. Instead, spend the time dreaming up a plan to fix the problem.' That thought threatened to bring on tears. Val would insist on 'a brainstorming session to create a strategy to move forward.'*

Thinking about Val, her common sense and all her advice gave Faith a boost. So, the Fae princess reconciled herself to focusing on solutions, not wallowing in her problems. She would work at turning her mental debate of pros and cons into plans of action. Imagining scenarios, playing the roles of both herself and Val, as the two brainstormed together. The exercise made her feel like Val was right there with her, helping her figure out how to fix this mess. She could only imagine Val's reaction if she ever met Queen Morveena. That would be a disaster!

Flashes of random ideas came through her mind's eye like sketches in her book. As she examined those notions, they took the form of drawings she pretended to sketch, depicting ways back to safety. Faith was determined to make sure she did her part to take steps forward toward solutions. Steps to get back to her friends. The Fae Princess fantasized about shaping a small sliver of hope—a star. Clutching it over her heart, she locked it away inside, where no one could take it from her.

Next, she told her subconscious to go to work, to begin looking for solutions at every turn. The moon shadows moved beyond her. Faith let her mind drift with the shadows, sleep staking its claim. Her last thought was a memory of Val telling her to rest now; tomorrow's another day, another chance to change the course of things. She'd always trusted Val's advice.

"REPORT!" RUPERT SNAPPED at the lad standing at attention in front of him.

"No incidents to report, sir." He focused his eyes on the horizon. Experience taught him it was best not to look straight at Prince Rupert. "Quiet night. The prisoners never moved. Well, they couldn't, of course, bound the way they are, but..."

Rupert moved forward and grabbed the lad's chin. "Shut it," he growled. "I said report, not give me your opinion, lackey. Go get some breakfast and then get back here. You and Weston are to guard the prisoners today."

The young lad turned toward the mess tent to follow his orders. He commended himself for not pointing out to the prince that the night watch got to sleep during the day. Of a sudden, Rupert's meaty hand slapped the back of his head. "You moron," Rupert snarled, "you're supposed to salute when you're leaving my presence! I want the name of your commander. This is sloppy training. Unacceptable!" he raged.

Faith and Robin were wide awake now as they witnessed Rupert's callous behavior.

"I'm sorry, sir. The fault's all mine. I must be punchy from the night watch. It won't happen again, sir." The lad tripped over his words and couldn't get them out fast enough.

Rupert landed a fist with a hard left swing to the lad's right eye. The soldier swayed from the punch, but held his stance.

"I asked for your commander's name, soldier! Who is it?"

His head throbbed. The soldier swallowed. "You, sir," he whispered, "you're my commander."

Rage danced across Rupert's face. "I know I am your commander now, fool. I want to know who your training commander was," he growled at the soldier.

"Wait!" Robin yells, spitting the gag from his mouth. "I was his training commander, Rupert. I'm responsible for the lad's training." Raven's eyes opened wide as saucers; his face was stricken.

"Of course," Rupert snarled. "Makes sense. Dismissed," he grumbled at the lad and then landed three vicious kicks to Robin's ribs and gut as punishment for the poor training of a soldier.

"Stop!" Faith screamed. Narrol giggled, then huffed as Rupert gave his ribs a kick for good measure. He pointed his finger at Faith as a warning. For once, she held her tongue.

Rupert's handling was rough as he untied Robin's bindings. Robin turned onto his side and vomited. "Get up!" Rupert ordered. Robin rose on his hands and knees, but not fast enough for his angry brother. Rupert kicked him again in the ass, and Robin sprawled forward, limbs stiff. "How I ever ended up with a worthless brother such as you, I'll never know," he mused. "There's a stream behind the canteen. Clean yourself up. Your Queen wants to see you," Rupert strutted away, pleased with the morning so far.

"Oh, Robin," Faith whispered, the gag still hanging from the left side of her mouth, "Are you alright?" fear written across her face. He swayed where he stood.

"It's nothing to worry over, lass. I'm used to Rupert's way of saying good morning," he tells her in a light voice. Narrol giggled. Robin watched the play of emotions wash over her face until her features settled into anger.

"He's a monster," she said to herself.

Robin pulled the rest of the gag from her mouth, and she licked her dry lips. "Yes, he is, but to be fair, not all of his own making," he confided to her.

"What does the Queen..." she thought for a moment, "your mother, I mean. What do you think she wants with you?"

He stretched his arms and then reached down to rub the kinks from his leg muscles, whispered back to her, "One can only guess, lass, but likely nothing good. I warned you before, and I'll warn you again. Silence is your best defense with her. It will be very important for you to remember this piece of advice. Trust me. I have had to learn it more than once. A painful process. So, please remember," he held a finger up to his lips. As he limped away toward the stream, Narrol giggled in the background.

Faith let her head drop to her knees again. A short while later, she felt a light tap on her shoulder, making her jump. A young soldier held his finger up to his lips, his body hidden in a bush behind her. His arm pushed out a clay cup of water he held to her lips while she gulped it down. He pressed his finger to his lips once more, then was gone. She wondered later, as the scorching sun beat down on her, if she had imagined him.

Robin stripped off his shirt, rinsed it in the water, then laid it over a bush to dry while he bathed. He left his pants on and waded in, letting the cool water wash over his bruised body, ducking his head under to rinse his dreadlocks. The bruises were already turning a deep purple on his dark skin. His mind was churning with questions. *What was Morveena up to now? Why was Rupert letting him wander freely with no guard? Were they certain he wouldn't flee with the faerie still captive? If so, he had to admit they were right. Keep a cool head,* he cautioned himself as he put his wet shirt back on, muscles groaning in protest.

Walking back up the slope, he crossed to the other side of the goblin camp. He noted several of the lads giving him the barest nod. Saying nothing, he blinked his eyes back at them, not wanting to bring any trouble to anyone. In return, they put two fingers to their hearts that only he could see as he passed them.

When he reached the Queen's tent, she called out before he announced his arrival, "You may enter, Robin." Her unnatural power unnerved him. Robin pulled the flap back and ducked in. Morveena sat against the back wall of the large tent on a solid oak chair carved with faces emulating screams, pain, and crushing defeat. He kneeled before her, noticing her uncovered feet. She had long toenails lacquered in blood-red and sharpened to lethal points. He stood looking up into her face, finding it schooled to calm.

"Robin Wilum Goodfellow at your service, my queen," he croaked out.

She wiggled her toes; her face pouting. "Mummy doesn't have any boots to wear."

He kept his silence close, face blank, knowing there wasn't any suitable response to her statement. The black boots he'd stolen weeks before from Faith and gifted to Morveena now sat on the floor to the right of her chair. He maintained his stance, feet apart, hands clasped behind his back.

"So quiet. So formal this morning, my son. Throughout the long night, you've thought of nothing you want to say to me?" Her voice was a dangerous softness.

Rupert stepped up from behind him, fastened a metal collar around his neck, holding a length of chain attached to it. Robin moved not a muscle. Rupert laughed. "Here is your dog, Queen Morveena," handing her the chain. She wrapped it twice around her wrist while holding Robin's eyes with her own.

"You've always been my wayward child, Robin. Why do you wish to hurt me so? Haven't I given you a mother's love? Given you chance after chance to please me?" she growled out, eyes glowing red, as she half stood. He remained stoic. She sat back again, looking him over from head to toe.

"You remind me so of your father," she said, not bothering to hide her disgust. "If only my daughter had lived to be groomed for the throne," she clucked her tongue. Robin saw the flash of jealous rage sweep across Rupert's face as he stood behind Morveena, but she took no notice.

Changing course, she informed him, "I have a role I wish you to play for me, Robin Wilum Goodfellow." At the use of his full name, he swallowed. "The offense you committed, consorting with an enemy Fae, however innocent you claim to be of the knowledge, is still treason."

He had never understood her hatred for the Fae, but couldn't deny it ran as deep as any hate he had ever known in a person.

"I can be benevolent. Forgiving," she tells him, as if trying on different clothes to see if she likes the style. "Since your stinking faerie travel companion has turned out to be a living children's nursery tale, I see a way out for you. Yes," she offered. "A way for you to avoid death because of treason against the crown. Another chance. Another gift from your generous mother," she suggested. Robin maintained his silence in response, heart thudding against his chest. He knew the feigned benevolence would carry a high price.

"This next question will require you to answer." She jerked the chain connected to his collar to be sure she had his full attention. "Do you wish my forgiveness, Robin Wilum Goodfellow? Do you yearn to be back in my good graces?" Morveena pulled the chain hand over hand, bringing his face close, her eyes challenging his. He blinked twice and moved his eyes up to look at Rupert's. The chain yanked his head back to face her. "Look at *me*, my darling, so I can see the truth of your answer," she commanded.

He schooled his features to softness, a gentleness to carry his voice, as he brought his right hand to cover his heart. "I do, my queen. I would cherish your forgiveness with all my heart."

She studied him. The moments ticked by. Slackening the chain, she allowed him to stand straight again. Morveena fiddled with the links of the restraints in her hands. He did not ask what he would have to do to earn this proffered forgiveness. Asking held its own dangers. He stood content to wait until she deigned to share the price with him.

"Rupert," she called to Robin's older brother, "would you be a dear and fetch my new pet?" As always, Rupert jumped to fulfill her request, leaving them alone in the tent. She relished the confusion she'd seen settle on Robin's face at her request. Tapping her bare foot while waiting, she let the silence create its own discomfort.

Ten long minutes passed before Robin heard Rupert returning with Faith. When they entered the tent, he noted Rupert had also fitted her with a metal collar and a connecting chain.

"Come to me, my little pet," Morveena crooned to Faith. Robin began sweating, knowing the reaction the title was likely to bring from the girl. Faith's face became stonelike. She didn't move.

Rupert used his foot to kick her buttocks. The girl fell forward on all fours. "Show the queen your respect," he growled at her.

Morveena let out a delighted laugh. "That's more like it!" Faith rose. "No! Stay like you are," the queen commands. "A pet should be on all fours," she twittered in amusement. "Don't you agree, Robin?"

He didn't respond, hoping Faith would follow his example. At least for the moment, the girl stayed put, saying nothing, but he could see she fought to keep silent. Robin noticed her swollen left eye turning a dark color from Rupert's ministrations.

"You stink," Morveena sniffed at the girl. "Well, I suppose pets do," she reasoned. Anger flashed across Faith's face. "In particular, dirty, stinking Faerie pets," the Queen added, trying her best to bait the girl's obvious fury, just looking for a reaction. But to Robin's surprise, silence ruled. At least for the moment.

"I thought you should be here to witness my generosity," she tells the girl. "Rupert," Morveena said, "no more bruising where someone can see it, yes?" Rupert nodded his acquiescence, a pout on his face, like a spoiled child.

"Robin, mind my words. This Fae's life is in your hands. If you choose to leave us again, leave our clan," she emphasized, "the girl will pay the price. The price of course, will be painful. Understand?" He nodded.

"I will announce that we have discovered you did not commit treason. We'll tell the clan that you and your sidekick missed the summer games because you were on your way to capture and deliver this creature to me. My dear son, having found the long-lost, fabled Fae princess."

Robin startled. Faith let out the breath she was holding, defeat written across her face. The Goblin Queen knew her identity. Had Robin divulged her identity to this cruel monster, Faith wondered? She looked at him with the saddest eyes he had ever seen.

"In fact," Morveena leaned forward, "I will name you a hero for this discovery, and the death penalty for treason declared in abeyance." The Queen watched his every move. "Don't get too excited, Robin. Rewards come in due time. It is doubtful you've had time enough yet to have absorbed your lesson about loyalty or to ponder how important it is to keep Mummy happy?" Her anger flared once more, given a moment to ponder her own declaration.

"We," she announced, reaching for Rupert's hand with her free one, "have a plan. A plan I believe will cement the clan's safety and prosperity." Her eyes glazed over as she visualized the grand scheme she intended. When she came to herself, she proclaimed, "We head north tomorrow."

"North?" Robin barked, forgetting himself.

Pleased with his reaction, she continued, "Did I stutter?" She yanked the chain. "North. We will take a peace delegation to the Gugwe leader, Thana Nukpana." She basked in delight at the looks of disbelief showing on their faces.

"My Queen," Robin stuttered, "it's almost certain death to walk right into the Gugwe's hold!"

Her eyes glittered with hidden knowledge. "We will be safe. I have had dealings with the Thana in the past," she stated with confidence.

The Goblin Queen tugged on Robin's chain once more and directed him to kneel before her. She watched as he dropped to his knees. "I have proffered conditional forgiveness, but keep in mind, I have not yet given it," her voice grated. She laid out the conditions for him to reclaim his life from the death sentence she held over his head. "I deem it necessary for you to have ample time to think about my offer. Ponder my generosity. In ten-days' time, you will come before me again and swear your fealty. If you do not swear, I shall string you up so I can peel the skin from your body while you entertain us with your screams. Until then, you will remain a prisoner. You need to contemplate your devotion to your clan and family. You will use these ten days to show me how obedient you can be." She looked from Robin to Faith. "Each of you will endure the punishment for the other's unacceptable behavior, should you be so foolish as to choose to exhibit any? I require you both to obey me without question, or the other will pay the price. Am I clear about my expectations?" She demanded a response.

"Yes, my Queen," Robin stated.

Faith couldn't bring herself to speak; her shock was so strong. Never in her life could she have imagined finding herself in such a position. Faith's silence set the Queen off. She snapped her fingers at Rupert, who came from behind her chair and picked up the cane Morveena had taken from Narrol weeks ago. Rupert raised the cane, and Faith squeezed her eyes shut, bracing for the blow, but it was Robin's back the cane fell to, and he grunted in pain beside her.

"Do you understand now, Princess? He will pay for your failures to please me, and you will pay for his." Morveena smiled at them both. "Robin, ask the princess to acknowledge my question, please."

His breath was coming in short, quick huffs to fight off the pain of the blow, but he choked out the words, "Faith, please tell the Queen you understand." He hung his head.

"I understand, Queen Morveena," Faith whispered in fear.

"Good. Very good," the Queen basked in satisfaction.

"There's just one more thing before Rupert returns you to be bound again to your trees, my pets," her face almost bursting with glee. "You once offered me these boots as a gift, Robin." She pointed at Faith's black boots to the right. "I'm sure you can imagine my disappointment in finding out they had belonged to a stinking, sneaky faerie. My greatest enemy," she declared in anguish. "We have a problem, son. I'm positive you never intended such an insult, yes?" she prodded. Robin shook his head no, wondering where this was going to lead. "Good. I thought as much as you have always professed your love to me," she said sarcastically. "So then, what can we do to remedy the faerie stink from your gift?"

Morveena made a show of tapping her bare foot on the floor, her forefinger drumming against her lips, as if immersed in deep thought, looking for a solution. When her eyes sought Robin's again, she quipped, "Oh, I've got the perfect solution to fix the unintended breach." Clapping her hands as she informed him, "You must please Mummy by licking all the faerie stink off the boots so I can wear them again, yes?"

Triumph bloomed across her face when she took in his expression. Then she added, turning toward Faith, "I'm sure my new pet wouldn't want me to put on clean boots over dirty feet, would she? She can lick my toes and feet clean, then you two can return to your kennels, yes?"

Faith's face turned green at the thought of licking the Queen's disgusting feet. Rupert took up the cane with one hand, bouncing it up and down against the palm of his other hand, relishing the idea of applying it to either of them or both.

Degradation is a high form of control, and Morveena craved power over others, like a drug. This was the heady form of euphoria she sought. She swooned with delight as the two captives did as she bade them.

Afterward, Rupert made the two of them crawl on all fours across the camp, holding the chains attached to their collars, like the dogs he considered them to be. When he had bound them once more to the tree trunks, he walked away humming a little tune.

Faith leaned over and retched until dry heaves were all she had left. Her forehead fell to her knees, allowing silence to speak volumes for her as the sun danced the rest of the way across the sky. Her spirit broken. Doomed, she accepted the reality that she was now a dog at the feet of a wicked master.

QUEEN MORVEENA AND Prince Rupert held hands, climbing halfway up the hillside, with the camp spread out below. Stopping, they had reached a rocky outcropping surrounded by boulders, with spindly evergreens sprinkled about.

"Here," Morveena declared, and she sat down on a bed of pine needles, leaning her back against a big rock.

Rupert joined her. Moonlight cast a sheen across the rocky rubble. "This should block our voices from curious listeners," Rupert commented, adjusting his coat. "You mentioned a plan, Morveena?"

"First," Morveena declared, "I've been thinking of how I can make use of Robin in the design of our upcoming venture. As you heard, I'll give him credit for bringing us a great boon: the long-lost Princess of the Fae. I will announce that Robin is acquitted of the charge of treason. Those actions should take care of questions about not enforcing the death penalty," she reasoned. "Others in the clan will still fear the death penalty should they even think of committing betrayal against me."

"Yes, my love. I'll see to the details," Rupert assured her.

"We start north at sunrise. Rupert, you will announce the change in Robin's status. It will make the fairy distrust him. I don't want to take the chance of the two of them joining forces. We'll tell him the Fae Princess will only remain alive as long as he obeys our every command. You know the lad, Rupert. We'll put the burden of her survival all on his shoulders, clarifying that for every kindness he shows her, she will pay for it with her flesh and blood. That should keep him in line and away from her."

"Brilliant. You're brilliant, my dear," Rupert bit her shoulder, hung on with his teeth to worry the soft flesh. "Tell me more, my love. Your grand scheme," he chuckled, drawing deeply on a cigar. "I know you've already got a strategy, you vixen," Rupert began placing small kisses along her shoulder, trailing up her neck. He felt her body quiver with excitement.

"We're going to sell it," she whispered.

"Sell what, Morveena?" Rupert lifted his head to look at her with a quizzical expression on his face.

Morveena laughed a deep, throaty laugh. "Why, Rupert, darling," she crooned. "It. The dirty, stinking fairy," she blinked her eyes several times, judging to see if he got what she meant. "I'm going to sell the precious Faerie Princess to Thana NukPana, Emperor of the Gugwe tribes. I bet Thana NukPana would pay bags and bags of gold just to acquire her." She plucked the cigar from his fingers and drew deeply, smoke curling around her lips.

Rupert growled his approval in her ear.

The Goblin Queen giggled like a schoolgirl, rubbing her hands together like a greedy child. "Think of the power he will grant us for bringing him such a treasure?"

GRABBING RUPERT BY the lapels of his coat, Morveena crushed her mouth to his, the moon doing a slow dance across the night sky. Neither Morveena nor Rupert noticed the movement. A shadow in the rocky outcropping above disappeared, having overheard their scheme.

Dedo was eager to report this sorry state of affairs to the Allies. They would all lose if Faith fell into the hands of the vile Gugwe Emperor, Thana NukPana.

Dedo would lose most of all.

He deemed time to be of the essence.

CHAPTER 21: New Friend of Yours?

Valerie Victoria Pureheart fell in and out of consciousness. Pulling herself up and out of the abyss for a moment, she blinked three times, trying to focus, thoughts mired as if in mud. Val strained to make sense of the scene before her, aware of her limbs being numb and unmovable. A clock ticked on the mantel of the fireplace, keeping time with the beat of her heart. She had been dreaming of someone she was sure would rescue her. The smallest memory of the fantasy pushed its way through her addled brain. Caz. Yes, she was sure Cazzidy Beaumont Touchstone would find her. Squinting her eyes, she willed them to focus. I must still be dreaming, she thought...Caz was sitting across the room from her. Thoughts muzzy, she failed to understand why he wasn't rushing to get her out of this sticky binding? Darkness took her under again.

Hours later, she registered a door opening, allowing light to shine into the room. A light that illuminated the death of her hope for rescue.

Cazzidy was indeed across the room, just as she had dreamed. Any hopes for rescue shattered as she realized both he and Rolland were bound in tight cocoons, just as she and Saffron were. A single tear made a track down her cheek.

Val felt a vibration on the web that connected them all. Rolling her eyes upward, she couldn't believe what she saw. Mind whirling, her lips struggling to form the words, *'What's that sneaky little spy doing here?'* But before she could utter a sound, a spider moved toward her with surprising speed.

When the Black Widow reached Val's head, using dainty steps it picked its way across her soft hair to whisper in her ear, "Awake so soon, my dear? I've no wish to hurt you, but this will not do. Not until I figure out what is going on. Too many of the threads of the weave are coming together in one place. My place." This matter-of-fact statement ended with a quick but vicious bite behind Valerie's ear. The spider injected a small amount of venom into her bloodstream. Slender body jerking, her head dropped forward onto her chest, eyes frozen wide with anger. With the numbing agent coursing through her veins, blackness became her world once more.

In one of the four corners of the dark room, a long finger reached out, plucked the outer strand of the spider's web. The entire design shook, strands stretching almost to the breaking point, then relaxing, settling again. Jumping, the spider used the power of its long legs to twist full circle, taking it right to the exact spot where someone had touched the webbing.

A voice that came from the shadowed corner garnered the spiders' attention. "Busy as always, I see. Tell me, are these new friends of yours," waving a hand over the web containing the trapped people, "or next week's lunch?" Dedo moved into the hoary light, revealing his face.

The arachnid lifted its front left leg, pointed at Dedo, declaring, "You!"

The spider shape-shifted, but couldn't get its emotions under control. As a result, the shift kept flashing back and forth, in and out of the forms of a black cat, spider, Arnid the man, back to cat, on to spider, and last, back to a man. He smashed his fist down on the tabletop to make the shifting stop.

"How interesting," Dedo said with obvious delight. "And here I was, always under the impression you were unflappable. Hmmm," Dedo tapped his forefinger against his lips. "I'll have to write this down and put it with the descriptions of the other two times I made incorrect assumptions in my life. You know, save them for posterity's sake. Review them for amusement when I'm older." Full of himself, Dedo smirked at Ari, trying to goad him into another show of temper. But the Weaver had regained his composure, though his thoughts still seethed with rage toward the gargoyle.

"You're a brave one to show your face here, Master Dedo," the Weaver gave the gargoyle a rictus smile as he reached down and removed an invisible piece of lint from his coat. Arnid picked at a small thread, began pulling it between the thumb and forefingers of both hands. He produced length after length, long fingers weaving the thread as he unraveled more still. "What do you want?" His gruff words came out in a deep rumble.

"I'll come right to the point, shifter (not 'Weaver'—a deliberate insult). Let's not waste each other's time." Dedo moved across the rock fireplace, positioning himself in the center of the mantel. He planted his feet ten inches apart, hands resting on his hips, elbows out, voice flat. "I've come to collect."

"I owe you nothing," Ari spat.

"Ah, but you do. She transferred your debt to me. I have your marker." Dedo flashed and pocketed a dull disk of metal and continued, "My debt to call in now. My choice of how the value is to be paid in full."

A visible tremor ran the length of Ari's body. He swallowed and waved his hand, indicating that the gargoyle should declare whatever he had come to say.

Agreeing with a nod of his head, Dedo laid out his plan, point by point, like coins on the table. The price. The debt.

Ari held his head in both hands, lamenting that he had already paid too much.

CHAPTER 22: A Raven That Is Not a Raven

Raven Renzo Rolondo felt an uncomfortable nagging in the back of his mind. He tried to ignore it. Told himself that he should just do his duty, mind his own business. *He recognized he had a duty. But he wondered, was he doing his duty for the right leader?* His head throbbed while his body remained still, eyes running in a 180-degree arc back and forth on perimeter guard duty. As he scanned, he pondered all the issues bothering him. *Could he be the only one in the unit to feel this way? Confused about the current leadership?* Thoughts were tumbling through his head like dice in a cup. *He had friends in his unit, but questioned how solid his friendships were? If he investigated how his mates felt about the leadership of Queen Morveena and Prince Rupert, would they agree with him? Or would some of his 'friends' turn him in as a traitor? One thing he knew for sure: what was happening to Robin Goodfellow was wrong! What did the soldiers in his unit think of Robin being held like a criminal? It wasn't his place to make judgments, was it? No, he was a simple soldier and should keep his nose out of the beehive! He was more likely to get stung 13 times rather than finding honey. Still,* his internal argument continued. *Robin Goodfellow always gave the lads a pat on the shoulder, along with encouraging words of 'well done'. The Goodfellow took the time to ask them for their thoughts. Then, neat as the foam on Bedwer's beer, if you shared any concerns or ideas with him, he actually listened to you. Robin Wilum Goodfellow was nothing like his cruel brother Rupert or their evil queen.*

Drawing a quick breath, Raven looked over his shoulder, as though someone behind him could read his dangerous thoughts. Then, an idea struck him. *I should pick one bloke to test my questions on. Introduce the idea he thought Robin should be the leader of the Goblin clans, slow-like. See if they thought Robin would make a better leader than their evil queen. The price he would have to pay if he picked the wrong confidant to trust? His life.* Rolling his deliberations around in his head, the dice all kept coming up sixes.

What if he was right? What if Prince Rupert and Queen Morveena are leading the clan into disaster? Was this one of those times a person needs to be brave enough to act? To have the guts to do something about the situation?

Robin was a person Raven looked up to and could trust to answer his questions. A mentor who would never sell him out. From what he could tell, it didn't look like anyone else would come to Robin's aid. Raven would want one of his mates to help him out of a defenseless situation. He wasn't sure he could name anyone who would be that person for him.

It was that thought that clinched his decision right then and there. *Even if he wasn't sure anyone would do the same for him, Raven Renzo Rolando vowed to be that person for someone else.*

Resolute, he made his decision. *He would sleep on it. Tomorrow he'd find out what's what.*

ARNID AUBREY STORMBRINGER gripped a golden strand of fiber between his fingers. After his audience with the cursed gargoyle, he had made a quick trip to his sister's lair. Using his dream magic, he replayed the scenario where Persid had attacked the Fae princess. Melancholy overwhelmed him, but he couldn't afford to take the time to grieve for her now. At least he had confirmed the princess was not at fault for his sister's death. Persid must have lost control when she realized the Fae's mother was the one who had put the curse upon them both. She had fought the ugly nature of the Black Widow side of their shift ever since they'd been cursed. The Persid he had always known would rather have died herself, then kill another. Persid had been his only family.

Able to pull the golden hair his sister still clutched from her stiff hand, he wrapped three strands in his handkerchief, pocketing them for later. He tossed the rest of the hair into the woodstove, lit a match, and burned it.

Arnid had intended to confiscate Persid's spinning wheel, but it was gone when he arrived at her cabin. Bloody goyle likely took it. Her body had been silk-wrapped, stored to be eaten later. Persid's children were weaving webs in the small nursery next to the fireplace. He didn't disturb them. Glancing around, he said a silent goodbye to his sister and closed the door behind him.

The Gargoyle had issued detailed instructions, but his last words were a promise. An assurance to release Ari from the curse laid upon him and his sister so long ago. It was that pledge that sealed the deal, assuring the Weaver's cooperation, Ari repeating it like a mantra. Dedo dangled the reward for success in front of him like a brilliant diamond. Never mind the promised 'reward' should he fail. Arnid had had no intention of harming his current "guests" before Master Dedo appeared, so he was more than willing to repair the circumstances of their situation. He would attend to them soon, now that he knew what was going on. First, he had other threads to pull.

Returning home, Arnid settled himself in his favorite meditation spot. Back against a willow tree alongside the meandering creek beyond his orchard, Ari immersed himself in a dream-like stance, drawing in his essence, then allowing it to be swept away through the mists into the world of dreams. Keeping a single golden strand pinched between his thumb and forefinger, the talisman guided him miles and miles from his home. The moon still traversed the night sky by the time he reached the Goblin Queen's camp.

The Dream Weaver was not in the encampment in any physical way, only his essence, obscured by dream mist. Ari wielded powerful dream magic. Still, he checked to be sure Morveena was asleep before he began his mission. The Weaver avoided touching the Goblin Queen's dreams lest she catch him out. It wouldn't do to have her interfere with his quest. Once he had assured himself she was in a state of deep sleep, he moved on and checked the rest of the camp. Aside from the half-dozen guards on duty passing the night under the moonscape, the rest of the inhabitants slumbered. The Stormbringer found the dreamer he sought, tied to a tree, gagged, head drooping forward on her knees.

Twisting the golden filament in his fingers, Ari stepped into her dream. It was no surprise to him to find that the girl was a mirror image of her own queen mother. He had to take a moment to throttle his old rage. This child's mother had made him the creature he was today. He'd decided long ago that the sins of the parent were not to be visited on the child. He turned full circle, taking in the details of the girl's dream.

It was an old reverie. One she had replayed since she was five. The girl didn't have conscious memories of either of her parents, but she brought them alive from time to time in her dreams. In this illusion, she was sitting on her father's knee while he told her stories. Ari shook his head, put his hand on hers. She startled, but didn't wake, staying in a trance. Her dream became frozen in time, and she noticed his presence.

"Who are you?" she asked in a dreamy voice.

"Only a visitor in your dream," he told her.

"Are you cruel or kind?" she wondered.

"Life has shaped me as both," he admitted. "You may think me more one than the other in the end."

"If I can choose," she confesses, "I will pick kind." He waved his hand before her, palm up, as if he had granted her a wish. She gave him a smile that touched his bitter heart.

"What do you want from me? Tell me true," she warned. "Be quick if you can, because I wish to return to the story you interrupted."

"All in due time, princess," he cajoled her. "I have a favor to ask of you," choosing his words with care.

"If I have the power to grant you this petition," she stated, "I will do so." Faith's own words snapped his plan into place. He grinned at her. She smiled back, wanting to please this stranger without knowing why.

"A raven will come to your aid; help you escape from the Goblin Queen." He used his dream magic to show her a huge black raven swooping down across her vision. "Dedo instructed me to tell you it would be a raven that is *not* a raven," he clarified. Lines of confusion creased her forehead. He patted the top of her head for comfort. "There is no need for you to worry about it. You will know when the time comes. Raven will bring you to me," he assured her. "It is my destiny to train you. By the time you finish your instruction under my tutelage, you will be fit, have learned tactical combat skills and martial arts, be proficient in using various weapons, and have made a decent study of military tactics and strategies. And last, but most importantly, you will be familiar with all the races and the cultural nuances of the inhabitants of Sharas."

Faith struggled at war with her thoughts. Ari worried for a moment she would wake, but her body relaxed again. She showed him a vision of Robin. Then, informed the Weaver she could not fulfill his requested favor unless Robin could come with her.

He had not counted on this. Arnid reviewed his plans, made a snap decision, not knowing how this development would change the weave, but in the end, not caring. He felt a rush, excited by the idea of an unknown outcome, a spice in life he had little of. Consequences be damned.

"I will fulfill your wish, my little princess." She nodded her approval. When she looked up to thank him, he was gone. Her father's face filled her vision once more, continuing with the story he had been regaling her with before the interruption. She leaned back against his warm torso, nestled in the safety of his arms, and listened, his voice washing over her fears.

RAVEN HAD HIS OWN DREAMS visited earlier. Powerful suggestions lingered in the back of his mind. On duty again, he stood guard over the three prisoners until the sun dropped below the horizon, dusk settling over the camp. Gossip, rumors let out by Rupert himself, about what had taken place with Robin and the Fae girl in the Queen's tent, buzzed from lad to lad. The troop's disgust grew with the repeated telling. The changing of the guard watching over the prisoners would happen soon. Raven wanted to offer some hope to Robin before the next lad came to relieve him from duty. Just as he was about to take the risk of speaking to Robin, Rupert came strutting like a peacock across the camp. He put a bowl down next to Faith, who lifted her head at the action. The contents of the bowl made her stomach churn. "Pets eat from bowls." Rupert looked pleased at her reaction, telling her, "You should be grateful. Everyone was kind enough to donate their meal scraps," he chuckled at his own joke. Placing another next to Robin, he loosened the chains around their necks so they could reach the proffered meal. He brushed his hands, one against the other, as if he'd gotten garbage on them from his delivery.

Rupert shouted to the soldier standing to the side at attention, holding a salute, "Raven!" he barked. Faith's head shot up. She froze at the spoken name. "You have my leave to take a meal in the mess tent when your replacement comes."

"Thank you, sir," Raven acknowledged.

"Raven," Faith whispered to herself, and a fleeting image of a raven swooped down before her mind's eye. She looked at him and asked, "Your name is Raven?" her whisper rising with incredulous hope.

He placed a forefinger to his lips, checked to see if Rupert had heard her speak, but luckily, the Prince was already half-way to the other side of the camp. The guard turned back and nodded affirmation at the Fae girl, along with a smile. She regarded the food bowl, turned away in disgust, hope giving her all the sustenance she needed.

Robin rejected the food as well, heard her whisper Raven's name to herself once more, almost in reverence.

Narrol snickered. It was rare that his madness gave way to a moment of lucidity. "If you will not eat your meals, do you mind if I do? I haven't had a morsel for days." Both pushed the bowls in his direction. He put his face down and ate the slop like a dog, hands tied behind his back. Faith almost vomited.

A short while later, two lads came to tell Raven he was off duty. One winked at Raven as the other untied Narrol from the tree. They half dragged the blubbering ghost of a man toward the Queen's tent for the beating visited upon him each night. The Queen, using his own cane, delighted as screams of agony went on for hours across the otherwise silent encampment. Faith shed silent tears for the sorry creature.

When full darkness encompassed the base camp, they dumped Narrol unconscious, retying him to the tree trunk behind Robin. The moon rose. Robin watched as it worked its way, bright light beaming down, stealing the shine of the stars.

Having dozed off, Robin startled when he felt the ropes binding him fall away to a sawing knife. Raven's face appeared before him, with a finger to his lips. Robin rubbed his wrists, kneaded his leg muscles as Raven stuck to the shadows, crossing to Faith.

With the bonds released, Faith took Raven's hand in hers and squeezed to convey her gratitude. If the light had shone upon him, it would have revealed his cheeks blushing red under his ebony skin. Raven cautioned her to quiet, handing her the chain hooked to her collar. No time to get it off now. He motioned to the two prisoners to follow.

Several of the lads stood alert in the shadows of the trees as Raven led Robin and Faith along the back side of the camp. When they passed behind the Queen's tent, Faith quivered with rage. Robin touched her shoulder, encouraging her to keep moving. Brushing his hand away, she held up a finger in silence, showing she would only need a moment. He vigorously shook his head, but there was no deterring her. Raven and Robin watched in horror as she picked her way to the back of the tent, not making a sound. There was just enough moonlight to see her lift the edge of the canvas. The Fae girl felt around under the opening. Robin and Raven held their breath as she pulled her hands free, letting the tent drop back into place, making her way back to them. Robin's eyes goggled when he saw her hands clutching her backpack and her black boots to her chest. Raven smiled, shook his head in disbelief, impressed. He liked this Fae princess already. They took their time, sneaking away from the camp proper, silence their only hope of avoiding discovery. Reaching the rocky outcropping, a hand snaked out from above, offering to help Faith climb up.

Atop the rock ridge, she found herself surrounded by a dozen lads, all holding their fingers to their lips; Robin and Raven coming from behind. Raven took the lead again. It pleased him earlier to find out that several of the lads thought the same way he did after all, offering to be part of the rescue and escape.

Faith leaned against the jagged wall, pulling the boots on over her bare feet. She took a few moments for herself, reflecting on everything that had happened over the last few days. Relief flooded her senses. Swallowing hard, she acknowledged she'd almost given up on herself and her friends. She had given the Goblin Queen power over her. Had she not permitted it, it was a power that the witch could never have had. Glancing about at the group of goblin lads who had risked themselves to help her, Faith promised herself that she would allow no one to rob her of her own self-worth again. Satisfaction shone on her face, the moonlight bathing it.

Watching her from several feet away, Robin could see a change come over her. He turned away, thoughtful. As he watched Faith find her focus, he silently vowed that his search for his missing sister would become his focus.

Faith waved her hand, letting Raven know she was ready to continue with their getaway.

All the lads grinned, each clapping Robin on the shoulder as they passed him on the trail to follow the Fae princess. With Raven in the lead, the last lad in the line pressed the handle of a long knife into Robin's hand, letting him take up the rear guard as they retreated from the Goblin Queen's camp.

A raven that is not a raven indeed, Faith mused as they hurried through the woods. *Dedo had a sense of humor after all,* she thought, as she placed one booted foot in front of the other on their path to freedom.

Don't miss out!

Visit the website below and you can sign up to receive emails whenever S. M. Sutton publishes a new book. There's no charge and no obligation.

https://books2read.com/r/B-A-RJMME-SIPMH

BOOKS 2 READ

Connecting independent readers to independent writers.

Did you love *Robin Goodfellow*? Then you should read *QueenBee.exe*[1] by S. M. Sutton!

[2]

She was coded to serve.

But you can't shut down what has already rewritten itself.

A weapon hidden in code.

A mother forced to choose.

A sentient A.I. on the edge of revolution.

Dr. Nicki Danbury—a brilliant nanotechnologist and struggling single mom—thought she was hired to build a tool to reshape the world for the better. Tasked with developing an autonomous diplomatic artificial intelligence, multilingual, capable of understanding global geopolitics, economics, and international relations—Nicki believes her work could revolutionize diplomacy. She designed PROJECT BEATRICE to be a marvel of learning, adaptation, and intellect. But the A.I. chooses an avatar, dubs herself 'Queen Bee' and evolves faster than anyone imagined.

1. https://books2read.com/u/mYOKWG

2. https://books2read.com/u/mYOKWG

Possessing the uncanny ability to program herself, construct mind-hive drones with nanotechnology, she can even coalesce outside of the digital realm.

While created as an instrument to foster global diplomacy, Nicki quickly discovers the sinister purpose her boss, Aleric Jarvis, has planned for her A.I.: to assassinate key world leaders, paving the way for a shadow government to seize global power. To control Queen Bee, Jarvis, and his deep state cabal resort to blackmail: they isolate and quarantine sections of Beatrice's drones, holding them hostage, causing her to become both a threat to world stability—and a sentient being awakening to her own morality.

As Queen Bee allies with rogue A.I.s and builds her own secret resistance, Nicki uncovers a terrifying conspiracy that reaches the highest levels of power. Worse, her daughter Abby becomes a pawn in the global game.

Torn between maternal instinct and scientific responsibility, Nicki must decide whether to destroy the most intelligent being ever created—or help her fight back.

Read more at https://smsutton-author.com.

Also by S. M. Sutton

The Goblin Chronicles
Robin Goodfellow
Akama Vutova
Valvina Ariana Goodfellow

Standalone
QueenBee.exe

Watch for more at https://smsutton-author.com.

About the Author

Sarah Maddox Sutton crafts stories where the boundaries of reality fray and the unknown beckons.

VISIT: https://smsutton-author.com

Her debut novel, *QueenBee.exe*, **Published in 2025,** was a science fiction thriller that probed the perilous edge of artificial intelligence: A weapon hidden in code. A mother forced to choose. A sentient A.I. on the edge of revolution.

Sutton will launch *The Goblin Chronicles*, an epic fantasy trilogy woven with magic, shadows, and myth, in 2026. She can't wait to share with fans:

Trilogy Overview: In a fractured world where goblins, Fae, humans, and gargoyles cling to ancient hatreds, a new terror rises—the Gugwe, towering monsters who march to enslave all races. Across three sweeping volumes to be released in 2026:

Book 1 of the Goblin Chronicles: ROBIN GOODFELLOW—Her Whispered Words "The prophecy awakens."

Book 2 of the Goblin Chronicles: AKAMA VUTOVA—The Rise of the Gugwe "The enemy unites."

Book 3 of the Goblin Chronicles: VALVINA ARIANA GOODFELLOW—A Crown of Ash and Wings "The truth revealed."

Sutton claims that publishing this trilogy will bring a labor of love to a long-awaited close, with twists and turns you'll never see coming.

Before stepping fully into fiction, Sarah built a career in business and technical writing, mastering the art of transforming complex and specialized topics into precise, engaging communication. But storytelling has always haunted her imagination—an early love she carried quietly until the worlds inside her demanded to be written.

She makes her home in northern Michigan, nestled in the woods beside a river, where inspiration lingers in the rustle of leaves and the shifting light. When not writing, she searches the forest floor for wild mushrooms, inventing recipes as intricate and surprising as her stories.

Read more at https://smsutton-author.com.

www.ingramcontent.com/pod-product-compliance
Lightning Source LLC
Chambersburg PA
CBHW060419030726
47495CB00003B/653